The Death of Promises

David Dalglish

BOOKS BY DAVID DALGLISH

THE HALF-ORC SERIES

The Weight of Blood

The Cost of Betrayal

The Death of Promises

The Shadows of Grace (coming soon)

THE WORLD OF DEZREL

A Dance of Cloaks (August 2010)

Prologue

Patient devil, aren't you?" Jerico whispered as he knelt by a shallow stream running through the rocky terrain. He scooped handfuls of water and drank, doing his best to forget that the orcs often urinated along the banks. The last tribe he had seen was downstream but the gray scoundrels bred like rabbits in the Vile Wedge. Most likely hundreds of orcs had relieved themselves into that very same water far upstream...

He spat out what little he had not swallowed.

"Well, now I'm thirsty, sick, and still annoyed as the abyss," he said. He shifted his left shoulder, adjusting the leather straps wrapped around his forearm. A thick rectangular shield hung across his back, emblazoned with the emblem of the golden mountain. That shield, protecting nearly every vital part of his body, kept him calm enough to keep his back turned to his unknown stalker.

He looked past his broken reflection in the water. For two days he had felt a gentle voice of warning in his mind. It was the voice of Ashhur, his beloved deity, the one he served in full devotion despite what had happened. Despite the fall of the Citadel. Despite believing himself the last paladin of Ashhur. He had survived longer than the others had because Ashhur's voice was strong in his ear and he never doubted it. This time it screamed that death followed him like a shadow.

"You're no orc," he said aloud, his patience tiring. He hadn't slept in nearly two days. "You're too patient for an orc. So stop hiding. If you want to kill me, come and try. You want to talk, come and talk. If it's neither, then please go with Ashhur's blessing and leave me be."

"I do not think Ashhur would ever grant me his blessing," came the reply from behind him. "For I have killed too many of his failed, faithless children."

The paladin stood. The voice was too far away to be within striking distance...yet.

"Another dog of Karak, I assume?" he asked.

"My name is Krelln, worm. I've killed three just like you. Weak in faith. Afraid. Did you think you could flee to the Wedge and hide amidst the orcs and the ogres? You don't much look like a goblin, failed paladin."

Jerico turned and faced his mocker. A young man, even younger than he. Such a shame to see souls corrupted so early, Jerico thought. He wore heavy platemail akin to Jerico's, except Krelln's armor was black and charred as if it had come from the bowels of the abyss.

"Failed paladin?" Jerico asked, scanning the young man's face. Scars lined every inch of it. "A bold claim considering you've never met me before. What did I fail?"

"Twice I have seen you grab your mace and not once has it glowed. Your faith in Ashhur is nothing." He drew his blade and held it with both hands. It was enormous, with a serrated edge and a carved lion head as a hilt. Black flame rolled up and down the length of steel. "As you can see, my faith remains strong."

Jerico laughed, shifting his left hand in the straps that held his shield tight across his back. One pull and it'd be at the ready.

"Do you plan on killing me, dark paladin?" he asked.

"Your head will be a grand gift to his majesty. Keep still your weapon and I will be merciful."

"You don't know what mercy is, boy. Mercy doesn't exist in Karak's twisted world."

Krelln charged across the yellow grass. He swung his blade with all his strength. Jerico took two steps back, drew his mace in his right hand, and smoothly parried the curved tip of Krelln's sword. A grin crossed his face.

"Should save your strength," he told the younger man. The second swing came straight down, trying to cleave the paladin in half. Jerico took a single step to the side and let the attack smash a deep indent in the ground. The black flame charred the grass around it.

Jerico twirled his mace in his hand, his shield still carefully tucked across his back.

"You don't have the faith to fight me," Krelln snarled.

"And you don't have the skill to fight me. Go back to where you came. No one has to know you found me."

The dark paladin spat onto his blade. The saliva sizzled in the flame.

"Confidence is nothing. Faith is everything."

"Is that so? Let's find out." Jerico hooked his mace to his belt and stood unarmed. "Try to strike me down. I won't draw my weapon. Your sword will falter."

Krelln glanced about, suddenly nervous. He suspected a trick but didn't know what.

"You lie."

"Lying's not my style."

The dark paladin licked his lips. His hands shifted their grip on the sword hilt. Jerico watched it all, waiting. Waiting.

Krelln swung.

Jerico yanked with his left hand, freeing his shield. He took a step closer, thrusting his shield into the path of the blade. Right before the blow connected, the metal of Jerico's shield burst with brilliant white light. Krelln cried out as his eyes burned. When the sword struck, he felt his arms jolt in pain. A loud crack echoed in the valley. It was as if he hit a stone wall. Jerico shoved aside the blade and approached, still unarmed. Krelln thrust, only to have it blocked. The contact jarred his arms and shoulders. He felt his heart skip and his lungs quiver. The black flames on his sword dwindled to a shadow of their former size.

"Your faith is untested," Jerico said, lunging forward, his shield leading. Krelln swiped upwards, a desperate defense. The paladin met it with the bottom edge of his shield. A soft cry of pain escaped Krelln's lips. Sparks showered the ground. "Untested, and built on anger and ignorance. You say you've killed three of my brethren; I've killed nine of yours, Krelln."

The young man tried to lift his blade but his arms refused to move. Jerico kicked it from his hands. Krelln staggered back, terrified of making contact with the awful glowing shield.

"The others will find you," he said, his voice growing hoarse with fear. "Once Krieger finds out Lathaar isn't the last, he'll hunt you down and make a necklace from your guts."

Jerico halted where he stood.

"Who is Lathaar?" he asked. Krelln tried to flee. Before he could take a step, Jerico slammed his shield deep into his back. The dark paladin screamed as his cursed armor melted. He collapsed, his face smashing hard on the dirt. Smoke sizzled as the melted metal burned his flesh. He felt a foot press atop his back amidst the pain and the heat.

"Tell me, who is Lathaar?" Jerico asked again.

"I don't know," Krelln gasped. "He's...he's just another paladin. We thought he was the last."

"Another paladin of Ashhur," Jerico whispered. "Lord be praised...another lives."

He lifted his foot. The man squirmed to a stand and glared. Blood ran down his face from a broken nose. His hair was disheveled, and he weakly sucked in air while clutching his numb arms to his chest. Jerico waved him away.

"Go," he said. "I will show you the same mercy you offered me."

"Bastard," Krelln spat before turning to run. Jerico watched him for a few seconds before unhooking his mace.

"Three good men died to his hand," he whispered to it. "Fly true, Bonebreaker."

He flung the mace end over end through the air. It struck Krelln in the back. The powerful magic within the weapon activated. White light flared, and then Krelln's spine shattered to pieces. He fell limp, making only a soft, confused cry before death took him. Jerico slowly walked over and retrieved his mace.

"Karak take you in his arms," he said while kneeling beside the body. "And after an eternity may Ashhur forgive you and save you from that fate."

He buckled the mace and his shield and then prepared to dig. He would leave no man, not even a dark paladin, to be feasted on by the carrion creatures. Besides, he needed time to think. Things had changed. After all the years, the nightmares of the Citadel falling and the brutal battles with dark paladins that sought total victory against his kind, he suddenly knew he was not alone.

"Lathaar," he said, repeating the name Krelln had spoken. "Where are you now, Lathaar? How have you lasted when all others have fallen?"

Well, not all others, he thought. He had survived, and there was nothing special about him.

"I guess that's not true," he chuckled, patting his shield before digging with his hands.

It took the rest of the day to bury the corpse. It was hard work, but he was used to such things. At the setting of the sun, he decided it was time to leave the Vile Wedge.

"Forgive me, Ashhur, if I endanger your priests," he told the last sliver of light falling behind the horizon. "But I must go to the Sanctuary. I must find him."

As darkness came, he felt the gentle touch of Ashhur on his heart and knew the path he had chosen was the correct one. That didn't mean it would be easy, or guaranteed to succeed. But it was the right path, and he held faith in Ashhur's guidance. In the end, that was what truly mattered.

Part One

1

It was a sad place, this small clearing encircled by thin trees with branches that hung low to scratch at their faces as they entered.

"Death haunts these woods," the frail man whispered to his lover.

"I know," said the girl beside him. "Be silent. I want you to see." She stepped away from his arms and into the clearing. Her long black hair hid much of her naked body. Only the soft pale white of her legs and arms was visible in the darkness.

"Qurrah?" the girl asked softly.

"Yes, Tessanna?"

"Do you love your lover?"

"Of course," he said.

"I believe you," she said, her back still to him. "But I must know. I must." She spread her arms wide. Dirt floated upward on a silent wind as all about the creatures of the night fell silent. Qurrah watched as she placed her hands together and arched back her head. Dark magic sparkled on her fingertips.

The wind ceased. Tessanna sighed. She knelt to the grass, turning slightly so that Qurrah could see what she had done.

"A rose," Qurrah whispered. He stepped closer, mesmerized by the sight. Indeed, it was a rose, but not one of leaf and petal. It was white and ethereal, shimmering above the ground with a sad, drooping head.

"It is a ghost," Tessanna said, a strange twinkle in her eye. "A ghost of a rose."

"I was not aware soulless beings could have ghosts."

"All things have a soul, Qurrah, even flowers and trees and the creatures of the forest. In death, they are more understanding than we. But there are times, very rare times, that a tragedy too great can befall them and bind them here."

Tessanna swirled the dirt beneath the floating rose. Her smile faded and a black substance glazed over her eyes. A few whispery commands tore pieces of an ancient corpse up from the earth. The pieces whirled together, mingling with the essence of the rose. The stem became bone, the petals rotted strips of flesh. A single flash signified the union of the two. The girl took the rose and held it before her naked chest, her eyes peering at her lover's. A slow smile crept across her thin, angular face. Her eyes, solid black with only a hint of white at the edges, held him mesmerized.

She offered him the rose. He took it without a thought. Thorns of bone pierced Qurrah's flesh. Blood ran down his wrist. He opened his mouth to speak but no words would come. All he saw was twisting red petals of a long dead flower.

"Do you love me, Qurrah?" the girl asked. Her voice was thunderous in the silence.

"Yes," he gasped.

"Would you give your life to me? Would you die so that I may live?"

The redness swirled faster. The whole world was flowers. He tried to speak but the powdery taste of petals numbed his tongue.

"Would you, Qurrah?" the girl asked, suddenly shy and quiet. "Would you?"

The petals vanished, and he saw his lover standing before a vast emptiness. The sight lit his heart aflame. When she vanished within the dark, the flame died in painful agony.

"Yes," he gasped. "My life is yours, and I give it gladly."

The thorns withdrew from his flesh. The owls and the cicadas began songs anew. Tessanna knelt before Qurrah, who had collapsed to his knees. She took the rose from his hand

and held it to her chest. Blood, Qurrah's blood, ran between her breasts.

"I'm sorry, Qurrah," she whispered.

"What did you do to me?" he asked, his strength slowly returning. He couldn't believe the incredible relief he felt when the rose was taken from his hand.

"It is the rose of the maiden," she said. "Only those who are truly in love can touch it without feeling its anger. Those ruled not by love but by anger, or fear, or hatred, or vengeance...it brings those to the dirt for the forest to consume."

"You were testing me," Qurrah said.

Tessanna crushed the rose and dropped the pieces to the ground. The softly luminescent ghost appeared once more, hovering between them. Slowly it drifted downward, resuming its perch just above the earth. The young woman grabbed Qurrah's hands and pulled him to her.

"It will be the last time," she said, pressing her lips to his. "It has been many years before love was made before this rose. Would you, Qurrah? Would you let this be our wedding, the rose our priest, the forest our witness?"

The half-orc kissed her once more.

"Let it be done."

And they wed themselves there upon the cold hard earth, their love bright and alive. The ghost of the rose watched and approved. When the two lovers awoke, it was gone, having long faded with the dawn.

"It will be getting colder," Qurrah said. "We must get you some clothes."

"There is a village nearby," the girl said. "I saw the smoke of their fires."

"Then let us take what we must. The Sanctuary is still many weeks of travel."

Qurrah left the forest alone, Tessanna remaining back to linger among the trees. Not far from the forest's edge was the village nestled beside a small stream that Qurrah followed.

He waited there at the stream, feeling certain someone would soon come for water. He expected a woman, but twenty minutes later a gruff man with a bent back approached. He held a bucket in one hand and a worn rake in the other. His face and skin were the color of mud.

The man kept silent as he neared, and outwardly he showed no signs of surprise or worry. Qurrah could sense his fear. It was small and well contained. Surprised by such strength in a simple farmer, the necromancer felt his curiosity climb.

"We have no need for a priest here," the farmer said, falling to his knees beside the stream. He put down the rake, dipped the bucket into the water, and let it fill. "Not because you worship the lion, mind you. We have little money and even less food."

"I am no priest," Qurrah said. The man looked at him, the right corner of his mouth turning upward in a subdued smile.

"Then you're a murderer, a liar, or a thief. Don't think we'd appreciate any of those in our village, either."

Qurrah laughed.

"I come in need of aid, farmer. My lover and I have had many trials and we need supplies for the winter."

"Your name," the man asked. He cupped some water with his hand and drank. "Tell me your name, orc-blood."

"Qurrah Tun."

"Well, Qurrah Tun, I'm Craig, but friends here know me as Badback. You don't have any money to barter with, do you? Didn't think so. Let's be honest, Qurrah. I said you were either a liar, a murderer, or a thief. Tell me, which of the three is it?"

The half-orc glanced back to the forest, angry at how uncomfortable he felt before the farmer's eyes.

"The man who owned these robes was a priest. He died at the hands of an elf, and I took them from his body. I am none of what you say."

The farmer chuckled. Qurrah sensed the fear within him, tightening but still masterfully controlled.

"You stink of death, half-orc. You are a necromancer, just as I am a farmer, and you toil with blood no different than I toil the soil. If I turn you away, will you kill me?"

The half-orc glared at Badback, who ignored him as he looked at Tessanna peering out from the forest. Qurrah couldn't shake the feeling that something was amiss. The farmer took his bucket in one hand and his rake in the other. As he stood, Qurrah pulled down the cloth in front of the man's chest and then spat at what he saw.

"You pick a strange spot to live, priest," Qurrah said.

"All deserve to hear the word of Ashhur," Badback said. "Even the poor farmers of the land."

"I should kill you."

"For what transgression? Have I harmed or insulted you? Now answer my question."

"Yes," Qurrah said. "I would kill you if you refused."

Badback leaned against the rake. His eyes stared straight into Qurrah's.

"Then you are a child lashing at those who do not relent to your desires. I would give you the cloak off my back if you asked in humble nature. I still will. What supplies do you lack?"

"Clothes," Qurrah said, again caught off guard and hating it. "My lover travels naked and will freeze at the first snow."

"I will see what we have," Badback said. He turned toward the village. "Wait here. I would hate to have you startle anyone."

He returned much later holding a bundle of clothes and supplies instead of his rake and bucket. He handed them to Qurrah.

"The clothes should hide her nakedness," he said. "The blankets should keep you warm at the night. And the food will satisfy your worldly hunger for a time."

"I thought you had little to spare," Qurrah said.

"And we spare it, anyway. You have never understood, have you, Qurrah? Do you think us weak sacrificing meager provisions to a man in need? You know this not to be true."

"Why do you mock me?" the half-orc asked.

"I do what I do for the sake of my village. Now go."

He purposely put his crooked back to the necromancer and returned to his town. Qurrah clutched the supplies in his arms, feeling his anger boil. He was being played the fool, he just didn't know how, or why. And not just that. He was being treated the inferior. He could strike the man dead with a thought, but here he was, made to seem the beggar and the fool.

"What is the name of your village?" he asked, using magic to heighten his voice to a shout, for his throat was too frail to do so on its own. The priest turned and cupped his hands to his mouth.

"I think it best you not know."

That was the last he saw him. Qurrah swore to return. Once he had the spellbook of Darakken, once his promises were fulfilled, he would burn the entire village to the ground.

"Qurrah?"

Tessanna had ventured from the forest, her naked body a startling oddity among the dying grass and cold air. The half-orc handed her the clothes, which she held out to look at.

"Fairly simple," she said. "And the skirt is far too long."

"I'm sure you'll make it fit," the half-orc said.

Tessanna slid the dress on. It was rough and prickly, but it was still something. She took her dagger out from Qurrah's robe and used it to cut a thin strip from the bottom. She then tied it as a sash and tucked the dagger within. This done, she looked at Qurrah and giggled.

"You just can't stand kindness for kindness's sake, can you?" she asked.

Qurrah's glare was answer enough.

The food, dried and salted venison, did well to sate their hunger. Tessanna ate little for she wore a simple wooden ring that allowed her to survive on a single meal every ten days. While in the forest, they had lived on deer and squirrel, but there was little to hunt on the grassy hills and plains they now crossed. Some days they walked, but other days...

"Should we ride?" Tessanna asked the next morning, blankets wrapped about her body. "The ground is getting colder."

Qurrah sighed. While Badback had given them clothes, he had forgotten shoes for Tessanna to wear. The travel was wearing on her feet, and some nights she would rest by the fire with blood soaking them from toe to heel. She never complained, and by morning the blood was gone and the cuts nothing but scars. The ground had steadily grown rockier and their travel slower.

"Yes," he said. "I guess we can this day."

Tessanna smiled. She let the blankets drop. The cold air bit her skin, but she held in any shivers. With her hands above her head, she started swiveling her hips in a small circle, weaving to some unheard music. She placed one foot in the ashes of the previous night's fire. The ash sprang to life, burning although it had no fuel. Tessanna twirled, her other foot stepped in the fire, and then it roared high above her knees. It did not burn her.

Qurrah watched, mesmerized as he always was by the summoning. Her movements grew slower and slower, every twirl of her hips and gyration of her back intensely erotic. The first time she had ever shown him, she had been naked. He had immediately made love to her afterward.

"Seletha," she whispered into the morning air. The fire sprang like a river into the grass before her, pooling and growing. Her spell lashed it together, lifting the fire higher into the shape of a large horse. She slowly drifted her hands downward, magic flaring across her palms. The fiery form solidified, growing muscle and bone. When her hands reached her sides, the creature was whole and the summoning complete.

The horse lowered her head and raised one bent leg, her way of bowing. She snorted, plumes of black smoke blowing from her nostrils. Qurrah pulled his robes tighter about him, fighting against the fear that always filled his gut at the sight. It wasn't the supernatural aspect of the creature that bothered him. Before their first ride, he had admitted to Tessanna his fear of horses. It took all his willpower to sit atop the magical being without panicking.

"The Gods' Bridges are close, Seletha," the girl said, gently patting the horse's head. "Think you can get us there by nightfall?"

She clomped a hoof and nodded.

"Good. Let's go, Qurrah."

"Of course," the half-orc said. He had ridden Seletha twenty times since fleeing the confrontation with his brother. He had hoped to get over his fear. But of course he hadn't, and Tessanna struggled to hold in her laughter as he placed a hesitant hand atop Seletha's back.

"You've always been so good at mounting me, silly," Tessanna said. "Surely you can mount a horse without too much difficulty."

The half-orc rolled his eyes and then climbed atop the giant beast. The two rode atop Seletha bareback, one of the other reasons Qurrah tried to ride as sparingly as possible. By nightfall, his legs and back would ache and he'd swear any hope of producing children was lost to him.

Tessanna arced back her head and levitated herself onto Seletha's back, both legs bent and tucked on the right side.

"I hate this damn thing," Qurrah said.

"Shush and enjoy the ride," she replied.

The girl whispered to the horse and then they were off. So great was Seletha's weight that deep hoof prints marked their passing across the earth, the centers of each one lined with a tiny flare of dying flame.

2

Qurrah hunkered beside the fire, a deep scowl covering his face. He pulled his hood low over his head and muttered about the pain in his lower back. Tessanna cuddled beside him, quietly singing. Each note was slow and soft, her voice as cold as ice atop a river.

"We were made for joy, we were made for suffering. We feel love, and we hate who we love, and this is not real until we cry…"

Love swirled within his chest, and in such a manner, he touched her face as she sang. But she was the girl of apathy, and her face was stone against his touch.

"I will not cry 'til I die, and I will die when you come for me. Come for me. Make me real."

She ended her song, her eyes staring up at the sky.

For the longest time she remained silent. Qurrah brushed her face again, not hurt by the lack of emotion she showed to him. Ever since Aullienna's death, her love for him had come and gone, much like her personalities. He knew, given time, she would return his affection. If she didn't, he'd take her and give her no choice but to love him. Sometimes he wondered if that was what she preferred the most.

"The stars are beautiful," Tessanna said. Qurrah did not respond so she continued. "I used to wish upon them when I was a little girl. I'd wish for a bear to come and eat my father and then a great black hawk to come and let me ride on its back. Do you know what I wish for now, Qurrah?"

The half-orc shook his head. She stared at him, wanting to see his reaction.

"I wish for a way to replace what was lost. The girl you killed."

"You desire a child?" he asked, fighting anger at the guilt she cast his way. "One of your own womb?"

"I do," she said. Her voice was perfectly calm, yet a tear ran down the side of her face. "But I know I can't have one. No life sparkles inside me. So what am I to do, Qurrah? What am I to do?"

Qurrah kissed her lips and then used his thumb to wipe the tear away.

"Even if it takes all my life, I will repay you for my mistake. For my brother's pride. Perhaps, in time, I may give you a child."

Tessanna finally smiled.

"You just want me more often."

He laughed.

"Any more than we already do, I may injure myself."

She laughed, the apathy within her melting away. Underneath the ice, a smoldering fire flared. "How about tonight," she asked. "Always worth a try, isn't it?"

He kissed her again as he removed her dress. In the light of the campfire, her body was perfect. He could not see her scars or the bones of her ribs. Her slender hands removed his sash and parted his robe. She crawled atop him, her lips and tongue flitting across his neck.

Qurrah moaned and arced his back, and as he did, he saw the men watching them.

"Tessanna," he said, his entire body suddenly tensing.

"I'm sorry," the girl said. "I should have sensed them sooner."

And then they were atop them, pulling Tessanna off. A boot pressed hard against Qurrah's neck. Another crushed his right hand. Two men each held Tessanna by an arm. They all wore brown coats and grey trousers.

"Hold them steady," one man said to the others. "Seems they're both all riled up and ready to go." The man, the leader of the bunch by the way he yelled at the others, knelt next to Qurrah and spat. The half-orc swore death as the saliva covered his eyes.

"Looks like you won't get to have too much fun, but your girl there..."

"A toll!" one man shouted, and his cry was quickly repeated by the others.

"A toll! A toll!"

They jostled the naked girl this way and that, her slender frame lacking any strength to resist. Yet despite their cries and their looks, she did not appear afraid. Instead, she let out a tiny moan as she moved her hips back and forth.

Qurrah forced himself to open his eyes. He needed to know how many had attacked them. He counted only four, two holding Tessanna, another restraining him, and then the leader. Daggers were attached to their belts, but so far they remained undrawn.

"For what should we pay a toll?" Qurrah asked. His free hand crawled across the ground and tightened about the handle of his whip, which lay atop the fabric of his cloak, nearly invisible in the darkness.

"To cross the Gods' Bridges, of course," said the leader. "Tory's boys own it now, own the whole bloody Delta. If you want to cross, you pay a toll."

"We have no coin," he said, glancing at Tessanna. He wondered if he should act or wait for her. The ruffians had no clue what they held in their arms. No clue at all.

"Well ain't that a shame," said the leader, standing up and walking to Tessanna. He cupped her face in his hand, turning her chin this way and that. "But I'd say this pretty girl does have something of value. Doesn't she boys?"

All four cheered and whistled.

"Touch her and die," Qurrah said.

"Shut up," said the man towering above Qurrah, pressing harder against his neck with his foot. "Close your eyes and keep them shut. We gonna take our toll."

The leader grabbed Tessanna's hair and pulled her head back. She moaned, louder. A smile creased her face.

"You like that?" he asked her. "You want a real man, don't you, not some bony little orc runt."

21

"You couldn't handle me," she said. "You'd only end up hurt."

He laughed. The others only smirked and chuckled. They knew what was coming. Tessanna wasn't the only woman to sass off when they took their toll.

"Oh, is that so?" he asked before backhanding her across the face. As she spat blood onto one of her captors, he drew his dagger and held it to her neck.

"You keep that pretty mouth of yours shut," he whispered. "I've humped corpses before, you little whore, and we'd all have hours of fun with yours before you turned cold."

Qurrah watched his lover smile even as blood ran down her lips. He tightened his grip on the whip's handle, knowing the one who held him was far too interested in Tessanna's body to pay him any attention. The girl was playing games with them, with all of them.

"It'd be more than hours," Tessanna said, licking the blood with her tongue. "I'm fire, you naughty little boy, pure fire. I'd burn you the second you put that little weed you call a prick inside me."

Sparks of flame burst within her eyes. The leader glanced around, for the first time realizing he was not dealing with normal travelers. Qurrah saw this and chuckled. About damn time.

"What the abyss," the leader said, pressing harder against her skin with his knife. Her hair caught flame, then her shoulders, her chest and her neck. The fire hid her nakedness. The men who held her screamed, the flesh of their hands seared black. The leader thrust his dagger only to have the cheap metal shatter. Fire leapt across the broken blade, burning a thin line up his arm. He tried to run but Tessanna was not done. She whispered a few words of magic, paralyzing him where he stood.

The man holding Qurrah fled. Qurrah whirled immediately, fire consuming his whip. He wrapped it about the fleeing man's legs, tumbling him to the ground. The man screamed as the fire burned his ankles to the bone.

"Shut up," Qurrah said. The necromancer hooked his fingers in bizarre directions and let his dark power flow. The bones in the man's ankles snapped. The broken pieces tore out the black mess of flesh, animated with dark power. With a thought, he ended the man's screams, shredding his throat with his own bones.

Qurrah picked up his robe and put it back on. He tied the sash while he watched Tessanna have her fun. The two men that had held her had long fled into the night. Only the leader remained, held sway by the beautiful sorceress. She ran a hand down his face, smiling as one of his eyeballs popped.

"Do you still want to bed me?" she asked. Tears ran from his good eye, and he tried to speak but all that came out was a pathetic whimper. "Good. You interrupted my fun, so I'll have to have fun with you." She pressed her body against his. Her arms wrapped about his body and pulled him closer. She ground her crotch against his leg. She slipped a finger inside his mouth. His clothes burned away, as did his flesh. Still she caressed him. Still she held him against her.

At last she pulled back and cried out in ecstasy. She released him from his paralysis. His throat and mouth was so charred and burned he could not even scream. Nothing but a blackened mess, he collapsed to the ground, bled, and died. The fire left her body…at least the outward fire. Qurrah wrapped his whip around his arm, amused at how aroused his lover was.

"I told him he couldn't handle me," she giggled.

The next morning, Qurrah was first to awake. His whole body shivered underneath his blankets. He pulled them tighter about himself and attempted to return to sleep but the groaning of his stomach refused to let him rest. He had eaten nothing the previous day. Their provisions were running low, and he meant to stretch them as far as they could go.

"I should have made her teach me that spell," he muttered, thinking of the banquets his brother's wife Aurelia had conjured seemingly at will. The spell most likely required some sort of component to cast, but whatever it had been, Qurrah knew it would be easier to carry and obtain than his current stock of food.

Tessanna stirred at his voice.

"Getting hungry again?" she asked, rubbing the sleep from her eyes. He didn't answer as he opened the dried meat's brown wrapping. He tore off a chunk and ate, grimacing at how salty it was. He immediately craved water. The girl watched him, absently picking at her lip.

"Do we ride today?" she asked. Qurrah shook his head.

"The Bridges are near. I want us to be prepared in case our welcome is as kind as last night."

The half-orc took another bite. Couldn't Aurelia summon water too? He thought he remembered her soaking his brother once or twice in such a way. The elf was a walking supply caravan, he thought. Here he was, able to manipulate shadow, bone, and blood, and he would trade it all for the ability to conjure a tiny bit of water along with a sweetroll or two.

He finished the rest of the meat and then cast the wrapping to the dirt. Tessanna raised an eyebrow.

"Someone's being a pig. Where will we get more?"

"Those men that attacked us last night must live nearby," he said. He pooled saliva in his mouth and then spit, imagining it full of salt. "Most likely a village. If we meet them at the Bridges, we'll find out, and take what we need."

"Murder for supplies?" She wrapped the blankets around her so that only her head peeked out. "That's low even for us, isn't it?"

Qurrah opened his mouth to speak, then stopped. It was, wasn't it?

"They attacked us first," he decided. "If they dare touch us again, well, would you blame me for taking what they will no longer need after I send them to the abyss?"

The girl shrugged. She pulled the blankets above her nose.

"Will they try to hurt me again? I don't like it when people do that."

Qurrah offered her his hand, and was not at all surprised that she shrunk back from it. She had slipped into her childlike state. She seemed more like a six-year-old girl than the young woman she really was.

"I'll protect you, whether you need the protection or not," he told her. "Now get dressed. Those men likely saw our fire from their post at the eastern bridge, so we cannot be far."

"Qurrah?"

"Yes, Tessanna?"

She smiled an unseen smile behind the blankets.

"What are the Gods' Bridges like? I've always heard they're pretty."

"Come with me," he told her, once more offering his hand. "And we shall see together."

He took her hand and pulled her from the blankets. She kissed his cheek before putting on her dress.

"Together," she said. "I like that."

When they were ready, Qurrah scattered the last few ashes of their fire and led them west.

The Bridges had been constructed centuries ago by the gods Karak and Ashhur after they had Celestia split the land of Dezrel with the great Rigon River. Just before reaching the ocean, the Rigon River forked in two, creating a large delta. Each god had placed a bridge just south of the fork. Each had hoped this crossing would allow them to claim the fertile delta, and it was their twin claims that led to their war.

Karak had built his bridge across the eastern fork, and it was this bridge that Qurrah and Tessanna first saw.

"Oh, Qurrah," Tessanna said, smiling. "It *is* beautiful."

Twin lions carved of stone flanked the entrance. They were reared back on their hind legs, their front paws raking the air. Their mouths were forever open in a roar of battle. Three arches made of giant stones wedged together formed the bridge's structure. The first arch began where the ground sloped toward the river, and the third ended atop the bank on the far side. Two giant pillars marked where the arches met above the water. Qurrah had heard that the hand of Karak himself lifted and placed the stones into the water, and seeing its size, he held little doubt to its truth.

Carved into the pillars was a giant man standing beside another lion. Qurrah recognized the image, for he had seen a similar one when he visited the priests of Karak back in Veldaren. The top of the bridge was smooth flat stone. Along its edges were three more arches, significantly smaller than the ones underneath. The entire bridge was a chalky white, though in patches throughout there remained the golden color it had once been.

"Pelarak mentioned this in his journal," Qurrah said as he and Tessanna stared in awe. "He wrote that many of his order came here to study the bridge and learn its secrets. Those arches in particular interest them. Pelarak claimed their strength is far beyond the mere stone that makes them."

"I don't care about its secrets," Tessanna said. "But I must see it closer."

She led the way, and Qurrah followed.

Twelve men waited at the bridge's entrance. They wore the same brown coats and gray trousers as the men who had accosted them the previous night. A couple had swords attached to their belts while the rest carried daggers. All Qurrah could think was of how pitiful the men looked compared to the stone lions on either side of them. The men drew their weapons as Qurrah and Tessanna neared. One man perched at the foot of the left lion called out to them.

"Stop, now," he shouted. "That's close enough to talk."

"We don't wish to talk," Qurrah said, using magic to strengthen his voice so the others could hear. If he tried to shout, he'd tear an old wound and blood would pour down his throat. "We wish to cross."

"Well that's the problem," the man said, tossing a dagger up and down in his hand. "We're not sure we want you crossing, not after what happened last night. And I said to stop moving."

The couple continued anyway. The other ruffians grew nervous at their boldness while the apparent leader kept tossing his dagger. Qurrah eyed him closely. His hair was cut much shorter than the others, and he wielded the weapon with an ease that implied many hours of practice. If it came to killing, that man needed taken out first.

"Fine then, guess shouting isn't too civilized, is it?" the man said, hopping down from the lion's foot. "My name is Tory. It's nice to meet such a lovely couple."

Qurrah grabbed several bone pieces from his pockets and held them in one hand. His other caressed the handle to his whip.

"We wish to cross and find supplies within the delta," Qurrah said, letting them look into his eyes and see the lack of fear within. "And we will not be stopped."

"You killed a few of my men," Tory said. "However, I believe they were acting boorish, so unlike the example I try to set for them. For that I apologize."

"Accepted," Qurrah said. "Now will you let us pass?"

"No, not yet," Tory said, pacing between the lions. "See, I heard some crazy stories about a girl made of fire killing my men. Now I don't see any fire, but what we see is hardly what we get, is it?" He gestured to Tessanna. "Are you more dangerous than what you appear?"

"I've killed more than you," she said, her voice meek and shy. "Ten times more. Does that make me dangerous?"

Tory laughed, but Qurrah detected a bit of nervousness. The other men were getting antsy. They had gotten a good look at Tessanna's eyes and they wanted no part of her.

"That's what I thought," Tory said. "Such a beautiful thing, too. Are you both in such a hurry that you cannot stay with us in our friendly town? Riverend may not be the largest of places, or the most civilized, but the ale and food are excellent." He looked at Tessanna, a charming smile on his face. "Surely we could become better acquainted."

Jealousy flared within Qurrah.

"How dare you..."

"We could," Tessanna said, offering him a flirty smile back. "But as I told your dead men, you'd die the moment you touched my flesh."

The charming smile faltered.

"So be it," he said. He snapped his fingers. The men around him reached back and pulled out loaded crossbows from behind the lion statues. Qurrah tensed, his knuckles white.

"No one insults me," Tory said, the dagger in his hand twirling so fast it was a metallic blur. "No one."

Before the men could fire, Qurrah tossed the bones into the air. Dark power flowed from his hands, giving them life. The pieces hovered in a small circle, shining a phantom gray.

"You cannot win this," Qurrah said, his fingers outstretched. "Put down the bows and I will let you live."

"They're scared," Tessanna said. Her hands remained at her side, and she appeared bored of the situation. "They're scared so they threaten."

"Then let's remove their ability to threaten," Qurrah whispered. He formed a fist, igniting the power of the bones. The shards flew through the air, aimed straight for the crossbows. They punched holes in the wood, broke the fingers that held them, and snapped the strings. A couple fired, but the shots were erratic. Qurrah opened his hand once more. Half of the bone pieces returned, hovering before his face.

"Do you think your swords will kill me?" he asked. "Do you think you will get close enough to try?"

A few men grabbed their daggers but Tory waved them off.

"You may cross," the man said. "You are the stronger, without question." He gave one last longing look at Tessanna. "A shame, too."

The group of men parted, granting the couple passage.

"The western bridge is not far," Tory said as they passed. "My men will let you through without hassle. Try not to keep them waiting."

Qurrah grabbed Tessanna's arm and walked across the bridge, silent.

"We're not going to the other bridge," Tessanna said once they were beyond earshot. "And we're not going just because he said he wanted us to. You're such a child."

"We need supplies," Qurrah said.

"Keep telling yourself that," she said, kissing him once on the cheek. "But you won't be fooling me."

"I'd never try to," he said, glancing back at Tory. "But I think I might kill him the next time we meet."

"Try to make it painful," Tessanna said, her tiny mouth grinning. "All he could think about was raping me the entire time we talked."

Tory couldn't decide why, but the horrific laughter he heard from the two as they left the bridge formed a knot deep in his gut, one that would take many drinks to loosen.

3

R iverend was a quaint little town, at least to Tessanna's standards. It thrived off the crops it harvested from the fertile land that stretched for miles in all directions. But many travelers crossing between the two countries also stopped to rest and purchase supplies, and coin from all nations was welcome. The two passed a couple of stores, vague places that offered a few odds and ends, blankets, and waterskins. Tessanna's beauty and Qurrah's robes gained them immediate attention, though no one dared approach. Most just gawked from afar.

"We have a problem," Qurrah said as they stopped before the town's sole tavern. It was one floor with a rain-damaged roof and no windows. Beside the door hung a wooden sign with a crudely drawn mug overflowing at the top.

"I have many problems," Tessanna said, her hands curled around his elbow as she ignored the curious stares. "But what is yours?"

"We have no coin and no items to barter with. We need food, water, and something for your feet. What exactly are we to offer?" Tessanna gave him a dirty smile, and immediately Qurrah's face flushed. "We are not offering you, no matter how much it would gain us." He looked back to the tavern. "If we rest for a night, and then take what we want from their stores, none here could stop us."

"And if they try?" Tessanna asked. Qurrah shrugged, earning himself a glare and a jab from her elbow. "If you won't let me sleep with some lonely farmer for our supplies, I am most certainly not letting you kill for them."

"Then what else do we do?"

The girl tugged on his arm.

"For now, we go and get a drink."

Inside, the dirt floor was tightly packed and trodden upon. Two tables filled the right half of the room, while the left was made of a tiny bar with several carved stools. There was no one inside.

"Evidently drinking is not as popular here as elsewhere," Qurrah murmured.

"Oh it is," said a man coming up behind them, wiping his dirt-covered hands on his trousers. He slipped past them and went behind the bar. "It's just all the drinkers here are also hard workers, and if you haven't noticed yet, the sun isn't even halfway through the sky."

Qurrah smiled at the man and the man smiled back. He was far older than Qurrah and his face was gruff, but he seemed rather amused by his early customers. His hair was tied behind his head in a bushy gray ponytail. When he smiled, it seemed to pull his entire face to the sides, and his bushy unibrow actually separated.

"I have noticed, but neither of us are hard workers. Might we have a drink?"

"Sure thing. Take a seat." The man took out two wooden cups and filled them underneath the counter from a container they could not see. He set them down in front of them at their table. "My name is Erik. Enjoy."

"Before we drink," Qurrah said, pointing to the cups. "I must say that we have no coin to pay for these. I still would very much like a drink, and I would also like to pay you."

"Isn't that how the world always works," Erik said, waving them off. "You can have the first drink free. Consider it a welcome to our town. I'm afraid the rest of the town won't be so friendly to your problem, though." He plopped down at a seat behind the bar. "Not unless you're ready to work for a few coins, but neither of you looks like the sort to bend your backs in the sun. Those robes. You a priest?"

"No," Qurrah said, sipping from the cup. He felt the burning liquid on his tongue, fiercely bitter. He swallowed as quickly as possible. "Just a traveler."

Tessanna dipped her finger into the drink and then put it in her mouth, sucking off the liquid.

"Just travelers," Erik said, watching Tessanna. "You didn't arrive here just last night, did you?" When neither answered, the old man nodded. "See, last night I heard a bunch of ruckus while I was sleeping." He pointed at the floor behind the bar. "That is where my old bones rest, and that is where I woke up to two scared hogs begging for a drink."

Qurrah took another sip as the old man leaned closer.

"They told me the craziest story about this girl of pure fire, beautiful as a goddess and as dangerous as a snake. Said she just started burning, and then killed one of their friends. Now I hope I don't imply an insult, fair lady, but you do look as beautiful as a goddess."

"I'm not poisonous," Tessanna said, her finger pressed against her teeth as she grinned. "But I do burn people."

"Why do you tell us this?" Qurrah asked.

"Because a girl like that, well, she could do a lot of things that people here might appreciate. Might even reward them for doing these things."

Qurrah finished his drink and slid Erik the cup.

"What things?"

"Which bridge did you cross?"

"The eastern," Qurrah replied. "We've come from Neldar. We traveled through Omn too quickly to supply ourselves adequately before we reached the delta."

The barkeep nodded. It was a story he heard often. Most desperate travelers had run afoul with the law at some point in either Neldar or Omn and thought to start a new life in the west.

"Did you meet Tory when you tried to cross the eastern bridge?" he asked. When they both nodded, he continued. "He moved in here with a group of thugs from Mordeina. Started charging a toll to whoever crossed the bridges. If anyone was well armed he'd just let them go by; he was smart like that. Thing is, he started getting more and more money, and he's acquired a healthy collection of all things drunkards love up in his little shack north of town. Got to the point where even those with bodyguards had to start paying his toll...and the tolls themselves got much higher."

Erik walked around the bar and to the door. He glanced outside to ensure no one was nearby. When satisfied, he turned around and approached their table.

"We're neutral territory. With the stigma of the war hundreds of years ago, no country will touch us. Tory's started taking whatever he wants from the towns in the delta, and it's not just food." He looked pointedly at Tessanna. "He wanted you, didn't he?"

She nodded.

"I could tell," she said. "I always can."

"You're older than he'd prefer," Erik said. Qurrah watched as the old man's hands gripped the table to stop their shaking. "But you're beauty was enough to sway his tastes. We've sent our daughters south to Haven, but not always in time. And he's begun to go there now..."

Erik had made this offer many times before to travelers passing through his little town. Never once had he seen such rage as he saw in Tessanna's eyes.

"Little pissfire comes here with men and weapons and thinks he can take what he wants," she said, her eyes staring into nowhere. "Do the girls live after he is done?"

"He keeps them," Erik said. He gripped the table harder. A few tears trickled down his cheek. He was too old and tired to hold them all in. "Keeps them until they're all used up. My granddaughter, she..." He turned and wiped his nose on his sleeve. "She was never the same. She threw herself into the river one night. Said she was certain Tory would come for her again, and she couldn't do it. She'd rather die."

Tessanna stood. Her hands took the old man's and pulled them from the table. She gently kissed his shaking fingers.

"I'll drown them," she said. "In their own blood. I promise."

"He'll still be at the bridges," Erik said. "If he's not, return and I will lead you to his hovel."

"We need food, water, warmer clothes, and shoes for Tessanna's feet," Qurrah said. "Have it ready when we return."

The old man nodded.

"Go with Ashhur's blessing."

To this, Qurrah smirked. "We come bearing death. Ashhur will grant us no blessing."

⊲⊱⊳

"Should we wait until nightfall?" Qurrah asked as they headed into the lush fields north of town that were in various states of final harvest before winter. Tessanna shook her head. Her lips were thin and pulled tight against her teeth. It was rare for her to be so angry, but the abuse of such young girls appeared to be one of the things that could pierce her apathy.

"I won't give him a chance to take another," she answered. "He might have a girl waiting for him, just waiting like a little gift when he returns with his men. I won't let him. I won't."

It took only an hour before the bridge grew within sight. The small gray shapes of Tory's minions littered the construction. They must have spotted them, for at once they rushed across the bridge and lined the near side.

"They fear us, don't they?" Tessanna asked.

"They are right to," Qurrah said.

"They're not afraid enough. Not yet."

Tessanna did not slow as she neared. Seven men remained of the original twelve that greeted them earlier. Tory did not appear to be one of them. As the guards leered and made their crude comments, Tessanna grabbed the nearest ruffian by the throat and shrieked. The force of her yell knocked them to the ground, all but the one she held. His flesh turned gray, his hair shriveled white, and the cartilage of his nose and ears curled inward to the bone. On and on her shriek continued, a horrific wail of death. The flesh peeled off his skull and his teeth cracked free from their gums.

She let him go. He fell to the ground looking freshly dug from the grave twenty years after his death.

"Where is Tory?" she asked the others as they lay stunned. None answered, for they could not hear through the ringing in their ears. She grabbed the shirt of another man and pushed. Magical energy slammed against his chest, tumbling him off the bridge and into the water below.

"Where is he?" she screamed.

"West," one said. He was curled against one of the arches that lined the side of the bridge. His hands were pressed against his ears. Blood covered them. "If you're looking for Tory, he went west, to the other bridge. We haven't done anything, we swear!"

Tessanna stared into his eyes, the black orbs peering into his soul.

"Did you ever take one to be your own?" she asked in a voice so calm and soft it seemed impossible to have been the same voice shrieking louder than thunder.

As the man stared back, he felt claws within his mind, feasting on his thoughts like a ravenous being. Through it all, a single question pulsed like a heartbeat, and he knew what it was she asked.

"No," he said. "It just wasn't…no."

Tessanna released him and turned to her lover.

"Let's go," she said.

"Do we let them live?" Qurrah asked, pointing to the men that were slowly getting to their feet.

"Only the one with the bloody ears. The others forfeited their lives long ago."

Qurrah opened his pouch of bones. The men saw this and fled, racing across the bridge like scared children. Only the one remained, perched against the side with his eyes still locked on Tessanna. He watched, mesmerized, as bones flew past his face and into the necks and skulls of his comrades.

When Qurrah turned around, he saw a swirling black portal hovering above the ground. Tessanna stood before it, her eyes shimmering purple.

"There are shadows in the trees," she said. "Enter."

He did as he was told. She followed him in. The portal closed behind them, leaving only the stunned survivor to flee back to Riverend, deaf but alive.

◁◈▷

They stepped out underneath a great canopy of trees. All around Qurrah saw sturdy brown trunks. Tessanna grabbed his hand and together they weaved through the trunks and brush that scratched at their legs and tore their clothes. The light grew brighter, the trees grew thinner, and then they exited the forest directly east of Ashhur's bridge.

It looked similar to Karak's, but instead of three arches on the bottom it had five, and the upper side were formed into a single, triangular mountain. Giant stone soldiers flanked the entrances to the bridge, wielding a sword in one hand and an hourglass in the other. Standing between these two statues was Tory, surrounded by ten of his men.

"He is deadly with knives," Qurrah said, glancing at his lover. "I would hate to see you cut, so be careful."

"You see me cut all the time," Tessanna replied. She started walking toward the bridge. Qurrah took out his whip and followed.

"You took longer than I expected," Tory shouted as they approached. He seemed jovial at sight of them, clearly unaware of what had transpired at the eastern bridge. Qurrah uncoiled the whip from his arm and let it burst into flame. Tessanna held her arms at an angle from her sides, magic pooling about her fingertips. All white left her eyes as ethereal black wings stretched from her back. Tory took a startled step backward, placing bodies between them.

"I said you can pass," he shouted. "There's no need to fight."

"I know what it is you need," Tessanna said. Her voice pulsed and changed with each syllable. Coupled with her wings, she seemed an otherworldly demon, furious and beautiful. None had the strength to face her. Tory's men turned and fled.

"Wait!" he screamed. Flaming leather snaked in around his ankle. He screamed as the fire bit in deep. He screamed again as Tessanna hooked her fingers toward his men and hissed in a language he had never heard before. Screams of the others joined his own. His paid lackeys fell where they stood, covering the bridge with blood that poured out their eyes, mouths, and nostrils.

The whip left his leg. The skin there was black and blistering, and pain flared throughout the right side of his body. Desperate, he drew his dagger and hurled it at the girl with black wings. She never moved. His aim was poor, and instead of piercing her throat, it stabbed into her left breast. Blood poured across her dress, staining the brown fabric a deep red. Qurrah snarled in anger, but the girl reached out her hand to calm him. She showed no sign of pain, no sign of injury. Just anger.

"You could have lived," she said, pulling out the dagger and dropping it. She passed by the two statues, gently touching one as she stepped onto the bridge. "People take what they can when they are the stronger. Every city, every land, even in nature, this is done. But you took what never should be yours to take. You took what I cannot forgive."

When her wings brushed the sides of the bridge, they parted like smoke only to reform on the other side. Tory fell to his knees, crying from the pain in his ankle.

"Please, I didn't do anything," he begged. "I never harmed you, I never harmed you, I never..."

Her fingers brushed his lips. He quieted.

"You cut me," she whispered.

Through her fingers, he felt his life pass. The cut on her breast closed, its bleeding halted. Upon his own chest, he felt a searing pain and the wet sensation of blood. He pounded the bridge with shaking hands, pleading as his bladder let go.

"Kill him," Qurrah said, disgusted. "He begs worse than a dog."

"Not yet," Tessanna whispered. She knelt close, so close her warm breath blew against Tory's ear. "Where is your home, dog? Where do you keep your girls?"

"Outside Riverend," he said in between sobs. "I'll show you, please, just don't kill me."

"Crawl there," she said. "On all fours, just like what you are."

Tory did. He crawled like a dog across the grass and dirt as tears streamed down his face. He had looked back at the bridge only once, but it was enough to send a fresh wave of terror through him. His shack was a mile southeast of the bridge. It was a long crawl.

When Tory reached the building, he collapsed and clutched his burned ankle. His crying had become soft, continuous sobs. The shack, while large, appeared in poor condition. No noise came from within.

"Mind if we take a look inside?" Qurrah asked. Tory gestured toward the door but said nothing. The necromancer yanked it open and went in, Tessanna following.

On one side was a large bed stuffed with feathers. On the other was a stack of barrels filled with alcohol. In the middle was a large table, poorly carved and cut. Laying on the table, her arms and legs bound behind her back, was a girl no older than twelve. She was naked, her dress torn and bunched at the waist. Bruises covered her body. Between her legs was a dried pool of blood. She was gagged and blindfolded. At the sound of their entrance, she quivered and sobbed quietly.

Qurrah approached the table, feeling his own revulsion rising. He had killed children before, but always it had been quick and merciful. What he saw now would result in the same outcome, but far from quick, and far from merciful.

"It's alright," Qurrah said. His raspy voice only startled the girl further, so he reached out and removed her blindfold. She looked at him with brown eyes that were already filled with tears. "It's alright," he said again. "We're here to help you."

"She will hurt for years," Tessanna said, removing the gag. "I doubt she will conceive children. What is your name, girl?"

"Julie." Her lower lip quivered, and she appeared on the verge of losing control. Tessanna shook her head and put her finger to the girl's lips.

"Be strong now. I made a promise, and I always keep them. You're scared, aren't you? Scared he'll return? I know how to fix it. I know how to make things right." She glanced at Qurrah. "Bring him inside."

Julie closed her eyes and turned away when Tory came crawling in. Bruises covered his hands and knees. Sweat poured from his face. He kept his eyes to the floor.

"Look at him," Tessanna said, wrapping the little girl in her arms and rocking her side to side. "Open your eyes and look at him. He won't hurt you anymore." Julie did look. Her legs squirmed, instinctively closing her knees and thighs tight. She was yet to speak, but Tessanna sensed within her a toughness that made her proud.

"How many days?" she asked. When the girl did not answer, she looked to Tory. "How many days, dog?"

"I don't know," he said. Qurrah wrapped his whip about Tory's neck and pulled it tight.

"I could set it aflame," he said as the man gagged for air.

"Fifteen," he gasped through clenched teeth. Qurrah released the whip. Tessanna stroked the girl's hair. Fifteen days. Fifteen days of being a toy for so many men, taken again and again as blood pooled between her thighs and her bruises darkened.

"Drowning is too good for you," Tessanna whispered. "But it will have to do."

She released the girl and placed her hand atop the table as she whispered a few words of magic. The blood that had dried suddenly turned wet and sticky. It ran down a table leg, collecting in a small red puddle on the floor. Thin ropes of it stretched out and wrapped around Tory's hands and feet. As he let out a cry of shock, a long red tendril wrapped around his neck and choked in his scream.

"Watch, Julie," Tessanna said. Larger and larger the blood puddle grew, pulsing with frightening strength. "Watch how even your monsters can die. You aren't helpless. Not to them. Not to anyone."

The tendrils dragged Tory by the neck toward the pool from which it stretched. The man's head hovered an inch above it, his mouth open and gasping for air as the blood swirled. Qurrah crossed his arms and watched, fascinated. He had seen blood magically enhanced and controlled but this was something special.

"Do you remember everything he did to you?" Tessanna asked Julie as she held out her hand. The girl took it as she nodded. "Then will you be strong for me? Strong for yourself?" Again the girl nodded.

Tory fought against the bonds, but they were too tight. He was losing feeling in his hands and his head felt as if it would explode.

"Put your hand here," Tessanna said. She held Julie's hands in her own, gently guiding them atop Tory's head. She pressed it firm. A shiver went through her. "Now kneel down and whisper to him. Just one word. Will you do that for me? Whisper just one word?"

Julie looked back and forth, her teeth chewing hard on her top lip. But something about Tessanna's eyes soothed her, and so she nodded again.

"I will," Julie said.

Tessanna knelt down and whispered the word to her. The girl seemed to understand. She left Tessanna's arms and knelt beside Tory, her hand still atop his head. The man's face was above the pool of blood, his chin dipping in and out of its disturbingly warm surface. Julie looked the man in the eyes, remembering how he had hurt her. Remembering the other men that had taken her, beaten her, and shouting things she did not understand. When he looked back at her, she saw no shame, no remorse, just cowardice and fear. She found the courage to say the word.

"Drown," she said, and then she pushed. The tendril snapped down. Tory's face smashed into the pool. Julie yanked back her hand as blood splashed in all directions. He shook and struggled, his head completely submerged. Screams bubbled up from beneath. Tessanna held Julie's hand as they watched.

When he was dead, Qurrah pulled his head out from the blood. His face was smashed and broken. Tessanna smiled even as her emotions faded away into apathy.

"You're safe now," she said to Julie. "You were strong, and now you're safe."

"Let's bring her back to Erik," Qurrah said, wrapping up his whip and opening the door to the shack. "He can find where she belongs."

Tessanna took Julie's hand and walked her home.

Erik was waiting for them at the entrance to his tavern. He had dragged a stool outside and propped it next to the door. At sight of Julie he straightened in his seat, and a grin spread across his face.

"He's…he is, isn't he?" the old barkeep said. "Ashhur be praised."

"Ashhur had nothing to do with this," Qurrah said, glancing down at the girl. "She has been tortured for days. If anything, he should be cursed for allowing such a thing to happen."

"We all see things as we wish," Erik said, offering his hand to Julie. "Come with me, child. You're from Haven, aren't you?" The girl nodded and accepted his hand. Erik smiled and gestured to a burlap sack bundled next to him.

"Food, water, and shoes for your lady," he said. "Should last you at least two weeks."

"It will last us far longer," Qurrah said, hoisting it onto his back.

"Light eaters?" Erik asked.

"Very," Tessanna said, giggling at his quizzical look. She knelt before Julie and placed her hands on either side of her face. "You be strong now," she whispered. "Be strong, and the hurt will go away."

"I will," Julie said.

"Sure you folks can't stay a night or two," Erik said. He gestured about. "People will be in a festive mood hearing the young devil's dead. A lot of parents here got daughters that can finally return from Haven, and plenty others that already buried their own would love to toast your health."

"We must move on," Qurrah said, digging through the pack. "And there we are." He pulled out a pair of rough leather moccasins and offered them to Tessanna. She put them on and smiled.

"Much better," she said.

"Might I ask where you're headed?" Erik said as the two prepared to leave.

"To the Sanctuary," Qurrah answered. "Do you know the way?"

"A semblance of a road leads out from the western Bridge," Erik said, his hand on Julie's shoulder. "Follow it until it turns completely north. Farther west you'll see some mountains. The Sanctuary's built into their base. You'll have no trouble finding it."

"Many thanks again," Qurrah said.

Qurrah and Tessanna camped miles past the western bridge, having crossed out of the delta and into the land of Ker. They had ridden Seletha to make up for the time they had lost, and the ache in Qurrah's back constantly reminded him why he hated doing so. The stars were blocked by a line of clouds that had come rolling from the north. Fearing rain, the two huddled close, their backs against the trunk of a giant tree that sprouted like a lone fixture amid the great pasture.

"What did you think of her," Tessanna asked, breaking the silence they had shared for the past hour.

"Who? The girl?" Qurrah asked.

"Julie. I like that name. So simple and pretty."

"Why do you ask me this?"

Tessanna turned and buried her head in his chest.

"Because she would have been a good daughter. I would have understood her, and she would have understood me."

"We could have kept her," Qurrah said. "No one would have known."

Tessanna smiled.

"You know we can't. Not yet. We're going to do some fighting at the Sanctuary, aren't we?"

The half-orc stroked her hair.

"If we must. Lathaar told Tarlak that few there knew of the tome's existence. They should be unprepared for our arrival."

"Lathaar left far before we did. If he warns them?"

"Then more will die than I'd prefer."

They quieted for a bit. Tessanna stared at the clouds, her mind drifting far away.

"He's almost there," she said, her voice dreamy. "He doesn't know we follow, but he fears it. He doesn't know about Aullienna. If he did, he'd ride faster. He'd know we chased." She wrapped her arms around Qurrah's neck. "I would have been a good mother for her," she whispered. "Do you believe me?"

He kissed her forehead. "Of course I do."

She pressed her face back against his chest, hiding the few tears that dripped down her cheeks.

"Then why'd you kill Aullienna," she whispered as the rain drowned out her words. "Why?"

4

Lathaar rode down the well-trodden path, branches flashing by either side of him. He knew he should be patient, but the forest was nearing its end. He held his sword high, using its light to see in the darkness. Rain had come and soaked the ground. The cold tried to chill his bones but he refused to let it. Fire and blankets awaited him. After weeks of riding he was about to arrive at the Sanctuary.

The trees grew thicker, their branches intertwining above his head. The leaves had long since fallen, and in the glow of his sword they appeared crisscrossing veins marring sight of the sky. Not long, he thought. Not long at all.

He let out a whoop as his horse suddenly burst through the trees and into open air. Towering before him were the Elethan mountains, shining purple in the reawakening stars. Cut into the stone was the Sanctuary. The entrance was built of wood harvested from the nearby forest and used to form the doorways and the roof. Beyond, chiseled in the rock, were circular pillars and great square sides. A lantern shone from a window in each of the four towers that stretched up from the corners. Lathaar swatted his horse on the rump and urged her on.

There was a single door to the building, roughly the size of a man and reinforced with bars across the front. A small window filled its center, also protected by bars. Lathaar hopped off his horse and banged just below the window with his fist. He waited a few minutes, then banged again. After the second time he heard commotion from the other side of the door and then a voice spoke through the window.

"What's all the fuss?" the voice asked. "Speak your business so an old man can get some sleep."

"I am a weary traveler searching for shelter," Lathaar said. "Might I enter?"

"What's your name?"

In answer the paladin drew his sword and let its light shine across his face.

"Good lord, you're back," the person on the other side exclaimed. "We've been hoping for your return."

Lathaar heard bolts being slid from the door, followed by a loud crack. The door swung inward. An old man dressed in white robes stood there, a large medallion shaped like a mountain hanging from his neck. His hair was in a frazzled mess.

"Lijah!" the man shouted. "Come get his horse and take it around back." A young boy appeared from further in. His face was scarred with acne, and his left hand a tangled mess. With his good right arm he reached out for the reigns. Lathaar handed them over, smiled at the boy, and then outright grinned at the old man.

"Been a long time, Keziel. I see your hair hasn't fallen out yet."

"Still your tongue and get in here," Keziel said. "I have a guest that's been dying to meet you."

Keziel grabbed his arm and pulled him inside. The hallway was cramped but the ceiling was incredibly high. Torches decorated both sides, lighting the place well. The priest turned and hurried past a few doors to a sharp right turn. The place rapidly expanded into a great room. A fire roared in a giant oven, and various rugs made of animal skins lined the floor. Sitting on one before the fire, turning pages to a small book, was a man dressed in platemail. Upon seeing Lathaar, he startled to his feet and grabbed his mace, which rest next to him against the wall.

"Draw your sword," the man said, flicking his head so his long red hair did not block his vision.

"What nonsense is this," Keziel shouted. "Put that down!"

"I said draw your sword," the stranger insisted. His free hand reached back and grabbed a handle on the shield that hung from his back. Lathaar grabbed the hilt of his sword and drew it, holding it before his eyes so that the blue glow illuminated the features of his face.

"It is drawn," he said. "Now what is it you wish from me?"

To his surprise, the stranger suddenly relaxed, and he lowered his mace.

"Ashhur be praised," he said. "It's been so long."

"What's going on here, Keziel?" Lathaar asked. He remained still as a stone, tensed for a trap.

"This is all just a misunderstanding. Jerico, did you have to get him all riled up?"

The man Lathaar assumed to be Jerico pulled his shield off his back and held it before his chest.

"Lathaar, paladin of Ashhur," he said, a huge smile overcoming him. "You are no longer alone."

And then his shield flared with the light of Ashhur, as equally bright as the glow that surrounded Lathaar's sword.

"Your name," Lathaar said, his mouth dropping open in shock.

"Jerico of the Citadel, paladin of Ashhur. The more attractive of the two last paladins."

Lathaar was still too stunned to argue as his mind tried to wrap around the joyous fact that he was no longer the last.

◦✠◦

So how did you survive?" Lathaar asked once the two were seated comfortably before the fire. Lathaar's armor was piled into one corner, waiting to be cleaned. Jerico's was beside it, with the square shield propped atop. Each held bowls of warm soup that Keziel had brought them.

"I dreamt of the Citadel falling," Jerico explained in between sips from the bowl. It tasted of potatoes and broth, and he loved the warmth down his throat. "It was too real to be just a dream. I would have thought it a warning from Ashhur, but it was too sad, too...final. I wasn't far from

Mordeina at the time, and I assure you, that was not a good place to be. All the priests and paladins for Karak came out in force, in far greater numbers than you'll ever see in Neldar."

"I've fought plenty," Lathaar said, blowing against the steam that hovered above his own bowl. "I spent much of the past two years either with Tarlak or the priests here. I've got quite a tale for you, once you have the time to hear it."

"I have a few of my own," Jerico assured him. "But Keziel has already told me much of what you've done. Slaying Darakken, eh? And what's this nonsense I hear about an Elholad?"

Lathaar grinned and pulled out his sword. At his command, it shone pure white, so bright and powerful that the metal seemed to vanish away within the glow. When he sheathed the blade Jerico gave him a few joking claps.

"It seems Ashhur had a plan sparing the two of us, although I cannot claim such amazing exploits as you. I returned to the Citadel after six months, just to be sure no dog of Karak waited for me. It was there I found Bonebreaker." He pointed to his mace. "Do you remember Jaeger? Big guy, hair redder than mine? That was his mace. I found it just laying in the grass, abandoned. I took it and then fled to the Vile Wedge. Killed a few orcs, maimed a few goblins, and just roamed. Didn't know why, or what I was waiting for, but then a young paladin of Karak mentioned your name before I killed him."

"I've become something of an obsession for them," Lathaar said, a bit of joy leaving his eyes. "Especially one in particular. But that is for another time." He slurped down the rest of his bowl. "For now, I need sleep."

"Amen to that," Jerico said. "I'm glad you arrived, though. Ashhur brought us here for a reason. I hadn't seen Keziel since the Citadel fell, and when I return, you show up within days of my own arrival."

"I'm not sure I want to imagine why," Lathaar said, grinning. "I've seen what he'll throw at just one of his paladins. What does he think the two of us can handle?"

Jerico laughed.

"I'll pray for both of us. Good night, Lathaar."

"You too, Jerico."

Jerico left for the only spare room while Lathaar curled his blankets tighter and scooted closer to the fire. After the month of riding, he finally felt at home. Still, sleep proved elusive. His mind kept drifting back to Tessanna, black wings arching out her back as she howled in the rain. He had seen that face before. He had seen it on Mira. Come the morning, he planned on finding out just what Keziel knew.

Prayer dominated all the morning rituals of the Sanctuary, and the sound of worship to Ashhur was constant. Keziel, being the eldest, attended the youngest at the prayers, and counseled those who were troubled. Lathaar remained patient, letting him complete his rounds before he would take him aside to talk. To pass the time, the two paladins sparred.

The ground was rough and cold but relatively flat on the north side of the Sanctuary, so they scraped a rough circle into the dirt. Lathaar wielded his longsword and shortsword, while Jerico twirled his mace while his shield remained on his back.

"Been a long time since I sparred with a paladin," Lathaar said, stretching his arms. "Brings back plenty of good memories."

"You were Mornida's pupil, weren't you?" Jerico asked. "Thought so. I remember hearing all this nonsense about prodigy and whatnot, some whelp of a kid five years younger than me that Lolathan died healing."

"He was not punished by Ashhur," Lathaar said.

"Easy there. Didn't say he was. But I remember the whispers."

Lathaar grabbed his ankle and stretched.

"Going to ready your shield?"

Jerico shrugged. "I don't tell you when to draw your swords, do I?"

"Very well."

David Dalglish

Neither wore their armor at Lathaar's insistence. It was just a harmless sparring match, not a competition, and he trusted each other to be skilled enough with their weapons. With a nod, they began.

Lathaar slashed with his longsword, keeping his shorter blade back and ready. Jerico parried it aside, grinning as he did. When the shortsword thrust in, straight for his gut, he had already stepped to the side. As it passed his exposed skin, he slapped it away with his mace.

"So you survived all those fights how?" he asked. "Surely not battle prowess?"

"Amusing."

Lathaar stepped closer, swinging both blades in a high arc. Jerico blocked the first with his mace, angling the hilt of his weapon to push the second hit down so that it passed harmlessly before his leg. When the shortsword cut back and thrust, Jerico finally pulled down his shield. The fine edge turned against the brightly glowing surface. If he had been of evil nature, Lathaar's arms would have jolted in pain, but instead he felt just a mild push at the contact.

Jerico placed the shield before him, covering all but his feet and the top of his head. Lathaar could not see, but he knew the way the paladin's eyes were glinting that he was smiling.

"I may not be the best fighter," Jerico said from behind his shield. "I'm probably not even good at it. But I'm harder than the abyss to kill."

"We'll see about that."

Lathaar feinted twice, and neither time budged the giant shield. He thrust both his swords from one side, hoping to curl around the right edge of the shield. Jerico shifted, smashing away the swords as if they were nothing. Lathaar felt his arms pushed back from the contact. He gave his opponent no rest. Again his swords slashed out, this time from either side. Again the shield pushed them away, batting left and right. His swords accomplishing nothing, he tried a new tactic. He slammed his entire body against the shield, hooking the hilts of his swords against the edge. His body shook with the contact. He spun off, pulling with his swords to toss Jerico's shield out and wide. Finally, his opponent was exposed.

And so was he.

The two were so close that Lathaar had no time to react before the ridged edges of Jerico's mace rested against his neck.

"You were doing so well," Jerico teased. "And then you had to do something stupid."

"I don't know what to do," Lathaar said, pushing the mace away with his fingers. "I've never seen anything like what your shield has become."

"No one has. I asked Keziel, as well Lolathan and Mornida at the Citadel. No paladin has been given the blessing that I have. It's always the weapon we hold that projects our faith and gains Ashhur's blessing. I guess for me, I've always viewed my shield as my greatest weapon."

"I'd never outlast you," Lathaar said, spinning his swords. "And you'll never make a mistake. That's how you lived all these years, isn't it?"

Jerico kicked the dirt and blushed a little.

"You make me sound so much better than I am. I have a big shield and Ashhur's made it glow. Let's not get carried away here."

Lathaar smashed his swords together, showering sparks to the ground.

"Again. I'll figure out how to beat you. I just need some time."

"You're welcome to try," Jerico said, hoisting up his shield so that his eyes just barely peered over. "Ashhur knows it's been awhile since I had some competition."

Lathaar tensed, thinking over several routines for attack, when suddenly Jerico lunged, his shield leading. Before he could move, the gleaming object slammed against his arms. He braced his legs to stop, but he was off balance and Jerico knew it. The shield lowered, and too late Lathaar understood why. A foot swept underneath, taking out Lathaar's legs. The paladin hit the ground, gasping as the air was knocked from his lungs. Jerico stood over him, grinning.

"That's to make sure you don't get comfortable," he said. "Don't think I'm going to sit here all day letting you hack at me. Understood?"

He clipped his mace at his belt and offered his hand. Lathaar took it, shaking his head as he stood.

"I thought we'd practice, and maybe I'd teach you a thing or two. Guess it's going to be the other way around, isn't it?"

Jerico tapped his forehead with his forefinger.

"I had five years of training at the Citadel beyond what you were given. And don't think you've fought any more, or suffered any worse, than I have since the Citadel fell. Normally I'd try to be gentler about this, but we're the last. We have no chance for error and no room for pride. The next time we spar, we wear armor. Understood?"

"Yes, master," Lathaar said, doing his best to swallow his bruised pride.

"Come on, now," Jerico said, smacking him on the arm with an open palm. "No pouting, and no master, or teacher, or whatever else you can think of. I'm your brother in Ashhur and that's more than good enough for me."

Lathaar stood, sheathing his swords and then brushing off the dirt from his clothes.

"You going to be alright?" Jerico asked him.

"Yeah, yeah." He bowed to the other paladin. "I just expect a bit more maturity from myself. We'll spar again tomorrow, and it'll be far closer than today, I assure you."

Jerico grinned. "Now that's more like it."

Lathaar searched inside the Sanctuary, but it was outside that he found Keziel.

"I wouldn't think the cold air would be good for an old man like you," he said, bowing before his elder.

"The air's cold everywhere, and a walk amid nature does me far better than the dim light inside." He continued to shuffle along. "You have something on your mind, child? Out with it."

"Have you thought about the curse on the girl I told you of last night?" Lathaar asked.

"If Calan cannot cure it, and believes that I cannot as well, then I trust his judgment," Keziel said. "But you knew this before you ever came to me. What is it that really bothers you?"

"It's about Mira," he blurted. "I think there's more to her than what you told me."

"I told you everything you needed to know," Keziel said, his eyes fixed firmly ahead. "She's a special girl, one rarely born upon our world. Protect her, keep her safe, and nothing else should matter."

"But I've found another," Lathaar said. The old man halted his walk and stared at Lathaar with disbelieving eyes.

"You shouldn't lie to an old man."

"No lie. I have seen another, by the name of Tessanna. I witnessed her magic, and even fought against her. She rivals Mira in power, and she may well be her twin."

Keziel resumed his walk. "What I can tell you will not ease the fears in your heart," he said. "And it will not aid you in choosing your next path. Are you sure you want to hear it?"

"I must know," Lathaar said. "I made a promise to a friend."

Keziel sighed and scratched his long white beard.

"I don't think even Mira knows what she really is. Few do. Are you sure you want to hear?"

Lathaar nodded.

"Very well," the old man said with another sigh. "Then listen carefully."

The paladin did listen. And when Keziel was done, Lathaar knew a lot of riding awaited him in the coming months. Tarlak needed to be told. Mira too. And Keziel was right; his fears were not eased. Not in the slightest.

Where is it you think you're going?" Jerico asked him as Lathaar saddled up his horse.

"Stonewood forest," Lathaar replied, pulling tight one of the leather straps. "I need to find Mira and bring her to Veldaren."

"Who's Mira? You have a love I don't know about?"

Lathaar chuckled.

"She's a young woman. She helped me defeat Darakken not so long ago."

"What's so important about getting to her?"

"Too long a story to tell." The paladin hoisted up a rucksack just behind the saddle and began tying it on. "At least at this moment, anyway."

"So I finally find you and now you're going to leave me? So rude, Lathaar. I expect better from a fellow paladin."

Lathaar laughed.

"I assumed you would come with me, whether or not I asked you."

Jerico leaned back against one of the wood beams that made up the stall.

"You assume wrong," he said. "I'm still needed here. Ashhur has been quite clear about that during my prayers. If you bring this Mira girl here after you find her I'll travel with you to Veldaren."

The two paladins embraced.

"I know what you mean," Lathaar said. "I hear his warnings too. Five days is all I ask. Stay safe until then, and throw me a prayer or two."

"Toss me a few as well. I can't imagine what need I have here in the Sanctuary, but if something or someone is crazy enough to attack here, I may need all the help I can get."

At this Lathaar turned, hiding the trouble on his face. Jerico caught the look and refused to let it pass.

"You know who approaches, don't you?" he asked.

"Five days," Lathaar said, his back still to Jerico. "Four if I leave now and ride hard. They should not have caught up to me, but if they did… just be careful."

He mounted his horse and grabbed the reins. Jerico frowned, displeased with how much he was being kept in the dark. As Lathaar rode south, Jerico decided he and Keziel needed to have a nice, long chat.

Once he was several miles from the Sanctuary, Lathaar closed his eyes and did his best to clear his mind as he rode along a faded road once traveled by pilgrims seeking healing from the clerics of Ashhur. It was many miles between them, but Mira had communicated beyond farther.

Can you hear me? he whispered in his head. No voice responded. The sound of his horse's breathing grew louder in his ears. The clomps of the hoofs were like thunder.

Mira? Can you hear me? I've returned.

His eyes flared open as a female voice suddenly pierced into his mind in a cascading shriek.

OH GODDESS HELP ME!

He awoke still atop his horse. The sun had set, and when he looked around, he realized he had traveled many miles since he could last remember. He rubbed his eyes. It felt like knives shredded everything within his skull. The fear in Mira's voice lingered within him. He remembered what Keziel had said, and his gut sank further.

"Please help her," Lathaar prayed. "Keep her safe until I arrive."

He stopped his horse and dismounted. There was no time to build a fire, so he pulled out his blankets, wrapped them about his body, and laid down to sleep. He let his mount wander in search of food and water, knowing she was well-trained enough to return before sunrise. The surrounding landscape was full of hills, and plenty of springs ran between them.

Lathaar thought of calling out to Mira again, but the ache behind his eyes deterred him. He needed rest, and he needed to hold faith in his god that she would be well when he arrived. He offered another prayer for her safety before succumbing to sleep.

Jerico had hounded Keziel much of the day, until finally the old man promised to tell all he knew once the sun was down and the rest of the Sanctuary was asleep. The paladin waited by the fireplace, polishing his shield to pass the time. When the priest finally entered carrying a plate with bread, butter, and a wide knife, he sighed at Jerico.

"Thrilled as I am to find another paladin alive, you certainly aren't helping me forget the worries of this world," he said.

"That's what I am here for," Jerico said, putting away his cloth. "Prayers aren't enough for what I do. I carry my shield and mace for a reason, and that's because this world is trouble."

"In trouble, really," Keziel said, sitting in a wooden chair next to the fire. He cut a slab of butter with his knife and began slathering it across the bread. "Something is coming, some event that all three gods have been preparing for. My heart tells me Mira has her part to play."

"Who is Mira?" Jerico asked. "How you speak of her, I guess my question should be *what* is she?"

"Mira is a daughter of balance, granted life by Celestia's own hand. She has been made in the goddess's image. Our order has written of several daughters of balance, and they always have pure black eyes and long hair dark as the night. Their mothers conceive without need of a lover and then die in birth. These daughters are barren, at least we believe so, for none are ever recorded as being with child."

Jerico shifted by the fire, trying to imagine what one such girl would look like.

"Why does she make them?" he asked.

"Because Celestia represents the balance between Ashhur and Karak. She wants their war to wage eternally in punishment for their transgressions against her and her world. As she sleeps amid the weave of fate, she can sense turning points in time. When the world would turn too far to the side of either brother god, she gives her power to a mortal girl, a girl whose entire fate is devoted to preventing any disruption to the balance."

"So this Mira girl, she's one of these daughters?"

Keziel took another bite of bread.

"I am certain of it. I once thought that her purpose was the slaying of the demon Darakken, and I still may be correct. But if Lathaar is correct, and a second daughter has been born, then something far greater is at stake."

"Why would it matter?" Jerico asked. "If Mira's was to prevent things from descending too far to darkness, why couldn't this other girl be to do the same?"

"With the destruction of the Citadel, it would seem likely," Keziel said, licking butter from his lips. "But not once has anyone recorded two daughters of balance existing within fifty years of another, let alone at the same time. Let me show you why."

He cleaned the butter off his knife and then balanced it on the tip of his finger. With subtle twists of his wrist, the knife began to teeter.

"Imagine the left side being Ashhur, and the right, Karak," he said as Jerico watched intently. "Our world constantly shifts between the two, as is the nature of such a war. But sometimes things are not even, such as when the Citadel fell." He shifted his finger more, so that the knife was perilously close to falling off the right side of his finger. "It is then a daughter of balance is born."

As Jerico watched, Keziel tapped the left side of the knife with his other finger. The knife rocked back and forth for a moment and then settled down into a gentler balance.

"As you can see, once a daughter of balance intervenes, everything is chaotic. The future is uncertain for a brief stretch of time. And if a second daughter exists…"

He smacked the knife with his finger so that it began to rock violently, and then hit it a second time. The knife careened off his finger to the stone floor, the clear ring piercing the quiet hall. Both stared at the knife, not saying a word. Keziel took another bite of bread, chewing it as he thought.

"I fear Celestia has grown desperate. The world may be approaching a point where one side must win, Karak or Ashhur. If this is true, then Mira may well be the key to victory. I respect the goddess's desires and commands, but I would greatly prefer Ashhur to take control of this world than let it descend into Karak's madness."

Jerico grabbed one of his blankets, wrapped it about his body, and lay down upon the stone.

"And this other girl," he asked. "The one Lathaar met in Veldaren. Isn't it possible she too has her part to play, for good or ill?"

"I'm sure she does," Keziel said, rising from his chair. "But from what he told me she is far from a beacon of light. She is dangerous, a wild creature. Go with Lathaar when he returns to Veldaren. He will need your help to deal with the threat she might pose."

Again Jerico remembered that look on Lathaar's face, and as he watched the flickering flames he prayed that the five days passed quietly. He found sleep in the simple logic that whoever this other daughter of balance was, she couldn't possibly have reason to venture across the rivers to come to the Sanctuary. In that simple but proud building of wood and stone, he could think of nothing anyone might want. Nothing at all.

But Keziel could.

5

Seletha halted at Tessanna's gentle insistence. The road they traveled had turned sharply to the north, and sure enough a great chain of mountains loomed to their west. The peaks were purple and red, and Tessanna commented on their beauty.

"We are not far," Qurrah said. "It is only a two-day ride, given Seletha's speed."

"She's a good girl," Tessanna said, brushing her side with her fingers. "Aren't you, Seletha?"

The horse snorted. Bits of flame and black smoke came from her giant nostrils. They had ridden the entire morning, and still the creature showed no sign of exhaustion. Qurrah did not know how Tessanna had learned to summon the creature, but it surely was an amazing gift.

"Give me your arms," Qurrah said. The girl obeyed, circling her hands around his waist. He took them and held on as Tessanna nestled her face against his neck and sighed.

"I could stay like this forever," she said.

"Will you settle for a couple hours?"

"I will."

With a kick from Qurrah's heels, the giant steed galloped on, straight for the Sanctuary.

That night, as Tessanna slept in Qurrah's arms beside a dying fire, she first heard the voice. It wasn't like the others in her mind, the ones she heard and knew were her own. It also differed from the calm, powerful voice she heard rarely, the one that seemed to know so much about her and called her daughter. No, this one was an intruder, a frightened one at that.

Help me, please, please help, it hurts so much...

Tessanna tilted her head to one side, as if to listen more intently.

"Who hurts you?" she whispered, quiet so she did not wake her lover.

He hurts me. He…who are you?

She felt a squirming in her head, as if this foreign presence was realizing for the first time who she was inside. Tessanna latched on, trying to visualize who spoke with her. At once she saw, and she felt a similar spark of recognition within the voice crying for aid.

"My reflection." *My reflection.*

The presence in her mind pulled free, easily breaking Tessanna's grip in her shock. She had seen herself in her mind, yet so different. She wore a faded green dress of the elves. Her skin was healthy and tanned. And most of all, her mind was not broken. And for that alone, she hated her.

She started giggling. She couldn't help it. Back at the Eschaton tower, she had smashed her face into the lone mirror of her room. She hadn't understood then, but now she did. Shatter your reflection, the voice had commanded. Shatter.

"I'll see you soon," she said, a strange pleasure swarming through her body. "Mommy said I have to, and so I will. I always do what mommy says. And I think she wants me to kill you."

Qurrah stirred and asked groggily, "Kill who?"

"Nothing lover," Tessanna said, her voice warm. "Now sleep."

He did. She stroked his face, the image of her equal locked in her mind. She didn't know where she was, or how she would find her, but she held faith they would meet. She could be patient. As she imagined plunging her knife through that other girl's chest, another swirl of pleasure overtook her body. Let the conflict wait, she thought. The pleasure of the imagining was enough for now.

She slept, and for once Aullienna did not torment her.

Qurrah made little complaint about riding Seletha the following days. Tessanna thought she knew why. The

Sanctuary was so close, and within was a tome rumored to be of such power that it could sunder mountains, turn mere mortals into demons, and even put together the fractured pieces of a girl's mind. She wondered if he doubted his abilities to fix her. He probably did. He had begun to doubt many things since Aullienna's death. Understandable, she thought. She too had doubted since then. How many promises had her lover made? How many had he broken?

Too many, she thought. But not enough. She wrapped her arms tighter around him as they rode through the day. She would keep forgiving, keep forgetting, every broken promise. His love was the first she had ever wanted, and she was terrified of losing it. If each promise led to death, if she had to suffer pain to keep his love, well...

"My life has been pain," she said to Qurrah. "Do you think that is a lie?"

"No," Qurrah said, glancing back at her. "Why do you ask?"

"Because I lie to myself sometimes," she said. "I lie so the voices behind my eyes will leave me alone."

Qurrah laughed. He had no idea the thoughts running through her mind. She was just speaking nonsense, the craziness she often hid coming out in full bloom. She knew he thought this, and her shy self took over. Her face flushed with embarrassment.

"I'm sorry," she said, pressing her face against the cloth on his back. "Just stay with me, alright?"

"Forever and always," he said as the two rode on.

That night they huddled together as a cold rain pelted their bodies. Their fire should have died long ago, but a gentle exhale from Tessanna's lips every few minutes sent it roaring to life in defiance of the rain. In the distance, they could see torches burning in the towers of the Sanctuary. The two stared at them, as if in longing of the calm and warmth they represented.

"When will we take the tome?" Tessanna asked as she huddled with her head in Qurrah's lap, using his body for shelter.

"Tomorrow night. Let the priests be sleeping and unaware."

"What will we do?"

Qurrah stroked her head with his hand.

"Not far is a graveyard the priests use to bury their dead. I'm sure you sense it as well as I do. There should be a few salvageable corpses there. I don't know how strong the priests will be, but I'd prefer to gauge their strength on my undead before risking harm to you or I."

Tessanna leaned closer to the fire and blew across it. As the flames soared higher, she whispered her question.

"Do we have to do this?"

Qurrah nitted his eyebrows as he stared down at her.

"I doubt they will hand over Darakken's spellbook willingly."

"That's not what I meant," she said. "I mean me. Us. Am I really so bad, my mind that broken?"

"I made a promise," Qurrah said.

"And I would free you from it."

Qurrah stroked the side of her face with the back of his fingers as an image of Tessanna and Aullienna playing in the grass outside the Eschaton tower smoldered in his mind.

"The price," he said, a sudden weight overcoming his words, "the price we have paid is already too high to turn back now. I will not make what we have lost be for nothing."

"But…"

"No," Qurrah said, pressing his fingers against her lips. Tessanna shook her head, freeing herself from his hand.

"Do not think you can make up for her death," the girl said, her black eyes seething. "No spell, no action, and no promise will wash it away. Do what you think we should do, not what you think will atone for your sins."

Qurrah stared at her, waiting for the anger to melt away into shyness or apathy. It didn't. His guilt flared under her stare, and he turned, unable to face her.

"I must have the spellbook," he said to the ground. "Give me a chance to at least keep the promises I have made and not yet broken."

Gently, she pulled his lips to hers, even as the angry fire still burned in her eyes.

"Of course I will," she whispered into his ear after their kiss ended. "Keep loving me, and I will give you anything of me you wish to take."

The rain poured down harder, but they held each other tighter and weathered it as they always had.

The Sanctuary had once been two buildings, separated by a dirt path a mile long. The younger clerics lived in the southern estate, while the older clerics lived and taught in the northern one. After the Gods' War, and the world became a far more dangerous place, the priests had built upon the northern rooms with wood, enlarging it to accommodate the younger brethren. The other building was torn down and salvaged. The graveyard beside it, though, was left where it was. In time, the travel down the dirt road south was viewed with pride and reverence, an inevitable walk they would all someday take.

As Qurrah and Tessanna traveled down that road, mountains looming to their right, they could feel a great weight on their shoulders. So many feet had walked where they now walked, carrying upon their shoulders the enclosed body of their dead brethren.

"Do you feel it?" Tessanna asked as they walked hand in hand.

"Not ghosts," Qurrah said, his eyes flitting left and right.

"No...they do not linger in anger or sorrow. They hallow this road, and Ashhur grants their souls leave to gaze upon those who walk it. They watch for their brothers and fellow priests." She laughed. "I don't think they like us being here."

"Then they really won't like what I will soon do to their own bodies."

Wooden stakes outlined the graveyard, each one with a small symbol of the mountain across the top. Smoothed stones marked the graves. They had no writings atop them, just a single image of the mountain carved in the stone. Qurrah counted the rows, trying to gauge the number of graves.

"I don't know how many bodies will be usable," he said when he finished. "But we'll get a hundred if we're lucky."

"We're not lucky" Tessanna said, her own eyes closed as she counted in a different way. "And you will get only fifty."

Qurrah nodded, trusting her judgment.

"Fifty will do."

He spread his arms, closed his eyes, and inhaled deeply. The words came easily, for they were attached to so many memories. How many had he brought to life when Velixar first taught him the spell? Eight? Qurrah smiled as his eyelids fluttered. He had grown stronger since, and now was the time to prove it. He did not voice the concern, but Tessanna knew it anyway. Fifty corpses might be usable, but how many could Qurrah actually bring back and control?

He spoke the words, driving all his strength into them. Dark magic poured out his throat, seeping into the dirt of the graveyard. In it was a single command, strong in its insistence. Rise.

"Come and play, children," Tessanna said, dancing from gravestone to gravestone. She pirouetted on one, the tips of her toes circling above the symbol of Ashhur as rotten hands and feet tore from the earth. The girl saw the movement and laughed.

"I count twenty-seven," she said, blowing her lover a kiss. Rotten bodies in white robes that had faded gray continued their climb from their graves, tearing at the dirt that covered their eyes and mouths.

"Far more than eight," Qurrah said, his eyes still closed. He could sense more, lingering underneath the ground, awake but not obeying. He sent his will to them. Their revulsion to his desire angered him greatly. "More than eight," he said again before falling to his knees. Tessanna twirled in between the dirt-covered minions. Words escaped from her lips, soft and slippery. At once, the earth about them erupted into turmoil as bodies freed themselves from their graves. Pleased, the girl danced her way to Qurrah, who was gasping for breath.

"How many," he asked, unable to lift himself to his feet.

"Seventy more," she answered.

"You said only..." A coughing fit interrupted him. He hacked against his fist, pretending not to see the flecks of blood that speckled it. "You said only fifty here were usable," he said.

Tessanna poked him in the shoulder.

"Fifty usable that you could raise. You disappointed me. Bad Qurrah."

His pale skin flushed red.

"Give them to me," he said. "I can control them."

The girl sent her undead out of the graveyard in a chaotic march. Amid the sounds of their shambling, she crossed her arms at her lover and sighed.

"I'm not worried about your pride, I'm worried about you. Now get up before I steal away the ones you do control."

The half-orc snarled, his fingers clawing into the dirt. He pushed to his feet, fighting away the sudden vertigo that accompanied his stand. Tessanna just giggled at his glare and turned away.

"I want night to come," she said sounding so very happy. "I want to go play with our new pets. Can we play now, Qurrah? I don't want to wait."

"Dark will come soon enough," he told her, trying to ignore the nagging humiliation he felt in his chest. "Surprise is our greatest weapon."

"No," Tessanna said, twirling once more amid the graveyard, now a torn mess of open graves and scattered stone. "I am."

When the Sanctuary was dark and torches burned in the towers, Jerico slipped out the front doors. He wore no armor, though he kept his mace and shield buckled and ready. So many years hunted by servants of Karak had taught him such. He walked to the southern side, wishing to be away from the doors. He stared at the stars as he walked, surprised at how accustomed he was to their light. The other priests knelt beside their beds in prayer, but he needed something different. Something larger.

He slammed his shield down and knelt beside it. His mace he shoved headfirst to the dirt, bracing his weight against the handle. In the calm, he prayed, his neck tilted back so his pleadings could reach the sky. He always felt Ashhur was up there somewhere amid the stars, so to them he prayed for the safety of Lathaar, for guidance in his difficult life, and for the strength to continue his walk of faith. Sometimes he heard Ashhur's gentle voice in answer, sometimes he didn't. That night, however, he heard his words like a clear bell ringing in his head.

Arm yourself. The fallen brother comes.

Jerico lurched to his feet, his shield braced against his arm and his mace in hand. His heart pounded, the leather surrounding his weapon's handle growing sticky against his sweating palm. He looked all about but saw no foe.

"Fallen brother?" he asked the night. He was given no answer. His heart ordered him to remain, to await whatever it was that approached, but his mind kept lingering on his suit of armor, piled near the fireplace within the Sanctuary. As the cold air chilled his skin, he ran to the doors. He slammed them open, charged through the hallways, and then found his armor. Piece by piece he buckled it on.

"Lathaar knew someone was coming," he said as he pulled on one of his gauntlets. "That rascal knew it and didn't tell me. I swear, next time I see him I'm going to do more than just whallop him with my..."

It was then he felt it. Because of his close relationship with Ashhur, he was attuned to those things his master hated more than all else. Like a thorn in his mind, he sensed them, their number so large his chest tightened and his stomach twisted. More than a hundred undead were near.

"Burn it all to the abyss," he said, looping his arm through the leather straps of his shield before grabbing the sturdy handle near the side. Finished, he took his mace and slammed it against his shield. Soft blue-white light covered its surface, just as bright as it had always been. Armored and ready, Jerico turned back to the hallway, and it was then he heard the great explosion of shattering wood and metal. Inside his head, he heard Ashhur's cry of warning, loud and constant. The undead were inside the Sanctuary.

Jerico turned into the hallway, knowing his time was short. The clerics were asleep and not prepared for battle. If too many rushed in, they could flood the building, slaughtering everyone. He would not allow it. Down the thin passage he could see the remnants of the door, now nothing but tiny pieces that had been blasted inward. Pouring inside were the skeletal shapes of the dead. A few doors on the sides of the hall had been pushed open, and from within he heard the briefest of screams.

"This is holy ground," Jerico shouted, bracing himself in the narrow hallway. "And I will remove your blasphemy, no matter how many you are!" Only he protected the deeper parts of the Sanctuary. His shield shone bright. He could not fall.

The wave of undead slammed into him, rushing forward with mindless energy. The paladin gasped as his braced legs slid along the smooth stone. Gritting his teeth, he pushed with all his strength while crying out the name of his god. The light on his shield flared, and the flesh of the rotting skeletons sizzled and burned. Bones broke, flesh peeled, and the unholy creations shattered one after another as they crashed against his shield.

"Awake, brethren," Jerico shouted as he took a step forward, pressing against the throng. "Karak has come to call!"

His shield flared with light again, knocking the undead back several feet. In the brief respite, the paladin pulled back his shield and charged, Bonebreaker already swinging. The first to feel its touch exploded, every bone in its body now chalky white powder. He hacked a second and a third, grim satisfaction on his face from each kill. He was halfway to the door, and the flood entering had completely halted. His shield smashed the closest skeleton once, twice, bashing it back so that it collapsed atop the undead behind it. Jerico put his foot on its chest while he kept his shield braced high before him.

"Be gone from here," he said, holy power in his words. The boot sank inward as the undead shrieked, the dark magic animating it unable to withstand his command. Jerico removed the boot, took a step back, and then peered over his shield at the door. Bonebreaker was ready for another swing, but the wave had retreated, the undead shambling out into the night. Voices called out from behind him. The clerics had woken and come.

"Jerico!" he heard Keziel shout. The paladin glanced back, seeing the old man in nothing but a long white bedrobe. "What is going on?"

Jerico turned to the door and held up his hand to silence them. A man appeared before the entrance, shrouded in dark robes. Deep red eyes flared from within the cowl of his cloak.

"This is most amusing," the figure said. His voice was a frail hiss that echoed off the walls with unnatural strength. "But I did not come here to play. Give me the book, or more will have to die."

Jerico heard soft crying behind him as the clerics entered the bedchambers that the undead had broken into. Keziel placed a hand on the paladin's shoulder.

"You have our blessing," the priest said. With those very words, Jerico felt every hint of exhaustion flee his body. His shield and mace weighed nothing. He looked at the strange figure at the door and laughed.

"How many undead do you have, necromancer? I think more litter our floor than fill your army."

"As I said," the figure hissed, "I am not amused."

A ball of flame formed around his hands. Jerico pulled Keziel behind as he lifted his shield. The ball flew down the hallway and struck his shield with such force that he was lifted from his feet. His bulk knocked the cleric against the wall, and together they fell dazed to the floor.

"Look out!" Jerico shouted as he struggled to his knees. A second ball of flame roared down the hallway, and this time nothing stood between it and the clerics. Desperate, Jerico freed his shield from underneath his body and then flailed Bonebreaker upward. The very tip of the mace touched the ball of flame, and that was enough. He rolled against Keziel and covered both of them with his shield as the fire ignited. When the bright light vanished, it left behind a great amount of smoke but no dead.

"Is that the best you can do?" Jerico asked as he pushed against the wall to stand. He glanced back at the priests. "Get as deep as you can into the Sanctuary. No arguments."

"Not the best," the figure at the door said. "Just a warmup, if you will forgive the pun."

"Not forgiven," Jerico shouted.

"In the very back there is a room carved into the stone of the mountain," Keziel said, latching onto Jerico's arm and using it to pull himself up. "We can hide within."

"Go," he told them. "All of you. Now!"

The paladin faced his attacker. Fire swirled around both his hands, and in the demonic glow his face was visible, a tired gray visage with horrific eyes.

"He doesn't want us," Keziel said as the rest of the clerics hurried down the hall. "What he wants is hidden within the fireplace. Do not let him get it."

"Ashhur be with you," Jerico said. "Now get your ass out of here."

Keziel smiled, but it was sad and tired. He turned and ran.

"So honorable," the stranger said. "If you surrender, I will spare all their lives. Even yours. I just want what I have come to claim."

"Sorry to tell you this, but I don't surrender," Jerico said, readying his shield. "Never have, never will, especially to someone whose name I don't even know."

"Qurrah Tun," the stranger said, fire still surrounding his hands.

"Jerico of the Citadel."

"A pleasure."

Two more balls of fire flew down the hallway, roaring with power. When the first hit his shield, he grit his teeth and bore the pain. When the second hit, he gasped for air and felt his entire body slide back a foot. The heat was incredible, and he had to keep his head ducked behind the shield to keep it from being burned.

"If you burn off my hair not even Ashhur will keep me from you," he muttered. He peered over his shield as he took a step to the door. His foot stepped on a long leg bone, and for an agonizingly long moment Jerico thought he would to lose his balance and fall to his rear. Then the bone caught and halted. Qurrah saw this and laughed.

"You say you've defeated half my army," he said. "Let me show you how shallow your victory was."

Words of magic echoed down the hallway. The bones of the undead, the ones not made dust by Bonebreaker, snapped erect. They swirled around Jerico in an elongated sphere. The paladin kept turning, kept positioning his shield, but he knew there was little he could do.

"Die well," Qurrah said.

The bones shot as his body from every direction. Jerico closed his eyes and dropped to his side, his shield hiding his face and neck. The bones smashed against his legs but were unable to penetrate his armor. The first barrage over, Jerico tucked his knees to his chest and shifted his weight. He kept his face down and hidden. A small finger bone slipped past his defenses and struck his cheek. Blood ran down his face. He used the pain to focus. He could banish undead back to their plane with his sheer will. Could he do the same with their bones?

"In the name of Ashhur and through his power, I command you to be gone from my presence," he shouted, his will unshakable. All around him, the animated bones halted their movements. Qurrah snarled, trying to grasp them with his mind, but it was as if they had grown slippery to his touch. Again Jerico shouted out his command. This time the bones flew away as if a great wind poured out of him. The bones clacked against the wall and ceiling, all power gone from them. The paladin stood, his shield readied before him.

"No dying yet," he said. He wiped blood from the wound on his face and gestured to it with his mace. "And what was that about shallow?"

"Such a terrible pun," Qurrah said.

"Just learning from you."

"Hemorrhage!"

The light on Jerico's shield flickered for a moment before resuming its steady glow.

"Did you really think your spells could make it past my shield?" the paladin asked. He laughed when Qurrah did not respond. "You haven't fought many like me, have you? You're forgiven. It's what I do after all, forgive people. Beacon of light and all."

The red eyes narrowed.

"Tessanna," Qurrah said. "Remove this insect."

A young woman appeared in front of the door, her shadowy silhouette curling about Qurrah's body.

"As you wish, lover," he heard her say. She turned toward him. In the starlight he could see very little of her, but then brilliant yellow light arced between her hands. He saw her eyes. He saw her hair. Keziel's words rang loud in his mind.

...*pure black eyes and long hair that is dark as the night.*

"Not right," he said before diving into one of the side rooms. A bolt of lightning shot down the hallway, accompanied by a deafening thunderclap. The paladin scrambled to his feet, doing his best to ignore the sight of a dead priest torn in two. Lathaar's daughter of balance, the one he had seen in Neldar, had come to the Sanctuary.

"Don't want to play?" he heard the girl ask down the hallway. "But what if I want to play with you?"

From nowhere she appeared before him, giggling like a little girl. Jerico shouted in surprise. Bonebreaker swung out of instinct. The image broke when the weapon touched it, fluttering away in a thousand butterflies made of shadow. Jerico's mind raced, trying to think of an advantage he could gain. Against spellcasters, distance was his enemy. In the narrow corridor he could not dodge, only brace for impact and trust his shield. He knew that his greatest chance of victory involved close quarters combat, but the idea horrified him. Another bolt of lightning tore through the hallway, gigantic in size. His fear of her only grew.

"Get it together," he told himself. "Help me, Ashhur, I'm not sure how to get out of this one."

He took his shield, positioned it facing the door, and then leapt into the hallway.

Tessanna was waiting for him, still standing beside Qurrah. Black tendrils shot from her fingers, electricity swirling around them. Two wrapped around his ankles. Two more found his waist, and then rest tried to wrap about his shield. The holy light burned them away, but the ones around his body remained. The paladin screamed as dark energy poured into him. His heart pounded faster and faster, so much that he feared it would explode.

The momentum from his leap slammed him against the wall on the other side of the hallway. With all his energy, Jerico lurched forward. Unbalanced, he fell to the floor, his shield leading. The gleaming surface struck the other tendrils that stretched out from Tessanna's fingers, severing them. The paladin gasped for air as the pain slowly faded. If she was upset by this turn of events, the girl did not show it.

"Come dance with me, Jerico," she said. "Come play."

She entered the hallway.

He put one leg underneath him and pushed. He stood, tottering precariously. His arms shot out, pushing against the walls for balance. Labored breaths poured in and out of his mouth as he stared at the girl with blackest eyes.

"You want to dance," he said, "Then come inside and dance."

He turned and ran further into the Sanctuary.

"Coward," Qurrah murmured, taking out his whip.

"No," Tessanna said. "Only a fool would stand there and let me strike at him." She waved her hand, and at once the rest of the undead began entering the Sanctuary. "That should keep him defensive. Do you know where the spellbook is? I'd prefer not to have to kill everyone inside."

Qurrah closed his eyes and let his mind grow attuned to the darker world. He could feel the spellbook nearby, pulsing with a black energy. As to where exactly, he did not know.

"I need to be closer," he said. "Follow me."

"I'm leading this dance," Tessanna said, twirling in front of him. "So you follow me."

Again he felt his ego bruise, but the girl just laughed at him, laughing as she danced amid the broken bones and dead bodies that littered the hallway.

6

When Jerico neared the fireplace, he remembered Keziel's request.

"Book, huh?" he said, glancing about the room. He saw nothing, so he assumed it hidden. What the book could be, he didn't know. Given the power of the two intruders, it most likely was not some mundane object.

The clacking sounds of approaching undead jarred him from his thoughts. The sharp turn into the room was his best strategic point so he sprinted for it, his shield leading. He didn't even slow when the first undead turned the corner. His shield flared as he crushed three skeletons against the wall, their bones almost melting to its touch. Jerico spun, swinging Bonebreaker in a wide arc. It shattered the spine of the closest undead, then hooked upward to knock off the head of a second.

A swift kick and he was off the wall and back into the room with the fireplace. More undead came, but he smashed them one after another. They wielded no weapons or armor, and against the magic of his mace they could not withstand him. Bodies began to pile at his feet, and he used this to his advantage. He took a step back, and when an undead stumbled over the pile, he lunged forward and smashed it with his shield. The pile grew larger.

"Sing, song, sing a song if you have a song to sing," he heard Tessanna call as she approached. The paladin shook his head, trying to shake the fear of her from his mind. He had fought casters before, powerful ones even. She was no different.

"But when you sing a song until its done, the song sings no more."

Tessanna turned the corner.

Bonebreaker smashed the side of her face. Her skull cracked against the wall. The girl slumped against it, blood pouring from her nose and mouth. Her cheek was cut and mangled. Her black eyes stared at him, frozen in surprise, as a trail of blood painted the wall.

"Tessanna!" Qurrah shouted.

A whip snaked around the corner, wrapping around his wrist before bursting into flame. The metal of his gauntlets glowed red, and Jerico screamed as the fire burned his flesh. He twisted his wrist, dropped Bonebreaker, and then madly flailed at the buckles. Just as a strong tug came from the whip he flicked it free. The gauntlet flew around the corner, taken by the whip. Jerico reached for his weapon with his bare hand, but changed his mind when the whip lashed the ground beside it. Unsure, the paladin took a few steps back, his mind racing.

He looked at the girl still slumped against the wall before his pile of undead. He thought she breathed, but the wound on her head was horrendous. Her left eye was covered with blood, even the iris filled with burst veins. He could see her teeth through the tear in her flesh. Her cheekbones were a shattered mess.

"Celestia's going to be mad at me," he said before breaking into nervous laughter. The whole while he backed away from her body. He had his shield, and in many ways he could still use it as a weapon, but would it be enough? When Qurrah walked around the corner, and he saw the rage in the half-orc's eyes, he knew it wouldn't. Not even close.

"You," Qurrah said, his entire body quivering with anger. "You dared scar her face." He lashed his whip against Jerico's shield. "You're a greater fool than I imagined."

"Never claimed to be the smart one," the paladin said, taking another step back. There was just enough room to get some momentum before reaching the necromancer. Perhaps if he charged...

Qurrah gave him no time. A bolt of pure shadow flew from his hands, crackling with energy. Jerico braced his legs and let his shield take the blow. The power of it jarred his shoulder, and his elbow screamed in pain. Another bolt hit, then another. He had taken so many spells with his shield, and while the holy enchanted metal bore no mark, his own flesh was another matter. His entire left side turned numb as the shadow power slammed against him. He staggered back, collapsing against the wall. Behind him, the heat of a fire warmed his legs, alerting him to its presence.

"You are weak flesh and bone," Qurrah said, lashing out with his whip. "Do you know why you still stand? Let me show you."

Spidery words left Qurrah's lips. A fleeting image of white mist rising from his armor graced Jerico's eyes.

"You were blessed with strength not your own," Qurrah said. "Do you feel it now, how strong you truly are?"

A lash of the whip knocked his shield an inch to the side, exposing his face. The whip curled back and then lashed inward, burning his already bleeding cheek. The paladin cried out, his balance fading. He tried to raise his shield, knew his life was exposed, but his arm refused to cooperate. As he collapsed before the fire, he heard the half-orc speak.

"*Hemorrhage.*"

He felt the rupture just above his wrist. Blood exploded out of it, splattering across his face and chest. Dizziness claimed his mind, that which was not occupied with his screaming. Qurrah came and stepped upon his bleeding wrist, his heel grinding into the agony.

"Listen to me, and listen carefully," the half-orc said, his voice quiet and cruel. "You have scarred my beautiful lover. You will make amends."

"And if I don't?" Jerico asked in between labored breaths. Qurrah placed his knee on Jerico's other shoulder and knelt down so his face was inches from the paladin's.

"I will slaughter every single priest hiding in this building. It will be slow, and it will be painful. If you heal her, I will spare their lives."

"Either way, you'll kill me afterward," Jerico said. "How can I trust you not to lie?"

Qurrah stood, grinding his heel in semicircles.

"You sacrifice your life in the hope to save others. Is that not how your order works? Does it matter if I follow my word, if you do all in your power to save the innocents that cower in fear of me?"

The paladin nodded, trying to ignore the horrible pain spiking up his arm. Qurrah walked to where Tessanna lay. Slowly Jerico stood, keenly aware of the black energy sparkling on Qurrah's fingertips. Any false move and he would die.

"She is Celestia's daughter," Jerico said as he took an uneven step toward her. "Perhaps Ashhur won't be too upset if I heal her."

"Quit speaking nonsense and do your duty," Qurrah said, though his eyes had narrowed at the mention of the elven goddess. He watched as Jerico knelt and pressed the palm of his shaking hand against the wound he himself had created.

"Daddy?" she asked, her eyes closed and her voice drowsy.

"Shush, Tess," Qurrah said.

"You hurt me again, didn't you daddy?"

"Ashhur, forgive me if what I ask is wrong, but give me the strength to do what must be done," Jerico prayed. Healing light surrounded his hands, pulsing unsteadily. Tessanna moaned as it poured into her flesh. Her broken bones snapped together. Her torn skin pulled tight. She let out a gasp as dizzying waves filled her head.

"Be healed," Jerico told her as he removed his hand. Both men observed his work. The shape of her jaw was back to normal. Amid the drying blood ran a single scar from ear to chin. When she opened her eyes, even the burst vessels had closed.

"Good man," Qurrah said. He waved his hand. A wall of energy slammed into the paladin, throwing him across the room. He collapsed in a heap of armor and muscle. The half-orc knelt beside his lover, his pale hand slowly tracing the scar.

"How do you feel?" he asked her. The girl looked up at him and smiled.

"I feel awful. I dreamt my daddy hit me. Did he?"

"No," Qurrah said, kissing her lips. "Just a dream. You're fine now."

The paladin rolled to his side, eyeing a door a few feet to his right. Beyond it was the deepest parts of the Sanctuary where the clerics of Ashhur had hid. If he could reach them... He tried to stand, but his entire arm remained numb. He could see blood pooling underneath his body. He would die if he lost too much more. The wound needed closed, and he lacked the strength to do it.

With his good arm he pushed, grinding his teeth to focus against the pain. He stood.

"Where are you going?" Qurrah asked, sounding amused.

"Forgive my rudeness," Jerico said, touching his shield with his other hand. "But I should go."

The light from his shield flared a brilliant white, blinding the half-orc. He shielded his eyes with his arm, but it did no good. When the light ended, the door was open and the paladin was gone. Qurrah stood to chase but Tessanna grabbed his ankle.

"No," she said. "Let him go. Take what we came here for."

Qurrah rubbed the tears from his eyes, blinked a few times, and then accepted the girl's request.

"Very well. The book is very close, hidden where..."

He stopped when he saw the burning fire. A smile crossed his face.

"Clever," he said. "Very, very clever."

A wave of his hand scattered the logs. They rolled across the floor, spilling ash as their flame died. Qurrah reached into the black pile where the fire had been, ignoring the heat that burned his fingers. Deep within the ash he felt it. Excitement sparked inside his heart. With a cry of victory, he tore the tome free.

"The fire?" Tessanna asked.

"The book is impervious to it," he explained, wiping ash off with his blistered fingers. "Otherwise the priests would have burned it themselves." He stared at his treasure. It was large, but that seemed its only special quality. The bindings were plain leather, with a strap connected to an iron buckle to keep the pages closed. But within...

"Let's go," he said, offering his hand to Tessanna, who took it and used his strength to stand. "I must begin reading the pages. So many mysteries inside..."

Tessanna kissed him on the cheek.

"Go on without me," she said. "I'll be right there."

Qurrah, so enamored with his prize, nodded and let her go. Through the door she went, heading after the fleeing paladin.

><<

Just your wrist," Jerico muttered as he staggered down the hallway. "You've been stabbed how many times, and you're going to...going to bite it from a silly wrist cut?" Silly or not, he could see the veins pulsing in his arm, and the blood pouring from the grievous wound. He kept his left hand clamped just above the wound. If he had the time, he would have asked Ashhur for the power to heal it, but he dared not stop his frantic running.

The walls abruptly changed from wood to stone. The hallway turned a sharp left before descending five feet of stairs. Jerico, staggering along as he was, did not notice the change. His foot hit air where stone should have been, and then he was falling headfirst. He had a brief moment to swear a multitude of punishments against Lathaar before his head cracked against the cold stone at the bottom, knocking him out cold.

Tessanna found him there, his arms and legs sprawled about and his head atop a pool of blood. Not far from the bottom of the stairs was a solid wooden door, barred from the inside. The clerics hid within, she knew. She could smell their fear.

"So close, yet none dare come to your aid," she said, kneeling beside his unconscious form. "Did they hear you come? Do they know it is you here?" She took his bleeding wrist in her hand and blew across it. Fire burned within her breath, sealing the wound. Finished, she smiled and kissed his cheek.

"Qurrah didn't tell me, but you fixed my face," she whispered into his ear. "But you also broke it. You've left me a scar, paladin, so I shall leave you scarred as well." She kissed his face, her tongue flicking against his skin. As she pulled back her lips her tongue remained. The flesh underneath it blackened and burned under its touch. She ran her tongue across his face, so that a long black line marred him from ear to cheek.

"My scar will fade in time," she whispered. "They always do. Will yours?" She kissed him on the lips, thrusting her tongue into his mouth. It did not burn him. The girl sighed as she tasted blood. Reluctantly, she pulled back and climbed the stairs.

"May we meet again," she said, then glanced at the sealed door, all life draining from her face. "Your champion is dying at your door," she shouted. "Are you so cowardly you will hide within while he perishes?"

She turned and left, not caring if they emerged.

Qurrah was waiting for her at the entrance to the Sanctuary.

"Is he dead?" he asked her. Tessanna glanced at him, and then at the book he carried.

"Does it matter?" she asked.

"No," Qurrah said. "I guess it doesn't."

They left as the last few undead under their command collapsed into lifeless piles of bone, flesh, and rot.

The Stonewood Forest was a thoroughly unwelcoming sight. The trees were black as coal, and stubborn against any fire. The branches stretched high, interlocking into a thick canopy above. Lathaar knew that come nightfall not even the stars could penetrate the thick blanket of leaves. Deep within the forest loomed Elfspire, which had once been the tallest of the nearby mountains. Now it was a cracked and broken sight, rent in two by the release of the demon, Darakken. Much of the Stonewood Forest had been destroyed in the ensuing battle. The outer edges remained, and it was there Lathaar hoped Mira waited.

He dismounted upon reaching the forest's edge. He had ridden as fast and as far as he dared, and he was proud of his mount. "Go rest," he told her, patting her neck. The horse neighed and then trotted away, wanting no part of the forest. The paladin drew his sword and held it before him.

"Mira?" he asked, his eyes closed. "Mira, can you hear me?"

Lathaar?

"I'm here, just outside the forest," he said. "Are you hurt?"

He's been waiting, don't come, don't...Lathaar!

Her voice silenced in his mind. What Keziel had told him haunted his thoughts. "Every daughter of balance has died horribly," the Priest had said. "They are not meant long for this world."

"Survive a little longer, Mira," Lathaar said, cutting away the first of many branches in his path. "Not you, not yet."

He had six hours before dark. He could make it if he hurried.

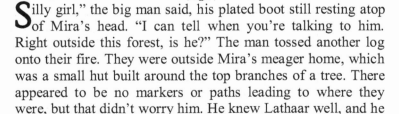

"Silly girl," the big man said, his plated boot still resting atop of Mira's head. "I can tell when you're talking to him. Right outside this forest, is he?" The man tossed another log onto their fire. They were outside Mira's meager home, which was a small hut built around the top branches of a tree. There appeared to be no markers or paths leading to where they were, but that didn't worry him. He knew Lathaar well, and he knew that he would do all he could to arrive before the sun fell below the mountains.

"He beat you," Mira said. Her voice was slurred as if she were drugged. She lay just inches from the fire, her hands tied behind her back with a barbed piece of metal. The man laughed, the sneer on his face vile.

"Did he? He never even drew blood, dear girl, so I'd hardly call that a loss."

He tapped his fingers against the sides of her face, pointedly reminding her of the tongue trap he had placed within her mouth. It was made of two pieces of metal. One lay horizontal, and was split in the middle so that her tongue could be pulled through. Its interior was lined with sharp teeth. The ends of the piece were two sharp spikes that dug into the sides of her cheeks. A second strip of metal wrapped around the first, the lower end designed to shred her tongue's sensitive underbelly while simultaneously digging into the bottom of her mouth. The other end ran to the back of her throat, where another spike jutted upward so any motion would cause her to gag on her own blood.

"You've been a good girl," he said, crushing the sides of her face with his hands. Mira held in her cries best she could, knowing they would only make it worse. The man tilted her head down so all the blood poured from the small, constant hole in her lips the contraption created. "You've behaved, but Lathaar's going to be here soon." He drew out a long piece of wire and held it in front of her face.

"See the edges?" he asked her. Mira nodded, having quickly learned it best to humor the man. He gently ran his finger across it, then showed her the drop of blood it had drawn. "Incredibly sharp, with lots and lots of teeth. You haven't tried casting any spells to escape, not after that first one."

He chuckled as he traced his bleeding finger along the bloody scar on Mira's abdomen.

"But you might get brave when your friend shows up. I'm going to wrap this around your fingers. It'll cut you, but keep your hands still and the pain should go away. Try to wiggle a finger or two, well…"

He jammed the wire inside her lower lip and jerked. Mira did her best to choke down her scream lest the contraption within her mouth tear her tongue to pieces. Blood poured down her neck, the pain throbbing with each beat of her heart. The man looped the wire around her fingers, a bizarre mesh that burned like fire. Even worse, her hands were beginning to shake against her will. She had eaten too little and lost too much blood over the past week. The fire on her hands burned brighter.

"Pass out if you want," the man said, smiling in satisfaction at his handiwork. "The false paladin has awhile to go before he arrives. I'm sure you'll be awake by then."

The girl projected a single thought across the forest before she collapsed. Lathaar felt his entire chest tighten as the words struck his mind.

Kill me.

As Lathaar neared Mira's home, he grew more and more certain of who had taken her. Few people knew of the girl's existence, and fewer still possessed the power to capture and torture her without being destroyed. The vile presence permeating the forest from her direction only confirmed his belief.

"Be with me," he prayed as he walked. "Keep her safe, and give me the strength to fight, to win."

He would need every prayer, every aid of Ashhur. Krieger had come to finish their duel. He approached her home without any worry of ambush. The dark paladin had a sense of honor about him, and burying a sword in his back would prove nothing. And that's what it was all about. Proof of faith.

All the trees surrounding Mira's home had been cleared years ago, allowing plenty of space to train, live, and play. Only a sliver of the sun peeked over the mountains when Lathaar arrived, flooding the area with shadows and thick beams of orange. Mira lay beside a giant bonfire, her green dress torn and covered with bloodstains. Standing over her, his foot atop her face, was Krieger.

"Greetings, oh great and powerful Lathaar," he said, bowing with all his weight atop of Mira. "You almost disappointed me. Nightfall is much closer than I anticipated. I'd hate to have an unfair advantage."

Krieger was a giant man, the sides of his face lined with scars. Without them, he might have been handsome. His long blond hair he had tied into a short ponytail behind his head. The bones of his face were sharp, so when he sneered his lips pulled back across his teeth. As he flashed his feral grin he pressed his foot down harder.

Lathaar drew his swords, horrified by the blood that poured out of Mira's mouth.

"She has done you no wrong," he said.

"That's why I had so much fun," Krieger replied, drawing his own swords. They were twin sabers, each fully consumed by black fire. He twirled them once in the air while he stared at the other paladin's weapons. "You've managed to keep your faith this time. Excellent. I would hate to be bored."

"I will kill you," Lathaar said. "You deserve no better."

"And Darakken is dead," Krieger continued, as if he had not heard a word. He paced around Mira's body. The girl made no movements. Lathaar could sense the dwindling life within her, like a dying fire in need of wood. He could heal her, if given the time.

"Dead, which is an impressive feat," Krieger continued. "You've grown much stronger, Lathaar, last paladin of a false god. Finally worthy."

"You have no idea," Lathaar said. "Elholad!"

Both his weapons flared with brilliant white light, and their weight nothing in his hands. He expected surprise, or worry, from the dark paladin, but instead he laughed.

"Karak tan my hide and burn me forever, you've even attained the holiest of blades. Ashhur must like you...or he has no choice, with all his followers dead and rotting."

He gestured around like a grand performer before an audience.

"This is our stage! This is our arena! I will prove the weakness of your god by slaughtering the last life that still clings to him like a frightened babe."

Lathaar smashed his blades together, remembering his one weapon of surprise he still carried.

"You're wrong, Krieger," he said, tensing his legs for an attack. "I'm not the last."

Krieger paused, his entire act halted, and that was all Lathaar needed. He lunged, his blades thrusting together in a sheer beam of white. When the black scimitars parried, they showered sparks across the grass. The contact was a test of their faith, and it was Lathaar's that was the stronger. Krieger's swords recoiled. Desperate, the dark paladin twisted backward, the light of the blades mere inches from his armor. The closest parts sizzled and faded gray.

The dark paladin continued his twist while lashing out with his right hand. Lathaar ducked under the attack, then slashed with his longsword. It cut through Krieger's armor as if it were cloth. A shallow cut in his side poured blood. The man showed no pain. Instead, he laughed and laughed.

"Another!" he cried even as he retreated again and again from Lathaar's attacks. "Karak be praised, I have another to slaughter, to test and torment. His name, paladin, tell me his name!"

"Jerico," Lathaar said. "And you won't live to meet him. It is my faith that is stronger. Your swords cannot withstand my own."

Krieger halted with his back against the giant tree in the center of the clearing. His grin was maniacal, his eyes, heartless.

"The false order of Ashhur has fallen," he said. "Chaos has filled the void, and from that chaos true order will come. Your faith is stronger, Lathaar, but your god is still a failed god. You have no idea how strong my faith is."

"I'm not afraid of you," Lathaar said.

"Give me time," Krieger said. "Felhelad!"

He slammed his scimitars together, and at their contact they burst into giant blades of pure shadow and fire. The fading sunlight sucked into the swords, darkening the entire clearing. The dark paladin grinned at Lathaar's stunned look.

"Our gods are brothers!" he shouted. "Did you think one would have a toy the other would not?"

"It doesn't matter," Lathaar said, narrowing his eyes and preparing for combat.

"But it does," Krieger mocked. "The great and powerful Lathaar...still not as special as he wishes to be. Not as strong. This is the duel I've sought all my life. This is the fight. Don't disappoint me, Lathaar." He held up his fist and showed a glowing orange jewel encrusted into his gauntlet. "A similar jewel is inside Mira's mouth. With a thought, I can activate its magic, splattering both of us with her brains. Kill me or I kill her."

Lathaar readied his swords.

"So be it."

Mira's eyes fluttered open at the sound of battle. Her entire mouth ached. Her tongue was swollen from all the cuts, causing the sensitive flesh to press harder against the ridges of the device. Even breathing caused her pain. She did her best to ignore it, for Lathaar had arrived. He had his swords drawn, and they shone with the light of the Elholad. Krieger was there too, his own black blades pulsing with power. She tilted her head just a little so she could better watch their duel.

The two charged, and in the twilight their god-blessed blades met. Lightning crackled at their touch. Both opponents glared at the other, their hatred open and growing. Krieger took the offensive first, alternating attacks with his left and right hand. Lathaar blocked each one, not bothering to parry. They wanted to test their strength. Each time their swords made contact their faith fought. Mira knew Krieger's bordered on fanatical. He would not falter, and he would not repent.

Lathaar however…she had seen him doubt. She had seen him lose his faith.

Stay strong, she said in her mind. She wanted to project the thought to Lathaar but she dared not interrupt his concentration. *Please, Lathaar, stay strong for me.*

Lathaar knocked aside a dual thrust by the dark paladin, then stabbed with his short sword. Krieger leapt back, slammed his foot against the tree behind him, then kicked forward. The two collided in a flashing explosion, sparks covering both their bodies. A glowing blade tore another cut across the front of Krieger's black armor. In return, a burning scimitar gashed the inner part of Lathaar's arm. The blood sizzled atop their weapons.

Mira knew them evenly matched. Neither would dare turn their attention to her, or the knife-edge they fought upon would balance toward the other. If she was to escape, now was the time. Slowly she opened her mouth as wide as it could go. The spikes tore into the sides of her cheeks, but at least she could no longer feel the edges pressed into the roof of her mouth and the upper part of her jaw. She took a breath, and then another. The spell she had in mind would require no movements of her hands, just the verbal components. She doubted she could pronounce them with her swollen tongue, but she had to try.

"Kel." The first part came easy, just a hard sound from the back of her throat. The tiny tilt of her tongue for the 'el' filled her mouth with pain.

"Lak."

Again the ridges tore into her tongue, but she could manage. She took a deep breath. The next syllable…

Vral was what she meant to say, but when she closed her mouth the piece attached to the back of her tongue gagged her. The involuntary wretches reopened the many wounds in her mouth. She wanted to vomit but knew it would destroy what remained of her tongue. Blood poured down her lips and across her chest. The pain was horrible. With blurred vision, she watched the two paladins. They seemed like statues locked in battle and bathed in light and fire. The hair on her neck stood as she wondered if Ashhur and Karak were watching, channeling their power into their champions to fight their petty brothers' feud.

Anger stirred in her breast. She would defy them. She would deny them their game, regardless of the cost.

"Kel," she whispered.

❈

"So how did this Jerico survive?" Krieger asked. They had fought for several minutes, and still his breathing had not turned heavy. "Did he cower in some hole as the rest of his brethren were slaughtered?"

"Cowering in holes never works," Lathaar said. "That's where your kind breeds."

The dark paladin slashed twice with his main hand, then curved a thrust low with his other. Lathaar blocked the first two, then parried the third away with his short sword. Krieger snarled, closing the distance between them while jamming both his blades at Lathaar's stomach.

"Have you forgotten where I first found you?" Krieger asked as their weapons clashed once more. "Cowering in a pathetic inn among beggars and drunkards and the lowliest of the low?"

"That just proves my point," Lathaar said, shoving the dark paladin away.

"Your faith was nothing then," Krieger said. "You think you can stand against me now?"

"My faith has been tested," Lathaar said. "Has yours?"

"Trust me," he answered, putting one foot forward while rearing back with his blades. "Seeing you alive tests me greatly."

Krieger struck with all his strength, a mammoth blow of unholy power. Lathaar crossed his swords and met them, determined to prove his own faith. Thunder crackled between them as the blades connected. The clearing had turned dark, and in that twilight the glow of Lathaar's swords fought against the sucking, greedy blackness of Krieger's fire.

Regular steel would have shattered, but neither possessed regular weapons. They bore the weapons of their gods. Flesh, bone, and will would break first. Each paladin fought on, determined that it would be the other that felt his earthly body fail.

❖

Mira took a deep breath and tried to clear her mind. Four times she had tried, but an involuntary gag or a shaking of her swollen tongue ruined each incantation. Through blurry eyes she watched the paladins. They were nothing but their swords now to her, black and white, healing and hurting.

"Kel," she said, tears streaming down her cheeks. "Lak. Vr..." The spike pressed against the back of her throat, tearing, but she had to ignore it. She forced the syllable out, no longer caring the damage that might result.

"Vral," she said, feeling the magical power beginning to flow from her body. One more syllable. Just one. Blood trickled down the back of her throat, but she swallowed it. Too much hesitation and the magic would leave her. Now or never, she thought. Now or never.

"Den," she gagged. Kellak Vralden. Shadow mist. Her flesh drained of all color, becoming a shifting form of gray smoke. The wire and rope surrounding her hands fell through her body, as did the awful contraption within her mouth. The metal plummeted down her throat and to the ground, a horrific sight of blood and torn skin. Attached to it was a small yellow gem that glowed bright in the growing darkness. Her body returned to flesh. Mira coughed and gagged, relieved beyond all description to have her mouth free of the device.

"Clever," she said, recognizing the yellow gem for what it was. She immediately regretted speaking. Her tongue was still swollen and sore. All she could taste was blood. Her fingers were a swollen mess, but nothing compared to her mouth. Krieger had been far more worried about what spells she might cast verbally. He had assumed removing semantic components would be far easier with her bound by rope and wire. For the most part, he had been right. But now she was free...

She pulled the gem from the device and rolled it in her hands. Neither combatant knew her free, focused as they were on their fight. That would end.

"No more games," she whispered. "No more fights. This torture is over."

She said a word of magic and then hurled the gem with all her might.

He was starting to slip. His strength, while great, was not enough. The light around the two swords faded, only a little, but it was visible to both, and both knew what it meant. Lathaar was about to break.

"Is this it, coward?" the dark paladin cried, ramming even harder against Lathaar's defenses. He slammed down with his swords, again and again. The weapons crackled, now the only light underneath the canopy of leaves. "I would prove my strength, but you prove your weakness!"

Lathaar wanted to say something, to counter with his own words, but his arms could no longer bear the weight. The twin scimitars came slashing in, the black fire surrounding them as strong as ever. He blocked, but his arms shrieked against the weight. The power from the blow knocked him from his feet. His short sword fell from his grip. darkness enveloped it as it left Lathaar's touch. The other faded in much of its brightness, no longer an Elholad. His faith was still strong, but Lathaar's will had been weakened and his resolve shaken. He no longer felt certain he could win, and in their fight, that was all that mattered. Krieger saw this and knew. He held his weapons high, gloating in their darkness. The gems on his gauntlets flared.

"I want you to know," he said. "I want you to see just how much Ashhur has abandoned this world."

He pressed the yellow gem beside his third knuckle. As the magic enacted, and he looked to where Mira had lain, he saw her resting against the tree in the center, pure hatred on her face.

"Boom," she mouthed to him as the gem attached to the small of his back detonated. Krieger howled as fire exploded around his waist. His armor twisted and shrieked amid the blast. The force took his legs out from under him, and in the air he spun and fell. Blood pooled underneath his body. He tried to move, but his legs felt strange and foreign to him.

Lathaar gave him no reprieve. He took to his feet and ran, his sword ready.

"You were beaten," Krieger spat as the other paladin hovered over him, his blade poised for a killing blow.

"But I wasn't abandoned," he said.

"Nothing's fair," Krieger said. "Nothing's right. But your death will be."

He slammed his right hand against the dirt, breaking a hollow jewel atop his gauntlet. Lathaar thrust his blade deep into the earth below, but it was too late. Krieger vanished in a puff of smoke and shadow, the sword passing harmlessly through the after-image of his body. Furious, Lathaar pulled free his weapon and kicked at the dirt.

"Coward!" he shouted.

"Lathaar," Mira said, still resting against the tree. "I need you, please."

She slumped against its base, laid her head against the bark, and then smiled at him.

"I stopped the game," she said. "I stopped..."

By the time Lathaar reached her, she had closed her eyes and fallen into a much needed sleep.

Krieger reappeared deep within the forest. From a pouch on his side he drew out a silver-blue vial and drank its contents, then broke the vial on a root beside him.

"That damn sorceress," he said between grunts of pain. He could feel his legs again, that was good. "I proved you weaker," he continued. "I was the stronger! I proved, I proved...Karak is the true god, you wretch!"

He fell back, his hands clasped around his waist. It would take months before he was back at full fighting shape. But the girl was free, and with her at Lathaar's side there was no way for him to fight a fair duel.

"Because of her, you think you are not abandoned," he seethed. "Because of her, you think your god saved you. You cannot win by your own strength so you coddle to others and act as if they were divine intervention." He sheathed his swords and struggled to his feet. His legs were uncooperative, and he walked as if he were incredibly drunk. At least they did work, however poorly. If his back had been broken, no amount of potion would have saved him.

"Come to me, Demonwail," he said, rubbing a red ruby on his gauntlet. Black smoke pooled at his feet, growing thicker and thicker while taking the shape of a demonic steed. The creature neighed in greeting, its hooves fire, its eyes shimmering ash. Krieger cast aside the broken pieces of his armor, knowing the weight would only slow him down. He used all the strength in his upper body to mount the creature, gasping in air at the pain it caused.

"Ride on," he told Demonwail. "Out of the forest. We ride to Karak's hand."

7

Mira dreamt of a field of roses, the vibrant red petals swaying in a soft breeze. A small patch of grass in the center was her bed. The sky was clear. Everything was at peace.

It's waiting for you, she heard a voice say. *Everything is well. The mirror must be shattered, Mira.*

She saw a dagger appear, floating above her breast in the hands of an unseen assailant. It twirled and then plunged into her heart. She felt no pain. Peace, pure peace, flooded her.

As it must.

A shadow fell across the land. Heavy rain clouds covered the blue sky as the roses wilted and died. She heard their cries, a swan song of crimson petals. A hand shimmered into view, still clutching the dagger. Crawling upward, the shimmer revealed more and more of her attacker. Mira saw a shadow twin of herself holding the dagger. She remembered the mind she had touched, the chaotic being that had heard her psychic pleas.

"Tessanna," she said, her voice a whisper. Thunder rolled through the clouds.

"Shattered," said the other girl. With a gruesome cry, she twisted the dagger and tore it through flesh.

Tessanna!" she screamed, waking from her nightmare. Lathaar's arms were around her instantly, his long brown hair falling down about her face. She buried herself in his chest, sobbing.

"It's all right," he told her, gently rubbing the back of her neck. "Everything's all right."

Mira sobbed, still hearing the shrieking of the flowers. Lathaar continued to stroke her head, but his mind had latched onto her cry of a name she had no business knowing. Troubling as it was, it was a departure from obsessing about Krieger, and his mind needed the distraction.

"I've healed you as best I can," he told her. "Keziel's abilities make mine look like a child's. Just a few days ride, and you'll feel right as rain."

"Thank you," she told him as her sobs slowed. "Thank you for coming for me."

The paladin nodded but kept silent about his own guilt. She had suffered greatly, all as a ploy to bring him to fight. Her mouth and hands were both terrible sights. All across her body he found cuts and bruises. Worst of all, he had let the man responsible escape.

"Mira," he asked, "how do you know that name?"

"What name?" she asked, wiping tears from her face.

"You screamed it as you awoke," he insisted. "Do you remember what it was?"

"Tessanna," the girl said. "I don't know who, just...I know the name. I think it's important."

Lathaar bit his lower lip. Keziel had been right. The two girls were identical.

"You need to come with me to the Sanctuary," he told her. "Keziel has things you need to hear, to understand. He knows what you are, Mira. Your eyes, your magic... he can explain."

Mira accepted his hand as she stood.

"I'm afraid to hear it," she said. "The world beyond my forest is a mystery to me. But I sense in your heart you feel it best, so I will go."

"Thank you," Lathaar said, standing. The two embraced. "Let's go," he told her when they separated. "I'm sure Jerico will be thrilled to meet you."

"Who's Jerico?" she asked, taking his hand.

"Jerico's a paladin like me," he said. "He's a bit older, carries this enormous shield. You know my swords? Well, his shield..."

They walked and talked as Lathaar told her all about the red-haired paladin, who at that moment was receiving a soft, burning kiss from the girl with the blackest eyes.

Several miles away, as the sun was just beginning its rise above the horizon, Tessanna touched Seletha's mane and whispered for her to stop. She readily obeyed. Qurrah leapt off the horse, ignoring the sharp pain in his back. Daylight was finally upon them, enough so he could read the words of the tome he clutched to his chest.

"Will it be dangerous?" Tessanna asked as she levitated to the ground. "Reading it, I mean."

"Stories tell of many who went mad looking upon its pages," Qurrah said as he stroked the cover with his fingers. "If this is true, my will is more than sufficient to overcome it."

"Be careful," the girl said, crossing her arms and twisting her body side to side. "I don't want to see you hurt. It'd make me sad, and I don't want to be sad."

"If I appear to be in pain or suffering, do not disrupt me," he told her. "If my concentration is broken, I might be lost to madness."

"At least you'll be with me amid it," Tessanna said. Qurrah was unsure if she was joking or not, so he let the comment pass. He put his back to the mountains and faced the rising sun. He undid the straps around the book, tossed them aside, and opened it. His entire body tensed, and he sucked in a single breath. Tessanna watched, her black eyes timid and curious. For a few moments he remained quiet and still, his eyes flicking over the page.

"Qurrah?" she dared ask.

"Lies," he said, exhaling. "But this doesn't appear to be spells, this is…"

He turned a page and read, his eyes darting over the words. Tessanna watched, curious but not wishing to intervene. He flipped another page, then another. His jaw dropped as he read, and his face locked in a stunned expression.

"This isn't a spellbook, not in the standard sense," he said. "No magical enchantments protect it, and it contains no inherent power." He looked up at his lover. "It has spells, many in fact, but all the stories, all the legends, were wrong."

"What is it, if not a spellbook?" Tessanna asked.

"There is only one person who could have written these words," Qurrah said, holding the book before his face as if it were made of gold. "This is Velixar's private journal, telling of the very creation of man."

⭐

Steady, Demonwail," Krieger told his horse as they neared the stone structure. Seven obelisks formed a circle around a faded carving of a roaring lion. Before the lion was a giant pit filled with ash. The statue seemed almost alive in the dim light of dusk, ready to devour those who came before it without proper sacrifice. Kneeling before it was a man clothed and hooded in black robes. The dark paladin dismounted, wincing in pain from his wound. He had not stopped to bandage them like he knew he should have.

Krieger limped to the altar, his hands on his sword hilts.

"Priests of Karak used to meet here at every full moon," the man at the altar said, not moving from his knees and his head still bowed. "They would cast a thief or murderer upon the flame, burning the chaos from his flesh. When did they stop coming? When did the rituals of old lose their power?"

"The world is losing faith in rituals and gods," Krieger said. "Even those who follow our ways are losing perspective. It's been so long since Karak and Ashhur walked this world that doubt has grown like a plague."

The bowing man nodded in agreement.

"I do not blame the commoner," he said. "We are responsible for shaping their minds. They will believe what we tell them, if our faith is strong. Truth comes from faith."

"I seek aid," Krieger told him.

"For your wounds?"

"I am no weakling needing aid of a healer," the dark paladin said, harsher than he meant.

"Neither am I," the other man said. He stood, kissed his fingers, and then pressed it against the nose of the lion. "Watch your anger. It gives you strength in battle, but you do not war against me."

"Forgive me, I would never insult the hand of Karak," Krieger said.

"That is a name I have not known in many years," the man said, turning to face the dark paladin. His eyes glowed a fierce red, and his face continually shifted its features so that every time Krieger blinked he would be unsure of what had changed and what had remained. Everything but the eyes. They never changed.

"You are the hilt," Krieger said. "The hand of Karak and his eternal prophet. What name do you prefer?"

"Velixar," the man with the ever-changing face said. "Velixar will suffice."

"Forgive me then, Velixar, but I do not need healing. I will bear the scars of my failure willingly."

"You've faced Lathaar many times. I expected him dead by now."

"The girl interfered," Krieger said. "That is why I come."

Velixar pulled his hood tighter about his face as the sun continued its rise.

"The daughters of the whore are well known to me. If you are asking me to kill her, then I must decline."

"She aids Ashhur," the dark paladin insisted. "The balance is tilting to our favor, and she has already stopped it once by slaying Darakken."

"Darakken was a reckless whelp," Velixar said, his deep voice rumbling in anger. "He deserved his fate. And you did not listen carefully to me, Krieger."

"You said the daughters were...daughters? There's more than Mira?"

The man in black laughed, a wicked gleam in his burning eyes.

"There is another by the name of Tessanna. That is why we let them be. The balance is not just threatened, my dear friend, it is spiraling out of control. The two still have their parts to play. Mira and Tessanna have intertwining destinies, and I will not act until I know how they will end."

Krieger kneeled and crossed his arms over his chest. "Very well. What would you ask of me?"

"Stay at my side. There are two I wish for you to meet."

"Who are they," Krieger asked, standing out of his kneel.

"The other daughter," Velixar said. "And my apprentice. He is the one, Krieger. With his aid, we can open the portal and free Karak from his prison."

"I would be honored," the dark paladin said. The man in black laughed, his deep voice an ugly contrast to the beauty of the morning. Amid the stones and the pile of ash he seemed as if he had always belonged.

Qurrah had slept little since obtaining the journal. Tessanna remained quiet, trusting her lover to inform her of what she needed to know. She wondered absently if he would still possess the ability to heal her mind. Perhaps he would, perhaps he wouldn't. It didn't bother her much, but she knew it would upset him, and she preferred him happy.

They prepared a fire, not at all worried that Jerico or the priests might be giving chase. Other than Tessanna's wound, which had healed into a faded scar, they had thoroughly dominated the followers of Ashhur. Besides, Qurrah's desire to read overwhelmed caution and stealth.

"Unbelievable," Qurrah said at last. He placed the journal upon his lap. "Just...unbelievable."

"Is it what you wanted," Tessanna dared ask him. He nodded, not understanding her question.

"Velixar lied to me. He claimed that Karak and Ashhur came here to make a better world than their own. He never mentioned they were fleeing like cowards."

Tessanna snuggled against his side, locking her arms around his side and resting her chin on his shoulder.

"Tell me," she said.

"There were more brothers," Qurrah said, staring at the cover as he tried to process all that he had learned from Velixar's own quill. "Karak was the god of Order, Ashhur of Justice. Then there was Thulos, god of War. They were to keep him from overstepping his bounds. They failed miserably. Thulos slaughtered the other gods and seized control of their world. Karak and Ashhur fled to Dezrel, hoping in its calm they could atone for their failure."

"Instead they warred against each other," Tessanna said, closing her eyes and sighing as she cuddled her lover. "It seems a bit of their brother's blood got into theirs."

"Evidently Thulos's war demons began going to other worlds, conquering all who would oppose. Even now they conquer, but Velixar seemed sure they could not make it here."

"Why not?" the girl asked.

"Something Celestia did after the other two gods arrived. I still have much to read, but he refers to it as the great secret. 'Only in absolute emptiness is there order' is the mantra he recites, but that is what he calls the truth. The great secret is the quest. I don't know what it is, for Velixar does not say. He claims Karak learned of it a few years after his imprisonment by Celestia."

"Karak's desire has always been to be freed," Tessanna said. "You know that as well as I do."

"But why keep the secret hidden?" Qurrah asked. The girl shrugged.

"Perhaps he's found a way, one he doesn't want put at risk?"

The half-orc scratched his chin.

"It would make sense," he said. "I've recently found where Velixar talks about his apprentices. They aid him in the quest, though he does not say how, only that Celestia must be weakened. His apprentices needed to possess enormous power to succeed."

"You were one of them," Tessanna told him. "One of his apprentices. Shame he is dead now. He could explain what it was he wished you to do."

"Yes," Qurrah said, feeling a darkening in his heart. He glanced at his lover. "Tessanna," he said. "I'm not so sure he remains dead."

She kissed his lips. "He's lived a long time. I wouldn't be surprised if he still does. You'll introduce me to him, won't you?"

Qurrah laughed. "If we do somehow meet him, yes, I would introduce you as my lover and as my wife. Will that suffice?"

The girl batted her eyes and shied away from him.

"I've always wanted to meet him," she said. "He always sounded like someone I would like."

"If he hadn't died, I never would have met you," Qurrah said.

"Then he died at the perfect time. Maybe he'll live again at the same perfect moment."

The idea seemed so simple it horrified him. Tessanna saw this and only laughed and crawled into a ball beside the fire to sleep. The half-orc watched her, realizing just how tired he was. The secrets of the journal could wait, he decided. He lay in the grass beside her, his arms curled about her waist. Together they slept as the sun rose higher into the sky.

✿

Qurrah recognized the feeling, a cold sensation of being seen and judged. His dreams crumbled and broke. He startled awake, his heart beating at a furious pace. Tessanna sat beside him, tracing images in the grass by charring it with her fingers, which sparkled crimson with magic. The sun was high in the sky. He shook his head, clearing the sleep from his mind while his lover began to talk.

"He's almost here," she said, her eyes not leaving her carving. "It can't be anyone else. The man without a face."

"I will not cower before him," Qurrah said, clutching the journal to his chest.

Tessanna glanced up at him, her face calm. "I know. Prove how strong you are."

The half-orc shifted the journal to one arm and prepared his whip in the other. As he stood there, staring about the hills, he felt a chill crawling in the back of his skull. He wore Velixar's robes. He held Velixar's private thoughts. He wielded Velixar's weapon. Everything he was, everything he seemed to be, had been shaped by the man with the ever changing face. And now, with his presence hovering about him, he felt nothing but fear.

"I am strong," he said, his hissing voice just a whisper. "And he will not show anger at seeing what I have become."

"There he is," Tessanna said, pointing. To their south was a twin set of hills, and walking between them appeared Velixar and another man wearing the black armor of a paladin of Karak. They appeared to be talking. If they saw the two lovers, they did not show it. They just marched on, coming ever closer. Tessanna slid over to Qurrah, wrapping her arms about his waist. The half-orc patted her hands, reassured by her presence. If anyone could match Velixar in power, it was her.

At last Velixar looked up and nodded at the two. He waved a hand at the dark paladin, who obediently ceased talking. They crossed the final distance as Qurrah nervously cracked his wrists, waiting to hear what his master would say.

"Qurrah Tun," Velixar said. The half-orc felt his heart tremble at the sound of his voice. He had forgotten how deep it was, how powerful. "Come to me."

The half-orc glanced back at Tessanna, who nodded her head and released him from her grasp. He took two steps forward. His heart raged in chaos. He should kneel. He had always kneeled. But his pride had grown with his power, and now he didn't know if he could. Velixar stared at him, his arms crossed and his red eyes blazing. The half-orc bent one knee and bowed to his master.

Velixar reached down his hand and pulled the half-orc to his feet.

"Stand," he said, a smile spreading across his face. "No longer should you bow to me. In my absence you have grown much stronger than you would have at my side."

"I was a coward," Qurrah said. "My weakness caused your death."

"I did not lie," the man in black said. "I said I would not die, and I remained true to my word. And you survived, Qurrah, cowardice or not. If you had died, however bravely, then all I have fought for would have been lost."

The half-orc shrugged his shoulders, not fully believing the logic but accepting the release from guilt nonetheless. He felt so young and foolish then, not sure of what to say or do before the ageless man. Thankfully, Velixar ended his confusion by pointing to Tessanna, who stood quiet with her hands clasped in front of her waist.

"This beautiful girl behind you," he said. "She is Tessanna, correct?"

"She is," Qurrah said, "though I ask how you know her name."

"Even the gods know her name," Velixar said, stepping past the half-orc to offer his hand to her. Tessanna stayed where she was, seemingly struck paralyzed by her nervousness. Velixar was not offended. He took another step and offered his hand again, as if approaching a shy animal. The girl kept her head low, her hair hiding her face. From that black curtain she peered out, unsure and embarrassed.

"Tessanna," Velixar said. "Have you taken my pupil to be your lover?"

"I have," she said, finally reaching out and taking his hand. It was cold and dry, but she was not disturbed. "And I have taken his heart and soul. He's mine now, all mine. Are you angry at me?"

Velixar laughed. "Do you know who I am?" he asked her.

"You're the lion's mouth," she said. "And Qurrah's to be your teeth."

Again he laughed. "Krieger," he said. "Come introduce yourself."

The man stepped forward and bowed on one outstretched leg.

"I am Krieger, dark paladin of the Stronghold. I have come to see the daughter of balance and Velixar's chosen apprentice."

"And so you have," Qurrah said. "Are we what you expected?"

"I expected a champion and a goddess. I see an orc in the prophet's clothing and a skinny woman too shy to say her own name."

Velixar narrowed his eyes and watched. He had known Krieger since he was a child, heralded as a prodigy within the Stronghold. But Qurrah was his pupil, and his chosen. He would see how he reacted.

Qurrah reached out with his free hand, his face slowly darkening.

"You've been wounded," he said. "And I am no orc."

Krieger felt the blood on his back growing hot with energy. In one blinding fast motion he drew his sword and placed it an inch from Qurrah's throat. The black flame blistered his skin, but Qurrah did not falter.

"You are a gray-skinned mongrel," Krieger said. "Velixar's pupil or not, you're still a child compared to me. You have no faith in Karak. Your lacking is a stink I can smell from here."

"I have faith in nothing," Qurrah said. He clenched his fist. The blood on Krieger's back burst outward. He screamed in anger and swung his sword. Tessanna moved between them, her bare hand catching the blade. Her skin was uncut by the edge, her flesh not burned by the fire. The dark paladin stared in wonder as the girl laughed.

"Bad paladin," she said. "No murder for you today. And you're on fire."

She waved her hand. The blood on his back erupted into flames that swirled about his entire body. He fell to the dirt and rolled to extinguish the fire. Another wave of Tessanna's hand and the fire vanished. The burns were mild on his body, though he coughed and gagged from the smoke and heat that had seared into his lungs. Velixar clapped, his vile laugh booming throughout the countryside.

"I've met many like you," he said to her. "But never one as amusing. Come, both of you have much to hear." He turned to Krieger and smirked. "I assumed you would react as such. You judge too harshly with your eyes. These two will usher in our greatest victory. Alert the Stronghold and the priests in Veldaren. The great purge will soon be upon us."

Krieger stood and glared at Qurrah.

"I will tell them," he said as he touched the jewel on his gauntlet to summon Demonwail. "But I do this out of my faith in you, Velixar. Nothing else."

"Karak wills it," Velixar assured him. "Now ride."

The dark paladin mounted his horse and then rode northwest. Velixar did not watch him go, seemingly fascinated with Tessanna.

"You lied to me," Qurrah said once Krieger was gone. He pointed to the tome. "Everything you told me about the gods was a lie."

"I have not lied," Velixar said, his face turning rigid as stone. "I do many things, Qurrah Tun, but I do not lie. You heard what you needed to hear. You have read much of what I held secret. I believe you ready now. Tell me, though...where is your brother?"

The half-orc sighed and pulled his hood lower about his face.

"That," he said, "is a long story."

They walked aimlessly among the hills as Qurrah talked. Velixar listened intently as Qurrah detailed the happenings after the man in black's 'death'. He told him of joining the Eschaton and of meeting Tessanna. His story continued on to Harruq's wedding to Aurelia. He spoke of the gradual change that had overcome his brother, feeling shame in his heart.

When he reached Xelrak's part he glanced at Velixar, his anger rising.

"Karak used him to turn my brother against me," Qurrah said. "He tore my life asunder to achieve some twisted desire."

He expected Velixar to be angry at his words. Instead the man looked at him and spoke as calm as ever.

"Karak used him to show you that your brother was already against you," Velixar said. "The conflict was inevitable; he just drew it to a head before you felt yourself ready. Karak did not make your brother react as he did. It is a shame to lose such strength, but we shall persevere."

Qurrah chewed on his lower lip as he thought about Velixar's words. It made sense, in a way. The man in black could see this and decided to further solidify his belief.

"Tell me," he said. "All that anger you felt, was it truly at Karak, or was it at your brother whom you loved and cared for? Would you rather hate Karak than your brother?"

"Yes," he said, taking Tessanna's hand into his own as they walked. "Yes, I would."

"Then give Karak a chance to prove his loyalty. We must travel to the Vile Wedge. I will explain in time, but that is our destination."

"But what is the reason?" Qurrah dared ask. "Why the conflict? What is the quest that you hide so tightly?"

Velixar chuckled.

"Come evening I will tell you," he said. "These are things that the daylight must never hear."

"Will you tell me something," Tessanna said, speaking for the first time since they had begun their travel. "Will you tell me what it is I am?"

Velixar thought a moment and then nodded.

"When the night comes, and you know what I desire, then I will reveal what you are. You both deserve to know."

Qurrah wasn't sure if he wanted to hear the truth about his lover, but he would not deny her that right. They traveled in quiet until the sun dipped below the horizon. Qurrah was not asked to continue his story, and for that he was glad. He did not want to tell of his niece, and how at the whim of Tessanna he had broken her mind so they might obtain Darakken's spellbook in exchange for a cure.

At Velixar's command they built a fire and gathered around to hear what the man in black had to say.

"What you have read is true," Velixar said as the last glimpse of sunlight faded. "Karak and Ashhur did come here fleeing Thulos. The war god is a powerful deity, and he consumed his home planet in a bloody conflict that lasted ages. He now goes from world to world, seeking nothing more than glorious war. He cannot come to Dezrel, though. Celestia has protected it with all her strength. It is why she now sleeps, her power drained in protecting us from those that traverse the realms."

"You've sought to weaken Celestia's power," Qurrah said. "You wish to remove that barrier."

Velixar laughed, and far away, a wolf howled in agony.

"Quite astute," he said. "That barrier must be shattered."

"But why," the half-orc asked. "Is Karak somehow trapped because of it?"

"No," Velixar said, his voice lowering. "No, that is not it. Karak has learned something during his imprisonment, something that I myself have shown him."

Tessanna nestled her head against Qurrah's chest as she spoke.

"What did the dark god learn?" she asked.

"Chaos," Velixar said. "Before order can be established, there must be chaos and death. Karak has seen his true goal, a world of perfect order. I will grant you an honor I have given no other; I will show you this perfect world."

He reached across the fire and placed a hand across each of their foreheads. At first they felt icy cold, and then the images came, sharp and unstoppable.

The ground was a barren eternity of blackened rock, burnt by fire long extinguished. Marching in perfect rows were legions of undead. They were men, women, and children of every race, from orc to elf. Overhead the sky was naked, nothing to protect them from the searing sun. Over the land they marched, no apparent goal than to move ever further. Standing amid them was Velixar, red smoke pouring from his eyes as he commanded each and every one of them.

The image faded with the removal of Velixar's hands. The two lovers stayed silent as the last of the black land faded from their mind.

"That is an ugly world," Tessanna said, breaking the silence. "Ugly. I want no part of it."

"You seek the end of all life," Qurrah said. "Everything burnt or turned to mindless undead."

"Order will be restored," Velixar said. "Everything will obey. Do you understand now? Thulos is everything Karak needs. His war demons will kill all life, and then our god will follow in his footsteps, establishing true order from the rubble."

"You need Thulos to free Karak first," Qurrah said, suddenly understanding. "You will unite the brothers."

"With their combined might we can slay Ashhur," Velixar said, his voice quickening as excitement flooded him. "Celestia will be powerless to stop us. Dezrel will be ravaged and burned, made to the world that you saw. And then they will continue on, bringing world after world to order." He pointed to the journal Qurrah kept on his lap. "Within there is the spell needed to open the portal. Incredible strength is required to cast the spell, as well as two people. I am strong enough, but for centuries now I have searched for another to aid me."

"You wish me to destroy everything, all that I know, just to free the dark god?" Qurrah asked.

"Darakken was strong enough, but he turned against me, becoming the demon instead. He buried that tome within his flesh so I could not obtain it. You have it now, Qurrah, just as you were always meant to. Everything is in place to bring Thulos into this world. I have found the final key."

"And what is that?" Qurrah dared ask.

"Her," Velixar said, pointing at Tessanna. "She is a daughter of Celestia, granted enormous power by the sleeping goddess. She is destined to keep the balance from tilting too far to Karak or Ashhur. But we can use her power as Celestia never would have imagined. She can aid us in opening the portal! Not even the goddess will be able to stop us!"

The girl shied back into Qurrah's arms as she heard those words.

"I don't like your world," she said. "There's nothing fun, just the dead and the ash."

Velixar laughed.

"That is why you do not have to live within it. Once Thulos has arrived, we can create portals to hundreds of other worlds. You may go into any one of them, with my promise that until your deaths the war machine of order will not follow. You can live peacefully until the end of your days."

Qurrah carefully shifted Tessanna beside him and then stood.

"I need to speak with you in private," he told him. Velixar waved to the emptiness beyond their campfire.

"After you," he said. The half-orc kissed Tessanna's lips and then ventured away from the firelight.

"Her mind is broken," Qurrah said once he was certain she could not hear. "I promised her I would mend the pieces."

"You thought Darakken's spellbook would have it," Velixar said. "There are many powerful spells within my journal, but not one such as that."

Qurrah sighed. He glanced back at his lover, a horrid ache in his heart.

"Then my word is broken once more."

"No," Velixar said, a glint in his eye. "I do not have the power...but Thulos and Karak are gods, Qurrah. Karak's power is chained by Celestia, but he and Ashhur created your kind. Healing her mind is well within their power. Aid me in inviting Thulos and I promise she will be healed."

The half-orc looked up at the stars, hating himself. He remembered the rows of marching dead. His brother would be amongst them, as well as his wife. Did they deserve such a fate?

He glanced back to the fire. Tessanna sat beside it, her dagger drawn as she viciously slashed into her arm. She was more nervous than she let on, he realized. Only the dripping blood revealed her worry. He thought of the scars that lined her arms, and the chaos that swirled behind her eyes. No, he thought, his brother might not deserve to walk among the rows of the dead, but his lover deserved the pieces of her mind to be made whole.

"I will help you," he said at last. "And Tessanna will as well."

Velixar clapped him on the shoulder, a smile creasing his face.

"I've always been proud of you, Qurrah," he said. "And you have made me prouder still."

"What do we do?" the half-orc asked, gesturing with the journal. "Should we begin?"

"Not yet," Velixar said. "We must cast the spell where Karak and Ashhur first entered this world. That is where the barrier is weakest."

"And where is that?"

The man in black grinned, a bloodthirsty hunger smoldering in his eyes.

"At the seat of the throne in Veldaren. I have not laid siege to it over the course of the centuries without reason. With its fall, we will be ready. But first we need an army. We go to the Vile Wedge."

"You made the orcs fight for you before," Qurrah argued, "but you cannot expect them to trust you now. You let them die upon the cities gates just so you could raise them as the dead."

"I do not need trust," Velixar said. "And I do not need obedience. The world is changing, Qurrah, and we are the catalyst. Once they were servants of Karak. It is time to restore the old order of things."

The man in black offered his hand to Qurrah. The half-orc bowed and clasped it in his own two hands.

"My life for you," he said. "And for her."

"Sleep now," Velixar said. "I will give you privacy. Come the morn, we ride."

With a fading of black mist he was gone, and Qurrah knelt alone in the darkness. He returned to the fire where Tessanna sat with her dagger in hand. Tears streamed down her face.

"Shatter my mirror," she said, the voice broken by the lump in her throat. "Not just that. Shatter everything, he says, shatter everything, and still you lie, still you hide, and Aullienna floats above it, floats, floats..."

"Shush," Qurrah said, wrapping his arms around her. She rejected his comfort, instead shrieking and flailing at him with the dagger. He leapt back, narrowly avoiding the bloodied edge. The girl stared at him, wildness in her eyes.

"When this is over we leave," she said, her lower lip quivering. "We leave Velixar. We leave your brother. We leave the gods and the goddess. We leave Dezrel, and we live together, just us. No plans. No destiny. No promises. You hear me lover? Will you come with me when all this is death?"

"I will burn this whole world to ash," Qurrah told her as he gently pushed the tip of her dagger with his finger. "I will keep my promises."

"How romantic," Tessanna said, her tears flowing once more. The edge left her voice. "How romantic, and how insane. You're acting like me, now, just like me. Just like me..."

She collapsed beside the fire. Sparks flickered into the air as the girl sang in a voice distant and lost.

"Run kitty-kitty," she sang. "Big dog's coming and he's coming for you..."

With a vicious kick, Qurrah scattered the fire. He let the darkness consume him, consume them both. As his eyes adjusted he spoke to where Tessanna lay.

"Insane or not, I am damn tired of breaking my promises, Tessanna. So I will see this to the end, whatever that end may be."

"I know," Tessanna whispered. "I just fear the end we bring. Shatter my mirror. Shatter it down."

Qurrah lay beside her and wrapped her in his arms. He placed his head on her neck and let his warm breath comfort her. The night would be cold without the fire, but they had blankets. He could deal with the cold, he just couldn't stand the light. He didn't belong in the light, not anymore. The light was for his brother.

"Forgive me, Harruq," he whispered, not caring that Tessanna heard. "Forgive me for Aullienna, forgive me for your wounds, and now forgive me for this..."

He closed his eyes and dreamt of a dead world where the mindless occupants marched forever.

8

At long last the Sanctuary appeared in view. Lathaar smiled, relieved at its sight. Curled in his lap lay Mira, her arms wrapped around his neck and her legs tilted to one side as she slipped in and out of dreams. He had done much to heal her wounds, but Krieger had left scars all across her body, and he dared not try to heal her mouth and tongue. The clerics excelled at healing. He would leave such miracles to them.

"We're here," he said to Mira even though she slept. "Praise Ashhur, we're finally here."

His joy faded as the Sanctuary grew closer. He could see the shattered remnants of the front door, and in his heart he knew who had come.

"Damn you, Qurrah," he said, spurring his horse on. "Damn you to the Abyss."

Jerico sat beside the door with his mace and shield at his side. He wore no armor. A long red scar ran from his ear to his chin. When he saw the two approach he waved and got to his feet.

"About bloody time," Jerico shouted to the approaching couple. "I hope you had fun, because I had a…"

He stopped when he saw Mira's wounds.

"What happened," he asked, grabbing the reins of Lathaar's horse.

"Take her," Lathaar said, shifting the girl off his lap and holding her. Jerico reached out and accepted her frail form, his mouth locked in a frown as he scanned her wounds. Her lips were scabbed and bloody. Cuts lined her face and neck. Her fingers were swollen and red. All about her dress were torn holes in the fabric, and at each one was a fading wound. As he examined her, he fought a shudder at how similar she appeared to the girl who had scarred his face.

"By Ashhur, what happened to her," he whispered.

"Inside," he said. "Find Keziel. I'll explain once she's been healed."

"I'm already here," the priest said, emerging from the building. "And I think we both have stories to tell. We had a visitor, Lathaar."

"The spellbook," Lathaar said. "Tell me, was it taken?"

Jerico glanced at Mira's wounded face, unable to meet the other paladin's eyes.

"Yes," he said. "It was taken."

Lathaar shook with anger.

"Who...how...damn it all!" He slammed his fist against the Sanctuary. Jerico put the girl down on the grass and let Keziel kneel beside her, healing magic already glowing on his hands.

"Watch your anger and your tongue," Jerico said. "Now tell me who did this, and then I will tell you who came for the book."

Lathaar told him of how he had found Krieger, and then of their battle. He skipped nothing. When he finished, Jerico smacked him across the shoulder.

"He sounds a lot tougher than most dark paladins," he said. "Don't worry. Mira's still alive, and that's what matters. As for your book, well..."

He glanced at Mira and pointed.

"Two nights ago, her twin showed up with a necromancer dressed in black. They attacked while we slept. I held them off, at least until most of the clerics could escape in the back. You think you did poorly in your fight?" He pointed to the scar across his face. "I passed out mere feet away from where the priests hid. One of them did this to me as I lay there, but did not kill me. Looks like it hasn't been a good few days for either of us."

"Amen to that."

The two stopped their discussion and looked to Keziel, whose back popped several times as he stood.

"She'll be fine," the cleric said. "She's already healed a remarkable amount, no doubt thanks to Celestia's power. Give her a day or two and I wouldn't be surprised if even the scars are gone."

"What's the plan?" Jerico asked. "We going to give chase?"

"Not yet," Lathaar said. "I need to keep a promise and return to Veldaren. Once Mira's better we'll begin. You in?"

"Course I am," Jerico said. "I think Ashhur gave us a solid lesson on the need to stick together."

"Amusing," Keziel said, "Now help me bring her inside, unless you think she should sleep on the grass in the dead of winter?"

"Lathaar, how could you!" Jerico said, faking shock and indignation. Lathaar rolled his eyes, picked up the girl, and carried her into the Sanctuary as all the while Jerico tried to laugh away the worry that squirmed in his gut.

On the western bank of the Rigon river, just before it emptied into the Thulon Ocean, stood Karak's counter to the Citadel. It was the Stronghold, a giant black tower with four obsidian lions guarding its corners. While Lathaar and Jerico waited for Mira to heal, Krieger rode night and day until he arrived at his refuge in the chaotic world of Dezrel. The sun was high in the sky, and the young apprentice watching the door threw open the gates and knelt in respect as the dark paladin arrived home.

"The Stronghold welcomes you," the apprentice said, his head bowed. Normally he would have offered to stable Krieger's horse, but he had seen before the magical properties of Demonwail and would not be made a fool.

"Where is Carden?" Krieger asked.

"The brethren are assembled for his sermon," the apprentice said. "It is the sixth day."

"Then he is in his study. The true god be with you."

"You as well."

Krieger marched inside as the great doors slammed shut behind him.

The first room of the Stronghold was designed with invasion in mind. All about the door were perches for higher ground, angled so that a trio of men with spears could hold off wave after wave of intruders. Farther back was a single barrier with four crossbows bolted across the top. Spikes protruded out of the barrier toward the door, so any charging the crossbowmen would impale themselves on the spikes first. The floor sloped downward so that if any went around they would find themselves still on lower ground.

Behind all the defenses was a large staircase leading both up and down. Krieger rubbed one of the spikes as he past the barrier, a habit from when he was a young apprentice. A thief had had the audacity, or more likely insanity, to try to rob the Stronghold. Krieger had caught him, and at the age of nine took his first life by slamming the thief against the spikes while he crept in the dark. Ever since, he had touched the spikes to remember the blood that had flown from them, and the initial thrill of watching another die at his own hands.

The second floor was more ornately decorated. Gold weavings covered the walls, showing ancient battles between Karak and the followers of Ashhur. Each wall had a marvelous lion, shining gold with bared teeth made of silver. What wasn't gold or silver was red, from the floor to the ceiling. Krieger loved the room. The 'gentle persuasion,' the dark paladins called it. Royalty and dignitaries were brought there to see the wealth and wisdom of Karak. If that failed, then they were taken to the 'hard persuasion,' which was beneath the first floor. Much as he loved the gold and red, the blood that bathed the floor of that other room always made Krieger smile.

Beyond that were rooms for sleeping, storage, and training. The dark paladin kept climbing, for he could hear the rough chants of his brethren. Every sixth day those at the Stronghold gathered for worship of their deity and to hear a sermon by the High Enforcer. The dark paladins were deep within the chant of loyalty. After that was the chant of obedience, and then the sermon.

On the sixth floor he joined his armored brothers in Karak. They knelt before a giant stage covered with a crimson curtain. There were no chairs, just wood floor, the stone walls, and the stage. To Krieger's right was a small door. He knocked twice, then entered. Inside was a gray-haired man dressed in polished black armor. A painted lion skull covered his chest, made deep crimson by the blood of his enemies. The man held his helmet in his hands, an ugly thing with the horns of a goat curling around the sides. The High Enforcer stood to greet his visitor.

"Welcome back, Krieger," Carden said, clasping the man's hand and shaking it. His voice was deep and old. It was a voice to be respected if not feared. "It is good to see you safe and well."

"Forgive me for not joining the chants," Krieger said, "but I bring matters that cannot wait."

"We have time," Carden said, sitting back down in his carved chair.

"I have spoken with the eternal prophet," the dark paladin said. "Darakken's spellbook is in the hands of his chosen apprentice. As we speak, they march toward Veldaren. The time has come, Carden. Ashhur's city will soon be burned to the ground."

"Karak be praised," Carden said, a great smile lighting up his face. "I prayed it would be within my lifetime that Veldaren fell, and at last Velixar is ready for it to come to pass."

"There is one problem," Krieger said. "Lathaar rides to stop them, and he is not alone. Another paladin has escaped our purging, one by the name of Jerico. I want their blood decorating my armor when we march victoriously through Veldaren's gates."

"We can send all our forces to guard the Gods' Bridges," Carden said. "Should they try to cross, we will slaughter them."

"No," said Krieger. "Give me ten of my brothers and we will kill them ourselves. Lathaar is mine. I shall have the privilege of slaying him."

"And it is you that let him live," Carden said as he stood from his chair. Though he stood a foot shorter, he still seemed a larger presence in the confined room. "In your pride you sought an equal fight. The death of all paladins proves Karak's greatness, Krieger, not your own physical prowess. The balance tilts in our favor because we are the stronger. It is Karak about to escape his prison, not Ashhur!"

Krieger knelt to one knee, feeling his face flush with blood.

"Forgive me, High Enforcer. I thought he was the last of his kind, and I underestimated the danger."

Carden waved him off.

"And now he is with another. The paladins of Ashhur were a worthy adversary, Krieger. You have not seen them in battle as I have. I remember this Jerico, an oddity with a shield blessed by Ashhur. We cannot let them continue to live just to satiate your pride." The old man collapsed in his chair and leaned back. An amused look came over his face, and his eyes twinkled.

"I have spoken with Pelarak," he said. "They've begun daily sacrifices to strengthen Karak's followers. A cloud of fear encircles the city. So soon, so very soon…"

The chant of obedience began to echo through the walls. Just three words, but they were spoken with power and conviction by all in attendance, over and over in perfect synchronization. I will obey. I will obey. I will obey.

"Do you hear them?" Carden asked.

"Yes, I do."

"They seek a leader," the old man said. "Their faith is strong, but many are young. A guide, that is what they need. A strong believer whose skill is unmatched."

Carden motioned to the door behind him that led to the stage.

"Give them your orders," the High Enforcer said. "Lead us to Karak's freedom."

"I will not disappoint," Krieger said, bowing deeply. He walked to the door, strangely proud of his damaged armor and wounded back. He bore signs of battle, and that was what mattered. As his hand wrapped around the handle, Carden called out his name.

"Krieger," he said. "Make sure it is the will of Karak, and not your pride, that guides you now."

The dark paladin did not reply. He opened the door and stepped onto the stage as the final chant ended. Thirty men, all dressed in gleaming black armor, knelt facing him. Krieger looked at each face as a heavy silence overtook the room. Some were young, brimming with faith bordering fanatical. Others were older than he, heavily scarred and bitter to the world. But a few stared at him with excitement twinkling in their eyes. They were the strong, the intelligent. They knew what Krieger's ascension to the stage meant.

"I have fought a paladin of Ashhur," Krieger said, his voice shattering the silence. "And still he lives. That is the nature of our enemy. Wounded, yes, bleeding yes, but still he lives. Another has joined him. Lathaar and Jerico, paladins of the Citadel. Their survival blasphemes against Karak. Their very breath insults our dark god."

As he talked he walked about the stage, shifting side to side so that the gruesome wounds on his back could be clearly seen. His voice grew louder, and his speech, faster.

"When the Citadel fell, we thought our victory complete. We have purged many, but the true faith is not restored. Not until Karak walks among us again can we say our purpose has been fulfilled! And he will! His prophet approaches Veldaren, and at long last our god's freedom is assured. But the paladins..."

He drew his sword and held it before him, letting all see the great black fire that surrounded his blade. Only Carden could claim a stronger flame.

"The paladins give chase! They travel with a witch of Celestia, the goddess who imprisoned our mighty god."

Krieger saw hatred growing among his audience. Good, he thought. Anger was very good. He pointed to the front row, where the youngest dark paladins knelt.

"You seven will be given chance to prove your faith to Karak," he said, pointing at each and every one of them. "You march for the Gods' Bridges. The paladins are wounded, as is their whore. When they arrive, show them your faith."

He spread his arms wide, waving to the rest.

"As for us... Veldaren will burn! Our time for war has come at last. We will march through the gates and join our priests of Karak as we cloud the city in fear and bathe it with blood. We will fight as the prophet sunders this world, and at long last victory becomes ours!"

The dark paladins drew their swords and held them high. The room darkened as the black flame flared from blade and axe. "For Karak!" they shouted. "For Karak! For Karak!"

Krieger beamed, the shouts causing the hairs on his neck to stand and a tight shiver to crawl up his spine.

"Arm yourselves," he shouted. "And prepare your provisions. Time is our foe."

"And every foe must be beaten," Carden said, joining him on stage. He strutted out with familiarity and an aura that made all in his presence bow.

"Krieger is the new High Enforcer of the Stronghold," the old man said, his deep voice losing no strength from age. "You will follow his commands, for they are the words of Karak himself. Now rise! Make ready! The time for war is now."

The dark paladins cheered his name and clanged together their weapons. As they left to prepare, the old man turned to Krieger and smiled.

"A sufficient speech," he told him. "Though your energy and conviction made up for your lack of grace."

"It is how I fight," Krieger said as he sheathed his sword. "And it is how I speak. Will you come with us?"

"My bones are old but my faith is still strong," he said. As if to prove his point he drew his own sword and plunged it two inches into the stage.

"Veldaren will crumble like a house of straw," Krieger said.

Carden tore his sword free and held it high.

"And we will be the fire that consumes it as it falls."

Mira had no horse of her own, but she was light and Lathaar's horse bore her weight with ease. She sat in front, his arm around her waist to hold her steady. Jerico rode several paces ahead, scanning the horizon for any sign of Qurrah and his book. They had been riding for several days, and after the fifth Lathaar finally told her everything Keziel knew about the daughters of balance. She said little, mostly listening. During their ride the next morning she finally spoke.

"Are you sure what he says is true," she asked. "About what I am?"

"I find no reason to doubt him," Lathaar said.

Mira leaned against his chest, closed her eyes, and then tilted her head so it rest sideways against his armor.

"Killing Darakken was my purpose, wasn't it?" she asked.

"We don't know that."

"And if I do have another purpose, what if..."

She said no more. Lathaar stroked her hair with his free hand. After twenty minutes of silence, she spoke again.

"I've had dreams," she said. "Good dreams. Peaceful dreams. And in each one I am dying." She felt Lathaar tense up at her words.

"That isn't your purpose," he said. "You aren't supposed to die. I won't let you be a martyr."

"Evermoon taught me to pray to Celestia," she said. "I know the sound of her voice. The dreams come from her, Lathaar. That girl, the one like me..."

"Tessanna."

"Yes. I think she is to kill me."

The path led them into a large forest, where the tree trunks were thick and the space between was large enough that they could stay mounted. They still had to be careful of footing, lest they injure their horses. Lathaar guided his mount side to side as he thought over his words.

"Celestia wants you to keep everything the same," he said, gently pulling on the reins to slow his horse. "She may want you to die to prevent more good. I won't allow it, Mira. I won't let you die just so she...just so..."

The girl smiled up at him and pressed a finger against his lips.

"I can read your mind, remember?" she said.

He nodded, trying to look calm as his face flushed a deep red.

"Careful back there," Jerico shouted, "I think I upset a gopher's home."

Lathaar checked the ground and sure enough found a deep collection of holes prepared like a deadly trap. He guided his horse around, glad that Jerico's horse hadn't injured its leg when the dirt collapsed underneath it.

"I missed you," Mira said.

"Missed you, too," Lathaar said.

The girl turned around and kissed his neck just above the top of his breastplate. Just as quick she turned back, nestled comfortably in his arms, and remained quiet for the rest of the day. Jerico looked to make sure they had avoided the pitfall, and as he did he noticed how red Lathaar face had grown.

"What the abyss is wrong with you?" he asked.

"Nothing," Lathaar said. "Nothing at all."

"Well hurry, still have a good week to reach the Bridges. This little shortcut through the forest will save us time, but not much. Oh, and Lathaar, may I remind you that while Ashhur doesn't require us to take an oath of celibacy, he does frown upon needless necking while my back is turned." Lathaar's face turned even redder as Jerico rode on, muttering something about youngsters.

Mira stopped them when the western bridge was finally in view. She had grown increasingly quiet as their journey progressed, to the point she said almost nothing to Jerico, and only the occasional comment to Lathaar. She cuddled him on his horse, slept at his side near the fire, and did little else. So when she held out her hands and ordered them to halt, it was their surprise, not her words, that made them stop short.

"What is it, Mira?" Lathaar asked. "What's wrong?"

"Can't you feel them?" the girl asked. "Waiting like snakes?"

Jerico closed his eyes and let his mind listen for the soft voice of Ashhur. "Dark paladins, seven of them. Someone isn't happy about our return to Neldar."

"This is worse than you think," Lathaar said, frowning atop his horse. "Qurrah was never in league with Karak's knights. If they're here, then more is at stake than we know. Neldar must be in danger."

"What do we do?" Jerico asked. They could see the magnificent arches of the bridge in the distance from their perch atop a hill. A small patch of trees filled the distance between them and the bridge. His eyes were good, and he could see waiting beside the arches were seven men in distinctive black armor.

"We can't go around," Lathaar said. "Our horses cannot swim across water that fast, and our armor isn't exactly light."

"I can get us across," Mira said, staring at the bridge.

"Yeah, I guess you might know a floating spell or two," Jerico said as his face perked up.

"No," Mira said, her face darkening. "You misunderstand. We will cross."

"Wait...you want to meet them head on?" Lathaar asked.

"There's only seven of them," Jerico said, scratching at his chin.

"They're dark paladins, not virgin squires. Seven is more than enough to be dangerous."

"I will get us across," Mira repeated. "Now move, or I go without you."

The two paladins glanced at one another, apprehensive about the idea, but Lathaar had seen Mira fight Darakken. He would trust her. Down the hill they trotted, through the woods toward Karak's bridge.

They were spotted the moment they left the forest. The dark paladins formed a line across the front of the bridge, eager for a fight.

"Arrogant," Lathaar muttered. "No hiding their numbers and no attempt at ambush. It's as if they want us to fight them or turn away."

"They're young," Mira said, her eyes rolling back in her skull. "Their faith is maniacal, blind." She flitted from one mind to the next. "None are afraid. They think our deaths will give them favor with the dark god."

"I haven't met a paladin for Karak I can't beat up, down, and sideways," Jerico said. "And no young pups will change that, either."

"You stay back," Mira said, her black eyes staring at him. "They don't know who I am. I will show them."

"Show them what?"

She smiled at Jerico.

"The goddess."

Mira leapt off Lathaar's horse. Before he could spur his mount faster, her bare feet were already hovering an inch above the grass. An unseen wind pushed her forward, as if she weighed nothing. Her arms trailed at angles behind her, like masts holding an unseen sail.

"Hey, wait!" Jerico shouted, spurring his own horse on as the other two left him behind. "Don't have fun without me!"

Mira saw that Lathaar was closing so she flew faster, her hair flailing wildly as the wind at her back soared stronger. The bridge approached at frightening speeds, but she knew that she appeared far more frightening to the dark paladins that waited. She slipped in and out of their minds, whispering echoing words as she did.

The goddess is coming. You are to die, mortals. Die to the goddess. Fear my eyes, my hair, my fire. The goddess is here.

She felt their fear growing, and to that she smiled. She had tried a similar ploy to Lathaar, and he had only grabbed her presence in his mind and demanded to know her name. Silly dark paladins, she thought. All faith but no courage.

Fire swirled around her hands as she came to a halt before the line of platemail, axes, and swords.

"I am a daughter of the goddess," she told them as they stared, frozen in place by fear and indecision. "And I demand passage. Will you grant it?"

"It is the will of Krieger, and of Karak, that none shall pass," the one in the center answered. While the others had long hair cut past the shoulder or tied in ponytails, he was completely shaven. "We are the embodiment of his will. And the goddess shall not break the will of Karak."

Mira laughed as the edges of white in her eyes vanished.

"Very well. Let's test Karak's will."

A ring of fire rose from the ground around her, blazing hot. The seven raised their shields, testing the heat. A razor blade of whirling air shot from Mira's fingers, slicing one in half at the waist. His body fell, blood and intestines spilling everywhere. She turned to another, who braced his shield. Again she laughed.

"Shut up, bitch," the man said, the lion skull on his shield gleaming in the sun. Mira clapped her hands together above her head. Lightning struck from the clear sky, swirling its power around her. The other dark paladins dodged, but the one who had cursed her kept his place. Arrogance, Mira thought. She pointed at his chest and winked. Lightning shot from her finger, crashing through his chest and out the other side. The blast lifted him into the air before flinging him off the bridge.

"We will not fall!" the bald one shouted, holding an axe in both hands. He prayed for aid from his dark god, and his request was granted. The black fire that surrounded his blade spread to all his flesh, protecting him from Mira's fire. The girl turned toward him, smiling as if it were a game. She remembered the times she had trained against Flowers, and later on the rest of the Doru'al. Even ten at a time she had won, and those demons were far quicker and stronger.

A wave of her hand and a wall of ice surrounded her. When the bald man shattered it with the hilt of his sword, a great flash of light blinded his eyes. Mira clapped again, and the horribly bright light struck them once more. The others charged, her fire wall dissipated. She twirled, blasting one with a solid ball of water and hitting a second with a chunk of earth she tore from the ground. A third swung his sword at her waist, desperately praying to Karak that it would tear flesh. Instead it passed through empty air, for Mira was no longer there.

She reappeared on the far side of the bridge, waving as if all was friendly between her and men she had just injured. As the dark paladins glared death, they heard the heavy sound of hoof beats. They turned and saw Lathaar and Jerico riding at full speed toward them, and with opponents on both sides, they knew their error.

"Kill the paladins while we can," the bald one ordered. "Close combat at all times. The girl will not risk hurting her companions."

The five charged, their weapons high and their shields ready.

"None of you are Krieger," Mira said, her bright smile fading just a bit. "But I feel better just the same."

She twirled her hands, opening a portal. She stepped through and appeared in front of the dark paladins. Before they could react, she knelt and punched the bridge. Another wall of ice rose up, blocking Jerico and Lathaar from reaching them.

"Mira!" she heard Lathaar shout from the other side.

I'm fine, she told his mind. *Please trust me.*

She stood, elegant and powerful. Ice swirled around her hands. She grabbed a man's throat, and then the ice found a new home. Frost shards exploded outward, piercing his windpipe. As the dark paladin dropped, the bald one stepped in and slammed his shield across her forehead. Mira fell, her vision swimming. She used her arms to roll to one side as an axe struck where she had been.

"Where is Krieger?" she asked them as she let loose a blast of pure white energy from her hands. Her target raised his shield and tried to block, but it just disintegrated the metal, then his armor, and finally blasted a hole in his flesh. His body sailed off the side and into the water. "Where is Krieger?" she repeated to the final three.

"He left us here for you," the shaved man said. "Said a daughter of the whore would be coming, and here you are."

"Your name," she asked.

"Fuck you."

Mira pressed her palm flat against the bridge and let her magic flow into it. The entire bridge rumbled on its foundations. The shaved man stumbled, and then she cast her second spell. Two cylindrical streams of water rose from either side of the bridge, spinning in the air. One hit his upper body while the other took out his legs. He hit the ground, cracking his head hard on the stone. The remaining two cried out the name of their god and charged, wanting Karak to think them brave and not cowards when they met him in his abyss.

"You know any way to get across?" Lathaar asked as the two paladins stood dismounted before the ice wall.

"Your girl has problems," Jerico said as he pressed his shield against the ice. "You do know that, right?"

"She's never like this," he said. "She's shy, and lonely...what are you doing?"

"Knocking down the wall."

He shifted his arms and pushed with all his might. The light around his shield flared brighter and brighter. Lathaar stepped back and crossed his arms.

"You're doing what?"

"Oh you of little faith..." They heard the sound of a thunderclap. "Sounds like your girl got another one."

He clamped his teeth together and grunted. The muscles in his entire body tightened. The light surrounding his shield grew even brighter. A long crack split the wall. Another joined it, arcing inward from the left corner. Lathaar felt his jaw drop as third crack appeared, spiking from the Jerico's shield to the lower right corner.

"Not right," he muttered as Jerico burst through, the ice wall crumbling to pieces around him. Jerico raised his shield above his head as the pieces fell. Several hefty chunks hit atop it, but he weathered them with ease. When the commotion was done the two saw Mira standing over a lone dark paladin. His face and hands were charred red, and his right eye looked like a blackened piece of fruit.

"Where is Krieger?" they heard her ask. Magic swirled around her hands. "Tell me."

"You think I'll tell?" he said with a pained laugh. She struck his other eye with a blast of lightning. The man screamed, and his back bent upward in a wicked jerk. He gasped for air as smoke escaped his open mouth.

"Tell me," she said. "Where is Krieger?"

"Mira, stop it!" Lathaar shouted, sheathing his blades and running to her. He grabbed her wrists and spun her around. Her entire body tensed like a cat before a pounce. Lightning crackled in her eyes, but then she saw him and stopped. Her hands unclenched. The magic left her fingers.

"I'm sorry," she said as Lathaar let go of her wrists. She wrapped her arms around his neck and pressed her face against his chest. Her tears ran down his armor. "I'm sorry."

Jerico stood over the dying, blind paladin. He hooked his mace onto his belt, slung his shield over his back, and then hoisted the bald man onto his feet. The man had no strength to resist as Jerico pushed him to the edge of the bridge, where the Rigon river roared beneath them.

"Why do you aid Qurrah?" he asked him. "What has that half-orc offered you?"

"Who is Qurrah?" the dark paladin asked. Jerico narrowed his eyes. All paladins of Ashhur could innately sense a lie, and he knew the man spoke truth. He didn't know who Qurrah was.

"Karak's army marches for Veldaren," he said. "Now give me an honorable death."

"Sure thing." He pushed him off the bridge. In his heavy armor, the man sank straight to the bottom.

"Don't do that again," Jerico said to Mira. "Revenge is too hard for a heart as soft as yours."

He left to retrieve his horse. Lathaar wrapped his arms around her as she continued to cry.

I tortured him, he heard her say in his mind. *Celestia help me, I tortured him, just like he…he…*

"You'll be okay," he said.

I've never…I have all this power and I lost control…

"You've fought before. Killed before."

But never this. Please forgive me, Michael. Never this.

Lathaar kissed her forehead and held her tight. She had called him by his original name before he had passed the Trials and become a paladin. It reminded him of just how young she still was, and how young she had been when he first met her, alone in a dark forest with only a demon to keep her company.

"I forgive you," he said, pulling her back and taking her hand. "Now let's get away from this place. Go back to my horse."

She sniffed, smiled a little, and then did as she was told. Lathaar pushed the remaining three bodies into the river, feeling grim satisfaction with each one.

"Five less servants of Karak in this world," he said. "Five less drops in a river."

"But even rivers one day run dry," Jerico said from atop his horse. He held Lathaar's reigns in his right hand. Mira rode atop the horse.

"Amen," Lathaar said, taking his seat on the saddle behind Mira.

9

Entrances into the Vile Wedge were few. The Citadel had guarded the lower portions of the rivers when it had still stood, preventing the dangerous inhabitants within from crossing by boats. No bridges remained across the bone ditch, the orcs name for the great chasm lining the eastern side. Scouts for Mordan sailed down the Rigon river on the west, reporting to the wall of towers than stretched for miles and miles. But to one skilled with dark magic, even the challenge of the giant rivers proved surmountable.

"Have you even been inside the wedge?" Velixar asked as they stared at the slowly flowing river, whose surface reflected back the stars in a beautiful display. Qurrah and Tessanna both shook their heads as they stood beside him.

"Marvelous place," the man in black said, smiling. "The orcs rule the majority, but it is a tenuous hold. Hyena-men, wolf-men, goblins, even the bird-men have their places, all castaways from the great war. They were made by the gods, then forgotten when their usefulness ended. But it is time to end their chaos."

He turned to Tessanna. "My lady, would you be so kind as to grant us passage across?"

"But, I'm not..." She stared at the opposite shore over two hundred feet away. "I don't know if I can."

Qurrah felt a spike of jealousy as Velixar put a hand on her shoulder her and gently nudged her closer to the water.

"You are as powerful as you are beautiful," he said. "And if you do not know if you can, then it is time you learned. You are the daughter of a goddess. Your limits are your own to discover...and then exceed."

Tessanna looked back to Qurrah, who only nodded.

"Very well," she said. "I could float us across, but you know that. This is a test. I don't like tests."

"My apologies, but I do," Velixar said.

Tessanna laughed.

"Aren't you so polite." Wisps of white ether floated like smoke from her hands. Velixar stepped beside Qurrah and whispered to him as a sudden wind screamed in from the south.

"How much have you seen of her power?" he asked him.

"More than enough," Qurrah replied.

"No," Velixar said. "There is never enough. There is always more."

Tessanna's black hair danced in the wind. Her hands spread wide, the white mist growing thicker and swirling around her fingers. She let out a tiny moan as her body lifted a foot off the ground, and her head arched back as she let loose her power. With a savage cry, she slammed her hands together. A white beam sliced through the river, accompanied by a great roar of moving water. She spread her hands. The ground shook. The river growled and tossed. And then a pathway opened, dry and barren.

"She could do more," Velixar whispered as both stood in awe. "And I will push her to it, whether she wants me to or not."

The blocked river tried to overflow its banks, but Tessanna curled her fingers and enclosed it. A white wall blocked both sides, stretching to the sky. The magical dam captured the water and pressed it ever higher. Despite the enormous power of the river, the girl walked through the pathway she had made with little sign of exhaustion.

"Don't hurt her," Qurrah said before walking through. "Just don't hurt her."

"I promise." Velixar pulled his hood low and followed. "And I keep my promises."

When they reached the other side, Tessanna turned and smiled.

"Wave bye-bye to the river," she said. Before either could react, she relaxed her body. The white wall vanished. The roar of the water was deafening as it collapsed downstream, overloading the banks and crushing trees that grew along its edge. The girl giggled at the destruction she caused.

"I may not like tests," she said, "but that was fun."

Velixar once again placed his hand on her shoulder and led her on. "Truly magnificent," he said.

⋈

It was Velixar's decision that they travel by day. Secrecy was no longer necessary. For two days they followed the river north. At the start of the third day, Velixar revealed a portion of his plan.

"There are three main orc tribes," he explained as they walked. "The Mug tribe is the biggest, followed by the Dun and the Glush tribes. A fourth tribe, however, has sworn off worshiping animals. Somehow they learned of their elven heritage and now worship Celestia, hoping the goddess will remove the curse that poisons their blood. They are a blasphemy against Karak and must be dealt with accordingly."

They came upon a crude banner made of two sharpened sticks thrust together in the dirt. Draped over the front was what appeared to be the skin of a wolf.

"We've entered their territory," Velixar said. "It won't be long before we find one of their camps."

"Why a wolf skin?" Qurrah asked as they passed by the banner.

"The wolf-men to the north often raid their homes for food. The orcs here use their skin to make their banners, blankets, and huts."

Tessanna started laughing.

"Bad doggie," she said as they passed by a similar banner. When both men gave her a funny look, she only laughed louder, the sound hollow among the quiet, dangerous land.

They traveled over the dry, yellow grass, until the encampment was within sight.

"There," Velixar said, pointing. "Karak has whispered of them for many years, but at last I see them with my own eyes."

Hundreds of tents covered the nearby hills. On each and every one was a triangle. Two lines stretched outward from the bottom. A tree, Qurrah realized. Drawn in the blood of animals was a tree, the old symbol the elves used for Celestia. For the first time Qurrah saw orc females, their sex no longer hidden behind heavy war armor. Their breasts were flat, and more muscle than milk. Children ran about, wrestling and playing games with rocks and toys carved from wood. In the center of the camp was a tent far larger than the others, with red trees on each side of the entryway.

"How have they not been conquered by the other tribes?" Qurrah asked.

"That is the mystery," Velixar said. He licked his lips. "Somehow they have held off any and all attacks. The other tribes talk of how a goddess protects them. This sort of blasphemy is dangerous, my disciple. It changes the order of things and renders the land even more chaotic. Follow me. We will show them their place."

Velixar walked down the hill, his arms held at his sides in an apparent gesture of peace. Guards lined the exterior of the camp, and when they spotted him they raised a ruckus in their native tongue. Orcs flocked together. Qurrah and Tessanna approached, hand in hand. The half-orc had never felt more conscious of his gray skin. He could feel his tainted blood coursing within him, and for the first time he saw their civilization.

"I could have been their god," he whispered. "Their deity."

"And I could be a goddess in any place I choose," Tessanna whispered. "But that is not my place in this world, and these huts are not yours."

A wall of spears surrounded them. Velixar halted, his hands still held high and wide. His hood had fallen low to cover his eyes, but beneath lingered his smile. Beyond the ring of orcs Qurrah saw women holding their young, watching. He was shocked when he realized many of them were praying.

A particularly large orc broke through the ring and shouted at Velixar in the orcish tongue. The man in black laughed and then spoke back in the same guttural language. The orc seemed surprised at this, and began questioning those around him.

"What is going on," Qurrah asked.

Before Velixar could answer, the big one turned toward the giant tent and shouted the same word three times.

"Darnela! Darnela! Darnela!"

"Darnela?" Tessanna asked.

"At last I understand," Velixar said, his grin growing. "An elf priestess of Celestia came and tamed them. She's filled their head with dogma of forgiveness and pathetic begging in hopes of revoking of their orcish blood. Keep ready, both of you. I find it unlikely we will get along."

In the distance they saw a sleek feminine form exit the main tent. She wore a cloak made of wolf skin. Her tunic and breeches were made of leather. She carried a scepter in one hand and a jeweled sphere in the other. She seemed a strange cross of elf and orc, elegance and roughness. All throughout the camp, orcs parted to grant her passage, bowing their heads as she passed.

"She's beautiful," Tessanna said.

"Yes," Velixar said. "And as dangerous as she is beautiful. I know this one. She has changed her name since we last met."

Qurrah felt his whip curling on his arm, bits of flame flickering from it even though he gave it no such order. Tessanna chewed on her fingernails as the girl approached. She had long hair, so long that it floated past the small of her back and beyond the length of her wolf head cloak. It was a dark brown, the same color as her eyes. When she saw

Velixar, a frown marred her beautiful face. The last of the orcs parted, and she stood before the trespassers to her camp.

"Greetings, Fionn," Velixar said, bowing low. "It has been too long since we last met."

The scepter shook in the elven priestess's hand.

"I am Darnela now," she said. "Do you bring your war and hatred to my orcs? They seek peace, dark prophet, and forgiveness from the goddess. We are not interested in whatever sins you bring."

"Your name used to be beautiful and pure," Velixar said, ignoring her question. "Yet you now claim a name meaning war and anger, all while preaching peace to the orcs, Celestia's cursed and abandoned?"

Qurrah winced as the whip tightened so much that his fingers tingled from the pressure. He dared not remove it, though, not with so many orcs with spears and swords desperate to attack.

"Be gone," she said. "Karak's taint is leaving their blood. We all see it plain as day."

"Indeed," Velixar said. Still grinning. "The...taint...is leaving."

Darnela took a step closer, glaring at the visage beneath the black hood.

"I swore to kill you, and I did," she said. "Celestia forgive me for thinking you would give Dezrel a gift and stay dead. Now leave."

"Qurrah," Velixar suddenly shouted. "Show our beautiful hostess here your weapon."

Slowly the half-orc let the whip uncurl and fall into his hand. The leather pooled upon the grass and then burst into flame. He watched Darnela's face, and he saw her rage grow. All around, the wall of orcs grew larger as guards from every corner of the camp gathered.

"I also made a promise," Velixar said. "I would use your husband's whip to return the favor for what you did to me. But not yet. You think these orcs your pets? You think they believe what you feed their minds? I speak the truth, Darnela, and even these shallow beings can feel and understand that."

He turned his back to her and gestured to the crowd. His voice boomed impossibly loud, every word he spoke thundering in the ears of those who heard.

"Orcs of the wedge, hear me! I am Velixar, and I speak with the voice of Karak himself!"

"Silence," Darnela shouted. The man in black turned and glared at her. For a moment they stared, their eyes locked. When the priestess did not attack, Velixar continued his shouting. Qurrah noticed he shouted in the common tongue of man, yet the orcs appeared to understand.

"What you have been told is true. You were once elves. You were cursed by the elven goddess, but that curse did not make you what you are today! Karak gave you the strength that saved you from extinction. Karak bound you together for war, and through him you crushed your enemies and fought for a place in this world. You feel that strength fading now, don't you? It is Celestia who cursed you, Celestia who abandoned you, and now you cry out to her like a dog licking the boot that just kicked it?"

All around orcs began shouting, some in defiance of what he said, others in response to their old bloodlust stirring. As Qurrah looked around, he could see Velixar spoke truth. Few orcs were as muscled as the orcs he had watched assault Veldaren years ago.

"Do not listen," Darnela shouted, magically strengthening her own voice as well. "He is a speaker of lies, a preacher of death. He would make you kill for his own gains, and when you died he would bring back your bones to fight again. He is chaos, he is slaughter, and he is the reason your kind was first cursed by the goddess!"

More shouting, more posturing with crude weapons. Tessanna clutched tightly to Qurrah's waist as she glanced about.

"I'm scared," she said, her face buried into his shoulder.

"Just stupid beasts with sticks," Qurrah told her. "You can defeat every one of them with a lift of your finger."

"But they're all scared," she said. "They're hurt, they're confused, and they don't know what to believe. The goddess weeps for them, Qurrah, can't you hear it?"

"I come offering what your kind has always embraced," Velixar continued. "I offer you war against those who drove you to this wretched land. You act as if your blood is a curse, but I call it a boon. Embrace your strength! Embrace your bloodlust! Darnela seeks only to pacify you and make you weak!"

"He lies!" Darnela shouted.

"Remember her own lessons! Let them show my truth! She wanted you to throw down your weapons, end your fighting, and turn away from all you once knew. You are a stone's throw away from being massacred by wolf-men, hyena-men, even the weakest of the goblin tribes. The elves have always wanted you dead. They know they cannot do it in war. But if they poison you from within? Look at yourselves, warriors of Karak, look at yourselves!"

Tessanna began to weep as a deep rumbling swept the camp. Darnela herself sensed the change. She had worked valiantly to redeem the souls to the goddess. She had preached over and over forgiveness and humility. And now, at the booming words of the man in black, it would crumble.

"You will die one day," the elf said to him. "And when that day comes I hope to look down from Celestia's paradise and laugh at your torment in the fire and darkness."

"Should that day come," Velixar said, his voice back to its normal volume, "I will rule as a prince. And even there I will seek to break the will of the goddess and storm your wretched home."

"Make them stop," Tessanna whimpered. "Please, Qurrah, make them stop."

"You will be buried underneath a wave of those you sought to make docile," Velixar said. He smirked at Darnela's anger. "Fitting, don't you agree?"

The priestess slammed her scepter and orb together. Flames consumed both, and a yellow pillar of fire fell from the sky. Orcs scrambled away as the pillar consumed her, swirling about her body as she prayed ceaselessly to her goddess.

"Kneel to me," Velixar shouted. "All who bow and confess their lives to Karak will live. Those who refuse will die by my hand!"

Dark magic swirled around his hands. He kissed the air as Darnela prepared her assault.

"Hold yourself together," Qurrah said, grabbing his lover by the arms. "What is the matter with you?"

"No!" Tessanna screamed, shoving him aside. She leapt in between Velixar and Darnela. Her right hand faced the elf, the left pointed directly at the man in black. She looked each in the eye as the orcs cried out in anger and confusion. Pure magical essence curled around her fingers, throbbing with her heartbeat.

"If either of you moves I will leave nothing but dust for the wind to spread," she said. Wisps of black smoke floated from the corners of her eyes.

"Of course, my lady," Velixar said, seeming unsurprised by her actions.

"Are you mad, girl?" Darnela asked. Her hair danced inside her pillar of fire. "Do you know what he is? You travel with him, yet still defy his will?"

"I don't need to know," she answered. "Let those who believe Velixar's words leave your camp in peace. The rest may stay under your command. Is this clear?"

"I accept your proposal," Velixar said, bowing. "Not your command."

For the first time a bit of anger flickered in his eyes, but Tessanna was unconcerned. She looked to the elf as the magic on her fingers crackled with dark lightning.

"Do you accept?" she asked her.

"You are a disgrace to the goddess," Darnela said, her jaw clenched tight. "But I will accept. Take the faithless and go."

Velixar looked around the camp. Almost half the orcs knelt, their heads bowed as the others nearby beat them and cursed the prayers they prayed. The man in black lifted his hands and called out to them.

"Come east, children of Karak. Abandon your weakness, for it is your blood that shall unite the tribes against Neldar!"

Hundreds of orcs took up their possessions and did as they were told. Tessanna remained between the two powerful casters until the stream of orcs had fully left the camp.

"I will see you again, Darnela," Velixar said as he bowed. "I still have a favor to repay you."

The priestess only turned and stormed off, the pillar of flame dissipating into fading embers in the air. When she was far enough away, Tessanna closed her hands and let go of the spells she had prepared. Velixar immediately grabbed her by the wrist.

"We will talk," he said, his red eyes seething.

"I know," she replied almost casually. He let her go and stormed away. Qurrah took her in his arms, holding her as her resolve vanished.

"Shush," he said, stroking her hair as he guided her east. "You did no wrong here."

"I know," she said, drying her tears against his robe. "But I risk what we have when I do this. He needs me, and he needs you, but he's patient, Qurrah. So patient, so dangerous."

"Why'd you do it, then?" he asked her. She looked up to him, kissed his lips, and then held his hand as they walked. She did not answer.

"Very well," Qurrah said. "I do not need to know the reason. I will still defend your choice to my death."

"I know," she said, gripping his hand tighter. "But it's good to hear you say it anyway."

Velixar was no stranger to leading armies, especially one made of orcs. They had little supplies, no food, and over three hundred mouths to feed. If they were to survive, they had to pillage. He marched throughout his small army, shouting and encouraging. He knew he needed a warchief, so he looked for the biggest and the strongest. He found his perfect candidate in a one armed mountain of muscle named Gumgog. His eyes were yellow, and his nose flattened upward like a pig.

"Celly wanted us to be nice," he said when Velixar asked why he left Darnela's camp. "Gumgog don't like to be nice. Gumgog like smashing, so you let me smash, me lead like you say."

Velixar grinned, liking the orc already. Where his arm had once been was now a giant club with a stone tied to the end. To call attention to himself, Gumgog took the second 'arm' in his other hand and used his entire body to slam it to the ground.

"GUMGOG SPEAK!" he shouted, and all around orcs quit their squabbles to listen. Velixar laughed. He had traveled with several warchiefs, some appointed by him, others already in power when he enlisted their service. He easily liked Gumgog the most.

"We going to the Mugs," Gumgog shouted to the three hundred. "We going to make them help us, maybe swear allegiance to us. Then we go to the Duns and the Glushes, and make them do the same! We make an army, and we follow the human in black. All hear me?"

When an orc near him raised a hand to speak, Gumgog gripped his giant club and swung in a great heaving motion that used his entire waist and chest. The stone connected against the orc's skull with a giant crack. The limp body flew ten feet before crumpling along the grass.

"Any others need help hearing me?" Gumgog bellowed. No help needed. All understood.

◁╳▷

"We can travel at least a day without food," Velixar said as he joined Qurrah and Tessanna by their fire. "I've got several hunting and butchering any animals we find, but the wedge is pitiful for living off the land. However, that should buy us time until we reach the first of the Mug camps."

"Who leads them?" Qurrah asked.

"Lummug," Velixar said. "At least, he did last I was here. You never know with orcs, do you?" The man in black chuckled. "No, and you never know about how children of a goddess will react either. You cost me troops, Tessanna. Even worse, you went against my will."

"I never swore my life to you," Tessanna said. She sounded sleepy, and her eyes drooped as she stared at the fire. "I swore it to Qurrah. And how many troops did you lose? A hundred? Two?"

Velixar narrowed his eyes.

"Those that died I would have brought back," he said. "At least six hundred would march by my side."

"How many orcs are there in all the tribes?" Tessanna asked. "How many thousands? You whine like a child."

She laid her head against Qurrah's shoulder and closed her eyes. The half-orc looked to his master, trying to gauge how much of his anger was truth and how much was bluster. He doubted Velixar had ever been challenged as he had been by Tessanna.

"Will the other tribes swear allegiance to you?" Qurrah asked, hoping to shift the topic of the conversation.

"In times past I have enlisted the aid of their warchief to keep the orcs in line. The time for such trickery is past. The orcs will swear their loyalty to me, and Karak, or they will die." He pointedly looked at Tessanna. "Does that please our princess?"

The girl smiled.

"Yes, master, but don't worry about pleasing me, I'm here to please you. Isn't that right, Qurrah?"

The half-orc stammered an unintelligible response. Tessanna laughed and buried her face into his robes. Velixar stood and turned his back to them, and in the light of the fire he seemed a hunched, angered demon.

"Sleep well. The Mug tribe will not follow, not until we show them our strength. You will kill tomorrow, both of you. Be ready for it."

"Yes, master," Qurrah said.

"And Qurrah..." Velixar shifted his head. "There is a world beyond you and your lover. Never forget that."

He left them to the dwindling light of the fire.

Tessanna's arms were empty when she awoke. She pushed herself up on her elbow and glanced around. The morning was still early, with only a sliver of the sun climbing above the horizon. The orcs were still asleep.

"Qurrah," she asked, rubbing away the tiredness from her eyes. She saw a hunched form far from the camp, sitting cross-legged with his back to her. She stood, pulled her thin clothing tight about her, and started walking. In the cold she could easily see her breath. The sky was gray and overcast. She wondered if it would snow.

The lone figure shifted, and as she neared she could see it was Qurrah busy reading Velixar's journal. Her slender mouth frowned at the sight of him, cold and shivering with the book on his lap.

"You should be by a fire," she told him. The half-orc looked up from his reading.

"The cold helps me focus," he said. "Velixar was right, Tessanna. That damn specter's always been right."

She sat beside him and wrapped an arm around his waist.

"What's bothering you, love?"

"I've become passive," he said, slamming the book shut. "I do as commanded, as expected. I disappoint him."

"That's easy to fix," she said, brushing away his bangs to kiss his forehead. "Take charge. Give your opinion, whether he wants it or not. You are no fool and no weakling. Even the wisest would listen to your advice."

"I plan on doing more than that," Qurrah said as they stood together. "Much more."

He returned to the camp. In her heart she wanted to follow, but she knew Qurrah needed to find the answer on his own. The life he had shared with Velixar was unknown to her.

So she stayed and watched the sun rise, letting the little warmth it offered seep into her pale skin and sad black eyes.

North of the camp Velixar waited, also watching the rise of the sun. He sensed Qurrah's approach but did not acknowledge him.

"Where is the next camp?" Qurrah asked. The man in black crossed his arms and remained quiet. "I asked where is it?"

"Several miles north. About four hundred orcs, just a pittance of the Mug tribe's numbers. Why do you ask?"

"When we arrive I will recruit them. I know what will make them bow."

"I have led many armies, Qurrah," Velixar said, raising an eyebrow. "And I have had thousands of orcs swear allegiance as my puppets. Have you?"

"I have the blood of orcs in my veins," the half-orc said. "And I will make them respect it. They will swear to you, all of them."

"They will swear to Karak," Velixar corrected.

"I don't care. I don't do this for him."

The man in black chuckled and gestured back to the camp.

"Yes, I know. You do it for her. For Tessanna. Whether she wants it or not."

"She does," Qurrah insisted.

"How many will you kill to heal her mind?" Velixar continued. "You would sacrifice this entire world just for that? And what happens, Qurrah? What happens when Karak comes and rids her of the child, of the apathy, of the wild animal? Will you recognize the girl that remains? Will the lives you have ruined be justified?"

The half-orc glared at Velixar, meeting the burning red eyes without fear.

"You question what I do? You question the very acts you yourself wish me to commit?"

"It is not the end, Qurrah, it is the means that matters!" Velixar insisted. "It is what we do, every bit of it, that defines who we are. I do not want you as my disciple if your allegiance to Karak is only of convenience."

He quieted as he turned back to the sunrise. Qurrah looked to the ground, remembering what he had told his brother when he questioned their killing of children. Take pride in everything you do, he had told him. So did he take pride in what he did now, marching alongside orcs in a campaign to release a war god into his world?

"You were so promising," Velixar said, breaking their silence. "For a time you saw what Karak offered. Everything you have now, Karak gave you. All you desired was power and the skill to use it, and I gave you both. In my absence you lost your way. You've succumbed to womanly flesh, forgetting that it is a pleasure, not a purpose."

"What is it you want from me?" Qurrah asked.

Velixar turned, and the force in his eyes sent Qurrah to one knee.

"I want you at my side, but not for her. Not to mend a mind that is beautiful in its chaos. I want you to relish, and worship, every second of what you and I are, and what we are meant to do. You once relished the thought of Neldar burning. I want you to feel that excitement once more."

"What of my brother?" Qurrah dared asked.

"Ashhur has corrupted him. I made a choice, him or you. You were always my disciple, and he, your bodyguard. Without you I have no need of him. So I chose you."

The half-orc stood, a sudden fear piercing his gut. He met Velixar's gaze.

"What do you mean you made a choice?" he asked, his voice nearly shaking with kindling rage.

"I killed Harruq's child," he said. Each word pierced Qurrah like a burning arrow. "I sent her into the woods and told her to play. It needed to be done."

"You?" Qurrah said, his fists shaking. "You turned my brother against me. You tore apart our lives like we were your playthings!"

"I did it with a heavy heart!" Velixar shouted back. "I had to make you see what you yourself were in danger of becoming. Harruq turned his back on Karak. I would not lose you as well."

A terrible silence fell between them. Qurrah felt all he knew flailing in a cyclone. He remembered the pain on Tessanna's face, and how she had shrieked against him in her sorrow.

"Do you understand now," Velixar asked. "Aullienna died because you thought of nothing else but your lover. You felt your end justified your means, but the truth is your actions should justify themselves. I will kill thousands, but I do it for my god, without remorse, without pity. You will kill as many, but what phantom do you do it for?"

"You think me a disappointment," Qurrah said, his soft voice gradually rising in anger and volume. "But I will show you the strength I have gained. When we reach the camp, I will make them bow and serve Karak. I will not cheapen my sacrifices, Velixar. I will not regret what I have done."

He stormed off. The man in black watched him go, his calm façade turning into pride.

"Welcome back, Qurrah," he whispered to the morning air.

Tessanna found him an hour later, marching north with nothing but his whip and Velixar's journal. His breath was labored and weak, and his stride unsteady, but his eyes were wide with fury and determination.

"Why did you leave me?" she asked him as she dismounted from Seletha.

"Do you want what I have offered?" Qurrah said, whirling on her and grabbing her shoulders. "Do you truly want your mind made whole?"

"I want what you want," she said, shying away from him.

"No!" Qurrah shouted, not caring that he spit blood as he did. "What is it that *you* want? Do you want me to change what you are?"

The girl bit her lip and shook her head.

"I like myself, Qurrah. I thought you liked me, too."

The half-orc collapsed to the ground and buried his face in his hands.

"Then what is it you want," he asked. "For what reason can I justify the massacre of thousands? I was to sacrifice this world for you, Tessanna. I still will. But I march with the murderer of my brother's daughter. Karak has guided my life as if I am a pet, trained to fight and kill, but for what reason?"

The shyness vanished as Tessanna heard his words.

"Velixar killed Aullienna?" she asked. The half-orc nodded. She knelt down and pulled his face up so they could look eye to eye.

"Do you know what I want?" she asked. Tears filled her eyes as he shook his head. "I want to live in a world where I don't feel my mother watching every step I make, preparing me for a fate I don't want. I want to live where no god will meddle in our lives and kill those we love to ensure our paths."

"How," Qurrah asked. "I would accept that so desperately, but how?"

"Velixar offered us escape," she said. "Thulos can send us away from Dezrel. We keep our promise, and he keeps his. That is what I want."

"But what we do, is it wrong?"

Tessanna crossed her arms and frowned at him. "Since when do you care about right and wrong? Too many people are suffering. I don't want us to be one of them."

The half-orc reached out, and this time she did not shy away. He pulled her close and kissed her lips.

"Before you I wanted nothing but power," he said.

"And you still should," she whispered. "I like it when you're strong. I always have. Don't change on me now."

For the first time since Aullienna's death, he felt the confusion that had clouded his mind finally lift. He kissed her again, nearly shoving his tongue down her throat as he held her tight.

"I've almost forgotten what it means to be stronger," he told her when their lips parted. "What it means to take a life and truly enjoy the taking. I will remember today. Come with me. The camp is not far. We've already passed several of their banners."

"Velixar and his orcs are not far behind," she told him.

"We don't need them," he said, taking her hand. "Not when we are together."

The girl smiled. "That's the Qurrah I fell in love with."

Hand in hand, they marched north, feeling warm despite the cold winter air.

10

The Mug tribe was the largest and the strongest of the orc tribes, with numbers in the thousands. Their territory was spread across the Vile Wedge, occupying more than a third of all the land between the two rivers. Camps waving the image of a bloodied wooden cup of ale dotted the entire wedge, each one ruled by a warleader who in turn pledged allegiance to Lummug.

"So what is the plan?" Tessanna asked as they walked through a small valley. Hills stretched to either side of them with towers built atop. Each waved a banner of a bloodied mug. Despite the drunkenness of the sentries within, it would not be long before one glanced down and spotted them.

"They will not expect attack during winter," Qurrah said. "Food is poor, and the cold is vicious against morale. Our campaign will be swift and short, and Velixar's undead will need little food."

At the end of the valley was the camp. Wooden palisades surrounded it, their tops carved into spikes. A giant door made of tree trunks remained wide open. Two guards slumbered in the cold.

"I know we have surprise," Tessanna said. "What are we to do with that surprise?"

"Make them kneel," the half-orc said, grinning.

"So dramatic," she said. "How about specifics."

"No plan," Qurrah said. "So no specifics. I will show them my power, and I will make them obey. The orcs are brutish children. They need to believe their lives are at stake when I tell them to bow. Nothing else matters."

Tessanna clutched his arm and kissed his cheek.

"It's going to snow soon," she said. "Will you be warm enough in these robes?"

"No," Qurrah said. "But I will survive. Prepare your magic. I think we have been spotted."

A horn sounded from one of the towers. A moment later the other tower joined with its own horn. The guards at the gate readied their spears as hundreds of orcs joined them, howling and bellowing. The air was cold, the morning dull, and the idea of combat both warmed and awakened them. They had armor made of leather, weapons of crude iron, and animal skins for warmth.

Qurrah cast a spell, and then shouted to the camp. His booming voice sounded like a deity taken the form of a spider or a serpent.

"Look upon me, orcs of the Mug tribe. I have the blood of orc in me, just as you. We come bearing an offer. Karak is returning to this world. His power will not be denied. An age ago your kind wielded swords and axes at his side. That is where you gained your strength. That is where you gained your bloodlust. I am a servant of Karak, as you once were. Kneel, and cry out his name, and I will give you everything. I will give you war against the humans. I will give you land to pillage and fields to burn. Cast off your worship of the wild animals of this world. Karak is your god. Will you serve him?"

The leader of the camp, a smaller brother of Lummug, pushed his way to the front. While he might have been smaller than Lummug, he still towered above the nearby orcs by a solid foot.

"Trummug bows to no one," he shouted as he raised a mighty axe high above his head. "Others bow to the Mugs. You take your god and leave. We not want him."

"You will serve," Qurrah said. "Or every one of you will die."

"Go get 'em boys," Trummug shouted. "Whoever brings me his head gets the girl."

A hundred orcs charged, whooping and hollering. Qurrah laughed despite the danger.

"At last a foe who relishes combat," he said. "At last a fight where neither side regrets the bloodshed." Dark magic flared across his fingertips. "It's about damn time."

"I will keep us alive," Tessanna said, a shy smile on her face. "You have your fun."

The first group of orcs neared, foaming at the mouth as they waved their weapons high.

"For the Mugs!" they screamed. Maniacal bloodlust coursed through their veins. The two strangers were unarmed and weak in form. They should have been an easy kill. Then the half-orc began casting. A black circle stretched from Qurrah's feet, consuming the grass. From the circle hundreds of tentacles crawled, sparking with electricity. Six orcs died shrieking as the tentacles lashed at their faces and chests, pushing aside the weapons they held up to defend themselves as if they were made of cloth. The gruesome sight slowed the charge, and that time was all Qurrah needed to cast another spell. The bones from the dead orcs tore from their bodies, showering blood in a gruesome rain.

"Kill the demon," Trummug shouted. "Kill him now!"

"Yes," Qurrah said. "Kill the demon."

The bones he commanded pelted the orc force, tearing at their eyes and exposed throats. Tessanna giggled at the carnage it caused.

"Qurrah," she said. "I want to have a little fun myself."

Her hands waved in circles that glowed a deep crimson. Two orcs collapsed, blood spurting from every orifice. She took control of the blood, giving it rigidity and energy. She stretched it into a long, bladed weapon. The bloodsword lashed through the orcs, mutilating flesh and severing limbs.

The tentacles vanished, their power spent. A band of orcs charged, furious at seeing so many of their brethren massacred. Qurrah knelt, placed his palms against the dirt, and spoke the words of a spell. When he pointed a finger, a shadowy ghost of a face rose from the earth, with black holes for eyes and a gaping maw that seemed infinite in depth. Then it shrieked. The sound slammed into the orcs like a physical force, shattering bones. They fell, writhing, convulsing, dying.

"No more need to die," the half-orc shouted, even as another wave of orcs neared. "Orcs have fought orcs for long enough. Karak offers the greatest war imaginable. Will you serve him?"

He received his answer in the form of a communal roar. The half-orc latched his hands together and pushed. Two black orbs shot from his wrists, merged together, and then grew to the size of a boulder. It rolled through the air, its surface shimmering like a bubble. The first orc to touch it watched his entire arm dissolve into gray sand. The next hapless orc had his entire upper body broken to the tiniest of pieces which fell like dust atop his collapsed legs. Orcs dove out of its way, but three more found pieces of their body vanishing.

"Do you see his power?" Qurrah asked. "The power of Karak?"

Tessanna punctuated his comments with a shockwave of her own. She laughed, and that laughter shook the ground all the way to the towers. It was as if Dezrel laughed with her, sharing in its contempt for the gray-skinned creatures. All around the orcs fell to their knees, only Qurrah and Tessanna remained standing, like gods among them.

"Bow!" Qurrah shouted. "Bow to those who would slay you without thought, so you may slay thousands of others!"

"Shut your trap!" Trummug screamed, slamming his axe into the dirt and using it to pull himself to his feet. "We seen your kind before. You promise us stuff to fight. Gold. Land. But you never keep those promises. You want us to fight and die, and then you move on while we lick our wounds and lose half our numbers to the winter."

"Fairly eloquent for an orc," Qurrah muttered.

"He is correct," Tessanna said. "You know he is."

"I do not bring the promises of men," Qurrah shouted. The rest of the orcs were getting to their feet, but they were not charging. They wanted nothing more than the two dead, but they would wait for their leader to give the order.

"What do you bring?" Trummug asked.

"The promises of Karak. The promises of a god. You are beloved in his eyes. He gave you strength and power. He saved you from extinction."

"Prove it," Trummug said. "Have him speak."

The half-orc glanced to Tessanna. A bit of worry crossed his face.

"What is it, lover?" she asked him.

"I can give him his request," he said. "I can, but…"

She understood. She put her hand on his lips and kissed his forehead.

"Do not fear him. Perhaps you needed this. You need to see what life you might lead."

He nodded, then turned to Trummug. "Very well. Have your men lay down their arms. Do not harm me, and I will let you hear his words."

The big orc gave the command. Qurrah walked the distance between them, feeling an ever-tightening knot in his stomach. He had never done this before, not once. He felt vulnerable, naked.

"Dark one," he prayed as he walked. "Accept this as a step of faith. Do not betray me."

Orcs grumbled and swore as the half-orc arrived. Trummug snorted.

"So, I'm not hearing anything."

"Kneel," Qurrah said. "Then you may hear."

"You want to make me a fool?" the big orc snarled, barely containing his growing rage.

"Cut me in half if you hear nothing," Qurrah said. "I will make no motion to stop you."

"The girl?"

"She will not stop you."

The anger had spread throughout all his body, but he held it in check. He slammed down his axe, then knelt as he gripped its handle. Before he could move, Qurrah thrust his hands against Trummug's face and met him eye to eye.

Karak, god of Order, he silently commanded. *Speak. Show him your paradise.*

At first Trummug's eyes widened, as if he suspected Qurrah of some sort of treachery, but then the glaze came over. A strong ringing filled both their ears. The sky went dark. The world was a haze. Qurrah had asked for communion, and his request was about to be answered.

><

Just under a mile away, his orc rabble marching behind him, Velixar broke into hysterical laughter.

"He is learning!" he cried, an enormous smile on his face. "Give it to him, Karak, give him his desire!"

All around orcs shied away from his horrific laughter, laughter that shivered their spines and struck dead the few birds that flew overhead. Laughter of a dead man. Laughter of an insane man. And none there could describe the pleasure he took within it.

><

From the ringing came a soft blowing of wind past the entrance of a cave. Trummug and Qurrah were lost within the sound, as if all time were halted.

"What you do to me?" Trummug asked, though his lips never moved.

Qurrah had no chance to answer.

You sought my presence, said the voice of Karak. Their entire world shook. The darkness recoiled, and spikes of red and violet danced within. *You wanted proof of my promise. You wanted my words, my voice. You are my children, cast away and given to me by the goddess. Accept my power, as you always have. Let the orcs become my banner carriers.*

"We will obey," Trummug said, still without moving his lips. Qurrah thought the darkness would end and the moment pass, but Karak's presence remained, his message not yet done.

Forgive my prophet, child. Forgive the loss of your brother. I have not yet turned my back on him, though he has turned his back on me. Velixar loves you, as you once loved him. Trust. Respect. The time will come when your power will surpass even his, and that time is not far away.

"I want freedom from this," Qurrah said. "I want a life with her, and nothing more."

Your freedom comes with mine. But once you have tasted the fire I offer...will you be so ready to flee it?

Red lightning consumed the dark. The black grew ever distant, until Qurrah realized he stared into the eyes of Trummug. The giant orc stood, his entire body shaking.

"What he say, boss?" the orc to his right asked. Trummug did not respond. "So we get to kill them?" the same orc asked, drawing his sword and turning toward Qurrah. The half-orc did not move. Trummug reached out and crushed the life from the orc's throat, all while still staring at Qurrah.

"Boys," he shouted. His voice gained strength as he talked. "The Mugs got a god smiling at us. All us orcs do. We gonna leave the wedge, and we leave it forever! Get the war drums, prepare the horde. We march to war!"

Qurrah turned to Tessanna and nodded. The girl smiled, but it was a nervous smile. She didn't like the way her lover looked. It was as if his face had darkened, a reverse glow that sucked in all light and denied it freedom. But he had his army, far larger than the one Velixar ruled. He walked over and wrapped his arms around her waist.

"I love you," he said.

"What did you hear?" she asked him. He opened his mouth to answer, then paused.

"It doesn't matter," he said. "Nothing matters but us. And we are one step closer to our freedom."

She kissed his cheek. It was colder than ever. When he kissed her back, a shiver traveled up and down her back. As his arms closed about her, she felt the chill subside. Karak's presence had faded. Qurrah's heart and soul were hers once more.

Velixar and his orcs arrived at the camp expecting war, but instead they were greeted like long lost friends. The Mug orcs cheered and offered ale and food, to which the exhausted and starving orcs gladly accepted. Qurrah waited for Velixar by the gate, Tessanna next to him with dagger in hand.

"You spoke with him," Velixar said when he arrived. "Not only that, you invoked his name. For the first time you put your trust in Karak. Do you see now that when faith is measured, the reward is greatest for those who believe without hesitation?"

"The orcs are yours," Qurrah said. "And Trummug will unite all the other Mug camps we come across in his name. Only Lummug can overrule him. Once the Mug tribe is in our hands, the rest of the tribes will step in line. The question is, who will be their Hordemaster?"

"I thought Gumgog," Velixar said. "He seems capable enough."

"Make him Warmaster," Qurrah said. "But Trummug has heard the voice of Karak. He should be the Hordemaster."

Velixar pondered over the decision. As he did, he watched Tessanna slice into her arm. The vicious cut splattered her dress with blood. Tears ran down her face, but she made no sound. When she caught him looking at her, she smiled.

"The cold makes it hurt more," she said, her voice like the purr of a cat. "But the pleasure's still there."

"Indeed," Velixar said, glancing back to Qurrah. "But will Lummug bow to his younger brother, I ask?"

"Of course not," Qurrah said. "We are instituting a new era for the orcs. The old must go. Lummug will die, and Trummug will rule, with all the orcs worshipping the name of Karak."

Velixar chuckled. "Very well. I will concede to your decision. Prepare the orcs to march. We have several more camps to collect before we reach Lummug's."

"Of course, master," Qurrah said with a bow. The man in black bowed back, feeling his joy increasing. His apprentice had finally gained the confidence to argue back, to disagree, and not out of arrogance. His plan was a sound one. Any orc blessed enough to hear the words of Karak deserved to rule.

"Well done, Qurrah," Velixar said as they entered the orc camp.

Gumgog and Trummug didn't just get along. They took to one another like brothers. The two were giants compared to the other orcs, and after an initial arm wrestling match, fist fight, and drinking competition, they were as close as any orcs would ever get. When Qurrah took them both aside to explain his plan, for Gumgog to be Warmaster and Trummug to be Hordemaster, both were thrilled beyond measure. They were also drunk beyond measure, which enhanced their reactions.

"But what, what about me brother?" Trummug asked. "He not like me being higher than him when me be smaller, and him older and he got this giant...what was me saying?"

"Your brother will bow to your reign," Qurrah said, "or you will kill him in Karak's name. Those are his choices."

"I'll beat him over the head for you," Gumgog offered. "One good whack, kapow!" He smacked their table with his wooden arm. The weighted stone at the end smashed right through.

"You, you a good friend, orc," Trummug said as he guzzled down his twentieth glass. "Good, good..." He vomited all over his chest. "Good friend. Kapow!"

Qurrah left as each shouted for more. A short, sweaty goblin dragged over a barrel and filled their glasses. The two raised them in a toast as the half-orc exited the tent.

"Kapow!" they shouted in unison before slamming their mugs together.

"Kapow!"

The next several camps quickly submitted to Trummug's command, grabbing all their supplies and weaponry before stepping in line. At Qurrah's request, they did not mention the required loyalty and worship to Karak. That would be for a later time, when Trummug was solidified as Hordemaster.

With numbers nearing a thousand, they planned their assault on Fortress Mug.

I say smash through by force," Trummug shouted, slamming an open palm against the table. "No sneaking and no talk. Brother's not gonna give up, and I don't want any rumors about me stabbing him in the back!"

"There will be no rumors," Qurrah insisted, his voice soft and reassuring. In the cramped tent, Trummug's shouts were painful to his ears, and he preferred to keep them to a minimum. "Any who question your strength will die by the sword. We cannot risk failure, though, and the last thing you want is a prolonged war."

"You call me a coward?" Trummug asked, his eyes bulging.

"I said nothing of the sort."

"You dare say me scared of war? War is what I live for!"

"You're trying to reason with him," Velixar said, chuckling from the corner. "I think we all can guess whether or not you will be successful."

"Very well," Qurrah said, plopping into his chair at the table. Tessanna sat beside him with her knees curled against her chest and her hands clutching the sides of the chair. She rocked back and forth as if she were mesmerized by the sounds around her. The half-orc gestured a finger toward Velixar. "Show me the wiser path."

Velixar stood, his grin dark and wide beneath the cowl of his hood. Trummug crossed his arms, confident he could not be convinced. His small, weaker council wanted him to sneak past the guards at night and slaughter his brother. He, in his orcish sense of honor, wanted to attack the city at dawn, with drums and horns announcing his arrival. He wanted to take the title of Hordemaster by force and war, not stealth or trickery.

"You say you are not afraid of war," Velixar said, pacing on the opposite side of the table from Trummug. "I believe you. Tell me, Trummug, who should rule the orcish tribes?"

"The strongest!"

"Yes, yes," Velixar said, his grin growing more smug. "The strongest. And who is stronger, my dear friend, you or Lummug?"

"ME!" Trummug smashed the table with both fists and flexed, his enormous muscles bulging under his armor.

"Of course. I would not have allied with you otherwise. So if the strongest orc should rule, and you are the strongest, how do we go about proving that?"

"By me chopping off Lummug's head, that's how."

Velixar clapped his hands and laughed, as if he had never heard such a brilliant idea.

"You're right, so it doesn't matter if Lummug has ten guards or ten thousand, you should rule. You're the strongest."

"That's right." He poked his chest with his thumb. "I'm the strongest."

"Then all the fighting and war you want is just a waste of time. The real test, the only part that matters, is the fight between you and your brother. So, the smart thing to do is to fight Lummug alone, right?"

Trummug scratched his head. Deep inside he could feel a throb he had never felt before, dark and sinister. He had felt it ever since he had heard the words of Qurrah's god, and now it pulsed with agreement. The man in black spoke truth. He didn't know how he knew, but he knew.

"Aye, it be the smart thing," Trummug said.

"So let us get you your brother. The more orcs that live, the more that join your army. You do want a grander army than Lummug ever had, don't you?"

"I will smash everything he thinks he's done!" Trummug shouted. "Get me to him. Once his head's in my hands, all orcs will call me Hordemaster!"

Velixar winked at Qurrah, who only threw up his hands in surrender.

"That is how you do it," the man in black said as he sat across from his disciple. "You just need to think simpler, less arguing, more coercing."

"You should fight his war," Tessanna said, her voice muffled by her knees. "You could bring the dead back, so no loss would matter. Less to feed."

"True, my dear," Velixar said. "But the orcs that live I can bring back. The dead, when slain, will stay dead. And raging orcs are far superior in combat to the mindless dead. And food will not be a problem. Fortress Mug has plenty of livestock for us to slaughter."

"So tomorrow we kill?" Trummug shouted, bored of the conversation. "Tomorrow me be Hordemaster?"

"If Karak wills it, yes," Velixar said, smiling at the orc. "But only if he wills it."

They left the tent to sleep. Come the morning, they would prepare their army. If all went according to plan, they would not need it, but all there in that tent knew that things rarely went according to plan.

Fortress Mug was like all the other orc forts: surrounded by wooden palisades with sharpened tips, covered with banners, and possessing a single gate to enter. Fortress Mug, however, differed by how enormous it was, encircling giant fields full of pigs and goats. A tent five times the height of any orc loomed in the center, surrounded by hundreds of other tents, home to the orcs that swore allegiance directly to Lummug. Over three thousand lived there by Velixar's estimate. A grand army, if united.

"Have we been spotted?" Qurrah asked Velixar as they stood at the outskirts of their camp and looked upon the fortress.

"I'm sure we have," Velixar said. "The walls are bristling with orcs. The question is, will Lummug still be inside his tent?"

"He won't leave until the fighting begins," Qurrah said. Velixar glanced at his disciple and raised an eyebrow.

"Do you know that for sure?"

The half-orc shrugged. "I wouldn't bet my life on it. I'd bet yours though."

The man in black laughed.

"Summon Trummug," he said when his laughter died. "It is time the orcs worshipped Karak once more."

Qurrah went to fetch him, leaving Velixar to grin alone. He had been in a joyous mood for days. Everything was proceeding without a hitch, and the inevitable release of Karak seemed closer than ever.

"Me ready to kill!" Trummug bellowed to signify his arrival. Velixar turned to him, his smile growing larger.

"A fine sight you are," he said, and he meant it. The orc's armor was cleaned and polished. Massive amounts of gray muscle bulged underneath. On his head he wore a helmet made of iron. Surrounding it was six pairs of antlers, positioned so that tens of sharp points stretched out from his eyes and mouth toward his enemy. Two sharp spikes stretched out from his shoulders, an addition made by Velixar. His gauntlets, also made of iron, were stained red from blood.

"Almost ready," the man in black said, admiring the sight. "But now you must accept the rewards Karak offers to those who keep his faith."

He placed a hand on Trummug's chest and closed his eyes. The orc fidgeted, unsure of what sorcery was about to take place. Then he felt the power flood into him. His muscles bulged. The armor, which had hung loose on him by Qurrah's demand, suddenly latched tight and firm. He held his giant axe in one hand, though he had always needed two to lift it.

"Karak made me strong!" he shouted, his voice carrying further than it ever had. Qurrah smiled, a sad smile. He remembered how Harruq had looked when infused in a similar manner. Even Trummug, with his armor and muscle, paled in comparison.

"Always bless his name," Velixar said, his voice captivating Trummug. "Let every kill honor your god. When you are Hordemaster, may every orc in Dezrel know the strength Karak offers."

Trummug held his axe high above his head and bellowed out a war cry.

"Send me to fight!" he screamed. "I'll go crazy if I don't kill!"

Velixar slammed his hands together and whispered words of magic. A black portal tore into the air, its destination unknown.

"Enter," he told the giant orc. "Slay your enemy, and take your place as ruler."

With a mindless roar, Trummug leapt inside, his axe high and ready. Qurrah followed with a silent Tessanna coming shortly after. Velixar entered last, but only after commanding Gumgog to prepare his army for battle. If the armies of the Mug Fortress poured forth, they needed to be prepared.

"We be ready," Gumgog said, saluting with his club arm. Velixar smiled.

"Failure would be most unwise," he said before vanishing within the swirling darkness.

><≡×

Qurrah was lucky enough to have ducked when he entered the portal, for otherwise a wild swing by Trummug would have taken off his head. The orc was storming about the giant tent in the center of Fortress Mug, screaming for challengers. Qurrah crouched lower and stepped back, cursing their luck. Lummug was not in his tent.

"Get back, dullard," he said, hooking his fingers and pushing them in the air. An invisible force pushed Trummug away from the portal so his axe did not harm Tessanna and Velixar when they appeared.

"We must find him quickly," Velixar said as he looked around and realized the problem. Trummug, nearly foaming at the mouth with rage, did not wait for council. He stormed out of the tent and shrieked at the top of his lungs.

"WHERE LUMMUG?"

Orc guards saw him and fled, wanting no part of the angry giant. Trummug raised his axe and chased, lopping off any heads within reach. Again he screamed for his brother, and throughout the entire fortress his voice thundered.

"Keep him alive," Velixar ordered as he held open the flap of the tent for Qurrah and Tessanna. "But make sure he strikes the killing blow against Lummug."

At first it didn't appear to be that difficult a task. Orcs fled in all directions, wanting no part of the strangers that had magically appeared within their gates. The curious or the slow found their heads chopped or their chests shattered. Then a giant swarm of orcs approached from the north gate, shrieking with battlelust. Within the mass was Lummug, his shield and sword held high.

"Take out his entourage," Velixar said. Qurrah chuckled.

"Is that what we should do? I might never have guessed." He prepared his magic as Velixar glared.

"Boys, boys," Tessanna said as she prepared her own spells. "Behave before I spank you both."

Trummug charged the orcs head-on as if he were impervious to any wounds. Qurrah and Velixar accompanied his charge with twin blasts of bones torn from the nearby corpses. Guards crumpled to the ground, gagging from torn throats and clutching massacred eyes. Tessanna kissed the palm of her hand and blew. Red smoke swirled like a snake through the air past Trummug and into the lungs and noses of the orcs. Those that breathed it in dropped their weapons and gagged, their eyes immediately swelling red with blood. Two dropped without uttering a sound. A third vomited his intestines. The rest fell, their stomachs bursting open and pouring blood across the grass.

"A magnificent spell," Velixar said.

"Thank you," Tessanna said, her voice calm and emotionless. "But I have better."

With their leader near, the rest of the camp had the courage to attack the three frail forms that stood seemingly unprotected. The girl twirled, her arms dancing through the air. Orange light shone from her fingertips. The blood of the dead orcs ran across the grass and pooled at her feet. Like a spider it latched upon her legs and climbed, swirling and covering her exposed legs. When it reached her dress it spread wide and covered it as well, so she appeared to have one long skirt of blood. With each of Tessanna's heartbeats it pulsed with life.

"Disturbing," Qurrah said, "but what does it..."

He stopped when Tessanna violently wrenched her body like some vicious dancer. The skirt spread wide, cracked, and then flew from her, the blood becoming snakes that flew with open mouths and dripping fangs. The snakes latched onto the gathering orcs, sinking their fangs into their necks and faces. Upon biting, the snakes dissolved back into normal blood, their poison spent. Orcs shrieked and scratched at their skin like it was on fire. They tore out their eyes so the pressure behind them would subside. They gnawed on their fingers, stabbed themselves with their swords, and writhed on the ground in unbearable agony.

"By the abyss," Qurrah muttered, watching the macabre display.

"I stand corrected," Velixar said. "*That* is a magnificent spell."

"Your pet," Tessanna said, still quiet and apathetic. She pointed to where Lummug and Trummug fought. "He's in danger."

The two men turned, having forgotten their reason for being there. The orc brothers were deep in combat, and it appeared Lummug had the upper hand. Despite his magical strength, Trummug was a much worse fighter in terms of skill. He swung wild and crazy with his axe, trying to use sheer strength to win. Lummug, the size of an ox himself, used his shield to absorb the blows before retaliating with his sword. His cuts were not severe, but they were quickly adding up. Blood soaked both their armor.

"Take his strength," Velixar said. "I will take his mind, but use a light touch. Our puppet must believe he won."

Qurrah thought over his spells, then settled on one he had used on his brother. He cast the curse. Invisible weights latched onto Lummug's arms and legs, making it seem his sword weighed thrice its normal weight and his shield was made of stone.

"You grow tired!" Trummug shouted, seeing his opponent's movements slow and his breathing quicken. "You're not able to face my strength!"

Velixar's spell was more subtle but far more dangerous to Lummug. His curse spread a thin veil of shadow over the orc's eyes. Lummug could still see, but what he saw was far from truth. When he saw Trummug swing his axe from below his waist, he positioned his shield to block. The blow never came, not from that direction. Trummug had lifted his axe high and swung straight down. No shield stopped it. The axe cleaved through Lummug's helmet, split his skull, and then buried itself in a mess of ribs, lungs, and heart.

With a scream of victory, Trummug tore free his axe and lifted the giant weapon above his head with one hand

"Lummug dead!" he shouted to the fortress. "Trummug Hordemaster now!"

Their leader dead, it was politics as normal for the rest of the orcs.

"Trummug!" they shouted. "Trummug the Hordemaster!"

The entire fortress erupted in cheers of loyalty. As Trummug basked in his glory, Velixar walked beside him.

"Do not forget what Karak has given you," he said. "Reward his faith in you by your faith in him."

"For Karak!" Trummug suddenly shouted. "For Karak, for Karak!"

The orcs outside the fortress took up a similar chant. For Karak! For Karak! The orcs within, confused though they were, joined in. They found the words pleasant to their tongues and the shout comforting to their minds.

For Karak! For Karak!

With the Mug tribe united in his name, it was only a matter of time before the other tribes fell in line. The army, numbering two thousand strong, marched east, a new standard for their banners. It was the skull of a lion.

Part Two

11

It had been a long night for the half-orc Harruq Tun.

"Try not to scream too much," his tormenter said as he pressed a glowing piece of coal against his neck with a pair of tongs.

A very long night.

"No screaming," Harruq said through grit teeth. "No screaming." He felt the searing pain against his flesh. He heard sizzling, his blood hissing and drying. He would have given anything to throttle the man, but the heavy chains around his body denied him his desire as he hung naked against the wall.

"I'm sure your friends are looking for you by now," the tormenter said. He pulled back the coal and admired his work. An ugly black burn covered the entirety of Harruq's neck. "Looking, but not finding."

The half-orc flung his head to one side so his long brown hair didn't cover his face, and doing his best to ignore the horrible pain it caused his neck. His breathing was heavy from the pain, but still he laughed.

"You have no idea," he said between labored breaths. "No idea how badly you just erred."

"Oh really?" the man said. He wore black robes with a feline skull hanging from a chain around his neck. His upper lip protruded a full inch farther than his lower jaw, so when he smiled he looked like a strange combination of horse and man. "What mistake was that?"

"Because I'm not the scary one," Harruq said. They were deep in the bowels of an old mansion, one with an owner rumored to be eccentric and lonely. Looking around at the various torture devices hanging from the stone walls of the cell, Harruq had to agree about the eccentric part. He did not, however, think the man was alone too often. Not in that cell, judging by the blood staining the floor.

"You're not the scary one?" the tormenter asked, humoring him.

"I'm the big one," Harruq continued. He was stalling, and by Ashhur the man didn't seem to have a clue. "Haern, he's the creepy one. Sneaky. Kill you before you know you're dead. But no, that isn't too scary, dying without knowing it. Aurry, however..." The half-orc laughed, then stopped to cough up and spit out a blob of blood.

"You mean your weak little elf woman?" the man asked him. He dug his fingers into the burn on Harruq's neck. Harruq sucked in air, denying the man the scream he wanted.

"She sees what you've done to me and she'll be hotter than a dragon napping in a wildfire. Haern's got some sort of honor. Aurry..."

The man in the black robes slapped him, then kissed the skull that hung from his neck.

"Karak protects me," the man said. "His power protects me from scrying. No one knows you're here. No one will hear you. No one will know you've died until I dump your body at the Eschaton's doorstep. Too late, then, too late for you."

Again Harruq laughed. And coughed. And laughed.

"What was your name again?" he asked.

"Karak has given me the name of Tormentus," the man said, glowing with pride. "His right hand in driving out blasphemy from this world."

Harruq lost himself in laughter so loud and chaotic he appeared delusional. Tormentus drove a dagger through the palm of the half-orc's hand, and even that did little to stop his laughter.

"Tormentus," Harruq said when he regained control. "You give yourself that name?" His laughter resumed, huge shuddering laughs that shook him against the chains that held him to the wall. "Run, children, Tormentus is coming, crazy man for a crazy god!"

The man slashed him across the face and neck with a knife, furious and humiliated. He had given himself the name thinking it would inspire fear in those he worked upon. On most it had, but this strange half-orc, who seemed impervious to any pain he caused, only found it hysterical. Suddenly he was ashamed of the name, felt almost childlike in its creation.

"You may know me as Gregor, if you would prefer," he said, wiping the blood off his dagger. "The name I held before Karak blessed me with his power."

"Sure thing," Harruq said. "So what is your last name? Cutall? Hurtme? Imakebooboos?"

"Enough!"

Gregor marched over to his rack of torture devices full of prongs, pliers, wrenches, strange shaped blades, and rollers full of spikes and rusty edges. The half-orc had dared trespass onto his property. His servants had subdued him with sleep scrolls they all carried. It took three to drag Harruq's body downstairs to his torture room and chain him to the wall. The half-orc had tested the chain's strength when he first awoke, then settled in and endured his punishment.

"What were you looking for," Gregor asked as he grabbed a device with a wooden handle and a small curved blade. "Eschaton do not steal or rob. What was it you sought in my mansion?"

"Just the usual," Harruq said. The man turned and approached with a sick grin on his face. "Thieves. Killers. Crazy people. You seem like all three. What you going to do with that, anyway?"

"Oh, this?" Gregor asked, smiling at his tool. "You keep laughing and mocking me. You ignore any pain I cause. So I'm going to cause you pain you can't ignore. And when you laugh, at least it will be at a higher pitch."

The room fell silent as Harruq realized what it was Gregor was saying.

"Now that's just too far," the half-orc shouted, straining against his chains. "You can hurt and kill me, but really, you can't be that sick."

Shouts echoed through the closed wooden door and into the room. Gregor glanced up the stairs, frowning at the intrusion.

"What is going on up there?" he shouted.

"I don't know," Harruq said. "You should go see, definitely, that is something you should..."

He stopped when Gregor back-handed him and then pressed the curved blade against his groin. More shouts came from upstairs.

"We can talk about this," Harruq said, all trace of humor gone from his voice. "Talk about this like men."

"Like men?" Gregor asked, a wild fear in his eyes. More shouts filled the room. People had entered the mansion. It did not take much thought to guess who.

"Like men," Harruq repeated with an enthusiastic nod.

"But you're not a man," Gregor said. "Not anymore."

The door exploded inward, and in stepped a furious Aurelia Tun. Fire danced on her fingertips. Gregor tensed the blade against Harruq while his other hand grabbed the half-orc by the throat.

"Stay back," the man ordered. "Stay back, or I cut him, and no priestess will undo the damage."

"Listen to what he says, Aurry," Harruq said, a slight quiver in his voice.

"You play some interesting games," the elf said as she looked around the room. She saw the torture devices, the wooden racks and the chains on the wall. She saw the blood pooled upon the floor. A sick room, she thought. Sick room for a sick man.

"Where are the others," Gregor asked. "The assassin, where is he? I see one flutter of gray and I cut."

"Cut him," Aurelia said, the fire leaving her hands only to be replaced by ice. "And I will do the same to you, except I will have far more time to make sure it hurts."

"She don't mean it," Harruq said, trying to smile. "You just let me go and we'll all be happy and leave..."

Gregor leaned closer and shoved Harruq's head against the wall. He knew he was in a tight spot, and the idea of the elf removing his own manhood did not appeal to him. Only by threatening the half-orc did he remain safe, but if he actually carried out his threat...

"Gregor," Harruq said, his voice soft as if he did not want Aurelia to hear. "Just be calm. She'll listen to me, you understand? I'm her husband, she obeys what I say."

"What do you propose?" Gregor whispered back. The half-orc ignored the horrible glare Aurelia gave him, for while his tormenter was an idiot, Harruq knew full well the elf could hear him despite his whispering.

"Just this," Harruq whispered before slamming his forehead against Gregor's nose. The blow knocked him back, and that slight separation was all Aurelia needed. A javelin of ice flew from her hands and pierced his back. Lightning followed the ice, reducing him to a dead, smoking lump of flesh and black robes.

Aurelia crossed her arms and stood at the top of the stairs.

"So, do I always obey what you say, dearest husband?" she asked.

"Clever ploy, nothing more," Harruq said, grinning. "Now please, could you get me to Delysia? I think I'm going to pass out."

True to his word, the half-orc slumped against the chains, unable to stand now that his adrenaline was fading. The elf pulled up her skirt as she walked down the stairs, not wanting to stain her dress on anything in the foul room. She kicked the curved blade Gregor had held, then looked up at the ceiling. A faded rune carved in blood covered it, designed to prevent magical scrying.

"The magic fades over time," she told the dead tormenter. "And the runes need reapplied. Just thought you should know." She looked over Harruq's wounds, wincing as she did. The man had done a number on her husband, but he had suffered through worse.

"Aurelia?" a voice called down the stairs. The elf turned and shouted back.

"Come on down, Haern. Found the big ox."

A blond man cloaked in gray appeared at the top of the stairs, twin sabers in his hands.

"The servants have been taken care of," he said. When he saw Gregor's body, he sheathed his swords. "And apparently so has the master."

"Har's passed out," she said, fiddling with the locks. "Care to help me get him out of these so I can take us home?"

Haern pulled out a kit from a pouch hidden beneath his cloaks. A minute later, all the locks were undone, and Harruq slumped into Haern's strong arms. The elf whispered words of magic, and then a blue portal ripped into existence, its blue light scattering the shadows of the room. Haern found Harruq's swords and armor piled in a corner and tossed them into the portal. He then dragged the unconscious half-orc in. Aurelia entered last, but only after tossing a ball of fire at the rack of torture instruments, setting them aflame.

◁✖▷

Harruq awoke the next morning at the touch of feminine fingers against his skin.

"Aurry?" he muttered, his eyes still closed.

"It's me," said a voice that was not Aurelia's. "Lie still. I just started."

"Hey, Delysia. Pleased as always."

The priestess chuckled despite her concentration. White light surrounded her hands, filled with healing magic. She focused on the brutal cuts Gregor had made, cuts that looked dangerously close to becoming infected. The light poured into them, killing the sickness and closing the wounds. Each cut took several minutes of concentration, and by the time she had the half-orc looking decent, her entire body ached and her head pounded as if filled with a thousand ogres banging drums.

Harruq lay still for most of it. The healing magic soothed most of his pain, but the ache in his muscles would not subdue for days, and the strange stretching and pulling of his skin against the wounds was uncomfortable at best. As Delysia cast her spells, he heard a door creak open, followed by shuffling of robes.

"So how's our half-orc doing?" asked Tarlak, the leader of the Eschaton mercenaries.

"Doing good," Harruq said, eyes still closed. "Remind me to never listen when you suggest splitting up patrols."

"Whine all you want," Tarlak said. "You're still alive."

Harruq opened his eyes and glared at the mage. He was dressed in a bizarre assortment of yellow robes, yellow sash, and long, yellow pointy hat. Delysia stood beside him, rubbing her pounding temples. They were clearly brother and sister, with matching red hair and green eyes. Tarlak stroked his goatee, all the while trying to hold in a laugh. The half-orc glared harder, determined to whallop the man if he dared mock his predicament.

"I heard you almost lost something precious," Tarlak said.

"Another word and I'll shove your hat down your throat and pull it out your rear."

"Very manly of you. Glad you can still do stuff like that."

"I swear, Tar, I will."

"Hush now," Delysia said, frowning at her brother. "Stop pestering him so he'll sit still."

"If you insist," Tarlak said, sitting down on the bed next to him. They were on the second floor of the Eschaton tower. Normally it was Delysia's room, but it often doubled as a ward for an injured mercenary.

"At least we got the sick bastard," Harruq said, closing his eyes and obeying a command by the priestess to shift onto his side.

"Yeah, about that." Tarlak took off his hat and picked at it. "Turns out that wasn't the guy."

"What?"

"Stay still," Delysia said, smacking him on the head with the palm of her hand.

"Thought you decided some Karak worshipper was doing all the mutilations?" Harruq said, doing his best not to move.

"I did, but that guy you killed...Gregor, right? Well this Gregor worshipped Karak, but he wasn't a priest. He was just some spoiled son of a rich man that fancied himself a chosen of our dear dark god." Tarlak put the hat back on his head. "That, and after you and Aurry so neatly dispatched him, we found another body near the castle. I won't bore you with the details."

Harruq raised an eyebrow at him.

"Alright fine," Tarlak said. "You know me too well. Extremities dismembered. Hands were sewn onto his face, palms covering his eyes. Tongue gone. Bowels burned. Oh, and the neatest carving on his chest. They made some skull out of twisted skin and bruises..."

"Enough," Delysia said, standing and holding her fingers against her chest. "Please, enough."

"Sure thing, sis," Tarlak said. He tipped his hat to the half-orc. "Get better. Tonight's going to be another long one, and like I say, no rest for the orcish."

"Thought it was no rest for the short?" Harruq said, immediately regretting it.

"Yeah," the mage said, a pall coming over his cheery attitude at reference to the former member Brug. "Well, no shorties around to keep going, so got to deprive someone of rest, right?"

Harruq did not respond.

"He doesn't blame you," Delysia said once Tarlak had left the room.

"He should," the half-orc muttered.

"You are not your brother," she insisted, gently running a hand down his wounded back. "And you are not responsible for him or the company he keeps. Even if you were, Ashhur preaches forgiveness."

The priestess left, not expecting a reply. She was right.

The rest of the Eschaton gathered around the fireplace on the first floor of the tower, drinking magically conjured drinks and discussing the previous night.

"Three bodies," Haern said, shaking his head and staring at the fire. "They're taunting us. No other explanation."

"Escalation does not mean taunting," Tarlak said as he came down the stairs. "Though it very well may be."

"When Antonil asked us to help patrol, it was a single body found every three days," Haern argued. "That night, and every night after, we have found a body for each night. They know we're looking."

"They?" Aurelia asked. She was seated in a luxurious red chair with a blanket over her. She took another sip of a hot brown drink that was deliciously sweet.

"That many bodies can't be one man," the wizard said. "And I still swear the priests of Karak are doing this."

Delysia came down the stairs looking pallid and exhausted. Her brother tossed a blanket around her shoulders and led her to a cushion beside Aurelia.

"He'll be fine," she said. "Whatever cut him was far from clean, but I think he'll..." She stopped, a spell of dizziness taking away her words.

"Thank you," Aurelia said. Delysia smiled.

"What if it is the priests," Haern said, his tone softer, more dangerous. "Will we finally strike at their heart?"

The women glanced to Tarlak, who sighed and began to explain.

"The priests have a hidden temple inside Veldaren. Very, very powerful spells hide its appearance, mask the evil energy within, and deny any attempts to scry its location. Supposedly it will reveal itself only to those who seek Karak's favor."

Aurelia leaned forward, suddenly very interested.

"But you know where it is," she said. "Somehow you found it."

Tarlak glanced to Haern.

"Not found," Haern said. "I have been inside its walls. The Spider Guild did not take kindly to my faith in Ashhur."

Delysia winced. She and Haern had spent many nights conversing underneath the stars. Haern had been a trained killer since birth, and so the opportunity to speak and think without fear of judgment or punishment had proven addictive. One night the members of the Spider Guild had assaulted them, dragging Haern toward the temple of Karak while leaving Delysia for dead.

"They thought to purge me of my belief," Haern continued. Old wounds drained the life from his eyes. "I memorized the way, and I will never forget that building, both the illusion and its true form."

"Then we tell the guards," Aurelia said. "The priests of Karak are forbidden from the city. Once King Vaelor hears of an entire temple he'll…"

"He'll do nothing," Tarlak said. "Because he already knows. Every king is informed on the first night they take the throne. They're also told, in no uncertain terms, that they will die should they try to remove the priests from the capital."

"How do you know this?" Aurelia asked. Tarlak feigned shock and insult.

"Why, because I'm a wizard, of course. I'm supposed to know these things."

"The temple's existence is common knowledge to the upper members of Veldaren," Haern explained. "The priests focus their attention on the wealthy, and gain safety and power through them. The priests of Karak bring only the most faithful and rich to their temple, and even then they bring them blindfolded."

"Why don't the priests of Ashhur do something about it?" Aurelia asked.

"Open warfare on the streets?" Tarlak asked with a chuckle. "Fun as that would be, Callan and his ilk accept the temple as a necessary evil. But we, however, do not fall under their jurisdiction."

"What was this about war on the streets?" Harruq asked as he came limping down the stairs. Aurelia frowned and rose from her chair.

"You shouldn't be up and around, you'll make yourself sick."

"Haern's beaten me far worse than this," the half-orc argued, though his voice was weak and unconvincing. He accepted Aurelia's arms and used her weight to reach her chair. She wrapped her blanket around him before sitting down beside Delysia.

"We don't want war on the streets," Tarlak said. "So we must be certain the priests are committing these murders and mutilations. But do we really have the strength to take them on, in their home no less?"

Haern leaned back and ran his hands through his blond hair.

"No. I don't think we do," he said. "But that hasn't stopped us before. We have never taken such a great risk, so if we do, we must do it with all our abilities. If the priests of Karak survive, we will be guaranteed retaliation." He looked around at his friends. "And I would not wish that upon any of you."

"We need to be more vigilant," Aurelia said. "We keep looking and keep searching. If we find and stop the priests outside the temple, they will view us as mercenaries performing a job. Those we kill will be faulted for being caught."

"Will that be enough to deter the killings?" Haern asked.

"It will be if we kill enough of them," Aurelia said, the hardness in her eyes frightening.

"Fantastic," Harruq said. "Why are they doing these killings in the first place?"

"Karak seeks total devotion," Delysia said after a long period of silence. "This means inhibition, compassion, and humanity must be purged. These mutilations, these sacrifices, are meant to show their faith. And I think we are ignoring one other aspect. Fear. There is a reason the bodies are being dumped for all to see."

"If it is fear they want, they're getting it," Tarlak said, remembering the talk he heard the previous day. "And it'll get worse, especially with how those three were found."

When Harruq asked how, the wizard shook his head.

"Some things are best to remain in the dark. For now, we rest, pray, and do what we do best for the rest of the day. Come night, we'll scour the city and hope to Ashhur we catch whoever's doing this before more bodies are found strung from...never mind. Good day everyone."

He downed the rest of his glass, made it vanish with a snap of his fingers, and then hurried up the stairs. To Harruq's questioning look, Haern only shook his head and shuddered.

That night the Eschaton gathered near the western entrance to the city. The air was cold, and they all wore extra layers underneath their armor and robes, as well as thick cloaks wrapped about their bodies.

"Harruq, Aurelia, you search the southern quarter," Tarlak ordered. "Del and I will scan the west. Haern gets the east. So far no one's been taken from the north, so we'll leave it be until they do."

"You going to be alright without me?" Delysia asked Harruq.

"Sure thing," the half-orc said with a wink. "Aurry will keep me safe."

"If you find any priests of Karak, use your best judgment," Tarlak said. "If they are too many, seek us out. Even if it is just one, treat him like a wild dragon."

"Yes, daddy," Aurelia said before taking Harruq's hand and pulling him away. Haern bowed, tied his hair behind his head, and then leapt to the rooftops.

"Come on," Tarlak said, casting invisibility spells over he and his sister. "Let's see if we can finally catch these murdering crows."

Despite the danger, the priests wore their black robes openly in the dark streets. Their success had emboldened them.

No man or woman who noticed them would dare point an accusatory finger come the dawn. Leading the group of five was Pelarak, the revered priest of Karak.

"Tonight will be special," Pelarak said, fingering the pendant shaped like a lion skull that hung from his neck. His voice was deep and firm, a powerful presence in the streets of Veldaren. "The fear we have caused is a pittance compared to our task tonight. Before the rise of the sun, the armies of Karak will conquer all."

"What about the Eschaton?" the priest on his left asked.

"They have a part to play in this," Pelarak answered. From his belt he drew a dagger. "Come. Our time is short."

They followed him north, heading straight for the fountain at the center of Veldaren.

⋈

One good sleep," Harruq mumbled, rubbing his eyes with his giant fists. "That's all I want. Why is it when bad things start happening, we always have to scour the city at night?"

"Such a baby," Aurelia said, jabbing him in the ribs with an elbow. "You're a step away from dead every time you plop down in our bed. What happened to this fabled orcish stamina we elves always heard about?"

"Bunch of lies," the half-orc muttered. "We like sleep, we like food, and we don't like staying up all night staring at empty streets."

The two were perched atop a building. Aurelia had used a levitation spell to bring them up. Other than a few drunks and stray animals, they hadn't seen a sign of life.

"People are becoming afraid," Aurelia said, frowning. "Staying home and avoiding the streets at night. But there is something else going on. Something... Harruq, look up."

He sighed and glanced to the cloud-covered sky.

"Yup, might rain. Perfect."

"No, look closer."

He did, and was stunned he had not seen it before.

"Oh gods," he said, his jaw dropping. "What does it mean?"

"We need to find Tarlak, now." Aurelia grabbed his hand and leapt them off the roof, using another levitation spell to slow their fall. Hand in hand they ran as far above them the red skull of a lion blanketed the entire western sky, a ghostly image shimmering across the clouds.

A s Haern leaned over the edge of a building, nothing more than a pair of eyes shining in the night, he heard a strange cry. He could not place it, but it sounded bestial and deep. The stranger part was that he heard it from the sky. He looked up, and there it was, a giant skull with its mouth opened in roar. It was blood red and hovered above the city like an angry god.

"Not good," he said before breaking into a sprint. Another roar thundered through the city, louder, angrier. Even without his exceptionally trained hearing, Haern could tell where it came from. He leapt from rooftop to rooftop, straight for the heart of the city.

W hen they heard the deep roar, they knew something was horribly amiss. Harruq drew his swords, and Aurelia summoned her staff and prepared her spells. They expected to see guards rushing toward the center, but so far the streets remained barren.

"Where are the guards?" Harruq asked as they ran.

"Afraid," she answered. "We underestimated what is going on. I'm scared, Harruq."

"We've faced worse," he said.

"No," she said. "Stop." She pulled on his arm, and reluctantly he slowed. He could feel his own horror growing at a rapid pace, a strange cancer that he was unaccustomed too. All he could think of was fleeing to the Eschaton tower and cowering away from the lion in the sky.

"It's magic," Aurelia said, brushing her hand across his face as she stared into his eyes. "Look at me. Look, and repeat after me. The fear is weak when the threat is false. Say it."

"The fear is weak when the threat is false."

Soft light flickered on her fingertips. "Again."

"The fear is weak when the threat is false."

Light flashed between them, but it did not hurt his eyes nor make him blink. The cancer in his stomach vanished.

"That should do for now," she said, kissing his lips. "Delysia can better ward us against fear should we find her. Come on."

She grabbed his wrist and pulled. The lion roared as if mocking them.

"Sooner we get rid of that thing the better," Harruq said, glaring at the lion as it glared back down at him. They ran until they could see the large fountain in the center of the city. They stopped again, but not out of fear.

"What the abyss is that?" Harruq asked. The lion in the sky roared, triumphant. The half-orc felt his swords shake in his hands. Aurelia wrapped her free hand around his wrist, needing its touch.

Five priests of Karak surrounded the fountain, whose waters ran red with blood. Pelarak stood at the north side, his hands raised and his eyes to the sky. The other four were on the opposite end, kneeling in prayer or chanting. Three bodies lay like the corners of a large triangle surrounding them. Their chests were wrenched open, their ribcages broken and twisted wide as if something had burst from within. Standing above the bodies were the lions.

They were larger than horses. Their black flesh rippled with muscle. They had no fur, instead covered with a smoldering coat of embers. In unison the three arched their backs and roared, and from their bellies streams of fire soared into the air. The lion in the sky roared back, pleased.

"What are they," Harruq asked, his eyes wide with terror.

"Lions," Aurelia said, gripping his hand tighter. "Servants of Karak. He's twisted them, made them...we need the guards, we need Tarlak. Where is everyone?"

The panic in her voice only worsened Harruq's fear. He could imagine one bearing down upon him, its claws made of molten rock, its fur burning his very flesh as its obsidian teeth closed around his neck...

"Faithless children!" Pelarak screamed, drawing his attention outward, away from his nightmarish vision. All throughout the city, his voice could be heard. "Behold the Lion that comes in the night seeking to reclaim his Kingdom. You have turned from Karak, willingly forgetting all that once made this city proud. Now you cower, fearing his judgment. Will you surrender? Will you accept the truth you have blinded yourselves to? Or will you give in to death, and in its embrace hide from your ignorance?"

The priest lowered his gaze and stared straight at the couple.

"Your brother was always the wisest, Harruq Tun," he said. "He approaches with an army at his side. Your master marches with him. Will you join them? Will you repent, and turn to the life you once lived? Or will you doom yourself and your loved ones by fighting against him?"

Harruq looked to his wife, and in her eyes he saw the floating corpse of his daughter. The half-orc met the priest's gaze, and he felt his fear shatter underneath his anger.

"I would rather die than become the soulless murderer my brother would have me be," he said.

Pelarak nodded, accepting the decision.

"So be it. Karak has given us his servants to prepare the way. It is in their teeth you will die."

The lions roared, all three leering at him with hungry eyes. Harruq snarled back and smashed his swords together. Aurelia clutched her staff, and a flickering shield of red grew around her. Two of the lions belched fire, the powerful streams ripping through the air, only to part against the elf's shield.

Aurelia twirled her hair and smirked. "That it?"

Pelarak chuckled.

"It is a pleasure to meet you, Aurelia Tun, however briefly. May you die with little pain."

At his command, the lions charged. They filled the entire street, one leading, the other two side by side behind. The ground shook from their footfalls. The night shimmered under the red embers of their fur. The couple held their ground. When the lions were about to reach them, and the foremost had leapt into the air, Aurelia knelt and pressed her fingers against the ground. A wall of ice grew straight upward, several inches thick. The entire wall groaned from the pressure as the first lion hit it. Hundreds of cracks filled the ice.

"Here," she said, pressing her hands against Harruq's chest. Red light surrounded their skin. "That will protect us from their fire."

She kissed him as he stared at the ice wall, which had begun to crumble.

"And their claws and teeth?" he asked.

"On your own there," she said as the barrier shattered. She flung boulders of ice from her hands as deadly concentration blanketed her face. Harruq stayed at her side, determined to protect her no matter the cost. The foremost lion snarled as the boulders crashed against its face and legs. A second lion leapt past with frightening speed.

"Come try me," Harruq yelled, running to one side and batting his swords together. The lion veered toward him, its mouth open in roar. A stream of fire shot between the gaping jaws and enveloped the half-orc. He crossed his arms and braced his legs, but Aurelia's spell held strong. The fire flickered across his armor and skin without burning. He felt the heat, and sweat poured across his skin, but he was not burned.

It seemed the lion was not surprised by his survival, for it leapt with its paws leading, obsidian claws hungry for blood. Harruq dodged to one side, slashing out with his magical blades, Salvation and Condemnation. The sister swords cut through the molten armor and into black flesh. Dark fluid seeped out, bursting into flame at contact with the crisp cold air. The wounded lion cried out in pain and wrenched its body away from the swords. When it landed further down the street, it spun, its eyes glaring with an intelligence that was terrifying.

As Harruq prepared for another leap, Aurelia used a spell to raise her high into the air. The other two lions belched fire and leapt skyward. Lance after lance of ice batted them back, angling them so their claws passed inches from her dress and their teeth snapped air instead of flesh. Frustrated, the two lions circled underneath, snarling up at her.

"Poor kitties," the elf said as more ice swirled around her fingers. "You want to come and play?" She fired thick lances of ice, which thudded against the muscular feline bodies. She wasn't harming them much, but at least the two lions were focused on her instead of Harruq. She threw two more boulders of ice. One missed while the other cracked in two as it collided against the spine of a lion. As its cry of pain ended, she heard a voice.

"Well done," Pelarak shouted. Dark circles sparkled on his fingertips. "But it is time your foolishness ended."

Aurelia felt a tingling throughout her body, and then the firm grip of gravity took hold. She hooked her fingers and cast another levitation spell, but the magic would not take. The elf fell, her green dress flapping in the air as the lions waited hungrily below. They were denied their meal. Strong arms gripped her as she passed by the houses, jarring her to one side. Together they rolled along the roof. She came to a rest still inside those arms.

"Having fun without me?" Haern asked as he helped her stand.

"About time you..." She stopped. "Are you alright?"

The assassin was clutching his amulet of the golden mountain as his entire body shook.

"The amulet helps," he said. "I will not cower before the demons of Karak."

"You poor dear." She put her hands on his own. White light flared as she cast the same spell she had cast on her husband. Haern's shaking subsided.

"Delysia and Tarlak will be here soon," he said. He grabbed her hand and held it firm. "Thank you," he said.

The lion in the sky roared once more, and it seemed the entire city shook under its power. The two lions leapt atop the building, the wood and plaster cracking under their weight. Their eyes shimmered as they tensed for a pounce.

"Can you keep the lions at bay?" Haern asked.

"Have so far, haven't I?"

The one on the right dug its claws, waiting for the slightest movement to react.

"The priests are mine," the assassin whispered. From a standstill he leapt twenty feet to his right, gently falling to the roof of another building. Both lions charged. One gave chase for Haern, but stopped when Aurelia pelted its side with a bolt of lightning. The force spun it sideways, ruining its jump. The thing tumbled to the street, belching fire all the way down. Aurelia fell as the other lion descended upon her. She had nowhere to go. Its muscular body was all she could see. She closed her eyes, hooked her fingers for one last spell, and prayed.

⋈

Haern jumped from roof to roof, his twin sabers held tight in his hands. He and Tarlak had spent many nights pondering what would happen if the priests of Karak revealed themselves to the city. Now, with the event upon them, it seemed all their preparations and strategy were as pointless as could be. The lion dominated the sky. If they did not end the fear that filled the city, Veldaren would be theirs.

He saw the five priests standing around the fountain that ran red with blood. He saw Pelarak, recognizing the leader. The others prayed and knelt while he watched and commanded. From the corner of his eye, he saw a flash of lightning knock back the lion that had given him chase. He didn't know if it would resume after him or return for Aurelia. He prayed Ashhur would watch over her, but he could not go back. Swords ready, he ran, nothing but a blur of gray in the night.

The houses ended, Haern catapulted himself into the air with all the strength in his legs. He dove for the fountain, his sabers leading like the claws of a bird diving for its prey. His cloaks trailed behind him, somehow silent though they thrashed wildly.

He fell amid the farthest two, his arms stretched wide. One saber pierced through the back of a priest's neck. The one next to him gasped, the curved blade cutting his throat. They died still kneeling in prayer, their faces slumped to the dirt. The one on the right had shifted from his prayers, as if he had heard the commotion. The other continued shrieking out his devotion to Karak.

Haern rammed both his sabers through the lungs of the one on the right. His back arched in pain. He opened his mouth to scream but the assassin had already angled a saber around, cutting deep into his neck. He let out only a gurgle of blood. Loud as he was, the other priest realized the sudden quieting of prayers. He opened his eyes, only to see a brief flicker of light before the tip of a saber pierced through his eye socket.

With a grunt, Haern kicked the dead priest off his sword. Before he could turn, he felt a weight press against his shoulder. Pain spiked through his body. The magical hand of Pelarak was upon him, gripping his body and sending wave after wave of torture. The priest watched the assassin writhe, all the while keeping his right palm stretched flat. Red light swirled around his hand, as well as Haern's body.

"You murdered my followers," Pelarak said. "They died quick, and with little pain. I will not grant you that same courtesy."

The light turned crimson, and Haern's screams grew louder. The whole time Pelarak smiled.

"Enough!" Delysia shouted.

White fireflies zipped around Pelarak's body, their light burning his eyes. One by one they crashed against his body, dissolving into luminescent sparks. Their holy energy burned delivered a throbbing stab against his soul. His concentration broke. The red light around his hands faded.

"So the priestess finally shows her face," Pelarak said as Delysia ran to Haern's side. He shrugged off the pain and let unholy energy gather at his fingertips.

"Same could be said for you," she whispered as glanced over Haern's body. He didn't appear too wounded, just in shock from the pain. He'd recover, if given the time. Time, though, was something she would have to fight for.

"You are a healer," Pelarak said as the darkness about him intensified. "Do you think you can withstand the purity of my hatred?"

Ten small projectiles flew toward her, their centers swirling an ugly brown while their outsides glowed black. Delysia put her hands out as if she were resisting a fall and then braced her mind. The projectiles hit, each one filled with an image and accompanying emotion. She saw fields of desecrated bodies. She saw innocents burning in fire. She felt anger, hatred, disgust and contempt. More images, those of mutilated children, starving women, bleeding animals and ruined forests, pushed into her mind. To each one she countered with the image of Aullienna smiling happy in her arms as she held her. All around were her friends. She remembered the joy and happiness, and against it the anger and vile images broke.

"Clever," Pelarak said as the mental link the projectiles had established broke. "But Karak has long wanted your meddlesome group removed. I have seen what you dare not see."

Two more orbs of dark memories formed at his fingers. He threw the first, then the second. His smirk was gone. The images he was sending hurt him as well, but against a priestess of Ashhur, they would be devastating.

Delysia prepared her defense. The image came, and it too was of Aullienna, running happily through the forest behind their tower. A pang of dread hit her as she realized what she was being shown. The girl climbed over a log, ducked through brush, and then found a stream. She giggled and smiled before diving into the water. The priestess tried to remember her happy, her laughing in her arms as a child, but all she could see was Aullienna flailing, water filling her tiny lungs and stealing away her life. The emotion coupled with the image was also something she had not expected: terrible, wracking guilt.

"You see the horrible things this world must endure because of the faith you preach," she heard Pelarak say. "You see the ruination that Ashhur breeds by your rejection of the half-orc's brother?"

The second projectile hit. She knew this one well, and against her weakened heart she could not shrug it aside. She saw Brug, lying numb and helpless on the ground as Tessanna stood over him with her dagger in hand. As the blade pierced through his eye, she shrieked and begged the image to end. Again she felt horrible guilt, this time coupled with regret. She could not bear it.

Pelarak smiled as the priestess collapsed to her knees, sobbing. Haern lay beside her, his eyes closed. Two of the most powerful defenders of Veldaren, both laid broken by his strength of will.

"Praise be to Karak," he prayed as he approached with death in his hands.

The flames felt much hotter than before. Harruq grimaced and hoped Aurelia's spell would hold out. The last thing he wanted to be was a charred meal for an overgrown cat, but he would be the first to admit things never went as hoped.

"Best you got?" he shouted as he ran down the street, the lion hot on his heels with fire shooting from its mouth. Harruq decided not to test his defensive spell anymore than he had to. He rolled underneath the first blast and dodged the second by ducking into an alley. The lion spun its body and dug its claws into the ground. Huge grooves cut into the dirt as it halted its momentum. Harruq clashed his swords together, taking strength from their magic.

"Don't think you can fit in here," he said to the lion. "But if you can, I don't think your claws can match my swords. Want to try it?"

Evidently it did. The lion snarled and lunged. Both shoulders slammed against the side of buildings. Their walls shook, charring black from the heat. Harruq leapt back, but only a little. The lion tried again. Beams broke. Plaster crumbled. Even if the buildings had to fall, it would reach him.

"Persistent bugger," Harruq muttered. When the lion charged again he lashed out, cutting a deep line across the bridge of its nose. The pain only spurred it further. Fire flooded the alley, and this time the half-orc felt his skin blister. The protection spell was nearly spent.

"Not good," he said. "Not good, not good, not good."

He cut at a searching paw, then went on the offensive. Salvation and Condemnation cut and spun. The lion could only bat at the swords, unable to use its greater size to its advantage in the cramped alley. When the paw struck blade, Harruq pressed with all his strength. The creature howled as it lost two claws, nubs of flesh hanging from them. The lion hobbled back, limping on its wounded right paw. Black blood poured across the dirt.

Harruq picked up one of the claws and hurled it at the lion, the mockery angering it further. It bared its teeth and prepared another blast of fire. The half-orc braced his arms, seeing nowhere to go. If he survived he could perhaps kill it before it recovered from the wound. The rush of fire, however, never came.

Three bolts of lightning slammed into its rear, the force knocking the lion to the ground. A whimper escaped its throat, strange and unbecoming. A lance of ice followed it, crashing against its face. The ice tore through its left eye, rendering it blind. The creature turned to run, but now Harruq was leaping out of the alley, his twin swords hungry. He slashed the tendons in its back legs, tumbling the lion to the ground.

Before it could stand, a final bolt of lightning struck from the sky. The giant body convulsed, and a stream of molten black gunk oozed from its open mouth. It moved no more.

"How in the abyss are you not a pile of ash right now?" Tarlak asked as he walked down the alley and slapped the warrior on the shoulder.

"Aurry," Harruq said. The wizard chuckled.

"Of course. Where is our lovely elf, anyway?"

The ground shook beneath them, and high in the sky the blood lion roared in exaltation. The two exchanged a single look, then without a word they ran toward the fountain, weapons drawn and magic ready.

※

As the huge teeth closed on her neck, Aurelia cast a desperate spell. Her body turned translucent, as if it were made of smoke and light. She fell through the roof, her body like a ghost. She landed beside a bed where two children cowered in the arms of their father. Their eyes were wide, and all shook with deep, constant fear.

"What's going on?" the father asked. Sweat ran down his chin.

"Get under the bed," she told them. At first they did not move, but then giant claws tore away the wood above their heads, and red light flooded the room as fire poured in. The elf hooked her thumbs and held her hands high, palms outward. A ward against fire materialized before the family, a shimmering concave barrier that darkened from orange to deep red as the fire parted against it. The father grabbed a son in each hand, held them to his chest, and then made a frantic rush for the door.

"No, wait!" Aurelia shouted. More of the roof tore away. The giant feline mass crashed down, claws raking and teeth biting. Directly beneath that mass was the family. The elf cast a spell on pure instinct. She clapped her hands, then opened them. A giant shockwave billowed out in a conic tornado of concentrated sound. It struck the lion as it descended. The creature bellowed in anger as it flew through a wall and out onto the street. As the spell ended, she heard one of the boys crying as if far away. Everything else was drowned out by the ringing of her ears.

"Stay inside," she said, though she did not hear the words. She ran to the opening in the wall and looked out. The lion was struggling to stand on a broken leg. Another marched in circles around it protectively. From her vantage point she had a clear shot at both. Ice formed and cracked around her hands. She pointed her fingers, and then the ice fractured and flew. The hundred shards grew larger until they were long as arrows and wickedly sharp. The pacing lion saw the attack and leapt before the wounded one, roaring as the ice shards pelted through its thick skin and into the muscle beneath.

As Aurelia prepared another spell, the two fled toward Pelarak. The wounded one trailed behind, still limping, but the distance was not far. Unable to see, the elf jumped through the hole and landed on the street. She saw Pelarak before the fountain, the blood-stained water swirling like a living snake around his legs and arms. His eyes looked to the sky, his mouth open in worship.

Lying before him was the still body of Delysia Eschaton.

12

Haern sensed Pelarak's approach as his wits slowly returned to him. He heard the priest's cold thanks to Karak. Nearby Delysia sobbed. The assassin let a slit of light enter an eye. He saw Pelarak standing over them. He was smiling.

"Only in absolute emptiness is there order," he heard him say as he put his hand on Delysia's pale forehead. The unholy energy surrounding his fingers crawled into her mouth and nose like vile worms. The priestess' neck snapped back, and wide-eyed, she stared at the sky. Coughs retched from her throat. Haern felt a sickness stir within him. He had watched Brug die, powerless to help him. He would not suffer that fate again.

His arms weighed a thousand stone, but still he lifted them. Numb fingers closed around the hilt of a saber. The darkness was crawling deeper into Delysia. Her heart was pure, and the presence of unholy energy filled her with unbearable pain. All doubt and fear within her was magnified tenfold. Her spine locked tight, and she had no control over her body. She knew she was gagging. She knew she was dying.

Haern took two deep breaths and flung the saber. The blade spun through the air, its aim true. The curved end sliced across Pelarak's wrist, leaving a shallow cut. The pain jerked his hand. The darkness snapped out of Delysia's body. She collapsed, her eyes open, unseeing. The priest clutched his bleeding wrist and glared.

"You will suffer dearly," he snarled.

Haern laughed weakly, an exhausted grin on his face.

"I know," he said. "But at least you have something to remember me by."

Pelarak was not amused. He pointed his hooked fingers, a bolt of shadow shooting from his palm. Just before the bolt hit, Haern enacted the magic in one of his rings. He teleported ten feet into the air. The bolt harmlessly hit the dirt where he had been. Haern shifted in air, trying to angle his body just right. The magic in the ring would only send him straight ahead, and only once every few seconds. He would have one chance when he hit the ground. And only one.

The priest saw the assassin above and glared. He would enjoy extracting what little life remained in the priestess. As for Haern, he was a nuisance he had long tired of. He fired another bolt of shadow. Just before he landed, Haern enacted the magic of his ring. He reappeared forward, mere inches away from the priest. His elbow smashed against Pelarak's forehead. As the priest staggered, Haern reached for Delysia's hand. If he could just touch her, he could use the ring to take her with him and escape.

He brushed the cold skin of her fingers, but then a brutal pain stabbed his chest. Darkness swirled around his vision, and then he felt himself soaring through the air. He grabbed one of his cloaks and pulled it from his body. The cloak snapped firm, the magic within activated. Haern floated to the ground, blind, wounded, and half a mile from Veldaren's center.

Pelarak towered over Delysia, his breathing deep and controlled in an attempt to reign in his anger. He glanced about, seeing his lions battling in the streets and upon the rooftops. He had expected the Eschaton to prove a difficult foe, but this was beyond his original estimation.

"Underestimate your foe, underestimate your losses," he said as he knelt down and grabbed Delysia by her long red hair. He dragged her closer to the fountain, which still pulsed red with blood from the curse he had cast upon it. He placed her beside one of the mutilated bodies, then let go of her hair. All around lay his dead brothers, killed by perfect strikes from the assassin. They would suffice for reinforcements.

Pelarak took out a dagger, flipped the bodies onto their backs, and then carved a rune onto their forehead. He felt the lion watching him from high above. The power of Karak was heavy in the air. A glorious night, he thought. One he had waited many years for. He sheathed his dagger and let his faith fill him.

"I call forth your servants," Pelarak said, his hands to the sky. The water in the fountain thrashed and bubbled, the curse growing within. He felt tendrils wrap around his body, flowing with power. He gasped in pleasure.

"My faith denies this world," he shouted. "And I demand you burst the chains that hold you and give unto me your servants so we may cleanse this land!"

The runes on the dead priests' foreheads flared red before exploding upward in smoke. The ground shook. The sky roared. The bodies of the priests erupted in blood as from their chests lions emerged. At first they were the size of their worldly counterparts, but then grew larger and stronger once they were free of their passageway into Dezrel. The lions shook off the blood that stained their coats. They uttered quick growls to each other, greeting their fellow pack members. The two wounded lions joined them, dipping their heads in greeting.

Pelarak lowered his arms as he felt the incredible power fade from his body. His knees wobbled, and he gripped the side of the fountain to steady himself. He had not expected to need more of the lions, but battle was chaotic, after all. When he saw the lions looking at him, he bowed.

"I am a humble servant," he said. The leader of the pack sniffed at him, then nudged the unconscious Delysia with a paw. Pelarak stood and redrew his knife.

"Do not doubt my strength," he told the creature. "The Doru'al will walk this world again."

The pack leader roared, and the rest of his pack took up the roar as far away a different kind of pack gathered to face the new threat.

See now," Tarlak said as he watched the four lions tear into their world through the bodies of the priests. "That's not fair." They reached Aurelia, who stood shocked by the sight.

"Two are wounded," she said as Tarlak and her husband neared. "But even so, there are six of them. Haern's gone, and Delysia..."

She couldn't finish.

They watched as Pelarak drew his dagger and hovered over her still body. Tarlak's hands shook. He turned to the others, unable to watch.

"Not in vain," he said, the hard look in his eyes scaring the couple. "Not here, not now...and not in vain."

Lightning crackled around his hands, painfully bright. One of the lions spotted them and roared. Harruq turned, his swords drawn and his hands shaking. Aurelia's spell had done much to banish the unnatural fear from the aberration in the sky, but his normal fear went untamed. It grew when all six of the creatures turned and belched fire toward them. The awesome display nearly broke his spirit.

Aurelia latched onto his arm, a spell on her lips.

"There," she said. "You will be protected from the fire again. And don't run on me, Harruq Tun. Don't you dare run."

He faced the lions, which approached in a tight pack of power and muscle.

"I won't," he said.

As one the spellcasters unleashed blasts of ice and lightning. The front lions dodged, but those behind were knocked back. More blasts followed, and then came boulders of earth and ice, cones of air, and invisible walls of magic. Harruq watched the display, awed and humbled by Aurelia's and Tarlak's power. His swords felt small and useless in his hands by comparison. The lions shook their heads from side to side and endured the brutal hits, using their giant mass and momentum to continue forward. The three would be crushed.

"Not in vain," Harruq whispered, hoping he could keep such a promise.

Tarlak tried to lift one of the lions off the ground with a brute levitation spell, but the creature resisted. The wizard collapsed to his knees, exhausted. Aurelia fired lances of ice, but they were small compared to the previous barrage. Harruq stepped forward, prepared to sacrifice his life to give them time to escape. He was never given the chance.

A swirling beam of light twice the size of any man screamed between he and Tarlak. It struck the foremost lion, enveloping its entire body in pure magical essence. The power tore its skin and shattered its bones. A second beam followed, and this time the lions had no choice but to retreat. It struck another lion, but the creature rolled out from the blast. Melted rock poured from its nose, and its right shoulder sagged. Stunned, Harruq glanced back to see the source of the attacks.

"Tessanna," he said, his mouth hanging open. The crazed demoness had come. Stranger still she walked between Lathaar and another man, both wearing the gleaming armor of paladins. Tarlak looked back as well, and his entire body tensed at the sight.

"How dare she," he said, lightning crackled from his hands despite his exhaustion.

"No!" Lathaar shouted, stepping in front of the girl with the solid black eyes. The lightning had already been loosed. Mira brushed aside Lathaar as if he were a child, and then batted away the lightning with her bare hand. Tarlak's anger flared, but then Lathaar was running, his swords drawn and light flooding the street.

"Mira!" he shouted. "Her name is Mira!"

Harruq looked to the lions, but they were observing the new power they faced. When he turned back to Mira, he realized the clothes she wore were different. Her dress was beautiful and green, tailored similar to Aurelia's. Her skin was darker, and her whole body thicker and healthier. Again he heard Lathaar shout the name Mira.

"What the abyss is going on?" he asked.

The other man pulled his shield off his back, and the brilliant light joined Lathaar's so that the street was bright as day. All their fear and worry faded away.

"Behind us," the man with the shield shouted, positioning himself in front of Aurelia and Tarlak. Lathaar joined Harruq's side, glancing at him as he did.

"We fought together once before," Lathaar said. "Ready to do so again?"

Harruq nodded. The lions were snarling and belching fire, clearly unhappy about losing their numbers advantage.

"So who might you be," Tarlak asked.

"Name's Jerico of the Citadel," the paladin said.

"Good to meet you Jerico. Try not to die on me so I can greet you properly. Oh, and don't let me die, either."

The wizard held in a surge of rage as Mira stood beside him. He remembered Lathaar's words, spoken in a time that felt ages away. She could be her twin, he had said. He hadn't been lying. The anger passed as he reminded himself, again and again, that the girl with black hair and eyes was not the murderer of his best friend.

"The demons are scared," Mira said. She lifted her hands and let the wild magic within her pool around her fingers. "They know what I am. Even Karak fears me." She brought down her hands as the lions charged down the street.

"Time to justify their fear."

Aurelia and Tarlak fired twin streams of ice shards, but it was Mira's spell that sent the lions leaping to the rooftops. A maelstrom of swirling air and magic erupted from her hands, spanning the width of the street. It sucked in the other two spells, twisting into a vortex of ice and wind. While the other lions could flee, the one with the wounded leg only whimpered and braced for the hit. Its molten fur shredded away under the power. The ice sliced every inch of its flesh. Dark blood clouded the maelstrom, which dissipated when Mira ended her concentration. Ice and blood rained upon the street as the lion fell dead.

The remaining lions dashed from roof to street to roof as spells darted after them. Magical arrows, bolts, and beams of all elements lit up the sky. At last they reached the party, and the four leapt as one from the rooftops.

"About time!" Jerico shouted as one leapt straight for him. A glowing image of his shield flung outward and struck the lion. The power hit its stomach like a battering ram, killing all momentum. The paladin gave it no reprieve, striking at its sides with his mace as it hit the ground in a graceless tangle of limbs.

Harruq and Lathaar rushed their attacker, their swords hacking. The lion clawed and bit as its huge body slammed into the both of them. It rolled head over feet as it roared, the two fighters rolling with it. The fire of its fur was hot to the touch but Aurelia's spell spared Harruq. Lathaar had no such protection. The paladin screamed in pain as he stabbed again and again into the belly of the lion. The half-orc slashed at its eyes, scoring a wicked strike along the upper eyelid. He held in a scream when two claws tore across his arm, easily piercing his leather armor and shredding flesh.

The remaining two lions leapt at the casters, both eager to devour the strange goddess among them. Aurelia and Tarlak raised their hands and cast protection spells, but Mira would have none of it. She flicked a wrist at each of them. Winds pushed them aside. The first landed atop her, but it passed through her body like mist. The girl laughed.

"Something wrong?" she asked. Her hand reached out, ghostly and ethereal. When it touched the lion's skin the spell enacted. Golden light exploded all around her, painful to the Eschaton's eyes but absolute torture to the demons. The lion flew back from her touch, its right shoulder shattered. The other twisted in mid-leap, trying to hide from the glaring spell. It sailed overhead and landed behind the group. It leapt again, avoiding a blast of lightning. Tarlak looped his right hand twice, and then red webs fell from the sky. The lion struggled but could not resist their strength. It hit the street with a whimper, and lay there writhing against the webs.

It was given no chance to recover. Mira pelted it with a blast of white magic, so strong it peeled away fur and flesh so its bare ribs were exposed. The mighty lion died whimpering. Not far away, the lion with the wounded shoulder snarled in anger. Its pack was dying, and Karak was not pleased. It glanced back to Pelarak, who beckoned for it to return. The lion dodged a parting shot from Aurelia before racing back to the priest.

"Be healed," Pelarak told it as he put his hands on the wounded shoulder. Light poured across the shoulder, shaping bone and mending cartilage. With a pleased roar, the lion turned back to the Eschaton. Pelarak drew his knife and urged it on.

"The sacrifice will be made," he said. Words of magic poured from his mouth. Shadow and mist swirled around the dagger as he clutched it with both hands. Tarlak saw the spell, as well as his sister lying unconscious at his feet.

"We have to help her!" he shouted. He started to run, but the pack leader blocked the way. Nearby he heard growling and shouts of pain. Lathaar and Harruq had backed their lion against a wall, and between their coordinated attacks kept it cornered. Jerico's lion, on the other hand, was battered and beaten. Every time it attacked, Jerico blocked with his shield, letting the holy energy seep in and destroy the demonic flesh of the beast.

"I will keep its attention," Mira said as she stepped beside him. "Hurry to her side."

A thousand tiny arrows flew from her hands, adjusting their aim when the lion dodged. At their touch, the creature howled. The arrows did no permanent damage, instead causing sharp, stinging pains. Multiplied by the hundreds, the pain infuriated the beast. Aurelia increased its torment by zapping it on the nose with a bolt of lightning. Mad beyond reason, it roared and charged.

Tarlak ran unnoticed past the lion, his eyes locked on Pelarak.

B e darkness made flesh," Pelarak said as the spell neared its end. The verbal components were finished. He could feel the power swelling within him as he looked to the still form at his feet. He saw a woman, beautiful and devoted in her faith.

"Flesh so soft and a heart so kind," he said. "Sacrifice. Everything must involve sacrifice."

He knew her brother watched. He let that last bit of guilt plunge the dagger into Delysia's breast.

"No!" Tarlak screamed, a single spear made of fire sailing from his hands. Pelarak did not try to protect himself. He accepted the spear with closed eyes, letting the fire burn the flesh of his chest. The impact knocked him against the fountain. The edge cracked against his hip, and he fell to one knee as pain filled his drained body. The magic was gone. His soul felt empty. The dagger in his hands contained no magic, only a dark stain of blood.

The wizard slowed, tears running down his cheeks as he watched the shadow and darkness swirl into the wound on his sister's chest. He heard a roar from the sky. Karak was mocking him.

"Damn you, Karak," he said, his lower lip quivering. "Damn you and your priests too." He lifted his arms into the air, every bit of his power screaming into the spell. When he thrust his arms down, a bolt of lightning twice the width of an oak tree blasted the fountain, shattering the statue of a long dead king and spilling blood-water everywhere. Pelarak accepted the blast, knowing death was an inevitability for his faith and the path he walked. But death did not come. Karak's will was strong in the air, and his hands protected his most faithful priest.

When Pelarak stood, Tarlak knew damn well what he was seeing. Karak was not done mocking him. Then Delysia rose from the ground, the darkness settling upon her flesh. Slits opened across her face, shining red eyes underneath. Claws stretched out from her fingers, circular and long as swords. The creature looked to him and snarled, revealing rows of teeth sharper than daggers and just as large. He sobbed, the sounds of battle fading away. His sister...his beautiful sister had become...

He couldn't think it. Couldn't bear it. His sister had become a Doru'al, one of the trusted bodyguards of Karak. And now it charged, claws out and teeth ready. It would kill him, and he lacked the heart to resist. Defeated before a single drop of blood was drawn, he slumped to his knees and waited.

Jerico dropped his mace and flung his other hand against the inside of his shield. The lion had abandoned all form of tactic. Every time it swiped or bit, his shield was there. Instead, it flung its entire weight in hopes of crushing him against the side of a house. He could feel the wood cracking against his back, and his arms shook against the tremendous weight. He clenched his jaw and focus. His elbows would not bend. His arms would not move. Even if bones broke, he would not relinquish.

The holy power of his shield poured into the demon like a river. At last it fell back, its very being quivering. Too much had entered its body. It collapsed, white light wafting off its body like smoke from a dying fire. Jerico gasped in relief, his shield arm falling limp at his side. He retrieved his mace and took a look around their battlefield. Lathaar and Harruq still fought against their lion, but they appeared in control. He didn't see Mira or Aurelia, but he trusted their magic. Tarlak though...

He heard the wizard's cry, and at the sound he felt his heart sink. It was the cry of a broken man. He turned and saw the Doru'al stand, the body a blot of pure darkness hovering above the street.

"Don't give in," he whispered, but Tarlak already had. Jerico ran, his shield leading. Meanwhile the Doru'al vanished, only to reappear directly in front of the kneeling wizard. Claws closed around his neck as it lifted him with one hand. The creature snarled at him, its red eyes evil and heartless.

"Make it quick," Pelarak ordered as he staggered toward the pair. "He was an honorable man."

The Doru'al growled in response. The priest shrugged his shoulders and watched. With its free hand, it dragged a claw across his neck and sliced open a thin red line of blood. The pain sparked a bit of life into Tarlak. He clutched at the darkness and attempted to cast a spell, but claws closed tighter, choking away his breath. The creature nipped at his throat with the tips of its teeth. Mocking him. Warm, foul breath blew across the blood, further igniting the pain. Torturing. Mocking.

"Back!" Jerico screamed as his shield slammed into the Doru'al's side. The hit freed Tarlak from its grip. Jerico continued to pummel it with his shield as he shouted.

"In the name of Ashhur, the light, and all that is good, I cast you back!"

The creature howled, the darkness within its being hurt beyond measure by the holy light. Against his constant attacks, the Doru'al had little chance to escape or survive. Pelarak ended them with a curse. Darkness covered Jerico's eyes, blinding his sight. The paladin swung with his mace, hoping to kill the creature before it realized his weakness, but the hit struck the dirt. He felt something slice into his arm, and then a horrid pain pierce his side. He staggered back while pulling his shield close to his body.

"You may be light in this world," he heard the priest say. "But can you live in the darkness?"

"Can you?" Haern whispered into Pelarak's ear before burying both sabers through his back and into his heart. The darkness left Jerico's eyes. The Doru'al was gone. Marching down the street were priests of Ashhur. Their High Priest Calan led the way. Lathaar joined his side, horrible burns covering his face and hands. Calan approached and put his hands on the wounds.

"Be healed," he told the paladin. "And forgive us for our failure to arrive in time."

"Better late than never," Harruq said, tramping down the street. He held his right arm against his chest, and winced with every step. "But not much."

At this he looked to Tarlak. Blood ran down the wizard's neck as he knelt with his hands pressed against the stone. He stared at the remnants of the fountain, his mind cruelly remembering every detail of the dagger plunging into his sister's chest. Haern approached and offered his hand. Tarlak didn't take it.

"Get up," the assassin ordered. Tarlak glared, but Haern's look remained firm. At last the mage took his hand. Haern pulled him to his feet and then hugged him. "All is not yet lost," he said. "She still lives."

"But as that…that…" He didn't finish.

Mira and Aurelia emerged from around a corner, their lion slain. Mira brushed away a priest who came seeking to help, for she had not a single bruise on her. Lathaar went to her side, but when he tried to speak she shushed him by putting a finger against his lips. Her eyes looked to the stars where the red lion still shimmered.

"You lost this night," she said. She raised a hand. Her hair lifted as if amid an upward gale of wind. The white of her eyes vanished to black. The lion shook, and its color ran as if it were turning liquid. It gave one last furious roar before all its power broke. The red funneled down, swirling like a tornado, a tornado that ended at Mira's fingertips. As the last of the color swirled inside her hand, she clenched it to a fist. Her face grew hard as stone, and her eyes filled with anger and determination.

"Hope battles fear," she said, all eyes upon her. "And hope springs from faith."

She flung the power back to the sky, but this time a golden mountain shimmered before the stars. Its light was soft, its image subtle, but it was there. Lathaar squeezed her hand at the sight and kissed her cheek. She blushed.

"Come with us to the temple," Calan said as he wrapped an arm around Tarlak's shoulder. "We need to talk."

"Not yet," Tarlak said, pulling free from his grasp. He walked to where Pelarak's corpse lay amid the shattered remnants of the fountain.

"Karak has a way of bringing back the dead," he said. "But not this time."

He burned the corpse to ash, and then scattered it into the air. A high breeze caught it and sent it south, so not a speck fell amid the city.

That done, he accepted Calan's arm and walked to the temple.

Harruq remembered the first time he and his brother had come to the temple. Tessanna had taken into her own body a deadly poison flowing through Aurelia's veins, saving her. The High Priest Calan had cured Tessanna while simultaneously warning Qurrah of the path they walked. As Harruq approached its marble walls, he thought of those words and understood. So many had died because his brother chose the darkness. He had felt an outsider the first time he came, but now he felt somewhat at home. The peace and calm in the air was just what he needed.

Calan led them inside to the giant chamber for worship. Row after row of benches faced an altar covered with purple silk. Young priests rushed in from a side door, carrying blankets and food. The party sat together among the benches, with Calan standing in the aisle beside them. All along the walls torches flickered and shone.

"Sleep here this night," Calan said. "You need safety after all this, not more travel."

"We're most grateful," Aurelia said, offering thanks when it became clear Tarlak would not.

Calan handed them a few more pillows, then turned to Jerico. A smile emerged on his face, his tiredness and worry unable to hold it back.

"Praise be to Ashhur," he said. "Another paladin lives."

Jerico stood and bowed to the High Priest.

"My name is Jerico of the Citadel. I offer you my mace and my shield, should you ever need them."

"I pray not," Calan said. "How did you survive?"

As Jerico began his story, Lathaar slid beside Harruq and Aurelia. The elf was curled into his arms, her head resting on his chest. She looked asleep, but he knew she wasn't. The half-orc nodded in acknowledgment. He opened his mouth to say something, then stopped.

"I spoke with Keziel, the head cleric of the Sanctuary," Lathaar began.

"Don't worry about it," Harruq interrupted.

"I'm sorry, Harruq, but he…what happened? Is Aullienna alright?"

Aurelia stirred. She put her fingers against Harruq's lips to keep him from speaking.

"She drowned," the elf said, her voice soft and sad. "Brug is dead as well. Tessanna killed him."

The paladin's jaw clenched tight as he held back his anger. He could see the pain in Harruq's eyes, and he knew any condemnation against Qurrah would only worsen it.

"I'm sorry," he said.

Meanwhile, Jerico had finished his story and Calan had more pressing matters to attend. Tarlak remained silent and dejected. His face looked ashen. His eyes fixated on the floor. The priest knelt beside him.

"She is not dead," Calan whispered. "And I don't say this to offer some meager comfort amid your grief. The spell cast upon her is brutal, yes, but it does not kill the host. The Doru'al will use her life to cling to this world. If we act fast…"

"Enough!" Tarlak looked up. His eyes were red, and tears welled up, ready to fall.

"I know she can be saved," he said. "You think I don't know that? You think I don't cling to that hope? But right now she is helpless while the most vile and horrific thoughts are rammed into her mind by the demon that possesses her. Even if we save her, she might never be the same."

"You're wrong," Mira said. She had remained quiet ever since entering the temple, but now she stood, her shyness shedding away. "The suffering we go through does not change who we are, only reveal our true self. If you love her, then you will have your sister back once more."

Tarlak stood, taking his blanket with him. He looked around at the priests and the Eschaton, an angry defiance raging within.

"I may not grieve for her death," he said. "But I can grieve for her suffering. Now leave me be."

He moved to the other side of the chamber, wrapped himself in the white blankets, and did his best to sleep. Calan chewed on his lower lip as he watched the mage go, then stood and addressed the rest.

"Get some sleep. You all need it, and as do I."

With that he left for his own bedchamber. Exhausted and troubled, the rest of the Eschaton did their best to sleep.

Miles away, a shape blacker than the night fled west through the forest, guided by the whispers of the dark god. Deep within the shade, Delysia wordlessly screamed.

13

One day from Veldaren. One day, and Qurrah couldn't find Tessanna. He searched the camps where the wolf-men slept, but she was not there. He searched the legions of orc tents, but she was not there. He searched the tight packs the hyena-men slept and ate in. She was not there. At last he asked Velixar.

"She needs time," Velixar said. "Will you give it to her?"

He sighed and said he would.

"Good," the man in black said. "Wait until nightfall, then head south. Follow the stream. Trust me, Qurrah. It is for the best."

Qurrah had seen Velixar and Tessanna talking over the past weeks as they marched through the Vile Wedge collecting their armies. Some joined willingly, some did not, but the numbers of their soldiers and the power of their magic destroyed any who resisted.

The army began its march, but Qurrah stayed at Velixar's request. For a moment he felt panic seeing his army leave without him. He knew Velixar needed him, though, just as he needed Velixar. In the sudden calm that filled the army's departure, his fears and his doubts were free to torment him.

He knew he would meet his brother in conflict. The Eschaton would not let the city fall without a fight. Did he wish his brother dead? What about Tarlak and Delysia, who had taken him in? An image flashed before his eyes. It was of Harruq, his skin pale and his eyes lifeless. He was just one of hundreds, marching mindlessly to his command. Or was it Velixar's command? He didn't know. He didn't know if it mattered. Either way, the image churned his stomach and filled him with dread.

Night came. He followed the stream south. The moon was bright, and even without his orcish blood he would have had little trouble seeing. He had spent so much time with the army he had forgotten how much he enjoyed the quiet solitude of the stars. He kept his thoughts calm and controlled as he walked. He wanted to think of nothing. Once Karak was freed he could be gone from the worries, the fear, and the guilt Dezrel inflicted upon him. He would go where his brother never existed, and none would ever know the atrocities they had done or the murder they shared.

An owl hooted twice, and when he looked up to search for it he saw the pond. It was almost too large to call a pond, the banks stretching for hundreds of feet. The water was crystalline and beautiful. The surface was calm so that the moon and stars shone elegant upon the water. Standing before the pond, her arms at her side and her back to him, was Tessanna.

"Sometimes I remember life before you," Tessanna said. "All those nights." Qurrah nodded but said nothing. He did not understand what was going on, but he could feel the significance.

"Many nights were cold or lonely. Sometimes I had bodies for warmth, but always the night stayed cold. But there were good nights, Qurrah. I want you to know that."

She turned to face him. Her arms were crossed, and she looked so young.

"Since I've been with you I've known hurt," she said. "I thought I couldn't hurt anymore, but I have. I never thought I would ever need someone so much it'd scare me. But I do."

She uncrossed her arms. With slow, small movements, she let her dress fall to the ground, exposing her naked flesh.

"I love you," Qurrah said. "Everything I do, it's because…"

"I know," she said. "This body is yours, Qurrah. Many have had it, but tonight…" Gently she traced her fingers down her neck, past the curve of her breasts, and to her belly. "Tonight is special. Take off your clothes."

He did. His heart pounded in his ears. She was so beautiful, but what was going on? He felt he was swimming in power and drowning in magic.

"I want you to know I can live without you," she said as she dipped a foot into the pond. "I would hate every second, but I would live. Not after tonight. Velixar has given me something I never thought I could have."

She stopped walking when the water was up to her waist. She reached out a hand and beckoned him. In the dead of winter, he knew he should be cold. He knew his frail body would shiver and break in the water. But the water was warm to his touch. The sense of magic swarming around him thickened. At Tessanna's beckon, he embraced her.

"Tonight," she whispered into his ear. "Tonight, under these stars, in this water, I can conceive. Will you give this to me? Will you give this of yourself?"

He had never believed such a thing possible. But as she wrapped her legs around him and guided him into her, he knew the answer. Aullienna's face flashed before his mind. He had taken her from Tessanna, and tonight, he might somehow make amends.

"After what I have done," he said as his breaths quickened. "Of course I will."

Standing within the water they made love. Their movements were slow, careful. At last she wrapped her arms around him and pulled him below the surface, baptizing them in the name of Velixar and Karak. When he tore his head above the water and screamed out in ecstasy, he felt the eyes of gods upon him. His lover emerged with him, gasping in pleasure. A twinkle was in her eye. The act was done.

Tessanna was with child.

They elected to walk back to Velixar and the army. Qurrah felt he was exiting a dream. The cold of the wind came biting back, and he shivered underneath his layers of clothing. No matter how close to a fire he sat, or how much clothing he wore, he always felt cold in winter. Tessanna did not complain or show discomfort, but her lips were blue and her teeth chattered with each step. Despite all this, they wanted to walk. They needed to talk.

"Velixar offered this to me," she said, answering the question she knew her lover kept unspoken. "He said Karak knew my prayers though I never sent them to him. He told me to travel to the pond and wait for you there. If I offered myself to you, and to the dark god, I would have a child. A daughter." She looked to him, tears streaming down her face though her voice remained firm.

"I've always wanted a daughter," she said.

"I'm not ready to be a father," he said. "Our life, our actions...what will become of any child following our footsteps?"

She took his hand into hers and kissed his fingers.

"By the time I give birth, we will be gone from here. Our daughter can live a life free of this place. I can give her the childhood I was denied." She looked to the stars and giggled. "Mommy isn't happy with me right now, and she isn't happy with Karak, either."

"Will you still be able to aid me and Velixar in opening the doorway?" he asked her. To this she turned and glared.

"I am not weak now," she said, a sudden venom filling her words. "Never think that of me."

"I didn't," Qurrah said. "I just...wait a moment. Something approaches."

He stopped her, then narrowed in his eyes in the darkness. He saw a shape running toward them. It was humanoid, though its body was hunkered down so he could not see much else. Tessanna lifted her hand so that fire swirled from her fingers.

"Unbelievable," she said, licking her lips. "Karak has sent us a gift."

The shape slowed once it reached the edge of light created by Tessanna's fire. It was a being of pure shadow, its ethereal presence swirling like black smoke in the darkness. Glowing red slits for eyes leered at them. When the creature snarled rows of sharp teeth glistened.

"What is this thing," Qurrah asked.

Tessanna's hand closed, and the fire vanished. In only the starlight, the creature was free to approach. It stood directly before them and growled softly. Qurrah felt his skin crawl at the sound.

"I know this scent," Tessanna said, her hand creeping toward the thing's neck. "I know this body." The shadow being retreated before her hand, shriveling back like a snake shedding its skin. Qurrah startled at the revealed face and neck of Delysia Eschaton. She looked catatonic. Tessanna rubbed her neck with her fingers, then pressed them against her lips.

"I love the taste," she said, licking her fingers. With her other hand she drew her dagger. "The purity of her blood."

"What are you doing?" Qurrah asked. The girl turned to him and beamed. The wildness in her eyes horrified him.

"Isn't it clear? Karak gives me a child, so I take a child from Ashhur. She is a gift, a sacrifice, an omen. Choose whatever sounds best to you."

Tessanna stunned him by leaning forward and kissing Delysia's lips. Her dagger trailed upward, drawing a thin red line from the bottom of Delysia's neck to the cleft of her chin. She licked the blood from her dagger and giggled.

"I could get used to this."

"Enough," Qurrah said. "Send her back."

"Why?" she asked. "Do you care for her? She worships a false god, and even worse, lets such a perfect body go to waste."

The half-orc grabbed her wrist and held it firm. He glared at her, every part of his being refusing to back down.

"You have killed enough of those close to my brother," he said. "No more."

He was not prepared for the rage that seethed inside his lover. When she spoke her voice was calm, but her entire body shook and quivered.

"I have killed?" she said. "Is that how you see it? I killed Brug. It was my desire, my idea, that killed Aullienna. Is it? Is that how you sleep at night? Is that how you banish your guilt, by casting it to me?"

She yanked her arm free from his grasp. The love they shared just an hour ago seemed ancient and lost to Qurrah. Even worse, her words tore at his guilt-wracked mind. Again he thought of an undead Harruq marching at his command and felt his heart split.

"You don't understand," he began, but Tessanna cut him off by thrusting the hilt of her dagger into his open palm.

"Take it," she said. "Take it and listen. We are condemned by our actions, or we are free of them. We are murderers, or we are victims. You will kill again. Will you feel its guilt only for those you know? A life taken is a life taken, Qurrah. Will you succumb to guilt or not?"

He closed his hand around the dagger and looked to the imprisoned Delysia.

"I don't know," he said. "I don't feel guilt, I just...I don't want to hurt my brother. Not any more than I already have, even if he hurts me."

She slipped behind him, her hands trailing around his neck and shoulders.

"But the choice is the same for him," she whispered. "If he had never chosen his lover over you, then the hurt would never be. He chose his path. He chose his hurt. Will you be slave to it?"

He looked at Delysia's beautiful frozen horrified face. She was alive inside, he knew. He could smell her fear. His fist clenched tight.

"Be gone," he said, waving his hand. The essence of the Doru'al shrieked in anger but could not refuse the power of his words or the magic that spiked from his fingers. The girl collapsed as the rest of the darkness dissipated. Delysia gasped in air, her eyes locked open. The half-orc stood over her, dagger in hand. The hand shook.

"How many times," he said. "How many times must I question myself? How many times must I doubt the path I walk? How many? How many!"

The priestess coughed once, then blinked. Her fingers clutched the grass, a reflex as the woman gulped in air.

"I will not," he said. His heart was in his throat. He felt his soul quivering. "I will not do this anymore."

He knelt down, pulled Delysia's head up by her hair, and then sliced open her throat. Blood poured over his hands and onto the grass. She made no sound as she stared at him with eyes that were full of despair. He stared right back as deep inside him he felt something die. He dropped her head to the dirt and then looked to the dagger in his hand.

"There," Tessanna said as she wrapped her arms around his neck. "Now the blood is on both our hands, as it always should have been."

"A life for a life," he said, mesmerized by the crimson droplets dripping from the edge. "Will it be enough?"

The darkness swirled around them, then collected into a doorway that Velixar stepped through. Qurrah knelt at his entrance while Tessanna curtseyed. The man in black eyed the body, then clapped his hands together.

"All as I hoped," he said. He knelt and touched the body. Shadows lifted it from the ground. They took shape, becoming a long-legged, spindly-armed creature without eyes or a mouth. The thing held Delysia's body in its arms and sprinted east with blinding speed. Velixar bade his disciple to rise.

"A man dear to me passed away this night," he said. "And now they will suffer in turn. You are strong, Qurrah, and you grow stronger still. Come. Your army awaits."

"My army," he muttered. He clutched the dagger tight with both hands and looked at his master. "Please. Take us to my army."

Another portal of shadow opened. Velixar stepped through, followed by Tessanna. Out of sight, Qurrah finally let the tears free. He wanted to kneel and beg for his brother to forgive him, but instead he placed the dagger underneath his right eye and slashed downward. He screamed. His tears mixed with blood. Before he lost his nerve, he placed the dagger underneath his left eye and did the same.

"I will not cry for you anymore, brother," he told the darkness. "Let my tears mix with blood so I may remember this vow."

He slid the bloody weapon into the sash of his robe and stepped through. Neither Tessanna nor Velixar asked about the wounds upon his face. It was if, somehow, they understood.

Harruq awoke with a screaming headache and a throbbing pain in his side. He guessed the headache to be from hunger and exhaustion, and the pain from the hilt of his sword digging into his side. He rubbed his eyes and looked about. The rest of the Eschaton were asleep on the pews. A few torches flickered and died, bathing him in darkness.

Tun...

The half-orc spun, for the voice had come from behind. Nothing, just a closed door. He thought perhaps it was Haern testing him, but he was curled up in a bundle of gray robes beside Aurelia. It wasn't Tarlak either, for the mage slept in the far corner, twitching and shifting as if trapped in unpleasant dreams.

Betrayer...

He drew his swords. Their red light seemed demonic in the holy place. Harruq debated waking the others. So few would call him betrayer. Only Qurrah...

He felt a shiver crawl up his spine. There was another who would label him as such.

Do you suffer yet?

He knew that voice. That cold feeling. The man in black had returned.

"Show yourself," Harruq whispered. He stood in the aisle between the pews, constantly spinning and searching.

Listen to me, Harruq Tun. You can avoid more pain. You can avoid more suffering. Take your lover and go.

"What is it you want?" Harruq asked the silence. "What is it that brought you back from the abyss where you belonged?"

You lost a daughter. Do not lose more. You can still come to my fold. You can join your brother and fight at his side. Do not let pain cloud your judgment.

The half-orc approached the giant doors to the temple. His armor creaked, and he kept waiting for someone to wake from his noise. None did.

"I am not what you wanted," he whispered. "I am not what you tried to make me be. You failed, Velixar, and damn me for letting Qurrah fail with you."

My life for you. That was your promise. If you deny me what was promised, then I must take it from another, and another, until your life is either mine or ended. There is no other way. You and your friends killed one dear to me. I have done so in kind. Suffer, Harruq Tun. Suffer in your betrayal.

The half-orc kicked open the door, swords raised to strike. Velixar was not there, only the cold body of Delysia. His blood froze. His swords fell from his hands, and their loud ringing upon hitting the stone awoke the others. He staggered back, slamming the door shut to block the sight. He fell to his knees, his hands digging into his face. Her throat was cut, her clothes torn...but most damning was the single word carved across her forehead.

Tun.

"What's going on," Haern asked, the first to reach his side. When Harruq did not answer, he pushed open the door. All time halted for the assassin. He did not move. He did not breath. When time resumed, he sheathed his blades and knelt beside her body. He lifted her into his arms and carried her inside. The others were waking, each stirring from a deep sleep. Harruq kept his eyes shut, hating his brother more than he had ever hated someone in his life. And then he heard Tarlak's cry.

"What happened," he heard him shout. "No, she's alright she...she..."

He opened his eyes at the sound of Tarlak's weeping. Somehow the torches had been relit. Delysia lay on the floor before Tarlak's curled form. Aurelia was at his side, her arms around him. He accepted the embrace and buried his face into her bosom. Haern stood by them, tears on his face. Even Mira cried, overwhelmed by the sorrow her keen mind drank in from the room. Only the paladins remained firm.

"Hear me, Tarlak," Lathaar said, kneeling beside Delysia's body. "There is no emptiness in my words, only truth and compassion. She has gone to a place beyond our suffering. She dwells in a land foreign to our tears. Everything we feel, we feel for ourselves."

"My sister," Tarlak sobbed. "My only sister..."

Lathaar took her body into his arms and stood.

"Ashhur gave her life, and now he has taken that life back to his arms."

He carried her outside. Tarlak followed at Aurelia's insistence. Harruq stayed where he was. When the wizard cast his eyes to him he dared not meet them. When the door slammed shut, the half-orc thought himself alone. He was not.

"Get up." Harruq looked up to see Jerico standing over him, his arms crossed. "I said get up."

"Leave me be," Harruq grumbled.

Jerico struck his fist against the half-orc's face. The pain flared his anger, and he glared death at the paladin.

"What the abyss is the matter..."

"It is one thing to mourn," Jerico said. "But you aren't mourning. You're drowning yourself in guilt and grief. That was your name carved upon her forehead, wasn't it?" Harruq's look was answer enough. "Why, then? What is the meaning behind it? Answer me."

"A long time ago, me and Qurrah swore our lives to Karak," he said. He didn't want to, but he couldn't stop staring at Jerico's eyes. They imprisoned him. "I turned my back on Karak when I fell in love with Aurelia. Qurrah fell in love with a girl named Tessanna. Aurry pulled me away from the darkness, but Tess just pulled Qurrah further and further in."

"Tessanna is the other daughter of balance," Jerico asked.

Harruq shrugged. "Don't know what you're talking about."

"No matter," the paladin said. "Another time. So now Karak tortures you for your choice? He does not take kindly to those who escape his grasp. You may be just one life, but just as Ashhur celebrates with every soul that welcomes him into their heart, so too does Karak fume with each loss."

"Brug, Delysia, Aullienna..." Harruq shook his head. "How many will he take? How many will suffer for my sins?"

"None will, and none have," Jerico said. "Your sins haven't earned you the pain you feel. It is the good in your life. Karak could not hurt those you love without you loving them in the first place. Would you sacrifice everything good just to avoid your pain?"

"I've slain children," Harruq said, confessing though he knew not why. "And when my daughter was killed, I thought it punishment for my crimes."

"And so you felt the burden yours," Jerico said, finishing the thought. "Will you let every good deed you perform be overshadowed by your past? If so, there is no point. Go join your brother. Join Karak. But if you wish your sins forgotten, join us with Ashhur and accept the grace he freely offers. The darkness in your life is caused by others, not the past you seek atonement from."

Harruq fiddled with his swords, uncomfortable and confused. "You make it sound so easy," he said.

A bit of the hardness left Jerico's face.

"Trust me. It's a heavy burden, but I do not carry it alone. I'll be outside. You should help bury her. It is only right."

The paladin left Harruq alone in the chamber of worship. In the silence, he thought over Jerico's words. They did seem too easy, too simple. But how many days had he spent with the Eschaton without guilt, fear, or condemnation of his past? It seemed only his brother obsessed over who they had been. Qurrah never believed people could change. Perhaps that was why he seemed so alien to him now.

"If you're listening," Harruq whispered. "Help me figure this out."

It was the closest thing to a prayer he had made since the death of his daughter.

⋈

For a moment Haern and Tarlak wearily argued for an Eschaton burial, but Lathaar would hear none of it.

"You've buried enough," he had said to the wizard. "Let me bear the burden."

Lathaar carried her in his arms while the others followed him to the western wall. Two nervous guards stood before it.

"Open the gate," Tarlak said in a cracking voice. He produced his sigil showing his allegiance with the King. "Now."

The guards obeyed.

"They're just on edge after the spell cast over the city," Lathaar said as they exited the city. "I'd wager that they cowered and hid every time the lion in the sky roared."

They didn't go far. West off the road was a large common grave. In its center was a stone slab for those who preferred the burning of bodies to burial. Lathaar picked a spot on the edge of the grounds and nodded.

"There."

They had no tools to dig. Instead Aurelia raised her hands and whispered a spell. The dirt shook and cracked. A perfect slab rose into the air, hovered a moment, and then broke into tiny pieces. Lathaar set her body within the grave and shook his head at Aurelia.

"No magic for this part," he said. "Our hands will suffice."

Silence overcame them as each looked down at the still body. The word Tun glared out at them from her forehead. Disgusted, Mira took a handful of dirt and blew. White sparkles filled her breath. The dirt flew to the letters, smoothing and compressing until a thin layer covered them. Harruq was grateful, but when he opened his mouth to thank her he found it dry and uncooperative.

"It's always my job to say something," Tarlak said. Every bit of his being fought to collect itself, to toughen against his pain. It was a monumental effort, and all there could see the will within him was strong. Even so, Aurelia gently placed her hand on his lips and kissed his cheek.

"Not this time," she whispered.

Jerico and Lathaar exchanged looks. Jerico was the older, and by tradition was to speak at a burial, but Lathaar had known Delysia in person. Familiarity won out over tradition.

"All of us here," Lathaar began. "Every one of us knows how to kill. Every one of us has. But Delysia was a healer. What we accomplished through strength and magic, she did through love and kindness. As we made a better place through our sword and fire, she made a better place by her forgiveness and compassion. She touched each one of us, and saved so many. While we may harden our hearts against the world for her passing, may each one of us remember that the strength of her love and conviction is no less weakened, nor voided, by her death."

He took a handful of dirt and let it fall into the grave.

"She is with Ashhur now. Finish the burial."

When the last of the dirt filled the grave, Lathaar stabbed two thick branches into the earth, forming a simple triangle. Somber and exhausted, the Eschaton lingered, unsure of what to do. It was Haern who broke the silence, and it was a sentiment Harruq recognized. Harm had befallen them, and he wanted vengeance.

"I can lead us to the priests," he said. His sabers were already drawn. "We have tolerated their presence long enough."

"Delysia would not approve," Tarlak said.

"I do not share that sentiment," the assassin said.

Their leader glanced around, gauging everyone's feelings. He had denied retribution against Qurrah, and for that Aullienna and Brug had died. He had denied retribution against the dark priests, and now his sister lay buried before him. Could he do it again?

"My heart is not ready for battle," he said at last. "Not this night. But we will." He stared straight at the assassin and promised.

"We will."

Mira wandered amid the graveyard, her eyes closed and her arms outstretched. Her aimlessness reminded Harruq so much of Tessanna as he watched her. Her back was to him, so he could not see the horrible pain across her face. Only when Lathaar called her name did they see her torment.

"Too soon," she said. "They're too soon."

"What do you mean, dear?" Aurelia asked.

She pointed west. They followed her gaze, and there they saw the faint line of torches lining the horizon. Aurelia gasped, for her eyes were far keener than the others.

"An army," she said, as if she herself could not believe it. "Thousands strong. What devilry is this?"

Lathaar and Jerico exchanged a glance. They had not revealed their failure yet, but it seemed they had no choice.

"Qurrah has Darakken's spellbook," Lathaar said. He winced at the ashen look that covered Tarlak's face. "Please. I'm sorry. He attacked the Sanctuary and stole it from the hearth."

"It's not Qurrah," Harruq said, stealing attention away from the paladin condemning his brother. "It's Velixar. That's his army. He's done this before, several years ago."

"Doesn't matter who," Tarlak interrupted. "The priests were there to soften the city for the attack, and they did a damn good job, too. Do what you can. That army will be here by the dawn."

Haern grabbed Tarlak's arm and stopped his casting of a portal.

"Where are you going?" he asked.

"To warn Antonil," Tarlak said, glaring at the hand on his arm. "And then grab a moment of rest. I'll be worthless without it."

He yanked his arm free and finished his spell. He entered the swirling blue portal without another word. The rest watched him go.

"I'll start rallying troops," Jerico said, glancing back to the city. "We might have a chance if we hold the two gates. Karak's image in the sky will have shaken most of the guard's faith. We need to restore it."

"Ashhur be with us all," Lathaar said, bowing to the others. The two paladins ran back to the city. Mira followed.

"You both will be needed," Haern said, running a hand through his hair. "We've all seen what your brother and his lover can do. If Velixar is with them, even the city's walls will not be enough to protect us."

Harruq said nothing. Aurelia wrapped her arms around his waist and held him close as the assassin left. The two stared at the line of torches in the dark, Aurelia filled with worry, and Harruq with guilt.

"My brother," he said. "Because of my brother…"

"And therein lies the blame," Aurelia said. "Not you."

"Easy words. How many will die tonight?"

Aurelia pulled on his shoulder and forced his eyes to meet hers. She was a living blessing in the moonlight, a beautiful creature hundreds of years old and filled with grace and wonder. And she kissed the simple, plain man she loved.

"Not us," she said. "And remember which side of the walls you are on. You will fight to save, not to kill. Now come."

She took his hand and led him back to the city.

Tarlak closed the portal immediately after exiting, not wanting anyone to follow. While he had said he was going to speak with Antonil, he had instead sent himself to the Eschaton tower. With a wave of his hand, he opened the front door and rushed inside. The others had been too focused on Aurelia's description of what she saw to notice he had cast a divination spell. He had seen wolf-men, hyena-men, bird-men, orcs and goblins, all marching in unison. Not since the original days of the brothers' war had such an army existed.

He came to the Eschaton tower because he expected never to return.

His room was first. Tarlak scooped up scrolls from his shelves and tossing them into his hat, which seemed to never fill. He went to Delysia's room next, wincing at all the signs of the life. He took a few pieces of jewelry Brug had made for her and then closed the door. He skipped Haern's room, knowing the assassin always kept everything he needed close on person. Outside Harruq and Aurelia's room he paused, thinking of what they might want from within.

"Might as well check," he said, and placed his hand on the door only to realize it was ajar. His hair stood on end, and somehow he knew it was no accident or happenstance. Slowly he pushed it open, thankful it was well-oiled as to not creak.

Sitting with her legs curled underneath her was Tessanna, gently running her hand through the illusory grass Aurelia had created with her magic. With the door open he could hear her softly singing. His hands trembled. Brug had died by her dagger, and all the while she had laughed. Laughed. Her back was to him.

Helpless, he thought. Power swelled into his hands, begging for release. He held it in. Something was too sad about the scene, and then he heard crying.

"I'm sorry, Aully," he heard her say. "Big dog's coming, and he's coming for you..."

Her grief was so great he felt like an intruder in his own tower. Where was the simplicity he had felt only minutes ago? His hands lowered, and the magic around them faded away.

A piece of bone pressed against the back of his neck. He tensed, and his heart leapt as he heard raspy breathing from behind.

"A life for a life," Qurrah whispered. "You spared her, so I spare you."

The bone piece left. When Tarlak turned around, Qurrah stared at him with arms crossed and his whip in hand. The bone hovered in orbit around his head like a morbid halo. Two scars ran down the side of his face, angry and red. His tears have become acid, Tarlak thought. The contempt and vileness he saw in Qurrah's eyes made it seem almost possible.

"We've seen your army," the wizard whispered. "Do you come to conquer, or destroy?"

"You'll fight me either way," Qurrah responded. "So that is an answer you don't need. Your city is doomed. Tell my idiot brother to flee while he still can."

Tessanna heard their talking and stood. She smiled back to Tarlak even though tears ran down her cheeks.

"You know he won't," she said, answering for him. "Which makes it all the sadder. Tell them I'm sorry, too. But I will kill all of you if I must, as will Qurrah. Leave, Tarlak. Please, leave."

He walked down the stairs, slow and dignified. He would run from no one. When he reached the outside, he opened a portal to Veldaren. Thoughts raced through his head. Under no circumstances would he give their message to Harruq. He glanced back one last time at his home as a part of him realized why Qurrah and Tessanna had come back.

"You'll never have what they had," he said to the highest floor before stepping inside, unaware of the life already growing inside Tessanna's womb.

Antonil had slept poorly ever since the lion appeared in the sky. When its roar shook the city he had cowered like the rest of his soldiers, and the shame of it scarred his honor. Several hours had passed with him falling in and out of fitful sleep haunted by dreams of facing legions of dark shapes while he wielded only a broken sword. When the blue portal ripped open in his room, he lurched forward and grabbed his sword, which lay next to him on the bed.

"Easy," Tarlak said as he stepped out to find the tip near his throat. "It's just me, your local friendly wizard."

"Forgive me," Antonil said, putting the sword down. "I've just been edgy since, well...I'm sure you saw it."

"More than saw it," the mage said, his whole persona darkening. "Priests of Karak unleashed that blasphemy upon the sky. Delysia is dead. The priests killed her."

Antonil opened and closed his mouth. The grogginess in his head refused to clear, but piercing that grogginess was the gentle face and red hair of the priestess. His heart panged with guilt.

"We should have been there," he said. "My guards, my soldiers, we only cowered while you fought…"

"It doesn't matter," Tarlak interrupted. "What matters is that an army marches toward the city, almost ten thousand strong."

"Orcs?" the guard captain asked.

"Yes," Tarlak said. "But also hyena-men and wolf-men. Even bird-men march alongside. This'll make the orc attack several years ago look like child's play."

Antonil rubbed his thumb and forefinger against his eyelids.

"Are you sure?" he asked as he blinked away the rest of his sleepiness.

"No, I just enjoy waking people in the middle of the night and scaring them. Yes, I'm sure! Get your guards stationed, wake up every man who owns a sword, and then put them before the gates!"

Antonil leapt from his bed, still wearing the underpadding of his armor. He put the rest of his gold-tinted armor on in mere moments, buckling and strapping it on as he talked.

"If they aren't equipped with siege weaponry, then they're going to throw their numbers against the gates and see if it'll break. If we position enough weight on the other side, and place archers…"

"You don't understand," Tarlak said. He stepped back as Antonil swung an arm around, nearly clobbering him in the head in his attempt to fasten a buckle near the back of his waist. His room was well furnished but still small. Only the king had a gigantic room for his own inside the castle.

"The man in black, the necromancer who commanded the orcs that last attack…he leads this one as well."

Antonil paused, his sword belt in mid buckle.

"Are you sure?" he asked. Tarlak rolled his eyes.

"Didn't I answer that already?"

"Last time that man shook our walls with his sorcery," Antonil said. "He destroyed the western gate as if it were made of sticks and mud. Are you telling me that same man marches against our town with five times the numbers?"

Now it was Tarlak's turn to rub his eyes with his fingers.

"Did our great guard captain develop a hearing problem over the last five minutes?"

Antonil buckled his belt and sheathed his sword. He took his shield off a rack and slung his arm through the two straps. At last he donned his helmet. He looked regal and deadly in the golden hue.

"I must alert the king," he said.

"Send someone else," Tarlak said. "We need you at the walls."

"If anyone else tells him but me," Antonil said, a strange hardness in his eyes, "he will not believe them."

"So be it. The Eschaton will help you, but we will not follow the orders of the king." He grabbed the man's arm as he turned to leave. "Antonil," he said. "There is a very real possibility the city will fall. They do not march to occupy. They will kill every one of us, some even eating our remains. If that will happen…abandon the city. Please."

The guard captain pulled his arm free of his grasp.

"I will obey my king," he said. He left to visit the king's private bed chambers. Tarlak swore as he paced the small room.

"Everyone has to make things so bloody complicated," he said as crossed his arms and glared at the floor. If Antonil followed the king's orders, not a soul would be allowed to flee. He'd bury everyone in his paranoia and selfishness. Ever since the elven assassin had taken his left ear…

"To the abyss with it all," Tarlak said. "I just want to burn stuff."

He opened a portal to the city walls and stepped through.

14

At first the soldiers barred them from the walls, but then Haern showed them his sigil.

"My apologies, Watcher of the King," one of the soldiers said, offering a clumsy bow. He moved away from the stone steps, letting them pass. Haern led the way, followed by the paladins. All along the wall, soldiers prepared arrows and readied armor. Jerico guessed at the numbers, and was none too pleased with his estimate.

"There can't be more than three hundred," he said. Haern nodded as he scanned the horizon. They were above the western gate, which was sure to take the brunt of the attack. He watched the sea of torches marching closer, his stomach hardening.

"The king lost too many to the orcs' siege, and then the elves at Woodhaven," Haern said. "Three hundred archers and two thousand footmen are all he commands."

"Rumors say it's more than just orcs coming," a soldier beside them said. He looked old and grizzled. Neither paladin was familiar with Veldaren's military ranks but the man was clearly not of a lower station.

"Do they?" Lathaar asked.

"The whole Wedge is coming, the wolf and bird and hyena." The man nodded towards the torches, both his hands gripping his bow tight. He was missing two of his fingers on his left hand.

"And where did you hear this?" Jerico asked.

"That man," the soldier said, pointing farther south along the wall. It was still dark, but in the torchlight Tarlak's pointy yellow hat stood out above the metal and armor.

"Excuse me," Haern said, slipping past and chasing after. He found Tarlak cheering and slapping archers on the backs and arms, encouraging as only he could.

"Kill twenty of those orcs and I'll polymorph your mother-by-marriage into a goat," he said. "Fifty, and I'll make her a toad! Hate your hair? Hate your face? I'll change it too, only fifteen kills each. Oh, you sir, I'll even give you a discount, since you're nose is so..."

"Tarlak," Haern said, grabbing the wizard and turning him about. "We need to talk."

"Howdy Haern," Tarlak said, grinning at him. "Ready for some mindless slaughter?"

"I hear there are more than orcs coming," the assassin whispered. "What did you see?"

His grin faded, but when he saw others looking at him and perked right up.

"When they hit the walls they're all yours," Tarlak shouted. "So don't have too much fun as they pretend they can climb with their bare hands!"

He leaned in next to Haern and whispered, "All races of the Wedge, Haern. Every blasted mongrel. We're outnumbered ten to one."

The assassin grabbed him by the collar and yanked him closer.

"They will bury us," he whispered back. "The whole city will burn."

"Then we'll burn with it," Tarlak whispered. "Scared of a little fun, Haern? Besides, you're worth a couple hundred kills. I'm good for a few hundred as well. Aurry, Lathaar, Jerico...how many can Mira handle? We're their hope, their only chance, and I will not let us descend into cowardice and retreat. Now go back to the west gate and cause chaos like I know you can. That's an order."

"Yes, Lord Eschaton," Haern said, his voice and subsequent bow filled with sarcasm. He returned to the paladins and drew them close so others would not hear.

"Twenty thousand against our two, according to Tarlak."

Both nodded, neither appearing surprised.

"To the ground," Jerico said. "I will defend the west gate if it breaks. The troops there will need me."

Lathaar drew his swords, their glow shining bright in the night.

"I'll be there with you. I was not there at the Sanctuary. I will make amends."

Mira grabbed Lathaar's hand and squeezed it tight.

"I'll stay here," she said. "And I'll do what I can. They won't be ready for me."

"No one ever is," Lathaar said.

He kissed her cheek and joined Jerico and Haern down the stairs. Mira, a tiny, diminutive figure amid the bustling soldiers, waved. She looked so out of place, the man with missing fingers put his hand on her shoulder and asked her to seek shelter.

"No," she said, a bit of fire sparking in her eyes. "I'm here to protect you."

The soldier let her be, and if any raised eyebrows or gestured toward her, he only shook his head and sent them on their way.

Harruq and Aurelia stationed themselves at the southern gate, using a portal to get up top. At first the soldiers there startled and drew their swords, but a glare from the half-orc sent them back.

"Get to work," he growled. "We're here to help, and you best like it."

"Such a silver tongue for a brute," Aurelia said. She smiled and poked his side. "Save the gruff. It's going to be a long night."

"You mean day." The half-orc pointed east, where the first glimmer of sunrise pierced the sky. "It's already been a long night."

The distant army grew closer, the glow of the torches stronger. Aurelia watched, her brow wrinkled.

"Orcs see perfectly in the dark," she wondered. "Why do they carry torches?"

"Velixar's making them do it," Harruq replied, gripping his sword hilts for comfort. "Has to be. It's the fear, the numbers. Same for that damn lion in the sky. If he had his way, we'd throw open the gates the second he got here and beg him to command us."

"His priests failed," Aurelia said. "As will he."

"And if not?"

The elf crossed her arms and frowned at her husband.

"Alright mister, enough of that." She gestured to the soldiers about her, scared and exhausted. "For their sake," she said, her voice quieter.

He nodded and kept the rest of his fears silent. His mood brightened a bit when Tarlak appeared walking along the walls, slapping and joking with every archer along the way. When he reached the two, he smiled and tipped his hat.

"Ready for an orc roast of epic proportions?" he asked.

"More ready than I thought," Harruq said, smiling in spite of it all. "Good to have you here, Tar."

"Same for you," the wizard said, the joy and foolishness in his eyes bleeding away. His whole body was trembling. It seemed the specter of Delysia hovered behind his eyes, just waiting for him to break. The smile returned. With greater strength than Harruq could imagine, Tarlak pushed the ghosts away.

"It does mean a lot, you know," the wizard said.

"We know," Aurelia said. "You're a good friend."

"Aye," Harruq said, his hands latched tight around the hilts of his swords. Together the three waited for Karak's axe to fall upon their city.

The king slept in a bedchamber beside his throne room. Two guards stood beside the door, anxious and alert. The roars of the lion had scared them, and now they heard alarms of an orc army approaching. When Antonil pushed open the huge double doors to enter the throne room, the guards knew by his armor that the alarms were true.

He strode over to them and saluted.

"Wake the king," he ordered. The right guard tapped against the door. Antonil pushed him aside and slammed his fist against the thick wood.

"King Vaelor," he shouted. "Your majesty, you are needed."

He heard shuffling, then a clank of wood and metal as the lock was thrown open. The door crept open a crack.

"For what reason do you interrupt my sleep?" the king asked through the crack.

"My apologies," Antonil said after bowing. "An army comes, and I seek your council."

"Remain here until I am ready," his king commanded. The door slammed shut. Antonil opened his mouth to argue, then closed it. His blood boiled, and he slammed his shield against a wall, not caring that he dented it.

"Damn fool," he muttered.

His glare to the guards made it clear that repeating that outburst meant death. The two saluted, understanding perfectly.

Antonil paced before the door, seething as the time passed. He needed to be commanding his guards, positioning and rallying them into a fighting state. Instead he was stuck inside the castle, bereft of all news. Twenty minutes later, the king exited his bed chambers.

He wore armor made of gold. It was soft, impractical, but it looked beautiful in the torchlight, and Antonil knew that was what mattered to his liege. A garishly jeweled sword swung from a belt trimmed with silver. A red cape hung from his neck. Upon his head was the crown of Veldaren. It had once been a simple ring of gold with a ruby upon the front, but Vaelor had declared it unfitting of a true king, adding several large gems and rubies. Attached to the bottom of the crown was a veil of red silk, recently added to hide the loss of the king's left ear.

"Sir, your attire…" Antonil said.

"Is this not how a king should be dressed for battle?" Vaelor asked.

"My men have needed me," he argued. "Could you not have spoken with me before you dressed for…for battle?"

"Do you dare question your king?" Vaelor asked. He crossed his arms and frowned. He was not much older than Antonil, and when they were children training together they had been mistaken for brothers due to their similar looks. But now Antonil's face and hands were worn and calloused. The king lacked a single scar on his pampered skin. His beard was trimmed and hair neatly curled around his shoulders, not a strand too long or too short. Only his ear marred the image.

"No sir," Antonil said, bowing. "Forgive me, I am just worried. They are far more than I have ever faced. All the races of the Vile Wedge have allied against us. They will destroy every life in our fair city if we let them."

King Vaelor walked to his throne and sat down. "Do as you must," he said. "I trust you to keep our city safe."

"No, sir, you don't understand." Antonil stepped forward, his worry overcoming his discipline. "We have no troops mustered from the reaches of Neldar. The green castle, as well as all of the Hillocks, are most likely destroyed. If this were a siege, we could hold out for months. Lord Gandrem would ride the host of Felwood through the northern plains and crush our foes against our walls. So too would Lord Meren ride up from Angelport, a whole legion of his archers ready to feather our enemies."

Antonil knew he treaded on dangerous ground, but he had no choice but to continue. "But they will not," he said. "This is no siege. The beasts of the wedge will storm our walls. Our troops are weak in number and wholly unprepared. We should order the populous to ready a retreat. If one of the gates falls, we can…"

"What is this?" King Vaelor asked, his voice thundering in the empty throne room. "Retreat? You would surrender our walls to orcs and dogs? I will not be written into the history of our world as such a coward. Already Woodhaven has been lost to the elves because of your weakness. You will fight to the death to protect what we all hold dear. You have defeated the orcs once. You will do so again."

"It is not cowardice to think of protecting the commonfolk should we fail."

"But it is cowardice by failing those helpless before that battle was even begun!"

The guard captain turned away, his fury rising with the stinging mention of Woodhaven. He was arguing with his king. Had times truly sunk so low?

"Very well," he said, falling to one knee and bowing his head. "I will not fail you."

King Vaelor put his hand on Antonil's shoulder. "We will be praised in songs for ages to come after our victory this night," he said.

Antonil thought a funeral dirge was more likely. With his king's permission, he left to join his men.

When Antonil arrived at the western gate, he was immediately aware something was amiss. His generals had done well to position and defend during his absence, but they were all terrified. Even the grizzled old men who had fought many a battle appeared ready to cast aside their weapons. The guard captain bound up the steps and joined his archers, determined to find out the reason. When he saw the ocean of bodies approaching, he understood their fear.

Leading the army were the bird-men, clutching their torches in their clawed and misshapen hands. Long feathers stretched out from their forearms, a mockery of their lost ability to fly. Their heads were small, dominated by their giant beaks of all colors. Behind them were the wolf-men. They were bigger than the hyena-men, their skin gray and their bodies lean and muscular. Their backs were heavily curved, causing their long arms to drag near the ground. Their awkward walk vanished when they ran, their bodies balanced for running on all fours.

The hyena-men were the last of animal men, and their yipping was already reaching the city. They looked like smaller cousins of the wolf-men, except their skin was yellow and black and their legs better suited for walking and running upright. Then came the orcs, howling and waving their torches. Antonil frowned as he saw their banners. It was the lion standard of Karak.

"You're right to be afraid," a quiet voice told him. He glanced left to see Mira smiling at him with twinkling eyes. "But you needn't be. They haven't seen what I can do. Go down the stairs. The paladins are waiting for you."

"Paladins?"

He looked behind him, and sure enough he saw the telltale glow of white and blue. He gave one last strange look to the girl with black eyes and climbed back down from the wall.

"Paladins of Ashhur!" he shouted. Buried in the center of the hundreds of footmen lined before the gate shone two swords and a shield. "Come forth!"

Jerico and Lathaar knelt before the guard captain as the man approached.

"We come to offer our aid, and the aid of Ashhur," Lathaar said.

"If there was ever a time we needed Ashhur's aid, it is now," Antonil said. "But I thought only one remained."

"I hid, but no longer," Jerico answered. "I ask you let us fight alongside your men in defense of this city."

Antonil pointed to the locked and barred gate.

"I have heard stories of paladins fighting off hundreds before falling in death. Let's put those stories to the test. To the front."

"If the heathen creatures burst through, Ashhur's light will wait for them," Lathaar said as he stood. The two took their positions. Antonil watched them shouting and ordering around his men. The sun was rising, but darkness remained heavy in the hearts of his men. Fear was the weapon of Karak, and Antonil knew nothing turned aside that weapon better than a paladin.

"We will hold the gate," someone whispered into Antonil's ear. He didn't need to look to know who it was.

"If you are here as well, Haern, then I'm sure we will," Antonil said.

Archers and ground troops ready, the guard captain and his personal guards marched to the southern gate. They had half the ground troops but the gate was thinner and the street narrower. Antonil expected the strongest blows to fall against the west. When he arrived he saw his best general, Sergan, shouting with a voice rapidly approaching hoarseness.

"Greetings Sergan," Antonil said, saluting the old veteran. "Think we have a chance?"

"Compared to Woodhaven this will be a picnic," the man replied. "Long as we don't got elves shooting at us...hey, who the abyss taught you how to buckle a sword?"

Sergan stormed over to a young footman who appeared lost on how to strap his sword to his waist. The general grabbed it from him, flipped it around, buckled it tight, and returned to Antonil in the span of five seconds.

"It's always the simplest stuff," Antonil said, a grin on his face.

"Wasn't my trainee," Sergan grumbled. The two quieted as each looked to the men on the ground and walls and pondered the strength of their forces.

"Sergan..." Antonil began.

"We can hold," the general said. "Even if they send more than you're thinking, we'll hold."

"And if the gates fall?" Antonil asked.

"You mean like last time?"

The guard captain nodded. Sergan sighed and gestured wide with his hands.

"They won't find the going easy. Lead your men, and I'll lead mine. We'll hold. Believe it, and we'll do it."

"See you at the battle's end," Antonil said. He drew his sword and held it high, rallying the soldiers around him.

"A pint of ale for every man who beheads an orc!" he shouted. The men shouted back, but their cheers were hollow. After saluting Sergan, he sheathed his sword and marched back to the western gate.

When the last of the sun rose above the horizon, the priests of Karak made their presence known. They slipped out of the king's forest, garbed in their finest black robes. They formed a loose semicircle around the city with forty of their members. They spread their hands and faced Veldaren. They opened their mouths. A single, solid roar of a lion shook the city and filled all who heard with fear. Every third minute they released Karak's power into that roar, so that all within knew that a god himself had come to destroy.

Great master," the goblin said, groveling on his hands and knees as if Qurrah were a deity. "Men come to speak with you, and they kill orcs who say no."

"Where are they?" Qurrah asked.

"Leave us," Velixar told the goblin. "Our guests are here."

Marching through the horde of orcs were twenty-five knights arranged in rows of five. Their armor was black, their eyes were blacker, and waving from banners attached to their saddles was the skull of a lion. The half-orc glared, recognizing his new arrival.

"The priests herald our arrival," the centermost of the leading five said as he removed his helmet. "And now the last of the obedient are joined as one army."

"High Enforcer Carden," Velixar said, embracing the man after the dark paladin had dismounted. "It has been far too long."

"Aye, it has, prophet. And I am High Enforcer no longer. Krieger has assumed my mantle."

Krieger dismounted from the horse beside them and knelt.

"It is an honor to be at your side at the final purge," he said.

Velixar bade him rise. "The dark paladins have done far more than I in swaying hearts to the true god. It is I who is honored by your allegiance. The sun has risen, the walls are in view, and the great lion roars. The battle is ready to begin."

He turned to Qurrah, who along with Tessanna had remained quiet beside Velixar, wanting little to do with their new guests.

"Prepare the torches," he said to them. "Afterward, stay at my side."

"And us?" Krieger asked.

"Join the priests in their circle. Not a single soul is to escape. Let the lesser races shed their blood for Karak first."

The dark paladins rode out, their banners held high. They filled in gaps of the circle, and when the priests released the lions roar, they held their swords high and shouted the name of their god.

"When we start the fun!" boomed an intoxicated voice. Gumgog pushed his way through the orcs, using his club arm to beat senseless any who didn't move. His face was painted white, and on his chest was the skull of a lion. The orc lumbered up to Velixar and slammed his club to the ground.

"WHEN?" he roared.

"Calm yourself, Warmaster," Qurrah said, not giving Velixar a chance to speak. "Order the beast-men to raise high their torches. When the fire hits the city, order the bird-men to attack the western gate. You do know which is west, right?"

"Bwah hah hah!" Gumgog lifted his club arm and shifted his shoulder so he could point at the gate directly across from them. "That one. Gumgog drunk, and Gumgog want to kill, but me still know what is what. What about the south gate?"

"The hyena-men will assault that one," Velixar replied, grinning at Qurrah. "Keep the wolf-men back. Their use is later. When the gates fall, have Trummug unleash the horde."

"What Karak wants, Karak gets," the orc bellowed before turning around and beating his way back through the orc ranks. "Raise your torches!" he shouted throughout the army. "All of you, get them torches high!"

"Amusing orc," Velixar said, laughing. The fear wafting from the city was intoxicating, and by the smile on Qurrah's face he knew his disciple sensed it too. "Will you begin the assault on your own, or do you wish my help?"

"Let the first strike be mine," the half-orc said. "It is only just."

Tessanna kissed his cheek and stepped back, giving him room to cast his spell. The horde army completely surrounded the city, with the bird-men and hyena-men near their designated gates. They held their torches high as ordered. Qurrah closed his eyes and let the magic pour out. Dark words flowed across his tongue. He felt the torches in his mind, lighting his inner vision like stars across a sky. He grasped them as he would with a fist, except he used his power, his will, to command. The fires of the torches flared hot, blinding even in the morning light. With a triumphant cry he tore the fires into the sky.

They soared upward, yellow tails streaking after them as if they were comets. Hundreds upon hundreds dotted the blue, crackles of black within the heart of the flames signifying the dark magic that controlled them. With another cry, Qurrah sent them rushing toward Veldaren like a river of fire. They rained down upon the walls, the buildings, and the castle. Flesh, cloth, and wood blackened. The soldiers crossed their arms and ducked their heads. Screams lifted to the sky, first few but then many as the fires spread. Veldaren was burning.

Qurrah opened his eyes to witness the destruction of his spell. At his side, Tessanna slipped her hand back into his.

"Beautiful," she whispered into his ear.

The priests lifted their arms and opened their mouths. Karak's roar shook the city, this time angrier and ominous amidst the fire. Gumgog slammed the ground and roared for his army to attack. The bird-men squawked and charged the west gate, while hundreds of hyena-men yipped in earnest fervor. The archers along the walls released their first volley, and as the tips pierced the flesh of bird and hyena, Velixar lifted his eyes to the sky in thanks.

Veldaren's purge had begun.

"**B**ird-men to the west," Mira shouted, using magic to escalate the volume of her voice so that all the soldiers near her heard. "Hyena-men to the south."

"Fill them with arrows!" Antonil shouted as he ran up the stairs and joined Mira's side. The first volley fired, the twangs of bowstrings in perfect unison. Hundreds of arrows fell upon the bird-men, piercing their tough skin and shoddy armor. They ran with their heads low and wings spread wide, so those that fell were trampled without slowing the charge. They squawked with fanatical anger and determination. A second volley lessened their numbers even further, so that by the time they neared the gate they numbered only eight hundred.

The outermost gate was made of wood, with the inner side reinforced with iron. Lacking any sort of siege weaponry, Antonil wondered what lunacy made them think they could break through. Then from his perch he saw their sharp claws shred inches into the wood, showering the ground with splinters.

"Fire at will," he ordered his archers. "Focus on the door!"

"Yes sir," Mira said, a grin spreading across her face. Fire swirled around her hands, begging for release. She slammed them together, unleashing a giant funnel of flame. The fire struck just before the gate, incinerating tens of the grotesque creatures. Then the spell detonated. Dozens more flew back, leaving ugly, featherless corpses in the spell's wake. The archers along the wall assaulted the scattered remnants who tried to mass at the gate.

"Well done," Antonil whispered. "Better than hot oil."

"Perhaps not," Mira said. She pointed to the greater army waiting. "I think I made a friend."

There," Velixar said, his eyes locked on the fiery bomb igniting his forces on the western side. "Foolish to give away her position so early in the fight."

Darkness clouded his fingers, but Tessanna halted his spell.

"No," she said, glaring at the wall even as she laughed. "She's mine. She is me, and mommy wants me dead."

"The other daughter of balance?" the man in black wondered. He had figured the spell to be cast by Harruq's wife. "So be it," he said.

"Here kitty-kitty," Tessanna said, twin red orbs of magic growing inside her palms. "Big dog's coming and he's coming for you!"

She threw them, the force of the spell knocking her to her knees. Mouth agape and eyes sparkling, she watched her spell.

"Get back!" Mira shouted, seeing the two orbs rotating around each other as they approached. She spread her hands wide, mentally pushing Antonil and the other archers to safety. She had but a second to cast a shielding spell before the orbs struck.

"Mira!" Lathaar shouted as half the western gate swarmed with yellow fire. The fire burned hot and died, drifting to the sky in a putrid smelling smoke. The paladin cheered as it dissipated, for hovering a foot above the wall was Mira, her hair swirling and her eyes black as night.

"Get off the wall," she ordered the rest of the archers, who obeyed without hesitation. Antonil grabbed Lathaar's shoulder and twisted him around to face him.

"How can she survive that?" he asked.

"Better question," Lathaar said, pointing at the girl. "How can they survive *that?*"

A solid beam of magic over ten feet wide screamed straight for Tessanna, who waited with her right arm out and her palm open. When the blast hit, she opened her eyes, dark lust inside them. The white beam parted at her fingers and swirled around her body like water parting around a stone. Her arm shook. Her body wavered.

"Help her," Qurrah shouted, but Velixar shook his head.

"She doesn't need help," the man in black said. "Are you so blind to your lover's strength?"

The beam intensified in strength, and Tessanna's fragile body seemed ready to break, weak and insignificant versus the sheer power unleashed against her. But then she pulled back her hand and spun, her arms high above her like a dancer. Qurrah cried out, thinking the magic would shred her to pieces, but instead it swirled around her body like a funnelstorm. The white faded to red, then to black.

From within, Qurrah heard laughter.

The tornado froze with a vicious tearing sound. All its magic pulled in on itself, folding and bending into a single black orb the size of a pebble. It hovered above Tessanna's palm, which shook as she fought to control it. Shrieking, she hurled the volatile orb back at Mira.

Mira summoned her defenses, but when the pebble hit her translucent shield she knew her mistake. Pain sheared through her mind. A white flash marked the explosion, followed by a giant eruption of lightning and smoke and darkness. Her shield broke. Her tiny body flew off the wall. Haern was there in an instant, leaping through the air to grab her in his arms. With a thought, he teleported them to the ground and put her safely down.

"The gate," Mira cried, struggling against the assassin's arms which pinned her. "The gate, its vulnerable, the gate is..."

"The gate will break," Haern whispered to her. "Whether you protect it or not. Will you break with it, or regain your strength to fight again?"

Before she could answer, the great roar of the lion filled the city. It felt as if it rose from the dirt beneath them, lifting the dust and blowing the hairs on their skin. In the sudden silence following, Mira accepted his wisdom.

"Get them away from the gate," she said, pointing to the soldiers wedged in front of it. "Hurry."

Haern helped her to her feet and then turned, seeking Antonil.

"Get them back!" he shouted, waving both his sabers above his head to gain the guard captain's attention. "Antonil Copernus, I said get them back!"

❖

Tarlak and Aurelia watched as the hyena-men charged with frightening speed. The first volley by the archers fell far behind the coming force. The archers compensated for the speed for their second volley, killing twenty. Twenty, out of nearly nine hundred.

"Get them arrows out there," Sergan shouted as he paced before the locked and barred gate. "You want us to throw open the city so I can show you how to kill?"

"That can be arranged," Tarlak mumbled as the hyena-men spread apart to lessen the damage of the third volley. The makings of a fire spell was on his lips when Aurelia grabbed his wrist and stopped him.

"Velixar is out there," she said. "If he knows where we are, he'll counter. Wait for them to enter the city, where our magic will go unseen."

"Spoilsport," Tarlak said.

"Incompetent wizard," she shot back.

"Orc lover."

"Don't make me polymorph you."

The hyena-men slammed against the gate, their claws sharper and thicker than those of the bird-men. The soldiers inside the city shook from the combination of yipping, growling, and clawing on the other side.

"They're just overgrown mutts, you pansies!" Sergan shouted to his ground troops. "And archers, I want empty quivers by the end of this battle. Now get to it!"

The arrows rained down on the hyena-men clawing at the gate, but when one fell, those behind it pulled it back and tossed it to the side. Using the bodies of their own dead, they built walls on either side of the gate. Then, to Tarlak's shock, a squad of ten hyena-men came running forward with crudely cut planks of wood in their arms. They threw the planks atop the two walls of dead bodies. The hyena-men had to crawl underneath, but it worked. The archers could not reach the hyena-men that clawed against the gate, shredding the wood and twisting the iron behind it.

"That's got to go," Tarlak said. He glanced at Aurelia, who nodded in agreement.

"Make it fast," she said. "And whatever you do, don't make it flashy."

Below them a hairy arm burst through the wood in between the straps of iron. It flailed around wildly, as if hoping a victim was near.

"This is going to be fun," Harruq said from the front line. He ran up, both his swords drawn. With a single blow, he chopped the arm off at the elbow and kicked it to the side. Two clawed hands replaced it, prying at the wood to make the hole bigger. Harruq thrust both swords into the hole. They came back soaked in blood.

"That all you got?" he screamed to the other side of the door.

"Get back here, soldier," Sergan shouted at him. "You want trampled the second that door knocks open?"

"But we've got to..."

Harruq stopped as a loud explosion rocked the outside of the gate. Smoke poured through the tiny hole along with the scent of burnt fur.

"Gate's clear again!" he heard Tarlak shout. The archers resumed their firing.

"You want to fight at the front you do as I say," Sergan commanded, to which Harruq shrugged and obeyed.

"Wizards get all the fun," he grumbled as Tarlak and Aurelia pondered their next choice of attack.

As the hyena-men clawed and tore at the door of the southern gate, the last remnants of the bird-men fled the battlefield. Most had been killed by arrows or Mira's fire spell. Plenty crawled wounded along the ground, but none would come to aid them.

Velixar frowned in disgust.

"Such cowardly creatures," he said. "But expected. Ashhur did create them."

When the retreating bird-men reached the line of dark paladins and clerics they cried out for mercy. Instead the dark paladins butchered them with their weapons as did the clerics with their spells.

"Not a single kill to their name," Qurrah said. "What a waste."

"They will serve their purpose soon," Velixar said. "But for now..."

The man in black closed his eyes and began casting. Qurrah had taken the fire of torches the hyena-men and bird-men carried and the display had been incredible. Velixar took the fire from his thousands of orcs under his command. The fire swirled into the air, forming a giant streaking comet. Velixar forked his hands as he concentrated, breaking the ball of flame in two. Each one curled around, smoke and fire trailing after as they careened for the barred gates of the city.

Antonil was still ordering his men back when the ball slammed into his gate, blasting apart the wood and melting the iron. A cloud of heat blew down the street, killing fifty of his soldiers that could not escape in time. Antonil slammed his sword against his shield, even as his men scattered and broke ranks.

"To me!" he shouted. "Form up! To me!"

With pure will, Antonil gathered his army and reformed their ranks before the shattered remnants of the gate. They saw the ring of servants of Karak, and behind, the horde of orcs with their banners waving in the morning sun.

"As long we hold breath our city will not fall," Antonil shouted, ignoring the quaking fear in his heart. "As long as we hold firm, our enemy will break. Stand, men, stand!"

Lathaar held his sword high, as did Jerico with his shield. Their light shone across the soldiers, and as the two paladins prayed the soldier's fear melted like snow within a fire.

"If your heart is with Ashhur, then death holds no sway against you!" Jerico shouted. "Accept the light and fight the darkness!"

Their fear was great, but the light was greater. Their ranks tightened. Their swords stopped their shaking. Ready to fight, ready to die, the men at the western gate waited.

❖

Aurelia prevented the attack from being the disaster it should have been. As the comet of fire burned through the hyena-men and slammed against the gate, she leapt from the wall. She had no time to levitate, no time to think. She collapsed from the impact, and her teeth bit down hard on her tongue. Head bent, blood in her mouth, she raised her hands and summoned a shield of magic. She prayed it would be enough.

The fire burst through, shards of wood and iron exploding inward. Aurelia screamed, unable to hold the shield. But then Tarlak summoned an enormous blast of air from the ground before her, pushing the fire and shrapnel to the sky. Harruq ran to her side, ignoring Sergan's cries for order. As he sheathed his swords and took her into his arms, he saw hundreds of hyena-men yipping at him with hungry eyes. The gate was down, and their way was clear. Harruq ran to the side while the soldiers of Neldar collided with the claws and teeth of their attackers.

"I'll protect her until she's ready," Tarlak said as he hovered down beside them with a levitation spell. "Get yourself into the fight."

Harruq turned to the chaos of steel, fur, and muscle.

"With pleasure," he growled.

He let out a roar, his adrenaline taking over. He charged the gate. Soldiers had surrounded the entrance so that any hyena-men who entered found a circle of steel waiting. The hyena-men were dying far more than the humans, but sheer numbers pushed them back. Then Harruq joined. He slammed his way past the Veldaren soldiers, having no fear for the claws of his enemy. Salvation and Condemnation drank freely as he sliced and chopped. He did not retreat as the other soldiers did. Instead he waded forward, slaughtering any who met his charge.

"Hot damn," Sergan shouted, witnessing Harruq in action. "Now that's fighting!"

Not willing to let the half-orc have all the fun, Sergan took his axe and rushed to his side. Together they hacked and chopped until they were at the rubble of the gate. The entrance was narrow, and only three could come at once. The room to maneuver diminished, it favored the two even more. The claws of the hyena-men were no match for the weapons that tore through them. Their thick hide was no match for the enchanted steel and well-sharpened edges that cut them.

"Get ready to fall back," Harruq said through grit teeth as he disemboweled one hyena-man while stabbing the throat of another.

"Lead on," Sergan told him.

The initial rush of hyena-men had been scattered and uneven due to the destruction of the fiery comet that had broken the gate. The archers had done their best to thin their attack, but now the hyena-men pressed forward as a single unit.

"Back," Harruq yelled, turning and running into the city.

"Shields, now!" Sergan ordered, hot on Harruq's heels. The two split once they were past the gateway. Rows of soldiers took their place, their shields locked together into a single wall. The hyena-men hurled themselves with wild abandon. The men screamed, their shoulders throbbing and their wrists aching. But they did not move. Men behind them pushed forward, aiding those who were weak or wounded. The hyena-men howled and tried, but their momentum was broken.

Atop the wall, the archers emptied their quivers, for with their enemy packed and unable to move, they couldn't miss. The soldiers on the front started stabbing in between the shields, filling the street with blood. Harruq rejoined the two casters, knowing there was no place for him without a shield.

"You alright?" he asked his wife.

"Head hurts," she said. She leaned against the wall. Tarlak was beside her, staring at the intense combat.

"Any spell we cast will hit our own," he said. "Either that, or make our position known."

"They'll hold," Harruq said.

"Good," Tarlak said. "Because it's going to get harder."

As if on cue, the city shook from the roar of the lion, except this time the shaking did not stop. Harruq looked about, confused and worried.

"What the abyss?" he asked.

"No point staying hidden now," Aurelia said, gingerly rising to her feet. "The orcs are coming."

Harruq looked back at the row of soldiers guarding the door. About thirty had fallen, leaving less than two hundred to hold the gate. Several hundred hyena-men remained still, fighting and clawing with every ounce of their strength to enter. Of the thousands of orcs, if even half marched to their gate...

The half-orc charged the front line. Shield or no shield, he was going to fight, and he was going to kill, because the numbers they faced were about to get a whole lot bigger.

15

S tand firm!" Antonil shouted as the lion's roar filled their ears. It's effect was pitiful compared to the light of the paladin's swords and shield. As it died, they felt the ground beneath their feet shake. The orc forces were charging. The guard captain positioned himself in the center of the first line. To his right was Jerico, his left, Lathaar.

"Antonil," Jerico said. "Listen to me. When the orcs are a hair's width from sword reach, we need to charge."

"If we brace our shields then..."

"Guard captain," Jerico said, pulling on Antonil's shoulder to force him to meet his gaze. "Order your men to charge just before the strike. Trust me. Trust Ashhur."

The coming horde roared and bellowed. Half broke south, a giant river of gray flesh and armor. Antonil whispered a prayer for Sergan and his men.

"I'll trust you," he said aloud when finished. "We're all dead men anyway."

"Not yet," Lathaar said, overhearing the comment. "Not by a long shot."

He held both his swords high and shouted out the word 'Elholad.' His swords flared brighter than any torch, sun, or star. Those who saw it knew no fear. They felt the sun on their skin for the first time, knew comfort in the weight of their armor and the strength in the grip they held on their swords. The orcs passed through the ring of priests and dark paladins, not daring to touch any even in their frenzy. Archers released their arrows, but it was like spitting on a bonfire.

"At my command," Antonil shouted over the commotion, "I want you to charge as one. Do you understand?"

The soldiers shouted in unison.

The army closed the distance. Jerico stepped out from the front row and knelt to one knee. His shield leaned before him. Its light shimmered and swirled, as if a rainbow were trapped within the metal. The paladin closed his eyes and prayed.

The orcs were almost upon him. They funneled through the shattered ashes of the doors and into the giant gateway. Their axes and swords were drawn. Their mouths were open in mindless cries of bloodthirst. Jerico heard none of it. He felt his shield become weightless on his arm. He felt his heart stop. The whole world was silent. He opened his eyes. He felt his faith like a knife in his chest, unbreakable, immovable. In one smooth motion, he stood and pushed his shield against the air. A white image rammed forth, similar to his shield but larger and made of purest light.

Sound returned. The world resumed. Jerico watched as the glowing shield slammed the nearest orcs. They howled with pain, and every one toppled as if a hammer had struck their chest. Those behind tripped over them and died, trampled by the next wave of their comrades.

"Charge!" Antonil screamed. The men rushed forward, Lathaar and Antonil leading the way. Lathaar's swords sliced through gray flesh. Antonil's shield bashed and pushed, his sword cutting into any weakness. The orcs had no footing, no momentum. Those who funneled into the gateway died, their bodies becoming a barrier the rest had to climb over. And then Jerico joined them, his mace Bonebreaker more than living up to its name. He shattered the jaw of one orc, kicked his body back, and then crushed the skull of his replacement. Over a thousand orcs pressed and fought to enter the city but were held back by the front seven of Neldar.

"Fall back," Antonil shouted. The horde were pulling away, preparing for another rush. Many were dragging bodies and dumping them to the sides so they could have a clear battlefront. A few tried to give chase and deny the soldiers a chance to flee, but then Haern appeared in the gap between the two armies, a wicked gleam in his eye. He spun through the orcs, his curved sabers slashing out tendons and throats as he passed. The orcs tried to converge on him but he leapt further away from the city. He descended upon the orc army like a storm cloud.

Once outside the gateway he had even more room to maneuver. He double stabbed one's throat, then leapt into the air and jumped off his chest. He sailed over the orcs, his entire body rotating. Sabers slashed and cut eyes and faces. Those near his landing tried to flee. They died. When several rushed, hoping to bury him with numbers, he turned toward the gate and activated the magic of his ring, vanishing and reappearing past their blockade. He ran through the gateway, which was a bloodied mess. The rest of the soldiers were inside and in formation, while Jerico knelt once more, his eyes closed and his shield ready.

"What in the abyss was that, that...shield?" Lathaar asked Jerico. While the others around them were gasping for air, both paladins appeared to be only winded from the fight.

"Like that?" Jerico asked, his eyes still closed. A slight smile broke the corners of his lips. "I've done it only once, when I was alone."

"Can you do it again?"

He looked to the orcs, who were snarled and lining up for another charge.

"I don't know," Jerico said. "I'll try."

Antonil ran through his ranks, pulling fresh men to the front. When done he ran back with his sword high and gleaming.

"Charge at my command!" he screamed.

"Yes sir!" The soldiers' shouts were louder, heartier. They had withstood the first assault without nary a life lost. No longer did they feel they fought a hopeless battle.

"Get ready," Lathaar said as he stepped back to the line. "They won't be surprised this time around."

"We don't need surprise," Haern said, blood covering his golden hair. "We have strength they can't dream of."

The orcs entered the gateway with their arms crossed and their weapons held in defensive positions, but it did no good.

Jerico waited even later, hurling the magical shield into the gateway even as the orcs swung at his body. They flew back, screaming in pain. The ground became a tangled mess of limbs as they fell atop one another. Instead of charging, the orcs behind them retreated, wanting no part of that chaos. Lathaar and Haern attacked, giving them no quarter. Antonil raised his hand and held his army back, in case the orcs tried to assault. They didn't. Glowing swords and sharpened sabers slashed through those who tried to stand and fight. Even those who lay in pain found steel piercing through their throats and eyes.

Lathaar reached the end of the gateway and stared out at the giant mass sent to kill them. The orcs glared and howled, but dared not move. The paladin raised his swords high, and he laughed despite the blood that soaked his armor.

"Is this the great army of Karak?" he shouted. "Is this the legion that will wipe life from this world?"

His words carried, and one man amid the host of orcs heard and was made furious.

"That damn pally just won't die," Krieger spat on the ground and drew his scimitars. Beside him, Carden drew his giant sword and watched the black flame surround it.

"Leadership through action," the old man said. "Let us show our brethren the strength of Karak."

Side by side the two dark paladins pushed their way through the orcs, the flame of their weapons filling all who saw it with fear.

This is it?" Harruq shouted as he slammed the body of a hyena-man against the wall. Condemnation hacked off his head. Meanwhile, Salvation buried deep into the gut of another. The creature yipped and clawed the air. A twist of the sword finished it. All around him, men with shields charged forward, slashing at their enemies before falling back. Only Harruq remained where he stood, a bloodied behemoth towering over them. Claw marks marred his face and covered his arms, but their pain was insignificant. Side to side his swords swept, his long arms covering every inch of the gateway's width. His swords glowed brighter from the blood that stained them.

The orcs were the only thing keeping the hyena-men fighting. Many tried to turn and flee, but a wall of flesh and swords pushed them on. Many never even fought back as Harruq slaughtered them. He didn't care. He felt no guilt. His home was under attack, and he would defend it. Two claws slashed across his cheek. He tasted blood. In return, he slashed out the creature's throat and spilled its intestines along the gore-slick ground. Another leapt onto his swords just so he could bite his neck. The others charged, thinking him vulnerable. Harruq screamed, louder and crazier than the dying hyena-man. He flung him away, his vision red and his pain distant. Those that thought him vulnerable found their claws cut from their hands, their teeth smacked from their jaws, and their lives rent from their bodies.

"Pull back, brute!" Sergan yelled to him from behind the wall of shields. "Pull back before you get your sorry ass killed!"

The half-orc kicked a body off his sword, knocking down two more behind it. He roared out in mindless primal fury. Soldiers stormed past him, locking together their shields so Sergan could grab and pull him further into the city. Harruq pushed the general back and walked inside, wiping some gore away from his eyes with his thumb. When he neared Tarlak and Aurelia, he sheathed his swords.

"How many?" Tarlak asked.

"Lost count," Harruq said. The ground suddenly shifted on him, as if it was rumbling and bumping, but he was the only one to drop to his knees while the others looked on. He heard the other two talking, but their voices were strangely distant.

"He's lost a lot of blood," he heard his wife say.

"I'm fine," he said.

"Where's Calan?" Tarlak asked.

"I said I'm fine!"

The half-orc staggered to his feet and drew his swords. He knew it was morning, but the sky was darker, the city dark as well.

"We need more time," Aurelia said. She ran to the gate, lightning crackling on her fingertips. Tarlak pulled on the back of Harruq's armor. He tried to resist, but the ground betrayed him again. Salvation and Condemnation fell from his hands. The wizard sat down on his knees in front of him and took off his hat.

"Drink this up like a good little boy and we'll let you kill more baddies, alright?"

Tarlak pulled a vial out of his hat like a petty magic trick. He popped the cork off the top, pried open Harruq's lips, and shoved the silvery liquid down. The taste reminded him of somewhere, but he couldn't place it…couldn't…

He slipped into unconsciousness, still trying to remember.

◥◆◤

Aurelia watched as the last of the hyena-men fell to the swords of the Neldar troops. Orcs tried to drag away the dead, but the archers above fired volley after volley. The piles of bodies grew larger. In the momentary reprieve, Aurelia stepped just inside the shield wall.

"Kneel down," she said. Sergan, recognizing her for who she was, ordered the front to their knees. "Keep them off me," she said as she began her spellcasting. She had a small window in between the shoulders of the men to either side of her. She'd have to be careful. The orcs funneled into the gateway, ready to bury them in their numbers.

A bolt of lightning tore through their center, killing seven. A second took five more. Her hands stretched over the men's heads, and from her fingers flew a hundred arrows of fire. Those that avoided her spells hurled their bodies at her, but the soldiers had seen her power. Three shields pelted one orc's body as he tried to hack off the sorceress's fingers. Another had two swords pierce his belly and hold him back as Aurelia flung a ball of fire through the gateway and into the mass of orcs. It exploded over fifty feet in diameter. Orcs shrieked and died.

"Roast 'em!" one shouted beside her. The elf smiled amid her concentration.

"Sure thing," she said, ten black orbs dripping from her fingers. She flicked her hands, and the orbs flew into the charging orcs. Each orb exploded when it struck flesh or armor, engulfing the hapless victim in fire. Faster and faster her spells came. She hurled a ball of ice over the wall, crushing two poor orcs underneath. Magical arrows buried into gray throats. Lightning blasted huge lines of them to the ground, but still they came. The soldiers pushed them back, one even flinging his arms in front of an axe strike so the elf could complete her spell.

"There's too many!" Sergan shouted to her.

"Trust me," Aurelia said. Her head pounded, her back ached, and her fingers felt made of lead. "I know!"

She made a ripping motion with her hands. A wall of fire stretched from the ground to the top of the city's outer entrance. She cast the spell again, forming a second barrier of fire on the inner side. A few orcs howled as they were pushed into the fire to test its strength. Blackened and dead, they rolled out the other side.

Aurelia grabbed the shoulders of the nearest man and pressed her head against his chest. With eyes closed, she tried to gather her strength. She had used so much magic, it felt as if her eyes would melt out of their sockets and blood would seep from her ears.

"Well, hello," the man said. "Always knew I'd sweep you off your feet one of these days."

She opened her eyes to see the soldier she had collapsed against was actually Tarlak.

"Comfy?" he asked with a grin.

"You sure know how to ruin a good thing," she said, pushing away from him. "Did you find Calan?"

"Aye, I did," he said. "And I must say, they know how to have fun."

Aurelia raised an eyebrow, but the wizard just shook his head.

"Either you'll see it or I'll tell you about it later. For now, how are things here? Nice fire walls, by the way."

"We're holding," she said, rubbing her eyes with her fingers. "But once you and I are exhausted, and Harruq's bled out every bit of strength he's got, what then? They're so many..."

"At least we have the archers," Tarlak said.

"Yeah," she said. "At least."

Velixar said not a word as he watched the assault progress. Qurrah found it difficult to read his face, for every second the chin shifted higher, or the cheeks sunk lower, or the eyebrows changed color. His anger, though, was loud and clear.

"Ashhur has done well," Velixar said. "Guided the strongest of this world to his side and then brought them to fight against us. But I have done the same, have I not?"

"We are ready to obey," Qurrah said.

"I know," Velixar said. "Kill the archers."

Qurrah raised his hands and went over the words of a spell he had learned from Velixar's journal. He had become a master of manipulating the bones of the dead, but the spell he was about to try was far beyond anything he had attempted before. Just before beginning the spell, he tried something new: prayer.

Aid me in this, Karak, he prayed. *Prove to me your allegiance, and I will prove to you mine.*

Words of magic poured from his lips. Hundreds of dead lay piled beside the two blasted gates of the city. Every single one was an entity he felt in his mind, their death lingering in anger. He harnessed the power of that death and then turned it on their broken bodies. His hands hooked and curled. The words came faster and faster. In the dark recesses of his mind, he heard the growl of the lion.

In one giant explosion, the bones of the dead tore into the air, numbering in the thousands. There they hovered while beneath them blood poured down like rain.

"Let death ride along the walls," the half-orc whispered.

The bones swirled together, a storm of white and red. It started at the west. Like a floating meat grinder, it descended on the archers atop the walls. The bones pelted their bodies, tore across their skin, and shredded their flesh. From there it traveled south. Many archers leapt from the wall, accepting the broken bones in their legs or arms to the carnage they witnessed upon their brethren. By the time it reached the second gate, half of the archers had fled down ladders and steps. The other half died.

Qurrah was not done. He pulled the bone tornado higher, letting the blood and gore within it fall across the city. The tornado sucked in on itself, collecting into a giant grotesque ball of bone.

"Death is rain," Velixar said, seeing what was about to happen. "Let them learn it."

Qurrah slammed his fists together. The ball of bone exploded. The pieces pelted the city. The effect was dramatic. The stench of fear rose high from the city, and the necromancers drank it in with pleasure. Tessanna kissed Qurrah's lips, giggling madly as she did.

"Do it again," she said. "Break their buildings. Knock down the walls. Bones, Qurrah, the bones!"

The half-orc kissed her twice. "Perhaps later," he said.

"One of the gates will fall soon," Velixar said. "When that happens, the entire city will collapse."

"What if too many die before then?" Qurrah asked. "You have the strength to sunder the walls, so why don't you?"

The man in black laughed.

"Those who die will serve me in death just as well as they would serve me in life. Does it truly matter?"

"No," Qurrah said, staring at the western gate and wondering if his brother was inside. "I guess it doesn't."

"As for the walls...the soldiers are here for a reason. They are to fight, and they are to die. I would not deny them their right. Besides, we must save our strength. Breaking Celestia's will to open the portal to Thulos's world will require everything, Qurrah, and then even more."

Velixar gestured to the combat, his anger gone.

"Enjoy the battle. Enjoy the death. We have sown these seeds for centuries. Let us enjoy the reaping."

The smell of blood was overpowering as they neared the west gateway of the great wall surrounding Veldaren. This should have excited him, but the blood was not the intermixed carnage of battle. No, it was the stench of a massacre, and even worse, it was his army suffering the great loss of life. Worst of all to Krieger, the pathetic paladin Lathaar helmed the defense.

"This is no time for private duels," Carden said to Krieger as they approached. With the archers dead or hiding after the bone tornado, they approached the sundered gate without worry. "The paladin's death proves our strength, regardless the circumstances."

"Then my failure to kill him showed Ashhur's strength," Krieger said. "Or does it not work both ways?"

Carden turned, his eyes burning with anger.

"You are the High Enforcer now," he said. "Act it. Our enemies are strong and clever. We will overcome them by sheer faith and will, not by assumptions and ego. Draw your swords, paladin of Karak."

Krieger did. Beside him, Carden raised his enormous sword, the dark fire visible throughout the battlefield. All around orcs gathered. Their bloodlust was high, and the sight of the fire heightened it further. If only they could get inside. If only the gateway defenders could be broken.

"Paladin of Ashhur!" Carden shouted. "Your kind is dead. Your god is fallen. Do you weep for your souls, knowing no arms wait to embrace you in death?"

Lathaar emerged from the line of shields inside the city, the glow on his swords strong. Krieger felt his blood boil at the sight of him. He should have killed him when he had the chance, he realized. He could have slaughtered him as a faithless, broken man in a backwater village. That was the fitting end for him, not some heroic last stand in the greatest battle of his life.

"Ashhur be damned," Carden said, stirring him from his thoughts. "You were right. There is another."

Jerico stepped beside Lathaar, and together they raised their holy armaments, their glow combining into an awesome display. Carden held his sword near his face, letting its dark fire absorb the painful glow.

"His name is Jerico," Krieger said. "They are the last. We can eliminate their kind right here, right now."

"We cannot draw them out," Carden said. He turned to the orcs around them. "So we must meet them within. Orcs! Your cowardice ends now! You will charge, you will fight, and you will slaughter. Let the name of Karak sound from your lips!"

The force of his voice whipped them into a greater fervor. Krieger felt the authority in Carden's voice and realized just how much he still had to learn and grow in his faith.

"Fight hard," Krieger shouted, determined to fill the role he was given. "Break through the guards and you will have an entire city waiting. Pillage! Rape! Every sin, every vice, you can have it all!"

The orcs were screaming now, ready to tear apart their own kin to engage in battle. Krieger slammed his sabers together, the sparks showering around his enormous frame. As one, the dark paladins charged, the orc army hot on their heels.

"Let's see how tough you are," Jerico said, hurling another giant shield of light. Carden raised his sword and bellowed out the word 'Felhelad.' His sword became a blade of pure fire, its color darker than the night. When the shield of light approached he slashed the air, cutting it in two. A force struck the two dark paladins but they were not harmed and they were not held back.

"Ashhur be with you," Jerico said to Lathaar as he stood to fight.

"You as well," Lathaar replied. "Elholad!"

His swords became pure light, the counterpoint to the black fire that bore down upon them. Jerico raised his shield as Carden's sword slammed against it. He had never felt a blow he could not withstand. He had never tried blocking a Felhelad. He screamed in pain, needing every bit of strength to hold back the sword. Anger fueled his determination, and then it was Carden's turn to experience something he had never felt in all his long life: the holy retribution of Jerico's shield. His Felhelad jerked back, pain stabbing his hands, shoulders, and stomach. The struggle had been mere seconds, but each one stared at his opponent with newfound respect.

Krieger bore down on Lathaar, his weapons also Felhelads.

"Did you miss me?" he shouted as his sabers connected with Lathaar's swords. Crackling power swirled between them. Lathaar winced and pushed back.

"How's your back?" he asked. He parried a thrust, stepped aside, and then blocked a vicious chop. Behind him soldiers of Neldar readied their shields and stepped forward. The orcs had arrived, howling bloody murder. They filled the gateway, pouring around the paladins. The formation of shields wavered. Antonil shouted and urged them on, wading deep into the river of gray, but his valiant efforts were nothing compared to the hundreds pressing in.

Jerico parried a sideswipe with his mace, whirled his weapon around, and struck Carden across the chest. He was strong, but the power from his faith was in his shield, not his weapon. The mace recoiled, the enchantments on the armor too tough for his weapon to break. The dark paladin saw this and laughed.

"Those who cannot kill will be killed," he said, slamming his Felhelad against the glowing shield. Again they both recoiled, wounded by the exchange. Two orcs ran past Carden and leapt at Jerico, their axes swinging. Jerico blocked one, clubbed the second in the jaw, and then slammed his shield against the first. Three more moved to attack Jerico but Carden cut them down with one giant swing. Despite his lecture with Krieger, he was determined to finish off the stubborn paladin without interference. Black fire leapt around his fist, and shouting the name of Karak, he punched Jerico's shield.

Jerico knew what Carden was doing. Several of the stronger paladins of Karak could harness their faith into a single blow that could shatter stone and fell trees. The stronger their faith, the stronger the blow. He knew Carden's faith was immense. When the fist connected with his shield, he knew immense didn't come close. The center of his shield bowed inward, the metal cracking and melting. His arm shook in spasms while his fingers locked open. His mouth opened in a scream that felt unending. The pain stretched beyond intolerable.

When Carden's fist pulled back, Jerico collapsed to his knees.

"Still alive?" Carden said as he hefted his Felhelad in both hands and raised it for a killing blow. "Accept my respect as I remedy this."

Down came the sword.

Lathaar pressed the attack as the soldiers of Neldar made one last push to seal the gateway against the orcs. Krieger tensed his legs and braced against the powerful blows. He grit his teeth as his biceps throbbed under the strain. The dark paladin refused to budge when he reached the inner edge of the gateway, instead crossing both scimitars and locking Lathaar's weapons together in their center.

"Your city is falling," Krieger said as the veins in his neck bulged. "Your faith is a false hope to be extinguished. Karak is the true god. As you die, you will see the proof."

Lathaar met Krieger's stare without blinking. Human soldiers fought at his side, their coordination having beaten back the orcs to the broken gate. Screams of the wounded and dying filled his ears. As he poured his strength into his arms and swords, he saw the insanity lurking within Krieger's eyes. All around, people were dying. Those he could aid. Those he could heal. Those he could protect with his swords.

"We don't matter," Lathaar said, the knowledge striking him like a hammer. He pulled back, slashed Krieger's scimitars wide, and then rammed him with his shoulder leading. The dark paladin fell back, entangled in the horde of orcs behind him.

"Fighting to prove Ashhur's faith is folly," he said as Krieger slaughtered the hapless orcs that hindered his return to combat.

"Then why fight?" Krieger screamed as he slammed the hilts of his weapons together. The two interlocked when he twisted them, so that he held a long bladed staff instead of two separate scimitars. He twirled it in his hands as overwhelming rage burned in his heart. Several orcs tried to assault Lathaar, but Krieger beat them back, severing the head of one who did not react quickly enough. The paladin was his to kill!

"Thousands will die within these walls if I don't," Lathaar said, quiet enough to ensure the dark paladin did not hear. "That is all that matters."

He slammed his Elholads together, the bright light blinding the orcs that stampeded into the city. The human soldiers had spread out, their tight line bulging into a semicircle that threatened to break with every passing moment. Only Lathaar stood in its center, no orc foolish enough to attack. Lathaar, however, did not care about his duel. He didn't care about Krieger. All around were bringers of death, and he would end them. He spun, his swords cutting and slicing. Tens of orcs died as they tried to rush around him for the easier targets behind. Krieger lunged, twirling his staff as if it weighed nothing.

Lathaar batted aside his opening thrust, stepped closer, and slammed an open palm against Krieger's chest. Ashhur's voice was all he could hear. He didn't know what it was he did, but when his palm touched the black metal of Krieger's breastplate his vision turned white. Just as Carden had struck Jerico, Lathaar struck Krieger. The power hurled the dark paladin backward, through his troops of orcs and out of the city. Smoke drifted from the hole in his chestpiece. But Lathaar was not done. He sheathed his short sword and held the longer Elholad with both hands. Its blade stretched out another foot. It should have been unwieldy, but it was pure light, weighing nothing, killing everything.

A swipe to the right, and five orcs fell dead. A swipe left, and six more died. He whipped the blade around, cutting off the legs of a charging orc, and then slammed his Elholad to the ground. A shockwave of holy power lanced into the gateway, slicing through flesh and armor like butter. The orcs engaged with the humans, having lost their reinforcements, collapsed and fled. Shields pressed into the entrance, the Veldaren soldiers creating tight formations. Lathaar spun and saw the other dark paladin towering over Jerico as if he were a conquered prize.

"Jerico!" he shouted as he charged after Carden. The dark paladin was surrounded by soldiers of Neldar. The long black sword swirled around, slicing through shields and armor, but Antonil and his men did not let him rest, nor to score a killing blow upon Jerico. Time and time again he would swing his sword in a full circle, knocking away all who neared, and then try to stab the blade into Jerico's chest. Each time Jerico lifted his shield and blocked the blow. The shield's glow had faded, and he looked beyond exhausted, but he was stubbornly alive.

"Cowards," Carden shouted to the men who encircled him. "Will none of you stand to fight, or will you flee like diseased dogs?"

Antonil thrust at Carden's back, but he had been baited. Carden was ready. The enormous length of his blade should have severed his head and sent it rolling through the street, but the Felhelad stopped. Lathaar protected him, sparks exploding between them as their blades collided.

"Your faith isn't enough to challenge me, boy," Carden said.

"Ashhur thinks otherwise."

They pulled back and swung again. At the collision of their god-blessed blades, orcs and men alike shielded their eyes against the light. Lathaar and Carden pushed against each other with all their strength, locked in a stare of death. Whoever blinked, whoever faltered, would die.

"The city falls," Carden said through clenched teeth. "No heroism will save it."

"Shut up already," Jerico said as he swung his mace from his prone position. Bonebreaker struck Carden's ankle, bent in the metal, and then touched flesh. The magic within activated, and Carden screamed as the bones in his foot shattered. Antonil leapt in, thrusting his sword through the exposed gap in the armor underneath Carden's arm. Blood soaked his sword, but before he could twist it the dark paladin spun. His giant blade batting them all away like insects. But as the blade spun around, Haern appeared directly before Carden, a wicked grin on his face. He sliced his sabers across the sides of Carden's neck, severing an artery before somersaulting away.

Lathaar saw the blood, saw the pain, and knew his opponent beaten. In one single move, he spun a full circle and swung. The momentum and power pushed aside Carden's last attempt to block. The Elholad melted his armor, cut through his arm, and cleaved his body in two. The black fire around the Felhelad vanished.

Outside the gate, Krieger shrieked in mindless fury.

❖

What is the matter?" Qurrah asked. Velixar's face had grown ashen in a rare expression of sorrow.

"Ashhur has always been bitter in defeat," Velixar said. "Two of my dearest friends are dead. Still, we have not entered the city."

"Are you sure we can't play yet?" Tessanna asked, smiling and batting her eyes like a child. Meanwhile, a dark paladin rode up on horseback and saluted Velixar.

"A spellcaster has formed twin walls of fire at the southern gate," he said. "Their forces are ready to break, but we have no means to combat the magic."

"So damn stubborn," Velixar said, a bit of frustration leaking into his voice. Qurrah kissed Tessanna's lips and then bade the dark paladin to give him a ride.

"You cannot go," Velixar said. "You are too valuable. The portal must be opened, and if you are killed…"

"If I am killed," Qurrah said, "then I never had the strength to aid you in the first place. Our armies are dying. There is no honor in this, not for either side. Let death come swift."

The dark paladin waited for a sign from Karak's greatest prophet. After a moment, Velixar nodded.

"So be it," he said. "The south gate is yours. Return the moment our minions enter the city."

Qurrah bowed. The horse turned and rode for the south entrance.

"So few," Tessanna said, laughing at the man in black. "All our numbers, all our power, and we are held back by so very few."

"Valiant efforts disgust me," Velixar said. "The west gate is yours to destroy. Let in our troops however you see fit."

Tessanna beamed and blew him a kiss. "I knew you'd let me have my fun," she said.

She eyed the city as her breathing quickened and her pulse raced. Fire consumed many buildings. The smoke floated in a gentle breeze. Somewhere within was her reflection. Mother had told her to shatter her reflection, and she would obey. The pleasure in the imagining was overwhelming. But the men at the gate with their shields and swords were keeping her from her pleasure.

"Blood is a strange thing," she said. Her fingers crossed. Magic leapt out of her like a river. A hundred orcs lined before the gate lurched and howled as their blood exploded out their bodies. The blood flowed through the air in rivers, pooling above the ground as Tessanna held it firm in her mind. "It is our life, and at its loss we die...but no other substance in our world holds so much magic and desire for death. Well, other than you, Velixar."

The blood sank to the ground. It grew thicker, stronger, congealing and reshaping as necessary. From the great pool three forms stood, each with feminine features. They had no eyes, but they did not need them. They could sense the blood of their foes. Tessanna shook her fingers, and strange words poured faster and faster from her mouth. The beings grew larger, drawing in the blood from which they formed. Soon they were five times the size of a normal man. Around their heads blood congealed into long ropes of hair that flowed down to their ankles. Although they had no eyes, they did have mouths, and each one opened and let out a shriek that pierced the sounds of battle.

"You must teach me that spell," Velixar said as he watched in awe.

"Blood elementals," Tessanna said as she smiled. "Aren't they beautiful?"

The elementals marched toward the gateway where Antonil's men stood horrified. The two paladins rushed the front and stood side by side. Haern, however, had other plans. He weaved through the ranks of the soldiers to Mira, who sat resting against a wall.

"You're needed," Haern said to her.

"Haern," she said. "Will you protect me?"

He took her hand. "Until death, my lady. Now come."

The first of the blood elementals neared the entrance. It was taller than the walls, but rather than duck inside the gateway it struck with its fists. The stone cracked and crumbled. A second stepped beside it and rammed its shoulder against the wall. Soldiers dove back as the gateway collapsed in on itself. At first it appeared the rubble would still hold them at bay, but then the three grabbed chunks of stone and hurled them away.

Antonil stood at the front of his soldiers as the first elemental stepped through the wall and into the city.

"Can these things be killed?" he asked Haern.

"Everything can be killed," the assassin replied. "Be brave. Your men need it."

Mira raised her hand to the air, a tiny pebble of light swirling inside her palm.

"Demon elemental," she shouted. "Be gone from my sight!"

It raised its foot to crush her. The light shot from her palm, leaving a trail of red in its wake. When it hit the skin of the elemental it pierced through, traveling up its leg to its waist before exploding. The thing shrieked as it was severed in two, its upper body collapsing in a shower of blood. The legs toppled in the gateway. The magic holding the elemental together was broken. Streams of red poured across the feet of the soldiers. The second elemental stepped inside, bellowing in rage. Mira raised her hand, and another white pebble formed across her palm. The elemental, however, grabbed an enormous chunk of stone and hurled it at her. Mira released the light, shattering the stone into a giant rain of pebbles. Clanks and pings filled the air as the stone fell upon armor and shields.

Before Mira could prepare, a piece of the wall hurled through the air toward her.

"Get back!" Haern shouted. He took Mira in his arms and leapt aside. The rock smashed where she had been then continued, crushing several soldiers in its path. The elemental passed through the wall and into the city. At Antonil's command, his soldiers charged, hacking at the elemental's legs and feet. The swords cut through the thick dried layer that made up its skin and released the blood swirling inside. It poured over them all in sheets, coating their armor and weapons.

The thing let out a shriek, a strange sound akin to a wounded bird of prey. Furious, it slammed its fists to the ground, crushing men in their armor, then kicked a soldier so hard he flew through the air and landed atop a house. Two more it hurled back to the orc army. Still the cuts grew in number, biting into its skin and keeping it at bay.

Haern put Mira down far to the side of the entrance. The blood elemental was still visible, fighting against soldiers that came up only to its knees.

"It's just blood," the girl said as she watched the fight. "Just blood."

Fire enveloped her hands. She unleashed her power in a stream of flame, its width greater than the length of her own body. The stream arced as if shot from a cannon, striking the elemental in the chest at the height of its ascent. The elemental shrieked, its skin hardening into long black strips that fell from its body. Jerico slammed his shield against its leg, and then it went down. Antonil led the rest, hacking and cutting its body as it lay vulnerable.

The last elemental picked up giant rocks in each hand and hurled them at the soldiers slaughtering its sister. Both pieces shattered in the air, broken by unseen magic. Lathaar glanced down the street, and his heart lifted at the sight.

Marching in rows of five were the priests of Ashhur, their hands to the air and holy power crackling around them. Swords made of light sliced across the elemental's chest, face, and arms. It took a step forward, but Mira blasted it with a ball of fire. Antonil called back his men, knowing their part was over. More holy power washed over the creature, sundering Tessanna's hold upon it. With one last shriek, it crumbled. Blood showered down upon the gore-covered dirt.

"No celebrating yet!" Antonil shouted, running through his troops and forcing them to line up. "Form ranks, form ranks, the city is vulnerable!"

What had once been a chokehold was now a giant opening in the wall. Rows of orcs were raised their banners to Karak and cheered.

"Antonil Copernus!" one of the priests shouted from the formation. Calan stepped out and beckoned the guard captain to him.

"My gratitude for your aid," Antonil told the old priest, "but the orcs are about to charge and..."

"I know," Calan said, interrupting him. "Listen to me. Our wall has been breached. The city is lost. Take the king and flee. There are ways out to the King's Forest from the castle. The soldiers, peasants, the children...take them with you."

"Who will hold the wall?"

Calan gestured to his priests. "We can hold them for a time. Take your men and do what must be done to preserve the lives of our people."

Antonil glanced to the orc horde. He was terribly outnumbered, with a paltry force left to hold the opening. And once they fell, the city was doomed. Everything inside him hated the thought of fleeing, but he knew more was at stake than his pride.

"I will take my soldiers to the king," he told the priest. "Hold as long as you can."

Calan nodded, and he put his hand on the man's shoulder.

"You are a good man, a good leader," he said. "The people will need you in the coming months. Be strong for them." He turned back to the priests and raised his hands high above his head. "Let our voices be heard by Ashhur, and let our faith be a shield against the coming darkness," he prayed.

Calan turned back to the broken wall, braced his legs, and held out his left hand. Behind him the rest of the priests did the same. They closed their eyes, bowed their heads, and gave themselves to Ashhur. A white beam flew from each of their palms, collecting together into a massive stream. It bubbled outward, through the gap in the wall, and out into the field. There it turned back in on itself, sealing the shattered gateway away from Velixar and his horde.

"Soldiers of Neldar," Antonil shouted. "To the castle!"

The Eschaton there gathered together, watching the remaining troops march east.

"He doesn't believe we can hold now the gateway is destroyed," Lathaar said.

"He is right," Haern said. "The priests will hold them at bay until their strength fades. They are buying us time."

"What do we do?" Jerico asked.

"Follow him," Lathaar said. "Until we know more, we follow."

They did, even as the orcs hacked at the white shield with their weapons, ignoring the pain it gave them, for they too knew the shield could not last forever.

Once it fell, the city was theirs.

16

Qurrah eyed the fire with mild amusement. It was a simple barrier of flame that would burn for hours in a thick line, but inside the cramped gateway it was lethal. The orcs parted for him, recognizing his power and station. Only one did not move, and it was Gumgog, waiting for him with his real arm and his giant club arm crossed across his chest.

"I tried smothering the fire with orcs," Gumgog said. "But they just burned. Waste of orcs. You gonna put it out?"

Qurrah chuckled at the Warmaster.

"Yes. I will put it out. Keep back your horde until I say it is safe, understood?"

"Alright," Gumgog said. "You got some orc blood, so you be trustworthy, eh?"

Qurrah said nothing as he approached the fire. To his right he saw an orc crawling toward his army. His legs had been crushed by an ice boulder from Aurelia. He was in pain, but he was alive.

"*Kerlem frau spevorr!*" Qurrah shouted, stretching out five fingers. The orc shrieked as horrendous pain spiked up his back. Qurrah's hand shook, magic pouring out his fingers. Blood spurted out the orc's lower back. His tailbone tore through the flesh. The orc's shrieks grew louder as his ribs cracked and his muscles tore. With a cry of victory, Qurrah lifted his hand high. The spinal cord ripped out the orc's body, dripping blood and gore. The shrieks ended. With a word of magic, Qurrah lit the spine and skull aflame, burning it clean.

"To me," Qurrah said, beckoning with his fingers. The spine floated to his hand. He held it like a staff. Those who had watched the spectacle cheered and howled, not caring for the loss of one of their own, only thrilled by the awesome display of power. Both hands clutching the staff, Qurrah approached the fire. It burned strong, and it was so thick he could not see through it. He had an idea what awaited him on the other side. Aurelia or Tarlak protected the gate, perhaps even both. If he banished the fire, they would just recast the spell. He would have to defeat them, despite what Velixar might say.

Fifty feet from the fire, he slammed the bottom of the staff against the ground. A wave of counter-magic streaked toward the gate, invisible to the naked eye. The two walls of fire sputtered and died. The orcs cheered, but Qurrah did not move, nor did he give signal to attack.

Aurelia stepped into the gateway, her staff in her left hand. She glared at Qurrah but said nothing. Qurrah felt a chill at the sight of her, but he also felt excitement lifting the hairs on his neck. He could kill her. He *would* kill her. No guilt would claw at his throat. He let no worry eat his insides. Aurelia would die.

The elf hurled a lance of ice from her right hand. Qurrah struck it with the skull of his staff. The lance shattered into harmless frost and snow. He threw a bolt of shadow into the entrance. Aurelia summoned a magical shield, and his attack splashed and dissipated against it. Lightning sparkled on her fingers. With both hands, she clutched her staff and lunged the bottom half at him. From the wood, a giant beam of yellow streaked straight for Qurrah. He clutched his bone staff and slammed the ground. Another wave of counter-magic flowed, defeating the beam.

His pale fingers caressed the skull of his staff, coercing the magic out. The jaw clattered, and a haunting laughter came from within. Twenty orange and red balls shot from the eyes, dancing and twirling in the air before shooting straight for Aurelia. The elf leaned against her staff and summoned her shield. The orange balls exploded into fire and ash, each one sapping a bit more of her strength. When the last exploded, they stared at one another, neither saying a word.

Tarlak stepped beside her from within the city. Fire swirled around his hands. A ball of flame seared through the air, but Qurrah hooked his hands and stole control of it. The fire turned away from him and headed straight back at Tarlak. The mage crossed his hands and spread his fingers. A magical ward against fire surrounded his body, so that when the flame struck he felt little of its heat. Smoke filled the gateway, and for a brief moment Qurrah could not see the spellcasters. Then two blasts of magic, one fire, one ice, shot through the smoke, both in thick beams the size of his body. The fire Qurrah merely sidestepped, letting it kill several behind him. The ice he detonated early with a piece of bone from his pocket.

Qurrah whispered words of magic, letting the dark power flow from his tongue. Ten orcs collapsed and died, the bones from their bodies tearing through their flesh and into the air. They flew in a river toward the gateway, dripping blood. Aurelia created a wall of ice to protect them, but Qurrah blasted a hole in its center with a wave of his hand. The bone pieces shot through, striking her skin. Tarlak leapt in front and slammed his hands to the ground. A shockwave rolled outward, destroying the rest of the ice wall and turning the bone pieces to chalk. Before either could muster an attack, Qurrah hurled a wave of counter-magic with his staff. Both were knocked back, an alien feeling overcoming them as all magic was temporarily denied from their bodies. As the wave passed, Qurrah approached, for he could see how little strength they had left to fight him.

"Why?" Tarlak asked as he neared. "What honor is in this? What justice? What reason?"

"No honor," Qurrah said, washing another wave of counter-magic over them. "No justice. Punishment for a city that banished me. Vengeance against those who sought to kill me. Retribution against those who turned my brother against me. That is what I bring."

Harruq stepped in front of the gateway. He leaned against the side as if his legs could barely support him. He looked groggy and dazed, as if he had just awaken from a sleep.

"No one turned me against you," he said to his brother. "You did that yourself. You're a slave of Karak now, nothing more."

Qurrah laughed. He spread his arms wide, clutching his bone staff with one hand. It seemed the entire wall shook with his laughter.

"I am no slave!" he said. "And I am no servant! Do you know what I am, brother? Do you know?"

Harruq watched as Qurrah's eyes flared red, first once, then twice. It was like watching the first gentle flames of a fire kindling. Harruq knew those eyes. He knew that glow.

"I am Karak's left hand," Qurrah said, his hissing voice washed over by a deep, rumbling sound of foreign power. "I am his fire, and I will burn everything I touch."

His eyes shone a fierce red, glowing even in the morning light. Running down scars underneath his eyes were constant streams of blood that burned aflame, like the tears of a demon.

Aurelia unleashed a barrage of lightning, but Qurrah caught its power with one hand, collected it in a ball inside his fist, and then hurled it back. She screamed in pain as the last of her magical wards broke. She flew back, badly burned. Her thin form crumpled in the street. Sergan's soldiers swarmed over her, their shields raised to protect her from any more harm. Furious at the sight, Tarlak tried to cast a spell of fire, but a flash of red from the skull's eyes blinded him and scrambled his thoughts. Before he could resume, bone pieces slammed against his forehead and neck, beating him back.

Only Harruq stood against him. Qurrah looked at his brother with eyes that were not his own.

"You did not kill me when you had the chance," he said. "Somewhere within you is the desire to stand at my side. Join me. Velixar dreamt of you leading his armies. It is not too late."

Salvation and Condemnation shook in Harruq's hands. Sadness and rage whirled inside him, greater than Qurrah would ever know.

"You believe no one can change," Harruq said. "But you're wrong. You know nothing of me. Be gone from my home."

He slammed his swords into the sides of the gate. Stone shattered and broke. He struck the left wall with both his blades. The foundation shook.

"Die in darkness, brother," Qurrah said, a beam of black magic shooting from his right hand. Harruq screamed, his rage inside burning. He crossed his arms and let the blow hit. He felt the magic strike his skin but he did not care. He would not succumb to it. He would not fall, even if all the world came crashing down on his shoulders. White lightning crackled from his weapons. Qurrah saw him resisting. He poured all his strength into his spell. Harruq's entire body shook, and Qurrah thought him ready to fall, ready to die, but he was wrong.

"I am not the weaker!" Harruq screamed. He pushed back the magic. His arms flung wide, and inside the gateway a sound like thunder shook the Tun brothers. Salvation and Condemnation struck the stone walls at either side, and through the stone a shockwave rumbled, blasting away its foundations. The evil spell flew back from Harruq and assaulted Qurrah. He felt the pain sweep across his body. The force of it knocked him back, and he flew through the air as the gateway crumbled in on itself. When he hit the ground his body writhed in pain, from both the spell and the fall, but Qurrah's thoughts were far away. All he could focus on was how in those last few moments Harruq's eyes had shimmered gold.

Harruq!" Tarlak screamed as the gateway collapsed. Dust billowed everywhere, and he closed his eyes against the sting. As it settled, he saw Harruq standing before the rubble, his swords held at his sides. His entire body was lifting and falling with his breathing. Every muscle was taut. He looked like a paragon of strength, and Tarlak was awed by the sight of it. When Harruq sheathed his swords and turned, the image vanished.

"Where's Aurelia?" Harruq asked. He noticed the look Tarlak was giving him but misunderstood its meaning. "Where is she?" he demanded.

"She's here, lad," Sergan said, pushing aside the soldiers that still guarded her with their shields. "A little burned, but she's breathing."

Harruq rushed over and took her into his arms. Her dress was blackened across the front, and ugly burns marred her chest. Her eyes were closed, but her breathing was soft and constant. As he brushed the side of her face with his fingers, Tarlak cast a spell across the rubble, covering it with a thin sheet of ice.

"Let's see you climb up that," he said. He took off his hat and reached inside, frowning as he did. He had stashed a wide assortment of potions in his mad dash through his tower, but wasn't sure of how many. Four? Five? More? From within his hat he pulled out a single healing potion and sighed.

"Good enough," he said. He knelt beside Harruq and offered it to him.

"Thanks," the half-orc said. He twisted off the cork and gently tilted it against Aurelia's lower lip. At first she coughed, but Harruq was persistent. He covered her mouth with his hand, and when her coughing died she swallowed the rest on instinct. The burns on her chest lost their angry red. Her eyes fluttered open.

"Where...is he still here?" she asked.

"Qurrah's outside," Harruq said. "I sent him away."

"Good," Aurelia said, closing her eyes and leaning against his chest. "I'll sleep here for awhile then."

Sergan placed his soldiers in front of the crumbled gateway in case any orcs tried to climb over. This done, he hefted his axe onto his shoulder and stood beside the Eschaton.

"So what now?" the old veteran asked.

"Rest," Tarlak said. "You won't get many chances. Hop atop the wall and see how the other gate fares."

Sergan motioned for one of his men to climb atop and see. When the man returned, he looked baffled.

"It looks like a web is covering the entrance, sir," the soldier said. "It's white and it glows. Damned if I know what it is."

"Some sort of magic protecting the entrance," Tarlak said. "Consider it good. Keep your men sharp, and be ready for anything. Who knows what Qurrah and his minions might do to enter."

Sergan moved away, leaving the Eschaton by themselves. As Aurelia rested, the mage scratched his head and looked at the half-orc.

"Do you know what you just did back there?" he asked.

"Aye," Harruq said. "I did something I don't understand. Clear enough for you?"

"Not even close. You toppled the wall with your swords alone. We both know, enchanted or not, your swords don't possess that strength."

"What are you saying, Tar?"

Tarlak plopped down beside them. "I'm saying I have no clue what I just saw, Harruq, but it scared me to death."

"Yeah," Harruq said, looking down at Aurelia so he didn't have to face Tarlak's inquisitive gaze. "To tell you the truth, it scared me too. But I knew what I was doing. I just knew. And for one moment there, just one moment, everything felt right."

Tarlak paused, a strange worry churning in his gut. "We have to get to the center," he said.

"What? Why?" Harruq asked.

"Trust me on this, alright? We need to go!"

The half-orc lifted Aurelia into his arms and nodded. "Lead on."

They left Sergan to guard the remains of the gateway as they hurried north.

Qurrah returned to Velixar with his head hung low. Another dark paladin had offered him a ride back, which he took ungratefully. When he dismounted he knelt before Velixar and offered his apologies.

"I failed you, my master," he said. "The southern gate is sealed off with rubble. My brother defeated me."

"Stand, Qurrah, it is no matter." Velixar gestured to the white shield summoned by the priests of Ashhur. "Do you know what you see? A last desperate measure by a dying city. The wall is broken, the way into the city clear. It is now just a matter of time. When their strength fails, we will push through. And fail it will."

Velixar waved his hand over his throat, casting the spell with but a thought. When he spoke, he spoke not to those around him but to the entire city.

"People of Neldar," he said. "Your walls have fallen. Your last measures are failing. Your army has abandoned you to death. I am the word of Karak. I am his witness, his prophet, and his sword. Fall to your knees and worship the true god and you will live. Ashhur has not abandoned you, for you were never in his care. Cast aside your delusions. Worship Karak. Cry his name. Seek his forgiveness. If you do not, then you will die by the sword, and you will not rest. Your corpse will rise, and even in death you will serve. Choose, people of Neldar. Service in life, or service in death. You have no other choice."

Velixar smiled and ended the spell.

"I have long waited to give that speech," he said. "And it was as glorious as I had always hoped. Order Gumgog to bring his troops to the western gate. Our victory is near."

◁◈▷

Antonil rushed up the steps of the castle. The guards stationed there threw open the door so he could enter. He marched down the carpeted hall, feeling a strange anger at the luxury around him. He was covered in blood, and his boots left red footprints across the carpet. He took off his helmet and held it in his hand. In his other hand he held the hilt of his sword as it swayed in its sheath. Sitting on his throne, still wearing the ungainly gold armor, waited King Edwin Vaelor of Neldar.

"Your highness," Antonil said as he bowed on one knee. "We must get you to safety. The walls will soon be breached. There are tunnels to the forest, and from there we can flee to Felwood castle."

At first Vaelor only stared at Antonil as if he were staring at a half-finished puzzle.

"You wish us to flee," the king said at last. "You would let them plunder our city while we cowered in the woods. I will not be a beggar king. Lord Gandrem would sooner hold me prisoner and retake Neldar in his name after the orcs are slaughtered."

Antonil felt his cheeks flush red. He could feel the heat of his anger baking off of him.

"It is either that or death, my lord," he said.

"Is that a threat?" The king stood, towering over Antonil because of the raised platform his throne rest upon. "We will die fighting and in glory, not hiding. Is your spine so soft, you coward?"

At one time Antonil might have felt intimidated, but now he felt only fury.

"You bathe in scented oils and perfumes," he said, rising to his feet. "I have bathed in the blood of my friends and foes, yet you call *me* a coward?"

"How dare you speak to me in such a manner!"

Antonil put his helmet back on his head and glared at the pathetic man before him.

"I will save as many lives as I can and then flee this city of tombs. I swore to protect Neldar, and so I shall."

"Then you are a traitor to the crown," King Vaelor shouted. "How dare you commit such treason?"

Antonil turned and pulled the crown from Vaelor's head. In one smooth motion he placed it on the ground and then smashed it with his sword. Gems broke from the gold and rolled across the floor. He grabbed the king by the top of his armor and pulled him close so that he could smell the stink of blood on him.

"There is no crown," Antonil said. "And the blame is yours."

He stormed out of the castle. As he marched down the steps, the king rushed out, screaming at his guards.

"Seize him," he shouted. "He is a traitor, a coward. I demand you execute him!"

Antonil stopped and glared at the two guards. They looked between one another, their swords wavering unsteady in their hands.

"I will not spare your lives," Antonil said. "Lower your weapons."

To the king's horror they did as they were told and then joined Antonil in their march away from the castle. Vaelor returned inside, closing the giant doors on his own. It was the last time Antonil would ever see him.

◁╬▷

The priests' shield was weakening. It no longer harmed those that struck it, so Trummug had every orc in his army hurling his weapon at the shimmering white magic. Velixar laughed, enjoying every second.

"Let the dead rise," he whispered. Karak's power flooded his being. He shouted out the words of his spell. Over a thousand dead bodies of orcs, hyena-men, and bird-men rose from the ground, held sway by his command. A chill swept through Qurrah at the sight.

"Beautiful," Tessanna whispered.

In his joy, Velixar could wait no longer. A solid black beam shot from his hands and into the white shield, which flickered and bowed inward against the barrage. The ground shook as the priests' last protection for the city broke. The orcs needed no command. Into the city they poured, where the priests waited. Their strength was spent. Their role was played. They raised their arms to the sky and let the axes fall, knowing the Golden Eternity waited for them.

Velixar gave his last warning to the city.

"Your walls are breached. Your city is lost. Come out of your homes and kneel. Cast aside your weapons, your faith, and your lives. Serve Karak as you were always meant to serve."

The thousand undead shouted the name 'Karak' in perfect unison, the sound horrifying to every soul within the walls. Velixar cast one last spell on his orc army. They heard his voice in their ears, and the power of his command was great. Those that kneeled, lived. Those that did not, died. The orcs obeyed. The slaughter began. Those hiding behind locked doors and barred windows lived as long as the barricades held, which under the biting axes and raging muscle of the horde, was not long. In minutes, the entire west side of the city was filled with blood and the cries of the dying.

❖

"Shit," Harruq said as he heard Velixar's message. All around were the people of Neldar. They were terrified, and every one was filled with an instinct to flee. They had nowhere to go, no safe haven. And then they started kneeling. More than half cast down what meager weapons they had and kneeled. A few prayed. Others just waited for death.

"Cowards!" Harruq screamed to them. "Karak brings you nothing! He's no savior. He doesn't know mercy!"

"They're just scared," Aurelia said. "Put me down, Har."

He did as he was told. The sight of so many on their knees filled his blood with anger. How many had died to protect their lives? Would they blaspheme against the sacrifice made for them by their worship of a death god?

"Aurry," Harruq asked, "can you make my voice loud, like his?" He gestured west, toward the general direction Velixar's voice had come.

"I can," Tarlak said. "What you have in mind?"

"We go east," he said. "And we go fast."

He ran down the street, not caring if they caught up. His heart was racing. He could hear it throbbing in his ears. All about men, women, and children were opening their doors and kneeling. He wanted to shout and curse their names, but he did not. There were those loyal to Ashhur, he knew. He would call them to him. Those with the will to live. Those with the courage to fight.

Since the eastern side had no gate, and therefore no traffic, the more wealthy had built their homes within. Harruq watched as the homes grew nicer and the streets better cared for. At the end of the road he saw the wall, looming high above the homes. A glance behind him showed Tarlak and Aurelia both running after. When he reached the wall he stopped, not the least bit winded.

"Cast the spell," he said. Tarlak glared, still trying to catch his breath. He put his hand on Harruq's neck and then muttered the spell. The half-orc felt a tingle in his throat and assumed it ready. He sheathed his swords, cupped his hands to his mouth, and began shouting.

"People of Neldar! Come to the east gate! If you want to live, if you want to fight, then here is your salvation. Come east! Come east!"

He turned back to Tarlak and nodded. The mage snapped his fingers, ending the spell.

"So," Harruq said. "You two ready to make us a gate?"

He backed away as the two casters put their hands upon the stone. They muttered amongst each other, picking a spell to cast in unison. When decided, they began. Words of magic flowed from their lips. The wall shook as invisible waves assaulted the stone. Harruq watched as Aurelia grimaced, pain etched on her every feature. His heart ached at the sight. Their spell finished. The stone exploded outward, leaving a giant gap in the wall. Six men could walk side by side through if their shoulders touched.

The last of the rubble had not yet hit the ground when Aurelia collapsed to her knees. Harruq drew his swords and let her be. He faced the west. The road was broad. Many people could travel through. How many would come, though? How many?

"I'll be fine," Aurelia said as Tarlak helped her to her feet. "My head, I just can't think straight, I can't…give me a moment." She leaned against the wall and closed her eyes. Tarlak rubbed his temples, knowing how she felt. Near the end he had almost fainted. He doubted he could throw a fireball larger than his thumb.

"So we guard our new gate," Tarlak asked as the first few survivors came running toward them.

"*I* guard our new gate," Harruq corrected. "You two aid the refugees. They'll need protected." To emphasize this, he pointed to the ring of dark paladins and clerics that encircled the city. "They'll kill any that try to cross."

More people arrived. They held little, a few random provisions or possessions dear to them. The death and carnage on the opposite side of the city seemed worlds away.

"You be careful," Aurelia said, kissing Harruq before taking Tarlak's hand.

"Don't do anything dumb," Tarlak said, tipping his hat. The two followed the fleeing civilians out. Harruq did not watch them go. He didn't want the distraction, nor the worry. Blades in hand, he watched for the first of the orcs to arrive, all the while screaming above the crowd.

"Come east! Come east!"

"Come east?" Velixar asked as he heard Harruq's rallying cry.

"There is no east gate," Qurrah said. "Has he lost his mind?"

Once the entire orc army had funneled inside the city, Velixar ordered his undead to enter. They poured in through the broken west gate like a river of rotten flesh. Qurrah did not watch, instead focused on a dark paladin rider arriving. The paladin pulled heavily on his reigns to halt his horse.

"The people of Veldaren are fleeing," the rider said. "There is a gap in the east wall. One of their mages must have created it."

Velixar looked at his undead entering the city and wondered. "It is too far around to seal the other side," he said.

"Push our forces harder. We will overcome them from behind."

The man in black turned to Tessanna.

"Yes, lovely?" she asked him.

"Fetch Bloodheel," he ordered her.

She placed two fingers in her mouth and whistled. Neither Qurrah nor Velixar heard a sound, but the five-hundred wolf-men waiting behind them howled. From the giant pack a towering behemoth of fur, muscle, and fang emerged, his entire body decorated with the bones of dead foes he had eaten.

"We come to fight," Bloodheel said, his rumbling voice deeper than Velixar's. "But we truly came to feast. The city is bleeding. When will we taste blood?"

In response, Velixar pointed past the southern tip of the city's walls.

"The people of Neldar are fleeing the city to the east. Unprotected. Unprepared. Slaughter them all."

Bloodheel arched and howled to the morning sky, his yellow eyes shimmering with hungry lust.

"We will not fail you," he said. He dropped to all fours and began running. On either side the rest of the pack passed, howling and drooling.

"The carnage will be complete," Velixar said, a smile growing on his ever-changing face. "Praise be to Karak."

"Praise, indeed," Qurrah said as the wolf-men vanished around the walls of the city.

Well, here we are," Lathaar said as they arrived at the fountain in the center of the city. "Ready for some fun?"

"Always am," Haern said. He leapt to a nearby home and kicked off an open window to propel himself to the roof. From there he scanned the major roads in all directions. Thousands of people filled the streets, herding to the center and then turning east toward the supposed safety and freedom there.

"You see anything," Jerico shouted over the commotion of the frightened people. Beside him Mira clutched at her robes, her arms crossed and her hands shaking. The fear around her was leaking in, but the bloodlust from afar was worse. When Jerico saw her tired, crying face he only wiped the tears away with his thumb and smiled.

Haern turned his eyes west. All he saw was a sea of gray flesh and burning buildings. Its progress was steady. Every home was broken into and its occupants slaughtered. The orcs who couldn't find a warm body to butcher moved further into the city. The bulk of the army was on the main roads, but like a disease it had spread throughout the entirety of the western half.

"Almost time," Haern shouted back. He took three steps and then leapt to the top of the statue. From there he wrapped himself in his cloaks and waited. Swarms of men and women passed, the panic on their faces obvious.

The orcs' arrival was sudden. Thirty came barreling near, their axes and swords cleaving innocent flesh. Behind them, the few remaining humans knelt and cried out to Karak for salvation. The sound of their pleading was far worse to Haern than any scream of pain from the dying. He jumped, activating the power of his ring as he did. His momentum forward continued, even after his body vanished in a puff of shadow and reappeared ten feet west. He descended on the orcs as a swirling gray death. Two had their throats cut as he landed. A twist, a step, and two more dropped, tendons cut and necks bleeding. The orcs surrounded him, but the assassin had begun his cloak dance. The first to try a wild chop in the center of gray cloaks had three of his fingers severed. The axe dropped to the ground, soaked in blood. The orc tried to retrieve it with his good hand. He died.

"For Ashhur!" Lathaar shouted, slashing the nearest orc across the shoulder. They had encountered no resistance since entering the city. They were not prepared for the Eschaton that had gathered in the center. Most had their backs turned to them, fighting against Haern as he slaughtered their kind from within. When Lathaar tore through their ranks, the orcs knew their error. Any who turned to face the paladin felt steel biting into their backs from Haern. They screamed and fled, wanting no part of either.

"The west is dead," Mira said, watching them go. "Those who remain alive have given themselves to Karak."

She spread her arms, gathering her power. Her eyes closed as she focused on the magic that dwelled within her. From the sky a giant meteor of fire materialized, traveling at blistering speeds. It slammed into the street, crushing the orcs with the force of its impact. Houses beside it crumbled. Dust filled the air, blocking all vision of the road.

"South!" Jerico shouted, pushing his way through the crowd with his shield. More orcs had come, flooding the streets from the back ways of the western quarter. The paladin watched in horror as the orcs butchered over a hundred unarmed men and women. Only nine lived, all falling to their knees and shouting Karak's name at the top of their lungs. Jerico felt his mace shaking in his hand at the sight. The last of the human survivors ran past, and only he stood before the gray mass.

"Death's waiting," Jerico said, slamming his shield with his mace. "Come and you shall receive."

The orcs charged. He blocked the first strike against his shield, smiling at the sound of the weapon shattering. He stepped back and swung his mace, cracking the orc's skull open. Two more rushed, but he parried both their attacks, stepped closer to the first, and then slammed his shield across its face. Holy power flared, killing it instantly. Jerico backed off, rotating from side to side, letting the orcs endure the pain they felt every time their swords or axes struck his shield. Several tried to run past to flank, but every time he'd spin and slam Bonebreaker into their gut or face.

He was nearing the fountain when he saw a gray blur fly overhead. Jerico charged, knowing all too well what that meant. Howls of pain came from the pack as Haern did what he did best. Jerico struck down the two nearest, slammed aside a third with his shield, and then met Haern amid the bodies.

"Well met," Jerico said to Haern before running toward the larger group of orcs further down the street. At least thirty by his count. Probably more. He shouted the name of his god and met the charge. His legs braced, his shield raised, he felt the tremendous weight slam against him. Axes cut across his platemail. Fingers pried at his eyes and the open areas of his armor. The orcs tried to bury him beneath their feet, but he was a pillar of stone that would not be broken.

As the last of their momentum died, he screamed in mindless agony. He could feel the blood running down his body, much of it his. And then he pushed them back. A glowing image of his shield filled the entire street, its light blinding even in the morning sun. When he stepped forward the shield struck. The orcs shrieked as it crushed their bodies, broke their bones, and knocked them hundreds of feet back as a pile of twisted corpses that rained upon the street.

Jerico staggered, his strength fading. When he turned to the fountain he saw Lathaar making his stand against streams of orcs. Mira fought behind him, killing tens at a time with fireballs and lances of ice. Haern weaved around the sorceress, taking down any who avoided Lathaar and tried to attack the unarmored girl.

"Too many," Jerico shouted as he ran to them. "We go to Harruq!"

Over a hundred filled the southern roads. Some approached them at the center, while others continued east, slaughtering those who refused to kneel. He looked to the north, expecting the same scene, but instead he saw soldiers marching in rows. Their swords were drawn and their armor was caked with blood. Antonil led them.

"Pull back!" Antonil shouted to the Eschaton. "We will cover your retreat."

Lathaar swung side to side, forcing his opponents to step back, and that room was all he needed. He turned and ran east, grabbing Mira's hand as he did. Haern spun his cloaks to hide his form and then cut down the first two who tried to run past.

Before he was buried by the orcs, he activated the magic in his ring and reappeared on the other side of the fountain.

Antonil's men were down to two-hundred, having lost twenty during their march south from the castle. He positioned five at the start of the eastern road, saluting them with his sword.

"Hold," was all he told them. The men saluted and then turned to the mass of orcs. They locked together their shields, braced themselves, and prepared for death.

"They'll be slaughtered," Mira said as they ran.

"They sacrifice so we may live," Antonil said. "And may Ashhur forgive me for demanding such a thing from them."

The girl pulled her hand free from Lathaar's grip and turned back to the five. The orcs pushed and slammed against them, but they held firm, stabbing over their shields and pushing back the greater numbers. When over a hundred more orcs neared, the men only raised their swords high and cheered.

Mira did not understand what she was witnessing, did not understand the valor and courage driving them, but she knew she would honor it. They would not be defiled and made to suffer. She hurled a giant fireball as they were buried beneath the wave of orcs. It turned them to ash and slaughtered more than forty of the orcs they had fought.

"Come on," Lathaar said, taking her hand once more. An army on their heels, they ran.

✜

Stay hidden among the people," Tarlak told Aurelia as they hurried away from Veldaren. "If we can catch them off guard, the better."

The sea of refugees neared the circle of priests and dark paladins. A hundred were ahead of them, their legs fueled by fear and adrenaline. Their hearts in their throats, Tarlak and Aurelia watched as the first reached the black circle. The men and women tried running past. The dark paladins drew their swords, offered a prayer of thanks to Karak, and then slaughtered any who neared. Bodies piled at their feet, killed by their burning black blades. The priests poured prayers to Karak and touched those near them with their hands. Horrible pain flooded those inflicted, and wounds like knife cuts covered their bodies. Of the first hundred, only twenty made it past alive.

"Butchers," Tarlak said. "Take out the priests first."

"I'll try," Aurelia said. The two picked a target and attacked. Tarlak's priest was caught unaware and without any wards for protection. A bolt of lightning struck him square in the chest, obliterating his heart. Trailing behind it was a lance of ice by Aurelia. Her priest managed to bring up his hands, and a spell was half-finished on his lips when the lance punched through his throat and pinned him to the ground. They both turned on the final priest. He summoned a protective shield, but Aurelia's fireball broke its power, and Tarlak finished him with a barrage of twenty magical arrows.

The dark paladins attacked, cutting down those unlucky enough to be in their way. They split, one after Aurelia, one after Tarlak. Aurelia knew any spell she cast to protect herself would not be strong enough against their blades, so instead she did her best to keep them back. She tore up chunks of earth and hurled them at him. As he punched and pushed his way through she knelt and touched the ground. A patch of ice stretched from her fingers to his feet. In his bulky armor he had little hope of keeping his balance.

She tried to cast a spell, but then those behind her jostled her forward. The people were running scared, and there were too many for them to recognize the battle transpiring. She fell onto the ice, cracking her forehead. Purple lines marred her vision. She tasted blood. As if underwater she heard the rest of the refugees, their shouts and crying a garbled murmur. But worse was the knowledge that the dark paladin surely approached.

"I got you," a voice whispered, still muffled. It felt like swabs of cotton clogged her ears. Someone picked her up and balanced her on her feet. She looked up and saw the dark paladin dead, smoke rising from his armor. She glanced to her side to see it was Tarlak holding her. The two were levitating an inch above the ice. The swarm of people fleeing were avoiding the ice, and therefore avoiding them.

"They're dead," Tarlak told her. "Are you alright?"

"I can't think, I can't..." She closed her eyes and put her head on his chest. "I'm sorry. I'm not weak, not like this, shouldn't be, I shouldn't be..."

"Shush," Tarlak said. "We both are. My head is going to explode if I cast another spell, but we have no choice. More are coming, Aurelia."

She looked back to the city, and there she saw the wolf-men, almost five-hundred running on all fours. They were less than a mile away, yet already they could smell the fear in the sweat of their prey.

"I can't," Aurelia said, turning away. Her eyes downcast, she shook her head again and again.

"You can," Tarlak said, taking her head in his hands and forcing her gaze back up to him.

"No," she said, tears running down her cheeks. "Please, I can't."

"You will," Tarlak said. "And so will I. If we fail, we fail. But I will not let any more die, even if it means dying myself."

The ice below them faded, its duration ended. Tarlak lowered them to the grass, took off his hat, and reached inside. He pulled out a single vial. He had hoped for more but he had been too quick to scavenge items from his tower.

"Drink this," he told her. "It'll clear your head and make you feel like you just had a solid hour of sleep." The two stepped out from the stream of refugees running a blind east, with no goal other than to leave the city far behind. A few spotted the wolf-men, and their screams of fear alerted the rest. They fled faster, pushed harder. Those who tripped or were too weak to continue were trampled.

"Pay no attention to behind us," Tarlak said. "Stand still and cast until you can't cast anymore, and even then continue. If we take enough, then maybe they'll have a shot."

The wolf-men howled in unison, ready to kill, ready to feast. Aurelia drank the contents of the vial, all her will keeping her from gagging on the foul taste. Her mind did clear, and the terrible ache in her temples faded. She dropped the vial to the grass.

"Thank you," she said.

"Don't mention it," Tarlak said. He took out a wand from within his robe and held it with both hands. "Let's just hope I get the chance to make you another."

A worn and battered pair, they waited for the wolf-men to close the distance and the slaughter to begin.

17

Harruq stood before the gap in the wall. His head was down, and his hair covered his face. Salvation and Condemnation were at his sides, their tips jammed into the dirt. His eyes stared at the people that fled to him and the safety he had offered. Even in their panic, they made sure not to touch him. Something about him made them stay clear. He did not see, but those that passed stared in admiration or reverence. He was like a deity made of stone.

Several thousand men and woman had fled by the time Harruq saw the first orcs. They were scattered and few, the teeth lining the edge of a gaping maw swallowing his entire city. It was swallowing people he loved. It would not swallow him. The last of the refugees screamed for help, but he did not move. He would not reach them in time, and if he left the gap orcs might escape the city and give chase. So he watched, his heart too calloused, too exhausted, to feel anything more than anger as the innocents were butchered and mutilated before him.

"You will die before you pass," Harruq said to the first to approach. The orc ignored his words and hefted his two-handed axe above his head. Salvation lashed out and cut his throat in a single, blinding motion. The sword returned to its original position as the body crumpled before him. A second neared. Condemnation cut the axe from his hand, looped around, and disemboweled him. The orc crumpled, gasping out his pain. Harruq saw none of it, heard none of it. A strange anger had settled over him. It was not raging or burning; it did not consume him like so often anger had. Instead he felt it filling his veins like ice. As three orcs charged him, he knew without question they would die by his hand. There would be no pleasure in the killing, no thrill in the act, just a deepening of the strangeness enveloping his mind.

Harruq smashed away the axe aimed for his head, stepped forward, and buried one sword to the hilt in the orc's gut. His other parried away a thrust so that the orc holding the sword fell forward. Harruq's elbow turned his nose to a splattered mess of cartilage and blood. He then pulled free his sword and slashed the remaining orc's neck. Blood poured across the black steel. Four orcs lay dead at his feet. He stared down the street, where more than forty approached. They carried pieces of humans like trophies. His anger strengthened.

"Come and die like the animals you are," he shouted to them. He held his swords crossed above his head, a glowing 'X' that dripped blood. The mass of orcs charged. They had killed many, but not enough. They knew the innocents fled outside the walls. Only Harruq remained in the way. Only Harruq.

He swung with all his strength, the magic in the swords cutting bone like it was dry wheat. He took out the legs of the orc before him, stepped back, and then swung again. Three more fell, their armor broken, their chests and bellies pouring blood across the ground. As the bodies fell they formed a barrier to the others behind, one they had to stumble and climb across. Harruq gave no reprieve and offered no inch of ground. The orcs swung, cut, and bit, but he did not feel the tears in his flesh, did not know of the blood that poured across him. All he knew was the death in the eyes of those he killed, and they were many.

As the last of the forty died or lay dying, Harruq screamed to the morning sky, a single cry of anguish, sorrow, and anger. It echoed throughout the town, intermixing with the sobs of the trapped, the bellows of hatred, and the pitiful weeping of those whose lives now belonged to Karak. Qurrah did not hear the war cry, but he felt it in his heart.

❈

"Come," Velixar said as the last of the undead marched through the walls. "It is time we entered as the conquerors we are."

The man in black raised his arms to the heavens, his red eyes rolling into his skull. He opened his mouth and whispered, and his legions of undead obeyed.

Karak! they shouted. *Karak! Karak!* It rose high from rotted throats and mindless flesh. The walls shook with the cry. All who heard felt the lion's condemning eyes upon their backs. The dark priests joined the shout, and the lion's roar traveled for miles. The orcs took up the chant. Those who knelt, forfeiting their souls for their lives, whispered it. The entire city became a writhing cauldron of death, blood, and worship.

Karak! Karak!

But there were still those fighting against him and whose lips worshipped him not, whose hearts followed Ashhur even as they struggled to survive inside the maelstrom.

Karak be damned!" Harruq shouted as he cut down his orcish attacker. "You hear me? Karak be damned!"

He buried his sword deep into the gut of another, so that blood poured hot across his hand and wrist. He yanked out the blade and kicked the body back, another obstacle for the incoming mass. His anger had evolved. He felt it flooding his being with strength, wild and desperate to be used. His focus was no longer the narrow knife edge but instead wide. He saw everything, felt everything, as the battle grew desperate. Fifty more had come, and they charged and howled with wild abandon. Harruq braced himself and prepared for the onslaught, but then he saw they were running out of fear.

Harruq had but a few to massacre. The rest were buried by Sergan and his soldiers.

"Well met gatekeeper," Sergan said, his enormous axe hefted onto his shoulder. "So what's the toll? I can't pay in gold, but I got plenty of orc heads for you!"

Harruq wiped the blood from his weapons and sheathed them. For a brief moment a grin lit up his face.

"Two heads a man, can you pay the toll?" he asked.

"Two? Two! Bah, my men here got nine to a head easy, ain't that right?"

The soldiers, exhausted and ragged, raised their swords high and cheered.

"Go," Harruq said. To emphasize this he turned and pointed to the wolf-men charging the fleeing peoples of Veldaren. "They will need you more than I."

"Hear that?" Sergan shouted. "We got some mutts to kill. Stick tight, and we'll make it fine!"

He turned back to Harruq, his voice dropping to a whisper.

"Are you sure you can hold?"

"Until I'm dead, I'll hold," the half-orc replied.

"That's what I'm afraid of," Sergan said, but he smiled and saluted. The kindness vanished quick as it came. Shouting with a voice hoarse and dry, he hurried his men on. As the last passed, Harruq drew his swords and placed his back to them. His momentary reprieve was gone. Swarming onto the eastern road were over a hundred orcs. Harruq twirled Salvation and Condemnation, taking comfort in their strength.

"For Karak!" the orcs shouted as they charged.

"And Karak can have you!" Harruq shouted back.

His bravado was not false. He saw the hundred, and he saw them dead. It was his task to make it come to pass. From underneath his armor he pulled out the scorpion pendant Brug had made him and let it dangle from his neck. The pendant flared, its magic increasing the strength of Harruq's swords. The first to near him lost his head. The second fell with his body in two. The half-orc rushed the army, cutting and chopping with a viciousness beyond anything he had ever known. As the orcs climbed over piles of their dead, he took off their arms and legs, letting them add to the obstacle they tried to pass.

Three orcs ran around the side, where the pile of dead was less, and leapt over seven bodies. They were behind Harruq and beyond his line of sight. But there was one who could see them, one who ran along the rooftops with long gray cloaks trailing behind him. Haern leapt into the air, kicked off the wall, and descended upon the three. Each saber stabbed downward at a neck as he landed. A sweep of his legs took out the third. He cut his neck as he fell, bleeding out the orc before he ever hit the dirt.

Harruq heard the commotion and spun, Salvation lashing out. Haern blocked it with both his sabers, his blue eyes unflinching even as his arms quivered against the half-orc's amazing strength. Harruq realized who it was, nodded, and then turned back to the horde. Haern joined his side, and together they fought. As the piles of dead grew larger, the orcs pulled back. Their numbers were not enough. Their strength did not match up against the tremendous skill of their opponents. More were coming, however, their numbers building higher and higher. The two watched as the orcs cleared away the dead that blocked their paths.

"How the others doing?" Harruq asked as he gasped for air.

"They live," Haern said, estimating the forces arrayed against them. As he neared two hundred he stopped bothering. "We will die here, you know that right?"

The half-orc chuckled. "No, I don't. We'll hold, Haern. We have no choice."

The assassin dropped into a stance, one weapon high, one low, as the orcs prepared to charge.

"It's been an honor to fight beside you, Harruq Tun," Haern said.

"Aye," Harruq said. "Die well."

The orcs arrived, spearheaded by a brave few and followed up by a cowardly many. Haern jumped forward, slicing out the throats of two and tearing at the legs of the third. They fell, trampled by the others. The assassin leapt back, and this time Harruq unleashed a whirlwind of steel. The magical weapons tore through armor, shattered the shafts of axes, and broke the poorly wrought swords. Orc after orc fell dead, often in multiple pieces. With each spin Harruq took a step back, and with each step he left a trail of dead.

"Fall back," Haern shouted. Harruq did as ordered. Their opponents were too close, and as he retreated several axes cut where he had been. Haern lunged, parrying a few defensive swings before thrusting his sabers through eyes and mouths. Five died, but they were a pittance. The assassin retreated, unable to strike any more. Harruq protected his retreat, hurling a body against those nearest and then charging in. Blood poured across the dirt as he swung with both weapons left, then right, and then left again. Fearful of getting too close, several orcs hurled their axes at him, as well as the axes of the dead.

"Fight on!" Haern shouted, using his sabers to knock down or parry the axes. He leapt over Harruq's head and landed on the other side, batting away two more throws. His foot shot out, tripping an orc, and then he cartwheeled, his other foot breaking a chin. Axes hurled through the air where he had been. When he touched down he leapt again, avoiding a second barrage. More orcs charged, thinking him on the run. Instead, he activated the magic of his ring and appeared mere inches before them. Two impaled themselves on his sabers. The others trampled over them. Haern screamed as the weight pressed against his body. The dead orcs protected him from their axes and swords, but that mattered little as feet stomped across his face. He tried to activate the magic in his ring to teleport himself out, but the magic for the day was spent. Haern gasped for air, all the while cursing such a death.

"*Get off!*" Harruq screamed, slamming his shoulder into the group. Three flew backwards, the unlucky fourth gurgling as the half-orc tore out his throat with Salvation. Harruq spun, daring them to approach. Haern shoved off the bodies and staggered to his feet. His face was badly bruised, and every breath filled his chest with pain. All around the orcs encircled them, howling and taunting.

"Harruq," Haern said.

"Yeah?"

"Get down."

The half-orc obeyed. The two dropped to the ground. Haern screamed as his chest pressed against the dirt, but he would endure. Bright light flashed above them, and then lightning tore through the ranks of orcs, followed by a barrage of lances made of ice. In the span of seconds they were all dead. Harruq stood, stunned by the sight. Down the street came Mira, bits of ice still dripping from her fingers. Behind her were Antonil and his men, as well as the two paladins.

"Well met," Haern said, bowing to the girl with blackest eyes.

"Form up a line," Antonil shouted. His men spread across the street, seven deep, their shields interlocked. Lathaar and Jerico stepped beyond them and surveyed Harruq and Haern.

"Do either of you need healing?" Lathaar asked.

"Just my ribs," Haern said. "I'll be fine."

"Healing's for after the battle," Harruq said.

Their bruises and cuts denied their words, but the paladins let them be. Harruq stepped past them and saw the line Antonil was forming.

"No," he said. "No, get them out of the city. Get them out!"

Antonil turned to him and frowned. "And who are you to order me?" he asked.

Harruq stormed over, grabbed Antonil by the top of his chestplate, and yanked him close so that their eyes were inches apart.

"I know you," Harruq said, his voice quiet but shaking with intensity. "The people of Neldar will need a leader. Go to them. Let us die as we must, but take your men and go. That clear?"

Antonil pushed aside Harruq's hand, then nodded to the fields beyond the wall. The wolf-men were swarming through the refugees, though it appeared many fought against them. Brief flashes of magic, be it fire or lightning, dotted the battle.

"Protect us as long as you can," the guard captain said. "And I'll do my best to ensure you have something to protect."

Mira slipped past them all and stared out at the battle beyond the city. Her hands shook as she watched. She could feel them dying. Her keen eyes saw many wolf-men avoiding the fight, instead feasting on the slain. Others were circling about, killing those that scattered or dropped off as if it were sport. Deep inside, she felt her power stirring.

"We must hurry," she said before a sudden blast of wind propelled her across the grass faster than a horse in full gallop. At Antonil's order, his troops abandoned their wall of shields and marched outside the city. Only Lathaar and Jerico stayed behind.

"For Neldar," Antonil said, saluting them.

"For Ashhur," Jerico replied.

The four defenders faced the west. Scores of orcs were dead, and the rest who lived ignored the gap in the wall and instead tore into homes in search of easier victims. The attacking army had been devastated, of that there was no doubt. Still, the remaining orcs were more than enough to slaughter the fleeing peoples of Veldaren. But it wasn't the orcs that attacked.

Karak! Karak!

Marching down the street, far as they could see, came the undead. They jostled and bumped each other as they walked. Their eyes were lifeless but their voices were not.

Karak! Karak!

"There must be over a thousand," Haern said, feeling his gut sink.

"But they are dead," Jerico said, readying his shield. "To my side, Lathaar. You two, stay back until you are needed."

The paladins weapons glowed a fierce white, and the glow grew all the brighter as Lathaar turned his swords into Elholads.

"You've seen many things in your life," Haern said to Harruq as the undead army approached. "But you have never seen paladins fight Karak's undead."

Harruq guarded Jerico's right flank while Haern guarded Lathaar's left. The two paladins held their weapons high, their eyes closed, and their mouths whispering prayers to their god.

Karak! Karak!

Lathaar opened his eyes. "Stay with me," was all he said. He launched himself at the tide of dead flesh and bone. As the blades of light tore through the bodies the undead did not just fall. They shattered as the magic controlling them was scattered and broken. Fast as he could cut them down they came, packed together so tight that a single swing massacred three at a time. As the hands tore at his flesh and teeth bit for his arms, he leapt back. Jerico slammed his shield into the mass, screaming Ashhur's name. The rotten flesh melted against his shield like butter. He swung Bonebreaker in wild arcs, each blow blasting apart arms and chests. Deep into the army he ran, and when the undead tried to close around him Lathaar was there, cutting them down.

"Back!" Lathaar shouted, and Jerico obeyed. He bashed his shield side to side, beating away the clawing fingers. Lathaar cut a swathe of chaos through the ranks, circling in front of Jerico's shield with no fear of its holy power. As he circled back around to where Jerico stood firm, over a hundred undead lay in pieces across the ground. Blood ran from scratches across his exposed face and neck. Lathaar gasped for air. He and Jerico had rode night and day to reach Neldar, and their rest within the temple of Ashhur had been too brief. They were both running on adrenaline and faith.

Each was tested as they stared out at the mass of dead chanting Karak's name. They had killed but a tenth of their numbers.

"Even rivers must run dry," Lathaar said as he sheathed his short sword.

"Amen," Jerico said.

As one Lathaar lifted his sword and Jerico lifted his shield. The light upon them flared, powerful and dominating. Harruq felt a comfort in his chest, his heart longing for the peace he felt emanating within the light. The undead, however, shrieked and howled. Those nearest disintegrated, and those behind them tried to flee only to be pushed back and torn to pieces by the rest.

The light faded back to its gentle glow. Another hundred destroyed.

"An awesome sight," Haern said in the brief lull before the paladins attacked once more. Harruq nodded but could not find words to describe what he had seen and felt. Lathaar cut through the undead, holding his Elholad with both hands. Jerico waited, and when Lathaar needed to retreat he was there, his shield leading. As they fought Harruq twirled his swords, unable to stand by any longer.

"Tired of watching yet," he asked Haern.

"You know I am."

To either side they attacked. Haern's strikes were impossibly precise, cutting away tendons and muscle so that one undead after another collapsed, unable to stand or attack. Harruq was far less efficient. Salvation and Condemnation pounded through skulls and bone with brute force. Between them Lathaar twirled his Elholad and sliced through the bodies that swarmed about. When Haern found himself overwhelmed, he somersaulted back. Jerico was ready, slamming his shield into the undead while the assassin was still upside-down in the air.

Time crawled. Harruq felt he fought an endless wave of fingers and teeth. His armor was scratched and soaked in gore. His face and neck were covered with bruises, and every exposed bit of flesh was cut and bleeding. Any normal foe would have been exhausted and daunted by the enormity of death around them. But they fought no normal foe. Bit by bit they retreated toward the wall, unable to halt the wave despite their bravery. The bodies were piling up, their adrenaline was fading, and the armor on their backs was becoming harder and harder to bear.

Another hundred fell. The dead were crawling over the barriers made by their own fallen, yet still they came. Jerico could hardly swing his shield, instead holding it against his body as the blows rained down. Harruq swung his arms without feeling the swords in his hands. Haern's strikes turned slower, less accurate.

Another hundred fell. Lathaar took the front, his swords weighing nothing. He used wide arcs, striking any many as he could. He called out to Ashhur, but his voice did not have the strength it once did. The dead did not recoil at his faith. They came onward, dying, their bones shattered, their blood spilt and their skin torn and broken. Despite the losses, the undead continued their chant. *Karak! Karak!* They would not flee. They would not stop.

Another hundred fell.

"Come back," Harruq shouted as he kicked away the remains of a young man. "We'll fill the gap with their own corpses!"

Jerico whirled in a circle, Bonebreaker blasting away seven undead swarming about him. He turned in the momentary reprieve and fled back to the wall, following the others. When they were out, he turned and placed himself in the very center of the crumbled wall. He collapsed to one knee, his shield jammed into the dirt to support his weight.

"I don't know how much longer," he gasped. He could barely see through the blood that ran down his face from the multitude of cuts and swelling bruises. "I don't know..."

Lathaar stood beside him, his Elholads glowing as fierce and bright as they had at the start of their fight. The remaining hundreds of Velixar's forces jostled and approached, but for the moment they did not attack. Harruq collapsed against the wall and glanced back to the refugees. He saw no sign of Tarlak and Aurelia. The wolf-men were gone. The last remnants of Veldaren's people fled east. It would not be long before they were out of sight.

"They'll have a chance now," Harruq said, letting his gaze linger longer than he should. The undead were moaning and chanting, but holding still. They were a fraction of their former number, but still dangerous, still fearsome. Haern crouched, using every second to catch his breath.

"Why command them to wait?" Jerico asked.

"I think I know," Lathaar said, but he had no time to explain.

Rise!

The command rolled through the homes and echoed against the walls. Hundreds of dead men, women, and orcs rose, a single chant on their lips.

For Qurrah! For Qurrah!

At their sound Harruq closed his eyes and lowered his head.

"Look what your actions have done," Haern said. The bodies of young and old, men and women, stretched far as they could see. The number was far beyond their abilities, already stretched to their limit. They would all die, and as they were torn limb to limb, their murderers would shout and worship the name of Harruq's brother.

"Not my actions," Harruq said, opening his eyes and facing the horde. He stood before Jerico and held his twin blades before his face, letting their red glow seep into him. "Not my murders. Not my guilt. I will not be damned for him."

The undead lumbered forward, driven on by a single command: kill. The others readied their weapons and their hearts. They would all fight, and they would all die. But Harruq was not convinced. Gold shimmered in his eyes as he glared at beings robbed of their peace in death.

"A thousand beaten," he said through grit teeth. "Time for a thousand more."

The wolf-men split into two groups as they neared the fleeing people of Veldaren. Tarlak swore as they went to either side of the people, trying to surround and trap them.

"Don't worry about those who make it past," Tarlak said. "Kill those near us, and we'll draw enough to give them a chance."

"Of course," Aurelia said. She turned and kissed him on his cheek. "Thank you."

"That better not have been a goodbye kiss," the wizard said, winking.

"Keep your end up and I'll keep mine."

Tarlak pointed his wand at the river of black and gray fur. "Time to punish some very bad dogs."

A ball of fire leapt from the wand, shrieking through the air with smoke trailing after. It slammed into the center of their numbers and detonated. Waves of flame rolled out in all directions, burning dozens of wolf-men to death instantly. Many more collapsed to the ground from the force of the explosion.

"That was pretty," Aurelia said, lightning sparking off her fingertips.

"Five more charges," Tarlak said. "Got to make them count."

Aurelia launched a giant strike of lightning into the right wave. It bounced from one wolf-man to another, knocking at least thirty to the ground, smoke rising from their fur. She turned to the other side, the lightning replaced with frost. From her hands a blanket of ice stretched out for hundreds of yards. As the wolf-men ran across they slipped and slid, forming a barrier against those behind them. Over fifty tumbled or smacked into their own members until those behind started leaping over the ice or running atop the few, crushed dead.

Tarlak, sensing opportunity, sent another explosive ball of fire at the pileup atop the ice. Wolf-men howled as their fur burned and their eyes bulged in the heat. Unable to ignore the casters, twenty broke for them, the rest continuing straight for the unarmed people. Aurelia killed the first ten with bolts of lightning. Tarlak finished the rest with a ball of fire.

"Three charges left," Tarlak said as they spun about. The wolf-men were raking their claws along the sides of the columns of men and women. Children of all ages were the first to die, having fallen behind without someone to carry them. Tarlak felt the wand shake in his hand as he saw wolf-men stop to fight over the first scraps. He spent his third charge obliterating five wolf-men that had gathered around a single woman holding two crying babes.

"Come on," Aurelia said, taking Tarlak's hand and pulling him along as they ran. She cast weak bolts of lightning, striking dead one or two wolf-men as they neared. The wolf-men cut and bit through the slower stragglers, quickly approaching the larger sections of people. A whirl of her hands and fire sprang from the ground, burning hot and high as it separated the wolf-men from the refugees. Hundreds closed their eyes and leapt through, enduring the pain and burns to reach the helpless. Many others turned and howled at the two spellcasters.

Tarlak sent another fireball into their midst, roasting thirty more. Only one fireball remained in his wand. The wolf-men charged, their tongues hanging out the side of their mouths.

"Grab hold of me," Tarlak said as he clutched his wand with both hands. "Can you protect us against fire?"

"I can try," she said, "but why do you…"

The wolf-men neared, outnumbering them forty to one. Aurelia wrapped her arms around his waist as she understood.

"Keep your eyes closed," she told him. The words of magic for the spell were still on her lips as the wolf-men leapt at them, their claws stretched and hungry. Tarlak tipped his wand to the ground and shot the ball of flame at their feet. The shock struck them first, blasting the air out from their lungs. The heat followed, agonizingly painful. Aurelia chanted, even though she made no sound. She felt her spell weakening. Her head was light. Her eyes saw only black. The fire rolled on and on, and she felt the last of her power drain away. The protection spell faded, but it had lasted long enough.

Tarlak opened a single eye and looked about. Aurelia was in his arms, and he was hunched over her as if he had been terrified. Which was true. When he saw only charred remains of the wolf-men, he straightened and reached for his hat. He felt only smooth skin.

"My hat?" he shouted. "My hair!"

He spun around, looking for his yellow hat, and saw hundreds of soldiers marching toward him, Sergan leading the way.

"To the fight!" Sergan shouted. "Pick it up, before the crazy fire-kissing mage blows everyone to pieces!"

They marched on by, a few offering praise but most too somber to bother. The rest of the wolf-men had reached the refugees and were tearing through them in a merciless bloodbath.

"We need to draw them back," Aurelia said as the soldiers ran on. "But how?"

"The wolf-men aren't here to just kill," Tarlak said. "Oh, there it is!"

He found his hat ten feet away, most of its yellow fabric now black. He propped it on his head, mumbling about the stupidity of fire spells. Finished, he gestured to the carnage at hand.

"Look at them," he said. "We're too late."

Most of the wolf-men had stopped their chase, instead content to feed. Huge groups circled around masses of bloody bodies, howling and yipping in glee. Oblivious to the charging soldiers, they gorged themselves. It was only when Sergan's axe tore through the skull of a full-bellied wolf-man that they roared and charged. Only half bothered to stop their feasting. The other half, still eager for blood, resumed their chase of the fleeing peoples.

"Stay tight," Sergan shouted, and his sheer will alone kept his men going. Their armor was thick but the claws of the wolf-men were thicker. Giant waves of solid muscle and fur slammed against their ranks, raking, biting and tearing out throats. Over and over the wolf-men howled, knowing fear was their ally. Sergan swore as he saw many of his soldiers shying away from the yellow teeth and the bloodstained claws.

"They're eating your loved ones!" he shouted, grabbing a man who had turned to flee and spinning him around. "You gonna let them eat you too?"

Sergan did not wait for a response. Instead he turned around and buried his axe into a charging foe. The wolf-men pulled back and started circling, snarling, their mouths oozing blood and drool. Those that had fled were cut down immediately. Sergan shouted orders, determined to face the new challenge. The soldiers formed a circle of their own, and back to back they raised their weapons and hurled insults. Every now and then a wolf-man would near, clawing at an exposed leg or an unshielded arm. Every time an axe or sword awaited it, severing claws or slicing away tendons in the leg. Those that stumbled due to their wounds were killed before they had a chance to call for help.

"Hold on," Sergan shouted. "We got them now!"

It appeared they did, and that was why the wolf-men suddenly turned and abandoned the fight. Faster than any of the men could hope to run, they chased after their brethren and the fleeing Veldaren people. Sergan swore and gasped for air as one of his soldiers beside him slapped his back.

"We got them running," the soldier said. "Let's finish this."

"Aye," Sergan said, hoisting his axe onto his back. "Smart words."

"I'll agree to that," Tarlak said, also slapping the general on the back.

"Where the abyss did you come from?" Sergan asked, startled. Tarlak pointed back toward the city.

"You ran by us, remember?"

Before they could say anymore, Mira flew past them. Only the sound of rushing wind marked her passing.

"Who the blazes was that?" Sergan asked.

"Give chase and see," Tarlak said.

"Wait," Aurelia said. She walked through the tired men, and despite her exhaustion and wounds the regal sight of an ageless elf fighting alongside the mortal men filled them with hope. When she reached their center she closed her eyes and raised her hands.

"I have one last spell," she said. All around the men felt their skin tingle. As the spell ended, she collapsed into Tarlak's waiting hands.

"What'd that do?" Sergan asked.

"March and see," Tarlak told him.

Sergan gave the order, and to his shock his men raced away like horses, their arms and legs pumping faster than he thought possible.

"You going to follow?" Tarlak asked. Sergan glanced back at the mage, who was cradling Aurelia's head while she lay on the grass, and then the general realized his own troops were leaving him far behind.

"Wait up!" he shouted. He sprinted, his old bones running faster than they ever had in his youth. Tarlak watched him go. They would reach the wolf-men soon, but not before many innocents were slaughtered. Again they would be outnumbered, and he also knew the effects of Aurelia's spell. Once it ran out, the soldiers would be exhausted. If they did not kill quickly...

"You better enjoy this nap," Tarlak said. He shifted his hat and scratched the bald spot on his head. "Because I might need you to wake up and save my ass if those wolves come back."

The man pushed his way through the waves of fleeing people. In the distance, he could see Veldaren, now a smoking shell of its former glory. The sound of screams and crying were all around him, but they rolled in greater strength from the trailing end of the masses where the wolf-men fed. Three others followed this man, all attired in red robes and armor. They followed their leader, trusting him with their lives.

"Kill quickly, before they know any challenge them," the man said. The closest to him, a red-haired girl who would be beautiful but for the brutal scar that had taken her right eye, drew her daggers and smiled.

"Too fast and we won't get to have any fun," the girl said.

"Too slow and one of us won't ever have fun again," the leader said. He pulled his hood off his head, revealing long black hair that fell past his shoulders. None could see his face, for he wore a pale cloth pulled tight about his features. Only his eyes peered through two holes, the left a dark hazel, the right, a vivid red. The girl couldn't see, but she knew he was smiling.

"We'll do it perfect," she said. "Hate for us to die just when things were getting interesting."

The four neared the end of the refugees, with only a panicked few men and women in between them and the hounds that chased. The leader dipped his hand into a bag tied to his waist and pulled out a handful of ash. Tilting his head back he scattered the ash across his covered face. Instead of scattering in the wind the ash hovered about his body, held in place by powerful magic. When he lowered his head a haze surrounded it, obscuring his already hidden features.

"No hesitation, and no mercy," he said as he prepared his magic. His name was Deathmask, leader of the Ash Guild. With his home destroyed, and all his negotiations, contracts, bribes and wealth of his thief empire ruined, he was eager to show the wolf-men just how he had earned his title.

The last of the refugees fled past, and the four stood ready. Deathmask raised his palms to the sky, chanting dark words. A leading pack of ten saw them gathered in a protective circle around their leader, their daggers drawn and their red cloaks flapping in the wind. The foremost howled, and into the air they leapt, determined to crush the sudden resistance.

"Burn for me," Deathmask whispered, his spell completed. His fingers clenched into fists and then jerked downward. The grass before him cracked and broke as columns of fire tore into the air. Three wolf-men plunged through, whimpering as the flame ignited their fur and blackened their skin. The three guarding Deathmask launched into action as the remaining wolves descended. The lady with the missing eye jumped and collided in the air with her chosen prey. The wolf-men bit and clawed, but she kicked and spun, avoiding every scratch. Just before they struck ground she buried a dagger into each eye, scoring the first kill of the group.

"Behind you, Veliana!" Deathmask shouted. The lady did not check to see, instead trusting her commander. She dropped to her knees and curled down her head. A swirling black ball of molten rock flew above her, courtesy of Deathmask. It struck dead an attacking wolf-man, knocking his jaw clean off. Veliana stood and spun, daggers lashing. More had joined the initial ten, furious at being denied easy kills and feasting. Blood splattered across her from cuts across a surprised wolf-man's lip and nose. A sharp elbow to his gut doubled him over, and then her daggers finished him.

Smoke swirled around Veliana in a large circle as if escaping from some underground fire. Recognizing the spell, the lady faced her attackers and beckoned them to assault. Seven charged, howling for blood. Deathmask activated his spell as the first crossed the ring of smoke. Lava sliced through grass and formed a wall. Thin as a leaf, the melted rock splashed across the wolf-men, melting their eyelids to their eyes and coating their fur. As they crashed to the ground, howling in pain, the lava hardened, locking their bodies in strange, painful contortions.

The lava wall vanished as quickly as it appeared, but by now the wolf-men had no desire to engage. They leapt straight for Deathmask, who laughed behind the gray haze.

"Mier, Nien, care to keep me alive?" he asked. The remaining two of the four clicked their daggers together and stood side by side in front of their leader. Gray bandanas obscured their mouths and chin, but their brown eyes and black hair were mirror images of the other. Twins by birth, they were also twins in combat. Mier dropped to one knee and swept his leg underneath the first attacker. Nien plunged a dagger through heart before the wolf-man hit the ground.

While he pulled his dagger free, Nien spun and slashed the tendon above the heel of a second. This time it was Mier who buried his dagger into the heart of the fallen.

Simultaneously they leapt into the air as three swiped their claws and bit at them. As they spun and their cloaks swirled, eight pairs of throwing daggers flew down, piercing arms and legs. Both landed behind Deathmask, who stood with his palms open. Gray darts shot from his fingers, over a hundred in number. Six wolf-men collapsed as the darts pierced their skin before vanishing into smoke. They bled out and died.

"Little help here?" Veliana shouted, twisting and parrying the claws of two wolf-men that attacked her in a animal frenzy. Numerous cuts lined their bodies, all superficial. As Deathmask whispered a spell, Veliana at last failed a dodge. Claws ripped through the leather armor and across her chest. Blood poured as she screamed and fell back. Nien and Mier hurled daggers as they chased. The wolf-men tensed and guarded against the painful but shallow stings, buying Veliana time. Deathmask slammed his hands together, anger fueling his magic.

"You cut her," he whispered. His spell needed no semantic components. Just rage. "You cut her and now you'll bleed."

A vortex of gray smoke billowed from his mouth, arching through the air like a snake through water. It struck the two wolf-men, and instead of blowing across them it shredded their flesh as if the smoke were made of steel razors. Veliana sheathed one of her daggers and clutched her wounded chest. Deathmask felt his heart skip. The wound must have been deeper than he thought. Nien and Mier ran on, for they saw what Veliana did not: the remaining fifty wolf-men barreling toward her.

"Get back!" Deathmask shouted. The twins heard and obeyed. Veliana had fled too far out. She would need to save herself. Deathmask hurled several orbs of black fire, killing the nearest, but it was too little, too late.

"We could save her!" Nien shouted to his leader.

"They are not that many!" Mier agreed.

"At my side, she knows that," Deathmask said, his mismatched eyes flaring with anger. "Do not question me."

Veliana glanced at the wolf-men, saw their closeness, and then turned to Deathmask. She blew him a kiss, then started running for her life. She was the slower, and she should have been caught, but she was not. Mira arrived. Lightning, fire, and ice exploded through the wolf-men's ranks in a simultaneous barrage that left them devastated. Only a scattered few escaped, fleeing with all their speed toward the safety of the city. Deathmask sighed and pulled the cloth from his face. The people of Veldaren were safe, at least for now.

The four sheathed their weapons and bowed as Sergan and his men approached. They gasped for air, yet still offered a mild cheer.

"They're safe," Mira said, staring at the refugees that continued their eastward trek. She smiled at Deathmask. "Thank you."

"Alright, let's form up and get an idea what we got," Sergan said. He smiled when he saw Antonil and his troops in the distance. "Ashhur be praised," he said.

"Ashhur may not be to blame for this," Veliana said as she looked upon the smoking rubble of Veldaren. "But he certainly deserves no praise, not this day."

"Maybe," Sergan said, "but I've got breath in my lungs and a weapon in my hand, so at the least I'll praise him for that."

Deathmask chuckled. "Amen, I guess."

18

Walking through the streets of Veldaren, they seemed demigods. The orcs cheered and raised their weapons at sight of them. Those that knelt in prayer to Karak groveled all the lower when they passed. Qurrah felt chills at the reverence. Tessanna giggled, thinking it amusing. Velixar thought it was about damn time.

"At long last," Velixar said as they arrived in the heart of Veldaren, standing before the giant fountain dedicated to Valius Kren, the first King appointed by Karak while he still walked Dezrel. "The city is returned to the hand of its creator."

"There are still those who resist," Qurrah said, staring at the statue and remembering how it was there he had first met Tessanna. "My brother included. What will you do about them?"

Velixar did not answer. Instead he watched Tessanna as she approached the fountain as if in a trance. Her eyes were locked on the waters. A smile dominated her face. She drew out her dagger and stepped in. High above her head she raised her left arm and pressed the edge of her dagger against her pale, scarred flesh.

"It's been so long," she said, and the smile grew. She slashed her skin. The blood poured down, and as it did she twirled. Another cut. She gasped in pleasure. With every cut, Tessanna remembered the city as it had been. She remembered the soldiers. She remembered the thugs, the men who desired her. She remembered meeting Qurrah. The half-orc felt the hairs on his neck raise as she laughed, wild and free. Without punishment, without anger, without dismissal or disapproval, she bled into the water.

"I'm home," she said to the two as they looked upon her.

Qurrah reached out, and she took his hand. She stepped out of the fountain and pressed her body against his, the blood from her arm unable to stain his robes. He kissed her forehead twice, then turned to Velixar. Something in his glowing eyes disturbed him so he pressed the matter of his brother.

"The gap in the east wall," Qurrah insisted. "Many of your undead have been defeated, I can sense as much."

"They are no threat to us," Velixar said. "But that is no reason to let them live. He is your brother. The dead fill this city by the thousands. Raise them, Qurrah. Send them to the wall."

Qurrah glanced away, remembering the multitude of undead Velixar had summoned on many occasions. How many had he summoned at the Sanctuary? Twenty-seven? At last he turned back to Velixar, shame bitter in this throat.

"I cannot," he said. "What I would summon will be a pittance compared to the army you can muster."

Velixar crossed his arms and glared at his disciple.

"You have grown in my absence, Qurrah Tun, but not near enough. I said raise them."

Tessanna rubbed her fingers across the half-orc's face and brushed her lips against his ear.

"Listen to him," she whispered. "He sees the same that I see."

Qurrah stepped away from her and closed his eyes.

"So be it," he told them. "I will raise the dead that I can."

By now he knew every syllable by heart. The power did not come from the pronunciation. A mangled word only diminished the spell's strength, for the true power came from the well of his soul that seethed in black turmoil. His hands shook as he felt nervousness crawl around the back of his mind. His master was watching. His lover was watching. Would he disappoint them? How strong was he really?

He felt the essence of death floating around the city, thick and strong. In his mind, he demanded it to follow his will. The final words escaped his lips. *Rise!* he shouted. *Rise!*

The strength fled his body. The magic left him spent. To his knees he fell, and when he opened his eyes he sighed. He did not have to say the number, for he knew that all three of them could sense it.

"Pitiful," Velixar said. "A thousand bodies lay massacred within this city, the death still fresh within them, and you bring a mere seventy to their feet?"

"Forgive me," Qurrah said between deep breaths. "It is the best I could do."

"No!" Velixar grabbed him by the front of his robes and lifted him to his feet with surprising strength. Eye to eye they stared. Velixar's features swirled faster, cheekbones growing out and then sinking back as his eyebrows stretched longer and thinner. "You have *not* done your best. I had thought you would be tested with my absence, but I was wrong. Look around you, Qurrah. Those that fight against us fight with every last drop of their strength, and many beyond even that. When was the last time you were pushed? When was the last time you had to fight even when your mind was in agony, and it felt your very next spell would send you to death? When, Qurrah? When?"

"Never," Qurrah said as he glared, his eyes flashing red. "Let go of me."

The half-orc turned his back to them and pulled his hood low over his face. His pride was wounded, and his anger seethed. He had fought. He had bled. He had killed many, and his strength had grown by leaps and bounds, yet now he stood accused. Tessanna's words repeated in his head. *He sees the same that I see.* What did that mean?

He stretched out his hands. The words to the spell returned to his lips. He would show his master that he was not the failure he assumed. Deep in his chest he felt his power stirring. Perhaps he had not poured all he had into the spell. Perhaps, just perhaps, he could do more. His focus narrowed to a razor edge. Higher and higher his hands raised. The power built, and this time it was swirling out of control. He tried to harness it, to command it. He opened his mouth and shouted the words. Within his being he felt fire. His chaotic will stretched about the city, demanding the dead to rise.

The dead obeyed. Another ninety stood.

"I knew you could do better," Velixar said as the combined dead of the first two spells sauntered toward the center of town.

"Silence," Qurrah said, the venom in his voice startling. The half-orc fell to one knee and propped himself up with a fist. He gasped for breath. Within his head, he could feel the hundred and sixty, every one moving by his strength alone. It was a weight he had never felt so strong before. It was as if creatures lurked inside his eyes, clawing and biting. At any moment he thought he would pass out. But it was not enough.

"You wanted me pushed," Qurrah said as he stood. "You wanted me tested. So be it, master."

He raised his arms to the sky and began casting the spell one final time. Velixar's eyes narrowed as he stared, but Tessanna only giggled.

"At last," she said as the power of the spell built. Flecks of white dust gathered around the half-orc's frozen pose, swirling as if it were a child-sized tornado. Qurrah's eyes rolled into his head. Everything ached. Everything hurt. The well of his magic, something he felt himself attuned to, felt empty. Drained. But he remembered years ago when he had challenged Velixar's magic.

The well is limitless, he thought. The power grew steady. Its chaos was gone. With each passing second, he felt his soul rise. The hairs on his body stood. His mouth locked open, the last of the spell finished. The well refused to run dry.

"Rise!" he screamed, and for once his throat did not tear. Magic poured out of him. He demanded obedience of the dead, and the dead obeyed. His heart raced as his body wavered. Delirium overtook his mind. The well would not run dry. All around Veldaren the dead were rising, and still the well did not run dry. He tore his gaze from the sky and looked at Velixar, a wild smile on his face. For one heavy moment, Qurrah's eyes shone a fierce red.

"A thousand," he said, and then he fell. As he lay in the dirt the glow about his eyes faded away. He coughed twice, and then he began laughing.

"Go to him," Velixar said to Tessanna. The girl nodded, still smiling. She knelt beside Qurrah and stroked his hair.

"I can feel them," Qurrah said. "Inside me. They'll obey. They are so many...so many..."

Velixar bowed his head as he heard the words of Karak inside his mind.

He has felt my touch. It will not be long before Thulos enters this world and breaks the chains of the goddess. Praise be to you, my greatest servant.

"His eyes," he whispered.

There is but one way for me to escape my prison. You know this as well as I.

"I was to be your avatar," Velixar insisted.

Hold faith. I show you no dishonor, but if there is another, I would keep you by my side.

"As you wish," the man in black said. He raised his head and saw Tessanna staring at him.

"Qurrah is mine first," she said as she held her laughing, insane lover. "And when your god is freed, he is mine alone."

"He has tasted what I have always lived," Velixar said. "I will never take him from you."

Tessanna helped her lover to his feet. He gripped her tight, his fingers digging into her skin. With wild eyes he grinned at Velixar.

"A thousand," he said. "Are you still disappointed, *master?*"

The features on Velixar's face slowed in their shifting, and from within the frozen visage the red eyes glared.

"Follow me to the castle," he said. "And send your pets to the east wall. Let them finish off your brother. We have more important matters to attend to."

"As you desire," the half-orc said. He closed his eyes, and all throughout the city his undead heard his commands and obeyed. Velixar led them north toward the castle.

Qurrah's undead took up a chant, and when Velixar heard it, a frown burned across his lips. They did not shout to Karak like they should have. Instead, they shouted their loyalty to another.

For Qurrah! they shouted.
For Qurrah!
For Qurrah!

The guards had abandoned their posts. The giant doors were unlocked and unguarded. The three of them were alone, small figures in a giant city filled with fire, blood, and death. Velixar stared at the castle, a smile replacing the frown he had been wearing. He raised his arms as he saw the four crenellated towers, the faded gray stone, and the roaring lion carved deep into the walls at the base of each tower.

"Praise be to Karak," Velixar said. "I'm home."

The inside was empty and quiet. They walked across the carpet into the throne room. King Vaelor sat on his throne, and in the morning light that shone through the windows, he was an obnoxious yellow figure. At the sight of them, he stood and drew his sword.

"No king has surrendered this city," King Vaelor said, "and I will die before I become the first."

"You are not surrendering," Velixar said, marching ahead of Qurrah and Tessanna. "You are relinquishing the throne to its rightful heir. Karak built this city, and Karak demands that long forgotten loyalty."

"Blasphemy!" the king shouted.

Velixar laughed.

"Only an idiot would believe stating the truth to be blasphemy," the man in black said as he curled his fingers. "I have no time for you, worm."

His fingers uncurled. Blood collected around the king's eyes, and in one single crack the bones in his face crunched inward. The sword dropped from his hand. He fell forward and bled out on the carpet.

"Not the honorable death he most likely hoped for," Qurrah said. Velixar dismissed the dead king with a wave of his hand.

"None will remember his name," he said. "Fools and cowards are soon forgotten."

Velixar passed by the throne, gently touching its sides with his fingers. The ceiling was high, and behind the elevated dais was a wall covered with a giant, crimson curtain hung from a long, golden rod. Velixar grabbed part of the thick fabric in a fist and whispered a word of magic. Purple fire surrounded his hand. The curtain burned in a sudden flash, becoming ash without smoke or heat. Qurrah gasped at the sight behind the curtain, and even Tessanna grabbed her lover's arm and held it tight.

A single painting covered the wall, done with skill and detail beyond anything Qurrah had ever seen. Much of it was of a green landscape cluttered with small hills and a few sparse trees. A giant portal swirled in the center. Fire burned out of control within it. Standing before the portal were two men, strong and beautiful. Qurrah recognized one, for he was eerily similar to the statue he had seen inside Veldaren's temple to Karak. The two could have been twins, except for their hair. The one on the left was blond, the other, brown. Perched on the clouds above them watched a woman, her hair black as coal and her eyes empty orbs of shadow. The resemblance was unmistakable. She looked like an older, mature Tessanna.

"Right here," Velixar said, interrupting the long silence that had followed the painting's revealing. "Where this wall stands is where the gods entered. They created the painting to commemorate their arrival. The Kings of Neldar hid it not long after the great war, as if they were ashamed of those that had shaped the stone and created their city."

Velixar took out his journal and opened it to the center page. His hand quivered as he glanced over the words.

"So long," he whispered. "So very long."

"This is where we will cast the spell," asked Qurrah. "This is where we reopen the portal to their former world?"

Velixar brushed the stone with his fingers. The stone rippled like water against his touch. "Come, Qurrah. Let it be done."

Tessanna kissed his cheek. "Make me proud," she whispered. The half-orc joined Velixar's side. He glanced at the words on the page. They appeared simple, but he knew better. The strength required to open the portal would be enormous, otherwise Velixar would never have needed aid. He felt sweat trickle down his back as he repeated the words over and over in his mind.

"Wait," he said. "We should rest. We are both weary from the battle…"

"We should sunder the wall between the worlds while the chance is still before us," Velixar said, interrupting him. "Are you afraid, Qurrah Tun?"

"Of course I am," Qurrah said. "I am no fool. The power needed could tear me to pieces. And what of Tessanna?"

At this the man in black turned and offered his hand to the girl. Smiling, she took it.

"Your magic is instinctual," Velixar told her. "Given to you by the goddess herself. You will know when the time is right. Qurrah, I ask you, are you ready?"

Qurrah closed his eyes. He could still feel the weight of the dead he raised pressing on his mind, but it grew lighter with each moment. Within himself he had found a well of power that frightened and exhilarated him. Could he tap it again? He put his fingers against the wall and stared at the painted portal. Within the fire on the other side he saw raised swords and legions of armies silhouetted in black. Did he have the strength to condemn all Dezrel to such a fate?

He felt Tessanna take his hand. He glanced behind and saw the love in her eyes, the trust, and the fragile faith.

"Yes," Qurrah said. "I am ready."

Velixar began first, chanting in a deep, monotonous tone. Over fifty lines filled the page, varied in their pitch and pronunciation. Qurrah took a deep breath and joined in. At first he felt no difference from the other cantrips and spells he knew, but then the power hit. It was as if he had latched onto a carriage as it sped by with its horses at full gallop. Deep in his chest he felt a pull, and as he poured all his will into continuing the words, he felt his whole body trembling.

"Qurrah!" he heard Tessanna shout. The strain was horrendous. Every bit of magic shrieked out of his soul. His vision faded into a mix of red, purple, and yellow. Within the psycho-sight the words on the tome burned like fire. His voice rose higher. His throat tore, and as the blood ran down he knew he was going to die. At his side Velixar continued casting, even as the book shook in his hand and the red glow of his eyes dimmed to nothing. The wall before them raged like the surface of a lake within in a storm. All he could hear was a constant thunder, but whether it was real or in his mind he did not know. The words continued. The magic continued. His death grew closer.

"Take my hand," he heard a voice say, and in the madness he sensed a stability he had never thought possible. He reached out blindly. A hand took his, and its grip was iron. He collapsed, unable to see the words of the book but not needing to. Every thought, every image, every breath was dominated by the power of the spell. He screamed, and even as he screamed he continued.

A tiny sliver of blue swirled in the center of the wall. The spell was nearing completion. Qurrah tried to speak the final lines, the lines that would wrench open the wall and end Dezrel, but he could not. His screaming was too loud, the pain too incredible. Through tear-filled eyes he looked to Velixar and saw his true visage. He was a skull with eyes, bones with a robe, death in a body. His features no longer changed, for he had no features. Just his eyes, which were dull and colorless. He too was screaming, and his wail was the final blow against his shattering psyche.

"Forgive me mother," a voice said, its sound a perfect calm amid the thunder. "Forgive me, but I wish to be free of your desires, your eyes, your power. Please, mother. Forgive me."

Tessanna placed a hand upon the wall. Wind swirled in every direction. The ground heaved in protest. Images and sounds from the far corners of the world assaulted them, random and wild. Amid it all, the girl with blackest eyes felt at home. So softly she whispered the final words that neither had the strength to say.

"Take away it all," she whispered as the portal ripped open in a sudden, violent explosion of noise and air. Qurrah and Velixar flew back, their limp bodies rolling across the ground. Tessanna arched her back and lifted her arms as the chaos swarmed over her, followed by a blinding white light that quickly turned red. Her vision returned as the light lost its strength. The portal gently swirled, its being filled with what looked like millions of tiny stars. Compared to the original portal it was tiny, only the size of an ordinary man. Tessanna brushed its edges.

"I'm sorry," she said. Backing away, she laughed as she cried. "But I couldn't be happier, mommy."

Velixar was the first to his feet. "We did it," he gasped. His voice was raspy and weak, but with each passing moment it sunk deeper and firmer. "Celestia has lost! Ashhur has lost!"

Qurrah's haunting laughter echoed in the cavernous room. "Do you sense it?" he asked as he lay on his back. "Can you feel the hatred? The goddess is furious, Velixar, oh so furious."

The portal shimmered and shrunk as if in response. Qurrah and Velixar screamed in turn as they felt sharp pains spike into their minds. Celestia was trying to close the portal.

"Leave them be!" Tessanna shouted as Velixar fell to the floor and Qurrah rolled around on his back, his laughter and screaming an intertwined sound of lunacy. The castle rumbled as if the earth itself were angry.

"Desperation," Velixar said as his own screaming faded. "There is nothing she can do but strike at us in futile frustration." He knelt on knee and stared at the portal as a red liquid ran from both his eyes. A wave of his hand and the shimmering stopped. The portal swirled faster, stronger. The stars pulled back, leaving a deep blackness fixed in the center. The blackness grew.

"Something is coming through," Tessanna said as she backed away. Qurrah stood, turned to one side, and spat blood. He grinned as he wiped the back of his hand over his mouth.

"Who approaches?" he asked Velixar. "A lowly demon? A commander of an army? Or is it Thulos himself? Will he bow to you, or cut off all our heads before we can speak a word?"

Velixar pulled his hood low over his face and smirked. "If you thought the latter was the case, you wouldn't be smiling. Stay on your best behavior. While Karak has sought an alliance with his brother, the same cannot be said for Thulos. For centuries they have hunted for this world."

Tessanna wrapped her arms around Qurrah's shoulders and braced her chin on his shoulder.

"Unless its Thulos, we can kill it," she said. "So we might as well be polite."

Air hissed out of the portal as if it were exhaling, and then the creature stepped through. He looked human, albeit a magnificent version of one. Giant muscles flexed inside his crimson painted armor. Only his arms were exposed, the rest covered in well-crafted mail made of plate and chain. A golden helmet rest atop his head, its nose guard hanging long past his chin. In the back was a small hole so that the man's brown ponytail could be pulled through. Emblazoned across the chest piece, colored a vibrant yellow amid the crimson, was the symbol of a fist. Hanging from his hip was a giant sword sheathed in black leather, gems, and rubies. The man stared at them with wide amber eyes. His skin was bronze, and every inch covered with scars. When he spoke his language was that of the Gods.

"We have opened doors to many worlds, but this is the first brazen enough to open a door to ours," the man said.

"Who is the idiotic dabbler in magic that created this rift? Name yourself so that I may punish your stupidity."

The man from the other world drew his sword, its length nearly equal to Velixar's height. In response, Velixar bowed low and beamed a smile frightening in its authenticity.

"I am the one who opened the portal," he said, "and long have I desired such...idiocy. Do you know where you are, minion of the war god?"

The man glanced about, and the confusion in his eyes was like a crack in his armor of confidence. All he saw was a castle, one like thousands he had destroyed before, but the man with the ever-changing face spoke his language and knew of his master.

"I do not know," the man said. "But when you speak I have understanding. My name is Ulamn, General of the First Legion and servant to the war god. With whom do I speak?"

Velixar again bowed as he introduced himself. "I am Velixar, voice of the lion, and I welcome you to Dezrel, a world you have long sought after."

"The lion," Ulamn said. His sword lowered as his mouth hung open. "Do you mean...?"

In answer Velixar drew from underneath his robe a pendant he had held ever since the end of his mortal life. It was shaped like a triangle. In one corner was mountain, another a lion, and in the third, a clenched fist.

"Proof of my claim," Velixar said as Ulamn shook with rage. "I speak for Karak, and he welcomes you."

"The cowards fled here then," Ulamn said, gesturing about the castle with disgust. "Failing in their duty and unwilling to accept the consequences. For what purpose does Karak call upon the Warseekers?"

"Conquest," Velixar said. "He yearns to fight alongside his brother. But he has been trapped by the goddess of this world. If Thulos can defeat her, Karak will be free to join your side."

Ulamn sheathed his sword and crossed his arms. "Thulos is not one of mercy or compassion. Karak's cowardice..."

"Is forgivable," Velixar insisted. "Thulos may not be one for compassion or mercy, but he is one of honor. Let Karak atone his disgrace by serving. Do you dare tell me your master would refuse such a powerful ally as his own brother?"

Qurrah felt Tessanna tighten her grasp around his shoulders. Her hair tickled the side of his face as she kissed his ear. "When the soldiers come," she whispered, "who is subordinate to who?"

"I will speak with the war god," Ulamn said. His amber eyes widened with excitement. "We are always eager for new worlds to conquer." He bowed, and Velixar bowed back. Without another word, Ulamn turned and vanished back into the portal to his homeworld.

Velixar laughed, long and loud. The sound chilled Qurrah, but not as much as it once did.

"The war demons are coming," the man in black said. "Let Dezrel fear and the heavens shake with the coming rupture. Karak will be freed!"

"Amen," Qurrah said, a crooked smile on his face. Tessanna kissed his cheek.

"Amen," she said. She tossed her hair and giggled. "So many are going to die. We're bad, Qurrah, bad-bad-bad."

Qurrah only laughed.

19

They came in waves, thirty or so of shambling undead biting with bleeding teeth and clawing with broken fingers. Each wave threatened to break their line, but Harruq held firm as the wall of the dead grew ever larger. Lathaar's Elholad had faded, and he swung normal steel with exhausted arms. Even Haern's slender sabers felt like giant clubs to him. The potent magic in Bonebreaker kept Jerico dangerous, with even his mildest of swings smashing bone. Harruq, however, seemed no longer mortal.

Salvation and Condemnation blasted away flesh and sliced off limbs without pause. He no longer felt his arms, but he didn't need to. He just kept on swinging, the shower of gore proof enough that his numb hands still followed orders. Blood soaked him from head to toe, much of it his, but he didn't care. Any time his resolve threatened to break, or his exhaustion steal him away into unconsciousness, he heard the words that spurred him on.

For Qurrah! For Qurrah!

They chanted it, and in return he shattered their jaws and took the blasphemous life that enabled them to speak. To Harruq, it was a fair trade. The gap in the wall narrowed further and further, filled with corpses of all shapes and sizes. Harruq kept ordering the others back, until only he stood before a four foot expanse that the undead pressed through. They kept coming, kept trying to drown him in numbers, but his arms never ceased.

Haern wanted to say something, to hear his student speak, but dared not disturb his concentration. Lathaar leaned beside him and whispered amid the slaughter.

"What is he?" he asked.

Haern shook his head. "Just a half-orc," he replied.

"Ashhur is with him," Jerico said, hoisting his shield onto his back. "Even more so than with Lathaar and I. His will, his strength...but his body will break."

Tears filled Harruq's golden eyes. He didn't even see his attackers anymore. He just saw his friends, his family, and the face of his brother. He would kill them. He would kill all of them. For Aurelia. For Tarlak. For Brug.

And then the undead changed their chant.

For Aullienna! they shouted. *For Aullienna! For Aullienna!*

The sound was a horrendous blasphemy, the beautiful name of his daughter flooding the streets through dead throats and lifeless vocal chords. As Harruq cried, his heart filled with pain equal to the pain in his chest, his legs, his head. He couldn't think, he couldn't breathe. Too tired, too damn tired. Delysia. Brug. Aullienna. Was Aurelia still alive? Tarlak? He fell to his knees, his weapons falling limp beside him. The confidence in which he fought dissolved into emptiness. Deep in his head, he heard Qurrah laughing.

"Harruq!" Haern shouted, seeing his student's sudden collapse. Lathaar reacted first, slamming his shoulder into Harruq's side. The two fell to the side of the gap in the wall. Jerico smashed his shield forward, pushing back the undead.

"Harruq, snap out of it," Haern said, pulling the half-orc's face up by the hair. But Harruq's eyes were rolling into his head, and he kept shaking side to side. His lips were moving but nothing came out. Wisps of dark smoke rose from his tongue.

"Damn you, Qurrah," the assassin whispered. "What game is it you play now?"

He stood on stars hidden beneath glass. Blue fire rose and fell in a ring around them, and high above floated a small red sun.

"Where am I?" Harruq asked.

Qurrah pulled back his hood. His eyes were a deep red. His skin was ashen. With each word he spoke the blue fire flared higher.

"Where does not matter, dear brother, only why. Forgive me for such a ploy. To use Aullienna's death as a weapon against you is a cheap dishonor, but I needed you to fall. Your mind has grown stronger. Entering was no easy task."

"Such a shame," Harruq said. Seeing the stars below his feet filled him with vertigo, so he stared straight at Qurrah. His eyes reminded him of Velixar, and the chilling thought kept his mind sharp.

"Celestia's wall has fallen," Qurrah said. "As we speak, an army of war demons enters the city. There is no limit to their size, Harruq. Hundreds of thousands loyal to Velixar, and to me. We will lay waste to all life."

"Why?" Harruq asked. "What have you suffered to slaughter so many? What loss have you endured that is greater than my own?"

"We've been fools for a long time," Qurrah said. The blue fire soared to the crimson sun, a wall reaching millions of miles high. The red in his eyes deepened. "Your daughter died because of Velixar. He led Aullienna into the forest and planted the seed that eventually drowned her. Your hatred of me, your vengeance...none of it is just."

Harruq felt as if a knife had shredded his insides and then stuck firmly into his heart. His head swirled, much as the stars did below.

"I loved your daughter," Qurrah continued. "As did Tessanna. Our recklessness caused her death."

"What do you want with me?" Harruq asked, unable to meet Qurrah's gaze.

"Join me. Everyone will die. It is inevitable. Does it matter if life ceases its pointless cycle on this miserable stretch of rock? You, your wife, the rest of the Eschaton, just bow and swear allegiance and you will live."

"What life could I hope to live in a dead, desolate world?"

"We will leave it," Qurrah said. "When all is conquered, Velixar will open us a door to a new world, without our troubles, without our death. We can escape, go back to how it had always been. Dezrel will be but a sad memory."

Harruq looked back up to Qurrah, his lower lip quivering.

"Back to how it was?" he asked. Qurrah nodded.

"Back as if we never met Velixar."

"Back," Harruq said. "Back to killing children for your games? Back to trusting you and obeying your commands? You would sacrifice this world, and then ask me to sacrifice my very life to serve at your side?"

Deadly anger swarmed over Qurrah's face. "You will die otherwise."

"What you ask for is worse than death."

"So melodramatic," Qurrah said, his voice a vile hiss. "Is what I offer truly so terrible? What do you gain by fighting against me? Accept my apologies. Accept my mercy. Live at my side. Don't die beneath me."

A chuckle shook Harruq's belly, vibrating up his chest and out to his arms, until his whole body was quaking with laughter.

"One day I will die," he said. "But it will never be beneath you. You're as low as it gets, brother. There's no way to sink any lower. Get out of my head."

The fire sunk, the stars faded, and as the sun shrunk into a thin dot Qurrah sighed. The red of his eyes was all that Harruq could see, and in perfect silence he heard the words of his brother.

"So be it. My mercy is spent. You will break before me, and unlike you, I will not show weakness when I strike the killing blow."

Harruq did not allow him the final word.

"Even back how it was," he said, "you never would have stayed your hand."

The darkness broke, and he opened his eyes.

Damn him," Qurrah said, jarring out of a trance. Tessanna's hands wrapped around his body, holding him as he reoriented himself. The two cuddled against a wall of the throne room. Near them was the portal, which had been still ever since Ulamn's departure. Velixar was on the opposite side of the room, deep in prayer to Karak.

"He didn't accept," Tessanna said. "I told you he wouldn't."

"You give my brother too much credit," Qurrah said.

"And you give him too little. Will he die to your undead?"

The half-orc rubbed his eyes and then shook his head. "No, he won't. He's still strong, as are his friends. He's almost out of the city."

Tessanna nestled her face into the side of his neck.

"Have your pets keep chase," she said, giggling as if it were a humorous joke. "Day and night, they'll follow. Deny your brother sleep. Deny him rest. He will crumble." She grabbed Qurrah's hand and held it against her abdomen.

"Is it true?" he asked her. "Are you with child?"

"Of course," Tessanna said, her eyes sparkling. "Aullienna will no longer haunt me. I will have a daughter of my own. Cease your pets chanting of her name."

"Already done."

She wrapped her arms tighter about his waist and kissed his chin. "Ready to be a father?" she asked him.

"I do not run from my responsibilities," he said.

"That isn't an answer."

He frowned down at her. "It is the only answer I will give. Now please, I need sleep."

He shifted more of his weight against the wall and closed his eyes so he wouldn't see the frown he knew was across his lover's face. She wanted to know. He could feel her presence peering at the edges of his mind, her considerable mental strength curious to his inner feelings. Such feelings were well guarded, for in truth he did not know if he was ready to be a father. He wasn't even sure he knew what it meant to be one.

How many children had he killed? How often had he preached against bringing life into a world of suffering? In doing so, was he a hypocrite and a blasphemer against his own beliefs?

He didn't know. The stone was cold, the portal was open, and Karak was victorious. All other things were chaos. So he stroked her hair and enjoyed her touch while all around the city burned.

⊶⊷

Get him up," Lathaar shouted as he hacked at the limbs that pressed past Jerico's shield. "Even if you have to carry him, get him up!"

"I'll get right on that," Haern whispered, slapping Harruq across the face. The half-orc's eyes were vacant. More of the strange shadow floated from his open mouth.

"What is it you are saying?" Haern asked, leaning closer.

"Get out of my head," Harruq growled. His focus returned. "Where the abyss am I?" he asked.

"Later," Haern said, standing and offering him a hand. Harruq tried to accept, but his arms swung like wood, his fingers foreign and unresponsive. So instead Haern grabbed the crook of his arm and pulled him to his feet.

"Is our sleeping princess awake?" Jerico shouted. His entire body was braced against the river of undead, which moaned in futile anger.

"Can you feel your legs?" Haern asked, ignoring the paladin. Harruq shook his head. "Well, can you still run?"

"He better," Lathaar said as he lopped an arm off at the elbow. "Because that's what we're doing."

Jerico braced with his front foot and then used it to push off, hooking his shield onto his back as he ran east. Lathaar swung his sword in a single arc, cutting down the first bunch of undead that toppled through before he too sprinted east. Haern pulled the half-orc along. Harruq struggled to focus. Foot after foot. That was all that mattered. Swing a dead log that was his leg, plant down, and then swing the other. The undead poured through the wall, but they were slow and lumbering. Second after agonizing second the city grew

David Dalglish

smaller behind them, the chorus of moans becoming distant. Their pace slowed to a steady jog, which soon slowed to a quick walk. They all kept their silence. They were too exhausted for anything else.

◦◈◦

They had no tent, so instead they found a few withered trees, hacked off their limbs, and arranged them in a circle representing the commander's tent. The air was cold, and with the setting of the sun it had grown even colder. Fires dotted the hills, each source of heat heavily crowded. In the center of their circle a large fire roared, courtesy of Tarlak. Antonil and Sergan sat beside each other, huddled and dejected. The Eschaton sat with them, as did Deathmask and his group. Grief had come with the stars, and the night was filled with the cries of lost homes, friends, and loved ones.

"Let's keep this simple, no formalities here," Antonil said, breaking the silence that had fallen over them. "Tarlak, your Eschaton saved countless lives this day, so that is why I bring you all here. Ashhur forgive me but I must ask for even more. And Deathmask, the reputation of your Ash Guild and your defense of my people has also earned you a seat amongst us. Sergan and I will speak for whatever remains of our kingdom of Neldar. Do any object?"

"You might as well speak for Neldar," Tarlak said. "No one else will."

"I need to know what chance we have," Antonil said. He glanced around, meeting each and every pair of eyes surrounding the fire. "Start with the basics. Food. Water. Shelter. Can we manage?"

"I can conjure spring water from the ground," Aurelia said. She sat in Harruq's lap, her husband's arms wrapped around her to keep her warm. "And once we have a decent sleep, creating fire for warmth should not be a burden."

"A decent sleep may be a long time coming," Jerico said, pointedly glancing west. Twenty guards patrolled the area, ready to sound the alarm if a party of undead entered their camp.

327

"Any sleep will feel divine right now," Tarlak said. He brushed his goatee with his thumb and forefinger. "Though fire does us no good while traveling. How many with us are too old, or too young, to survive a journey in the cold? We have no blankets, no tents..."

"Let's not worry about what we can't change," Antonil said. "What about food?"

"Aurry, can't you summon some?" Harruq asked. "Same with you, right Tar?"

Deathmask chuckled at the half-orc. "Did no one bother to tell him of the components for mage banquets?" he asked.

"Components?" Harruq asked.

In answer, Tarlak reached into his pocket and pulled out a handful of small yellow gems. He handed one to the half-orc.

"Topaz," the wizard said. "The more the food, the more topaz we use. What, did you think those extravagant meals we fed you were free?"

"I have some as well," Aurelia said. "Enough to feed five for a month, but how many thousands are here? It will never last."

"Keep it simple," Deathmask said. "Plain bread. If we spread it out, we might have enough to last an extra week."

"Tarlak, Aurelia, do you mind being responsible for the food and water until another solution is found?" Antonil asked. Tarlak laughed.

"Sure, why not. I don't mind being a walking bakery."

Another moment of silence. Antonil knew the first part was easier, at least compared to what he planned to propose.

"So we have no shelter," the guard captain began, "and limited food. Where else can we go to seek aid? Omn is a brutal month away, through the deep of winter no less. We must go to the elves and request their aid."

"You're a fool," Deathmask said. "After you nearly start a war to remove them from Woodhaven, you think either race of elves will give food and shelter to so many refugees?"

"The one responsible for that edict is dead," Antonil said. His ragged face hardened. "And do you see any other option? If I must, I will have Scoutmaster Dieredon plead my case."

"They will turn us away," Deathmask insisted. "Mordan waged war to push them across the rivers, and then Neldar banished them from their lands. We are not welcome, and we are not wanted. You might as well turn us back around and march us right into Veldaren!"

"And if I thought it was the best path for my people, I'd be the first to kneel before the armies of the dead," Antonil shouted. "But I'll be damned if I watch the rest of this nation slaughtered by Karak's madness."

"Quiet down now," Tarlak said, stroking his goatee as he glanced between the two. "Deathmask, I understand your worry. Personally, I think the elves will be thrilled at the chance to thumb their noses at us, but does anyone here know of any possible alternative?"

Silence.

"I didn't think so," Tarlak said. "I don't know the prejudices of most here, but the elves aren't evil, and they aren't heartless monsters. There are too many weak and helpless here for them to fully turn us away. The bigger question is, do we seek help from the Quellan or the Dezren elves?"

"The Quellan," Aurelia said. She shifted in Harruq's lap. "They will help us. The Dezren will just turn us away."

"How do you know this?" Tarlak asked.

"Wait a second," Harruq interrupted. "What's the difference between, what is it? Quellan? Dezren?"

"Does no one tell this beast anything?" Deathmask muttered.

"Watch it," Harruq grumbled.

"The Dezren elves once lived in Mordan," Lathaar said. He had drawn his sword and laid it across his lap, his eyes staring at the soft blue-white glow. "King Baedan waged war, quick and brutal, to force them from their forests by systematic fires. Those fires spanned for miles and filled the sky with smoke and ash. The elves fled across the rivers and settled in what you know as the Derze forest. Many came to the Citadel for aid, but we…"

"You turned us away," Aurelia said. "Left us cold and hungry and scared as we entered a country not our own in search of a home." As she spoke, both Jerico and Lathaar stared at the ground in shame. "A kind word, a hand raised in aid, and we might have believed that not all humankind shared such hatred and disgust. You were the champions of the god of men. You turned us away. The Dezren elves will not give us aid."

"I was but a child at the time," Lathaar said in the following quiet. "I don't know the reason. Politics, perhaps, or maybe Sorollos's influence had grown too strong. But I remember your faces. So beautiful. So tired. I tried to offer some food to a small elven boy. My headmaster slapped the bowl out of my hand and ordered me inside."

"The Quellan elves share their hatred," Antonil said, his own voice turning ragged. "Why would they help us? It is they who helped the Dezren build homes in their forest while Vaelor turned a blind eye to their plight."

"Harruq," Aurelia said. "Tell them what your brother said to you, just before you fled the city."

The half-orc shifted, suddenly uncomfortable with the amount of eyes watching him. How many didn't know of Qurrah? How would he explain who he was, and what his brother had done?

"Qurrah," he said, trying to find a place to start. "He…just before we left, he entered my mind. He said Celestia's wall had fallen, and that thousands of demons were pouring into the city. I don't know what he meant, or if he spoke the truth."

"Celestia's wall?" Mira asked, startling those around her. She had remained silent for the meeting, but now seemed focused.

"Who is this 'Qurrah,'" Deathmask asked. "And what wall did he speak of?"

"Qurrah…" Harruq began.

"Was once a member of my Eschaton," Tarlak interrupted. "He has caused us much grief, and sides with the servants of Karak. He commands many of the army that overran Veldaren."

"Qurrah," Antonil said. "The necromancer you accused of mutilating the bodies half a year ago? He leads this army?"

"Yes," Tarlak said. "We did not kill him when we had the chance. Now we all pay dearly for our failure."

"The wall," Mira said. "Tell me, what is it?"

Aurelia started to speak, but Antonil held up a hand.

"It is my failure," he said, "and I will tell it. Only kings and guard captains are shown what is behind the throne curtains. It is a mural depicting Ashhur and Karak entering this world through a swirling door made of stars. Whenever a new king takes the throne the Quellan elves send a single diplomat, always with the same request. 'Will you guard that which all other Kings have guarded?' Most assume it means peace, or life, but that isn't it. Our scholars believe it is through that wall, that gate of stars, that the gods entered our world. The Quellan elves confirm this."

"Whatever Celestia guarded our world from cannot be ignored," Mira said.

Antonil stood and turned his back to the fire. His hands shook at his side.

"I swore to guard the throne of the king with my life, yet here I am. What has your vile brother done, Harruq? What has he released into our world?"

Aurelia brushed aside Harruq's arms and stood, placing her hand atop Antonil's shoulder. He flinched but did not push her away.

"The Quellan elves will fight them," she said. "No good would have come from your death, nor the sacrifice of the thousand that look to you for strength. Say the destination, and we all will follow. Give the word, and your people will gladly die in the cold, damp earth. It is better than the fate you spared them from."

"Is it?" Antonil asked as the guards at the perimeter called out warning. Undead approached. "Can you be so certain?"

＊＊＊

Wake, my disciple," Velixar said. Qurrah muttered and crept open an eye.

"Can it wait until dawn?" he asked. Velixar frowned, displeased at the lack of immediate obedience.

"Ulamn returns. Stand. Our new army comes."

Tessanna stirred at the sound of their voices.

"Our army?" she asked. Her voice was drowsy and her eyes still closed. "Do they march with our banner? Do they obey our commands?"

"In time," Velixar said. The portal swirled, the stars violent. "Qurrah, stand. Their passing will tax your strength."

Gently Qurrah slid Tessanna off his chest and to the floor. He staggered to his feet, brushed his eyes, and then screamed in horrid pain. Velixar grit his teeth, and his eyes faded. Ulamn stepped through, flanked by twenty guards. They held flags of the yellow fist. Weapons hung from their belts.

"The first of many," Ulamn shouted, and the others raised their fists and cheered. They marched forward, ignoring the three in the corner. Twenty more arrived wielding polearms made of a strange red iron that matched their crimson armor. Again Qurrah screamed.

"The pain will lessen with each passing," Velixar said, his voice raspy and weak. "Celestia has not yet given up hope of breaking our spirit."

"I can see that," Qurrah gasped as he crumbled to his knees. Thirty more soldiers entered. They held supplies for constructing tents and fortifications. The half-orc winced, his teeth locked tight so that his scream came out as a hissing moan.

"Try to rest," Tessanna said as she stroked her lover's face. "It is only pain. You have endured worse."

"That..." Qurrah said as he gasped for air. "That is a lie."

A group of forty marched into the throne room carrying long planks of wood atop their shoulders. Qurrah arched his back against the wall and smacked a fist against the cold stone. Sweat covered his face. Through blurred eyes, he saw Velixar did little better. His skin had turned pale and rotten. His eyes were tiny spots of red amid a dried up skull. Velixar pulled his hood low across his face and turned away from his disciple.

"Do you understand the power we control?" Velixar asked. "Without us they cannot enter. To defeat the armies of Celestia and Ashhur, they will need thousands of Thulos's war demons. If we break under the strain, they will be trapped here."

"Thousands," Qurrah gasped as another group of forty entered, marching in perfect formation with gigantic swords strapped to their backs.

"It will get easier," Velixar said. "I promise."

Ulamn finished ordering his men to set up camps along the outside of the castle and approached the necromancers.

"We normally have a hundred gatekeepers to share the burden of passing through our armies," he said. "To have only two will slow us greatly."

"We have time," Velixar said. "How many centuries have you searched for this world? A few extra months will be nothing."

"Thulos will not be able to enter," the demon general said. "You both are far too weak to support the entrance of a god."

"When Celestia is defeated, and her elves ash and bone, we will have the strength," Velixar said. "How many come with you?"

"Two hundred, for now," Ulamn said, glancing at Qurrah. "Will he survive?"

"He will," Tessanna said, answering for him. "I know he will."

"So be it. We will camp within the city. A battle has been fought here, and it will do us good to be surrounded by the bodies of the conquered."

Qurrah's scream interrupted them, which then turned to laughter.

"Is it true pain makes you stronger," he asked in between laughs. "Because you won't need a god after this. I'll be one."

"His madness is…" Ulamn began.

"None of your concern," Velixar said. "Go tend your army."

The demon general frowned but obeyed. Two more groups exited the portal before it shrank. The stars fixated in position. Qurrah gasped in relief as the light returned to Velixar's eyes.

"I will be in prayer," the man in black said before marching off. He could not bear to be in the same room as his disciple. He slammed the doors shut behind him, leaving the two lovers in silence. Tessanna knelt down and held Qurrah as he gasped in pain.

"I wish they would have let me sleep first," he said, the right side of his face cracking a smile.

"Sleep now," Tessanna told him, kissing each of his eyes closed. "Recover your strength. You will need it by the morn."

He did as he was told, far too weak to argue otherwise.

※

Mira slipped through the many fires, her heart panged by the sight of so many suffering. She wondered how many would never wake from their sleep. Ten? Fifty? A hundred? The cold would claim so many. She reached the edge of their encampment. A lone guard walked by, a faded cape wrapped around his body and his helmet pulled down to cover his numb ears. He nodded at her as he passed.

"A throne of a king," Mira said, her eyes staring off in the night. Visions danced before her, not of her own creation. "And a mural with the gods' entrance. Is this what you want of me, Celestia? Is this my purpose?"

She waved her hands, tearing open a blue portal. Her whole body quivered with fear and excitement. She knew who waited on the other side. Could she face her, knowing what her dreams demanded?

She didn't know, but she entered anyway.

◆◆

Tessanna stood as the small blue portal ripped open beside the throne. She smiled as a healthier, livelier version of herself stepped through. They stared at each other with gigantic black eyes, the eyes of goddesses.

"I dreamt you would come to me," Tessanna said.

"Is that all you dreamt?" Mira asked.

"No," Tessanna said, smiling at her sleeping husband. "I dreamt of my child. And I dreamt of you dying, my dagger plunged deep in your breast." She drew her dagger and licked the edge, not minding the blood that trickled from the cut she made on her tongue.

"I don't trust my dreams," Mira said. "I've defeated ancient demons, Tessanna. Armies have quivered and fled by my hand alone."

"And Qurrah quivers from mine," Tessanna said. "And he is greater than any army."

Soft white mist fell from Mira's hands as she summoned her magic. "Dreams change," she said.

"Never," Tessanna said. "Only we change. Our dreams stay the same."

Mira hurled a lance of ice, which quickly shattered from a wave of Tessanna's hand. Seven more lances followed, each one breaking as she laughed.

"Is this all?" Tessanna asked. "I thought you were supposed to be my mirror?"

Mira spread her arms above her head and glared. A ball of fire grew, shaking with intensity. With all her strength she hurled it across the room, but not at Tessanna. Instead it flew straight for Qurrah's sleeping body. Tessanna shrieked, twirling her hands on instinct. A wall of shadow cocooned him. The fire exploded, burning curtains and filling the room with smoke. Qurrah was unharmed.

Tessanna glared at Mira. She was no longer having fun. Mira saw this and smirked.

"I lived alone for so long," Mira said. "As did you. What would it be like to lose him and return to that loneliness?"

"Never," Tessanna hissed. Bolts of shadow shot from her hands, splashing across a magical shield.

Mira uncrossed her arms, and from the center of her chest a bolt of lightning streaked across the room. Tessanna caught it in her hand, laughing as she felt its power char her flesh. Her laughter ended when a second bolt struck Qurrah, dissolving her barrier around him. Qurrah, exhausted beyond measure from opening the portal and enduring the arrival of so many troops, remained unconscious.

"How afraid of loneliness are you?" Mira asked. Before she could hurl a second attack at Qurrah, the lightning bolt left Tessanna's hand, strengthened by a surrounding aura of fire. Mira brought up her shield and cried out in pain as she halted the spell. Tessanna gave her no reprieve. She locked her hands together, braced, and then fired a gigantic beam of shadow. Mira did the same, except pure white magic streamed from her hands. The two beams struck, the sound of their meeting a concussion of violent thunder.

"You will break," Tessanna said. "You have no idea the pain I can endure."

Suddenly, Mira halted her beam and hurled herself into the air with a levitation spell. Tessanna's spell continued onward, blasting apart the doors to the castle, destroying several homes, and eventually knocking a hole in the wall surrounding the city. She swore as several soldiers in crimson armor entered in a frantic search for the cause of the tremendous magical power.

"Stay out of this," she shouted to them. The men glanced about, saw Qurrah lying vulnerable, and ordered a protective barricade. Mira frowned at the sight, her one advantage now blocked by a wall of shields.

"You have no escape," Tessanna said. "You aren't strong enough to beat me, and even if I fall, others will kill you. This accomplishes nothing."

"Liar."

Mira rained fire from the ceiling, burning the stone to black. The fire did not pass through their shields, and Tessanna herself let several waves burn her skin and singe her hair. She laughed at the pain.

"A goddess fighting a goddess," Tessanna said. "Who wins? Who breaks the tie?"

"The angrier," Mira said. Lightning swirled about the ceiling, striking Tessanna over and over. Some she blocked with a shield, others she let hit her. Smoke rose from her eyes, and when she opened her mouth and laughed, putrid darkness floated from within like ash.

"You would strike my lover to defeat me," Tessanna said. "And you are wrong. It is not the angrier. It is the one most insane."

She raised her arms, and black ethereal wings stretched from her shoulders. They grew larger and larger, reaching from the ceiling to the floor. A single beat and she rose to equal height as Mira and then shrieked a wild, magical cry. The sound knocked Mira back and scattered her thoughts. The sight of the black angel awakened something inside her. She slammed the other side of the room with her body, then gasped at the pain. Her eyes flared a rainbow of colors. Wispy white wings grew from her back, attached to her shoulder blades by ethereal strands. White and black light shimmered in the room, and even the experienced war demons who had conquered many worlds stood with mouths agape.

"Insane?" Mira asked. "Is this what you call insanity?"

Tessanna snarled and cast a bleeding spell. The magic faded, losing all strength in the blinding white. She hurled fire and lightning, but this time it was Mira who let the spells hit, laughing as they splashed across her skin. They damaged her dress and burned her skin but caused no serious harm.

"Is this what we are?" Mira asked as she beat her wings, stretching the luminous white extremities throughout the room. "Is this the visage we will know beyond our death?"

Tessanna pulled her arms tight across her chest, her black eyes shimmering beneath a gray haze. Red seeped into her wings, the bloody crimson similar to the wings of the soldiers guarding Qurrah with their shields. Swirling darkness collected around her hands. She stared at Mira with a sudden calm, and at that look Mira knew what was happening. She could feel it in her own head.

Her children were fighting, and mother was coming to set things right.

"You're to die," Tessanna said. "I don't know why, but you're to die. It's the only reason I was allowed my child."

"Dreams, nothing more," Mira said.

"Lie to yourself if you must."

Tessanna locked her fingers together, pointed her hands at Mira, and let the full extent of her power unleash in a focused beam of red lightning. Mira thought to batter it aside with a shield as all other attacks, but she underestimated the power sent against her. Her shield shattered like glass, and then she screamed as pain immeasurable swarmed her being. Her wings dissolved, fading away as if they were but a dream. Magic abandoned her. As the electricity swirled around her body she plummeted to the ground, smacking against the unforgiving stone. Tessanna giggled as she heard the delicious sound of bones breaking.

"Stay away from her," she ordered when she saw the war demons leaving their defensive formation. "She is my kill, and mine alone."

Triumphant, she lowered herself to the floor, her black wings pulling back into her body. She smiled at the blood everywhere. Mira lay on her stomach, facing away from Tessanna. Directly before her was the portal, spinning steadily. She looked like a sacrifice to the mural, an offering in payment for the demon soldiers that had marched forthwith. But that wasn't what caused Tessanna's smile, nor was it the blood on the floor. It was the fact that Mira's shoulders and chest still heaved from her breathing.

"I expected more," Tessanna said as she drew her dagger. "So easily beaten? Mountains should have crumbled from our conflict, and entire cities leveled."

Mira opened her eyes and stared at the portal as she heard the voice of the goddess speaking.

"I've wanted this for a long time," Tessanna said. She could hear her mother's voice, the one that had told her to shatter her mirror. Finish it, the voice cried. End her. Destroy her life. The dagger, a single strike with the dagger!

"You still don't know what we are," Mira whispered. "And you think you will raise a child?"

Deep inside her breast she felt her power rising. It was the magic of the goddess, granted to her when she was just a babe leaving her mother's womb. That power had struck her mother dead, stripped her of all life so that it might pour into the newborn child. A spell repeated over and over in her mind, and gently Celestia whispered to the small, lonely girl.

You were not meant for this world, only to save it from itself. Forgive me, my daughter. Accept the dagger. Forgive your other. She knows not what she does, only that she does it for me.

Mira began whispering the words of the spell. The power in her breast strengthened and concentrated. Tessanna sensed the growing danger. All around them wind swirled, chaotic and directionless. Their hair whipped about and the dust of the ground rose to the ceiling. The nearby soldiers covered their faces and cowered. Tessanna knelt, smiling her insane smile. Her heart raced. Her head throbbed. Excitement tingled up and down her spine. All would happen as it was meant. She would plunge the dagger, shatter her mirror, and then rouse Qurrah from unconsciousness so he could hold her, maybe even make love to her.

Mira stammered more and more. She felt desperate and vicious. She was becoming a trap, one that would detonate with the force of an angered goddess. Tears ran down her face, continuing even when Tessanna pushed her onto her back. The dagger hovered in the air. If it plunged through her skin, Mira's magic would release in a devastating explosion, destroying Veldaren and closing the portal. Balance, so precariously trembling over permanent darkness, would be preserved.

Tessanna grabbed Mira's face in her hand and tilted it so they could stare eye to eye. Her other hand quivered with excitement as it held the dagger. Now. Her entire purpose was now. For one agonizing moment all her pieces were made whole, her mind was one, and in singular desire she plunged down the dagger.

Mira closed her eyes, knowing what her death would mean, what her sacrifice would gain. Knowing so many lives would be saved. But she remembered how Lathaar's arms had held her as she wept atop Karak's bridge, and that knowledge meant nothing. She would never see him again. She screamed, one of horrible sorrow and shame. The spell dissipated, the danger vanishing and she went against her mother's will. The dagger plunged into her breast. Tessanna gasped in pleasure, but the kill was not complete. She had missed the heart, and for a strange moment, she realized she had never aimed for it in the first place.

"Then why did I…" she asked before her mind fractured. The agony crumpled her to the floor as she held her temples and screamed.

"Lathaar," Mira whispered as she felt warm blood spill across her chest. "Please, help me Lathaar. Help me."

With shaking limbs, she slid onto her knees, the dagger lodged in her flesh. She glared at the war demons, who watched in admiration and horror. They knew her strength and were both in awe and terror of it. She looked away, unsure what such armored men with red wings meant. All she wanted was one thing. With the last of her power she staggered to her feet, opened a portal, and fell through.

Tessanna crawled along the floor, weeping all the while. Where she crawled she left a long red smear of blood. The soldiers parted for her. She clutched Qurrah's robes and used them to pull herself onto him. She beat against his breast as she wept.

"Wake up," she said. "Please, wake up, Qurrah."

The drain of the portal was too great. Her lover remained unconscious. As the war demons took up their shields and weapons, she laid her head upon his neck and bathed him with her tears.

"I was whole," she said. "I was whole, Qurrah, please wake up, I was whole. But now mommy's mad at me, mad at us both. She wants our child, please, Qurrah, please damn it, please wake up!"

She cried herself to sleep, still alone, still in pieces.

L athaar lay with his back to the small fire, one of many that warmed the sprawling camp. His body was exhausted, his mind begged for sleep, but still he stared into nowhere. Ever since his childhood in the Citadel he had believed he was to be a beacon, an example of a decent life in an indecent world. He knew he was far from perfect, but his failure to meet a standard did not remove the standard. He heard the weeping and terror of so many shivering beside fires as they too failed to succumb to sleep. He, the beacon, felt emptied and darkened. What hope could he offer them that would not stink of falseness?

A sudden rush of air stirred him, and he turned to see Mira collapse through a blue portal. She fell, still gasping his name.

"Mira?" he asked, pushing up to a sitting position. "Where have you…"

He saw the dagger in her chest. He swallowed his question. She lay on her back, staring up at him as she gasped in air. He put one hand on the side of her face and the other on the dagger's hilt.

"This will hurt more than it already does," he told her. She said nothing. Whispering a prayer, Lathaar pulled out the dagger. Blood poured across her dress as her scream of pain awoke many nearby. Without pause the paladin dropped the dagger and pushed both his hands against the wound. He closed his eyes, a twinge of fear in his heart. He was exhausted, mentally and physically. Ashhur had not gifted him with healing talent. Would he still heed his prayer?

"Please," he whispered. "I've nothing left in me. By your hand, let her be healed, for this I beg."

He felt no warm presence, no divine light, not even a sense of comfort. When he opened his eyes, he saw the white light fading from his hands. He pulled back, and through the hole in her dress he saw the skin knit together into an angry scar. Mira closed her eyes, sleep calling as the pain faded from her breast. She wrapped her arms around his neck and pulled him to her.

"I'm sorry," she said. Tears swelled in her eyes. "I love you, Lathaar, and because of that I've done something terrible."

"Nothing terrible can come from love," he said.

"You're wrong," she said, remembering the vicious hatred in Tessanna's eyes. "And now I've sacrificed us all."

He stroked her forehead with the tips of his fingers and held her in his arms until sleep stole her away from the world she was no longer meant for. And in the quiet he heard a voice, but it was not the deep calm of Ashhur. This one was feminine, peaceful, and in great pain.

Balance is broken, young paladin. There must be a victor. Will you fight for all things good? Will you protect my daughter?

"With my life," he whispered.

Then mind your faith.

20

She could see her breath in the air but she refused the comfort of a fire. Harruq still slept, which didn't surprise her. She had seen how exhausted he was. As a soft wind blew against her she shivered and pressed her arms against her chest.

"I must say, Aurelia, I was not aware elves were immune to cold. Silly me."

The elf rolled her eyes. Deathmask, wrapped in a thick blanket, smirked as he approached. "Then again," he said, "most elves would do anything to escape a human death caravan such as ours, so obviously you are not a normal elf."

"What do you want?" she asked, her voice as cold as the weather.

"Antonil is forming people into groups with the goal of each group sharing a set portion of food. You'll be needed soon."

"That's fine," she said, still staring past the hills where the ruins of Veldaren lay hidden. Deathmask turned to go but then stopped.

"You realize we won't have enough food," he said.

"We have no choice, if we ration…"

"We ration we make it farther, but not to the Quellan forest. And we have no tents, no blankets, just freezing water and conjured bread that will do little but dull their hunger."

Aurelia turned on him, anger in her eyes.

"What do you want," she asked. "You want to flee yourself? Abandon those you could help to save your own skin?"

"No, but I'd rather not die in a hopeless cause without…" He glanced behind her, and his bravado faded. He pulled up his mask from around his neck and covered his face. Aurelia spun, looking for what it was he saw.

Twenty shapes flew from the west, their wings red and their armor crimson.

"What manner of men are those?" Aurelia asked.

"No men of Dezrel," Deathmask said as he poured ash across his face. Ready, he tilted his head and raised his arms. Dark fire consumed his hands.

"Kill them quickly, before they know our power," he said. "If one escapes, they will track our location with ease."

Ice lined Aurelia's fingers. Side by side, they waited as the winged war demons flew closer. As they neared, they drew spears and swords and held them high, their red hue shining in the morning light.

"Surely they see the campfires ahead," Deathmask muttered. "They know our location. Why do they press the attack?"

"They want blood," Aurelia said. "So let's give it to them."

Lances of ice flew from her hands at tremendous speeds. The demons dropped and spun, expertly avoiding most. One had his wing shattered at the shoulder, while another dropped dead, a spear of ice pierced through his throat and out the back of his neck. Deathmask laughed at the display of power. The dark fire of his hands swelled. He focused on a single demon, watching with pleasure as fire surrounded him and consumed his wings in a single burst of flame. The demon plummeted, doomed to die by the long fall.

The remaining demons saw their attackers and spiraled to the ground, skimming above the grass in a collision course for the two spellcasters. Deathmask burned the wings of two more, clenching his fist and grinning with each body that rolled and bounced on snapping bones. Lightning arced from Aurelia's fingers, striking dead one demon before leaping to the next. Only ten remained by the time they neared them.

"Drop down!" Aurelia shouted. She fell to her knees and slammed her open palms to the grass. A wall of fire tore to the sky, and through it the demons flew. It only burned and maimed them, but it also hid their presence. As the last passed through the fire, Aurelia banished the wall and stood. The demons were spread out in two groups, each group looping around and coming in for another pass.

"Know any more tricks?" Deathmask asked.

"I don't fight flying men too often," Aurelia said.

"Neither do I. But I do fight over-aggressive ones."

Deathmask clapped his hands together. Dark magic sparked between them, and a loud roar erupted at their contact. Again he clapped, and the roar was louder, the black sparks stronger. Aurelia spun her arms, and a swirling column or air enveloped them.

"Here they come," she said, but Deathmask needed no warning. Grinning beneath his mask, he clapped his hands the third time as the first of the demons pushed through the wall of wind. A shockwave of sound and magic rolled in all directions. Aurelia felt it strike her body. Her lungs froze. Her heartbeat halted. For one agonizing second her body was a statue. The feeling passed, and her lungs and heart resumed their dutiful workings. Aurelia smiled as she realized the brilliant trap. Even Deathmask had been stunned by the spell, but they were on firm ground and could recover immediately. The war demons, however…

Aurelia gave them no chance to recover. As they spun and turned in a vain attempt to avoid the ground she blasted them with lightning and fire. Deathmask cursed them with pain and weakness, sapping their strength and clotting their minds. Several died from striking the ground. Only a few remained healthy enough to flee. Deathmask pointed them out and swore.

"Three," he said. "They're out of reach."

"Not yet," Aurelia said. The demons had flown straight into the air, hoping to gain enough distance to fly safely back to Veldaren. Aurelia stared into the sky, visualizing. She had to be perfect. She whispered the words to the spell, then stepped through the blue portal that tore open before her. She fought off the initial wave of disorientation, for she did not step onto land, but into freezing open air directly above the demons.

All three had been facing back, watching for spells to dodge. She killed the first with a lance of ice through the head. The remaining two turned to see her fall between them, lightning exploding from her hands. Limp and smoking they fell, very much dead. Aurelia's fingers danced the semantic components of a spell. Her fall slowed as a levitation spell took hold. Shivering in the wind she floated to the ground, smirking at Deathmask the whole time.

"Show off," he said as she gently landed. "If I wasn't insane, I would have joined you in opening the portal and…"

He stopped as if slapped.

"What?" Aurelia asked.

"A portal," Deathmask said. "Why don't we open a portal to the Quellan forest?"

"You're insane," Aurelia said. "I don't have the strength to move so many, and neither do you."

"Not a free form one," Deathmask insisted. "Think older, when portal magic was first discovered. If we carve the correct runes into the rock and then have enough of us join together, we can open a much larger portal. It would be healthy and strong and ready to move, say, thousands of people hundreds of miles away from chasing winged demons."

"How many do we have?" Aurelia asked. "You, Tarlak, and I would be hard-pressed even with the help of the runes."

"Veliana can cast spells, as can the twins," Deathmask insisted. "We can do this. Tarlak will agree. Trust me."

"If you say so," Aurelia said, trudging back to the camp where hundreds of hungry people waited for her to create them food.

"Are you insane?" Tarlak asked as he handed off a piece of bread. "What mushrooms have you been eating?"

"It'll take more time, and patience, but we can do it," Deathmask insisted. The three stood before long lines of people, each a representative of the groups Antonil had separated them into. Each person was given a loaf of bread and bit of cheese to divide up among his group. In the center of the camp Veliana had summoned a gentle spring for those needing a drink.

"We're talking an entire day, maybe two," Tarlak said. "Two days to carve the runes, ensure all of us know the words, cast the correct incantations, and then move everyone through while hoping no one has a slip of concentration that leaves hundreds of people stranded miles away from safety."

"That sounds about right," Deathmask said.

Tarlak sighed. He twirled his finger. A piece of bread appeared in his hand like some cheap parlor trick. Another twirl and he had some cheese. He handed both off to a haggard women with frostbitten fingers.

"Alright then," the wizard said. "Let's have a talk with Antonil."

✦

Absolutely not," Antonil said. "Even I know the risks of portal magic. What happens to those who might be left behind? Even worse, what happens if we are attacked in the middle of the ritual?"

"I have absolute faith in this idea," Tarlak said. He removed his hat and scratched at the bald spot on his head. "It's not like the portal is made of fire or anything."

"You need to trust us," Aurelia said. "You know our resources are limited. This is our best hope."

Antonil frowned and crossed his arms. He glanced about his camp, pondering the options.

"Guard captain," Deathmask said, stealing his attention. "How many did not wake up this morning? How many perished of exhaustion, of cold, of hunger or thirst or sheer hopelessness? I know the number, as do you."

Over a hundred was the answer. Under his orders, the soldiers had left them where they lay.

"We will not survive this journey," Deathmask said. "Even in perfect conditions we would be hard pressed, but we are in the dead of winter. One snowstorm, one torrent of icing rain, and all will die. Give us the order."

Antonil sighed. Aurelia felt a sinking feeling in her gut at the sight of the guard captain when he spoke.

"Do it then," he said. "And may Ashhur have mercy on us all."

The refugees collected around fires, huddled and quiet. Antonil had told them little of their plan, only that they needed to rest and stay warm. After his simple speech the guard captain retreated south to where a small cluster of trees surrounded a spring that emerged from one hill and vanished into the small cave mouth of another. The trees were barren, their leaves long since fallen. He had left his soldiers under strict orders not to follow. When he heard the soft hiss of a portal opening, he shook his head and sighed.

"I'm not one of your soldiers," Aurelia said, guessing his thoughts. "And even if I were, I would still come here."

He turned and faced her. His shoulders sagged, and his frown seemed permanently etched above his jaw.

"I don't know you well, Aurelia, but I know enough to believe there is a reason for this intrusion, and a good-hearted one at that. I don't want to hear it. My shame is…"

"Shut your mouth already," Aurelia said, and at her harsh words, he obeyed. For a moment she said nothing, only glared. At last she spoke. "Your men are dying. Your people are dying. They are cold. They are hungry. And they are terrified."

"I am well aware of that," Antonil said. His right hand shook, clutching the hilt of his sword.

"Who are you, Antonil Copernus?" Aurelia asked. "Do you know anymore?"

"I am a failure to my people, to my king, and to my kingdom. And what do I do now? I let them sit here, gambling on the whims of wizards and sorcerers to save their lives from demons and the dead. What would you tell me, that I did the right thing? That they need me? What would you tell me that I do not already know?"

"You are their king!" she shouted. Tears swelled in his eyes even as he adamantly shook his head.

"No," he said. "I have no bloodline, and no claim to a throne I abandoned."

"Open your eyes," Aurelia said. "You are no longer a guard captain. You are no longer a servant to the king, for you cannot be a servant to yourself. Every life in that camp needs to trust in something or someone to protect them and promise them a better life the day after tomorrow. Already they speak of you as king in their whispers. Take up the mantle."

"I am not ready," Antonil said, but the words came out weak.

"No one is ever ready," she said. She reached out and took his quivering hand. With her other she drew his sword, flipped the hilt toward him, and grinned.

"What is it you humans say?" she asked. "The King is dead, long live the King?"

"It is. So will the portal work?" he asked as he took the sword.

"I haven't the slightest idea," she said.

Despite his terror, King Antonil laughed.

"If you are ready," she said as he wiped his eyes, "then I have this for you." She removed his golden helm, held it to her lips, and kissed it. The helmet shivered and the gold drained away. The precious metal reshaped, and from the top seven spikes jutted into a warlord's crown.

"It is awesome," Antonil said as he stared at the gift she offered back to him.

"Just an illusion," the elf said. "But in times like these, illusions will suffice. Your strength will give strength to others. Now wait here for my return."

Aurelia did not want the newly crowned king to come strolling into the camp. No, he would ride in atop a horse and demand the courage and respect he deserved. They had no horses, but that wasn't a bother to her. A few well placed teleports and she was much farther south, staring out across a chill field. Several wild horses trotted about, nibbling from grass that still held a bit of green.

"Come to me," she said, casting a simple charm spell across the largest and most elegant. The beautiful beast strode up and snorted while shaking his head. His body was deep black, with only a thin line of white underneath his neck.

"It will be cold where I take you," she told the horse. "But you will be the mount of a king. A fair trade, yes?"

Another shake of the head, another snort. Aurelia giggled. She knew the creature was intelligent, but not enough to understand her words. Only pegasi were smart enough for that. But the horse understood her tone and could feel her desires, the charm spell made sure of that. She put her arm atop his neck and lead the horse through portal after portal.

"Holy piss bucket," Antonil said when Aurelia appeared before him with the horse.

"Such language for a king," she said. "Climb up. He will obey your commands. Just make sure I have a bit of time alone with him every night or he'll suddenly decide you're not near as friendly."

"I've been thrown before," Antonil said. "I'll do what I must to prevent that again."

<hr style="width:10%" />

King Antonil rode into the camp. He nodded at the soldiers that he passed. Every one, even those that stood slack-jawed, stood erect and saluted. The peasants that saw him cheered his name, the weather suddenly not so cold, the future not so bleak.

"At last our king wears a crown," one shouted.

"All hail Antonil!" shouted another. Slowly word spread from campfire to campfire. At Aurelia's instructions he circled the perimeter of the camp, letting soldier and commoner see his armor, his crown, and his steed. When he finally returned to his tent and dismounted, the entire place was stirring with shouts and songs.

Sergan waited for him, his axe hefted across his shoulders.

"About the finest damn thing I've seen in years," he said, his grin spreading from ear to ear. "And since when could you create crowns from dirt and horses from logs?"

"Since today," Antonil said. He went to hug the old sergeant, but Sergan stunned him by falling to one knee and laying his axe across the ground.

"I swear my axe to you, King Copernus," he said. "Will you accept this gift, humbly offered?"

"I accept it," Antonil said, "and I am humbled by its offering."

Sergan stood, and the two embraced. All around soldiers raised their weapons and cheered. The newly honored king winked at Aurelia, who had remained in the background, admiring her work. She feigned a curtsey, then laughed.

"Impressive illusions," Tarlak said, sliding up beside her. "So what is he really riding? A donkey? A large dog?"

"The horse is real," Aurelia said. "If it had been an illusion, I'd have made sure its face resembled yours."

"Touching," Tarlak said. "Now follow me. We've got a problem."

<hr>

I told you this was crazy," Veliana said, a large rock in her hands. "And I know I wasn't the only one."

They were gathered atop a solitary hill. Strewn about the dead grass were slabs of stone with runes carved atop them. Some were intricate in detail, while others were only half-finished. Deathmask stood where the portal was to go, a chisel in his left hand.

"Genius will always have its doubters," he said, waving the chisel about.

"So will madness," Tarlak said as he and Aurelia arrived at the top of the hill. "Funny how much those two have in common."

Mier and Nien laughed. The two were busy juggling stones, a chisel and a hammer. Oddly enough, with each pass the runes on the stones grew a tiny bit sharper and longer.

"Deathmask doesn't trust us," Nien said.

"Deathmask doesn't trust anyone, but this time he doubts us," Mier said.

"What are they talking about?" Aurelia asked.

"The portal..." Tarlak began.

"Will still work," Deathmask interrupted. "We just need to shorten the distance."

"What do you mean?"

"We're not enough," Nien said.

"Not strong enough," Mier said.

"Please, just one person at a time," Aurelia said.

"Even with all of us helping," Tarlak said, glaring at Deathmask as if daring him to interrupt again, "we're looking at hundreds of miles to the edge of the Quellan forest. Multiply that by the thousand or so we must transport and we'll all crumble under the strain."

Aurelia crossed her arms and stared at the stones. The others stilled their movements. They had all reached the same conclusion, but they wanted to know if the last major spellcaster agreed.

"You want us to make two portals," she said, glancing back up at them. "One halfway to the forest, and once we're all safe, one the rest of the way. Cut the strain in half."

"We'll still make far better time," Deathmask said.

"I know you're right, but the strain on all of us will..."

She stopped, for she sensed something both alien and familiar. It was an aura of brooding silence, constrained power behind a cracking dam. Gently limping, Mira walked up the hill.

"You're building a portal," the girl said.

"Aye, we are, my beautiful lady," Tarlak said. He frowned at the sight of her torn dress and multiple bruises. Lathaar had told him a little about Mira's trip back to Veldaren. Still, he was surprised by just how fast she had healed. Even the deep stab to her chest was only a vicious red line of scabbed blood. "Should you be up and about, hurt as you are?" he asked.

To this she said nothing, only trudged to the circle of stones. "Where will you take them?" she asked.

"Two hundred miles south," Deathmask said. "After that, another hundred."

"The Quellan forest," Mira said.

"Yes," Deathmask said. "That is our goal."

The girl smiled, but it was a dead smile. "You mustn't make two portals. One will suffice. I will hold it, and I alone."

The twins halted their juggling. Tarlak and Aurelia glanced about nervously. Deathmask only laughed.

"What sorceress do you think you are?" he asked her. "No, what goddess?"

"No goddess," Mira said, her black eyes flaring with sudden life. "But if you must judge me by my blood, then know me as Celestia."

She raised her arms, and at once the many runes snapped rigid. Fire burned across them, changing and reshaping the runes. She arranged them in a circle about the hill. Out of her mouth words of magic poured, quick and sharp. Clouds circled above, pulled in by the power that swept through them. Lightning struck the hill. In the deafening thunder a massive blue portal ripped open. Mira's dress flapped in the wind that swirled into it. The other casters stared in awe.

"I will hold the portal," she said, showing no strain from its size or distance. "I killed us all. It is the least I can do. Prepare your magic. The demons approach."

"Demons?" Deathmask asked. "What is she talking about?"

To this she pointed west. Tarlak cast a spell to augment his eyes, his jaw dropping open when it completed.

"We're in trouble," he said. "Someone find Antonil, we need people moving through this portal, now!"

Aurelia cast a similar spell, her heart sinking at what she saw. Soaring through the air in perfect ranks were hundreds of the winged men she and Deathmask had fought earlier. Many of them carried red banners marked with the yellow fist.

"An entire army," she said, her voice just above a whisper. "Are they what Qurrah has brought into this world?"

"Fight them," Mira said. "Unless mother denies me my strength, I will hold."

"Deathmask," Tarlak said, tipping his hat. "Care to fight side by side to protect our goddess?"

"I enjoy my life," Deathmask said, his hand dipping into the bag of ash hanging from his belt. "And I'll enjoy this battle as well."

21

Antonil ordered his people into a giant line stretching up the hill. Five wide they rushed the survivors through while the remaining troops of Veldaren flanked them on both sides. Mira stood beside the portal, her arms raised to the sky and her eyes closed. Her hair tossed about while her dress flapped against her legs. High above the clouds darkened and grumbled angrily. The two paladins stood at her side, their orders simple. Mira was not to be touched. The blue portal hissed and shook as five by five the people fled through.

"Do not panic, and do not stop!" Antonil shouted as he rode his horse down the long line of frantic refugees. "As long as you hold breath make for the portal!" He circled the greater mass of people at the bottom of the hill eager to join the line, again shouting his command. The soldiers flanking drew their swords and saluted, and the sign of formality and duty soothed those climbing toward the swirling blue magic.

Beyond the last few families and peasants, the Eschaton stood in a long line. They stared east with baited breaths. Deathmask's crew intermixed with them, magic sparking on their fingertips. They were eight in all, the first and strongest line of defense against the coming demons.

"Use everything you've got to get their attention," Tarlak said as the sky swarmed with dull red armor and beating wings. "Keep them on us as long as you can. With each volley, take a few steps back."

"As you wish, master wizard," Deathmask said, ash hovering so thick before his face his features were all but gone. "And no one be a fool. When the battle is lost, make for the portal. Dying here means nothing."

"Such elegant words," Harruq muttered.

"I don't exactly feel like dying here either," Aurelia said, but her voice was distracted. She was trying to estimate the number of soldiers that approached. By her guess, each banner that flew represented a unit of fifty, and she counted nine banners. She winced.

"Daggerwork may not be enough," Mier said.

"We need more than daggers," Nien said.

Veliana drew her own, kissed the blades, and stared at the sky with her lone eye. "Their armor is thick, but daggers will do just fine," she said.

The twins chuckled at her but said nothing.

"They're almost here," Harruq said. He could see the giant red wings, the crimson armor, and the wicked weapons hanging from their belts. Silhouetted by a blackened sky, they seemed a demonic army indeed.

"Let's give them a good welcome, shall we?" Tarlak said before beginning his spellcasting. Deathmask and Aurelia joined him, choosing their largest and flashiest spells. A ball of fire shot from Tarlak's hands, smoke trailing behind it. When it struck the first soldier it detonated, consuming more than twenty in fire. Aurelia's spell was a great barrage of ice lances. Forced to evade, the demons broke their perfect ranks as ten of their own plummeted to the ground. Deathmask's was the worst. In the center of their ranks a small ball of shadow appeared unseen. At his command, it exploded, filling the sky with thousands of black-tipped arrows. Most bounced off the armor the demons wore, but their wings carried no such protection. Deathmask laughed as he saw more than fifty drop to their deaths.

"You need to teach me that spell," Tarlak said with a whistle.

"You would not want to learn," Deathmask said. "Not while the golden mountain hangs from your neck."

"Damn," Tarlak said. "That's a shame."

So instead he prepared a second fireball as a great swarm of metal descended.

Ulamn hovered high in the sky, a banner carrier holding flight beside him. The general swore as he saw the spells decimate his army. He had expected a ragtag band of survivors for him to slaughter, but powerful spellcasters? Even worse, he saw the swirling blue portal atop the hill the mass climbed. But Ulamn had conquered many worlds, and fought with spellcasters greater than those arrayed against him.

"Send a single unit after the casters," he ordered. "Have the rest assault those atop the hill. I want that portal closed."

Two demons beside him tucked their wings and dove, screaming out their general's orders. The army split in two, each curling around the initial defense line and hooking back to the hill. Antonil's men raised their shields and shouted. Their time to fight had come.

◆◆◆

Damn it, they're not taking the bait," Tarlak shouted as he blasted several demons with lightning as they passed.

Make for the top," Haern said. He turned to Harruq and motioned for him to follow.

"But Aurelia needs me," the half-orc protested.

"Now!" Haern shouted. He leapt more than twenty feet into the air, his sabers drawn. The few demons foolish enough to fly near screamed as their throats were cut and their wings severed. Harruq snarled and gave chase, running outside the line of Antonil's men to avoid the throng of refugees.

"Eyes ahead," Veliana said, twirling her daggers.

A unit of fifty dove for the line, their ranks spread wide to lessen the damage of magical attacks. Lightning and ice struck down several, but then they closed the gap. Mier and Nien let loose their daggers, hurling four at a time into the air. The blades shimmered purple with magic. Those that tried streaking straight at Tarlak veered off, unable to withstand the barrage. Veliana crouched before Deathmask, ready to defend. Deathmask curled his hand, sapping the strength from the first to near. The demon struck the dirt ten feet before him, his wings unable to keep him afloat.

"Get down," Veliana said as two more arced close and swung their long glaives. Veliana jumped into the air, her legs tucked against her chest. As she fell backward her daggers lashed out, perfectly timed. The long blades cut beneath her, her twisted body slipping in between the wooden shafts. Her left dagger cut straight through one's neck, spewing blood. Her right severed tendons, and unable to bear the pain the demon dropped his glaive and ascended.

"Mere distractions," Deathmask said as he stood, hurling small bolts of fire to keep away a few circling demons. "They will kill Mira while we play."

Aurelia had no protector, so she relied on her own magical strength. As the demons came whirling in she tore the dirt from the ground and hurled it high. The demons bounced and slammed through the boulders. Many fell unconscious while others veered away from the dangerous trap.

"Make for the portal," the elf shouted.

She hurled the boulders, crushing a few remaining demons that circled above them. Turning about she saw the true battle raging. The shouts of dying and panicked rolled down the hill. The elf closed her eyes, her mind focused on Mira at the top. She felt her body shiver, and when she opened her eyes she stood beside the girl, the tempest wind blowing her hair and dress.

"By Ashhur's girdle, get down elf!" Jerico shouted behind her. She obeyed without thought. The paladin rushed past her, his shield high. Steel collided as a war demon struck where she had been. The demon hollered as holy light leapt up his weapon and into the scarred flesh of his hands. Jerico pushed aside the sword with his shield, raised Bonebreaker, and struck. The demon dropped, his skull shattered.

"Nice of you to join us," Lathaar said as he slammed his swords together. All about demons winced and averted their eyes.

In the brief reprieve Aurelia looked down the hill, studying the fight. Demons had slammed into the shield walls on either side of the refugees, using brute strength and size to push their way through. Antonil's men had held held firm, however, and men of valor fought against the crimson armored demons. Lining the ground on either side were scattered corpses of demons. She saw more than fifty, a true tribute to Antonil's training. The king rode along the west side, his sword held high.

"Hold firm," he shouted. "Hold fast, hold firm, and make for the portal!"

The people of Neldar did as commanded, and five by five they stepped into the blue and were gone.

"Behind us," Lathaar said. Jerico turned, chuckling at the sight. Four demons flew close together, their swords stretched before them. They were planning on ramming the paladins with their speed and weight to knock them aside.

"You'd think they'd have learned by now," Jerico said. He stood before Mira, his shield high. Singing a song to Ashhur, Jerico braced his legs. A glowing image of his shield leapt into the air, ten times the original size. The demons collided with the image as if they hit stone. Bones broken, they collapsed. Lathaar circled Mira, his swords whirling in a blinding blur of a white. Both were Elholads, and in the paladin's hands they weighed nothing and cut everything. Broken weapons littered the ground, along with severed limbs and pieces of armor.

Still the swarm increased. A wave of twenty banked from the sky straight for Mira. Lathaar stood before them, his weapons crossed. Jerico knelt behind Mira, catching his breath. He knew the demons Lathaar did not kill would try to circle back around. Aurelia tossed lances of ice, softening the wave for Lathaar.

"Hold me fast Ashhur," he prayed. "And your will be done."

He stood firm, a tribute to heroic paladins of old. His twin Elholads slashed and cut. The demons' armor meant nothing to him. Their weapons were nothing as well. Spears and swords clacked off his armor, but they would not pierce flesh. One after another he cut them down, severing them into pieces. The bodies of his foes crashed off his body, even their momentum nothing to him. Ashhur's will was done.

Aurelia stared with mouth agape, for not a single demon had survived. Jerico stretched as high above a demon hurled his spear.

"Easy enough," he said.

His eyes opened wide as the spear punched through his platemail, into his back, and out through his underarm. Aurelia shouted his name as he fell to his knees, only his shield propping his body to a sitting.

"Easy," he gasped, the pain incredible. "Easy."

His head slumped and his eyes closed.

"Jerico!" Lathaar shouted, turning toward his friend.

"Hold your post," Aurelia shouted. Furious he turned to her, but she did not back down. Instead she pointed to the line of fleeing peoples still over three hundred in number. "Hold your post, or all of them will die," she said. The fury in his eyes shifted to understanding. He nodded.

"Ashhur be with us all," he said, turning back to the demons that circled the sky. The only other of his kind lay dying, and he could only turn his back and guard his charge. The light on his blades lessened, and he felt their weight once more.

⚔

Haern led the way down the line, a blur of gray in the dim light. Many of the war demons had landed, preferring solid ground over tumultuous wind. Despite their valor, Antonil's men were falling, exhausted and outmatched in skill. The demons that punched through slaughtered men and women, soaking themselves in the blood of innocents. Haern leapt into the air, landing on the back of one demon with an elderly woman hanging limp from his spear. His sabers sliced the arteries in the demon's neck. As the demon fell he leapt again, ten feet up the hill atop a second. He landed with all his weight on the demon's neck, snapping bone.

Harruq followed in a less precise manner. He barreled through combat, not fearing the swords of either man or

demon. Condemnation and Salvation tore through crimson
armor, spilling an even darker shade across the red mail.
When he saw two demons assaulting a soldier cowering
behind his shield, he roared and slammed his shoulder into the
nearest. As the demon flew he planted his foot and swung,
severing the second at the waist. Harruq gave the soldier no
time to thank him before he was off, chasing Haern up the hill.

"Wait up, damn it," he shouted. "I'm not a leaping frog
like you are!"

He caught movement from the corner of his eye.
Instinctively he braced his shoulders, turning to one side as a
spear skewered where he had been. The attacking demon
slammed straight into him, and in a mass of muscle and armor
they rolled, crushing a hapless man in their way. Harruq
growled as the demon scowled behind his helmet.

"Thulos will burn your world to ash for this cowardice,"
the demon said. He tried to strike with his spear but Harruq
pinned his arm with his knee.

"You're the one attacking unarmed men and women,"
Harruq said. The demon's body pinned Condemnation
underneath him, but Salvation was free. The problem was the
demon gripped Harruq's wrist and held back the killing thrust.
Slowly the tip quivered in the air.

"You're strong, and you speak the god's tongue," the
demon said. Veins pulsed underneath the scars across his face.
"Pull back your blade and join us. We have positions of honor
for your kind."

Harruq laughed, but amid his struggling it sounded more
like a cough.

"I'll tell you what I told Qurrah. Not...gonna...happen!"

Down went the tip, through flesh, past bone, and into
dirt. The demon's arms went limp. Harruq pulled himself free,
yanking out his swords in the process.

"Getting so tired of people trying to recruit me," he said.
"And in the middle of battle for god's sake."

He turned to the portal and ran.

King Antonil ducked his head as a spear thudded into a shield held by one of his men. His heart was heavy for he could see just how many of his soldiers lay dead. Even worse, the men, women, and children he had sworn to protect. Blood soaked the hill, the bodies of the slain a barrier needing climbed. His horse charged across the grass as he swung his sword at any nearby enemy. In spite of his exhaustion, his guilt, and his sorrow, he shouted for all to hear.

"Keep climbing! Keep running! To the portal, to safety, do not stop! Do not stop!"

A war demon slammed to the ground before him and swung his glaive. Antonil jerked the reigns, and without hesitation his horse jumped. A sharp neigh filled the air as the glaive tore flesh, but nothing stopped the enormous weight from crashing atop the demon. As his body crumpled beneath the hooves he heard the labored breathing of his horse turn into a dying whinny.

"I'm sorry," he said as he dismounted. The horse's front legs collapsed, a giant pool of blood covering the ground below. The king looked about the darkened hill. The clouds had turned even thicker so that it seemed night had fallen. There were no torches, no starlight, just the brilliant blue glow of the portal. He trudged toward it, but three demons landed before him with their swords and axes drawn. They saw his crown and knew they found a chance for glory.

Antonil saluted, determined to kill at least one before he died. He was never given the chance. A bolt of lightning shot past the king, hitting the first demon in the eye before leaping into the chest of the second and the throat of the third. All three fell, wisps of smoke rising from their bodies.

"Hope I wasn't intruding," Tarlak said as he grabbed Antonil's wrist and pulled him on. "Now let's leave before their friends show up."

King Antonil followed the yellow robes as if they were light in a giant fog. All around he saw chaos, men missing limbs and women bleeding from giant gashes across their arms and chests. Some were armed. Most weren't. Climbing adjacent the trail of bodies he saw the four members of the Ash Guild, a deadly combination of daggers and death magic striking down any demon who dared near. They offered no aid to the wounded or those in combat, only pressing onward toward the portal, toward escape.

"How many have made it through," Antonil asked as they neared the top of the hill.

"Can't say for sure," Tarlak said, his eyes constantly darting about in search of threats. "At least half. More than half, actually, maybe a lot more. Hundreds at least. Watch your head."

He hurled another bolt of lightning, a joyless smile on his face as he pegged a demon out of the air. With the vast bulk of the Veldaren people escaped, the rest of the demons had taken to circling above, preparing one last assault on Mira and the portal.

"How does she still stand?" Antonil asked, shaking his head. Near a hundred corpses surrounded her, the vast bulk wearing the crimson armor of Thulos. Lathaar stood at her side, his weapons tipped to the dirt, his eyes scanning the sky. When the Ash Guild arrived he saluted them. They did not salute back. Instead, they dived through the portal, their part of the battle finished. The king shook his head, disappointed but understanding. It was not cowardice that caused them to leave, just self-preservation.

Antonil heard a primal roar from the half-orc. He glanced back, in awe of the sight. Harruq was soaked in blood. Cuts covered his arms and hands, yet he grinned with a maniacal glee. The demons seemed to have labeled him as a special prey, for while all around him men, women, and even soldiers hurried to the portal unabated, wave after wave dove for Harruq. The half-orc took them in stride, slamming them away with his powerful swords. As Antonil watched, Harruq sidestepped a thrust, beheaded the attacking demon, took two steps back, and then buried both his swords into another demon's chest. Even as he flung the body away another took its place, striking downward with a gigantic axe.

Swords together he blocked the blow, grinning even as the muscles in his arms twitched. He muttered something, but Antonil couldn't hear it. Then the axe shook, its haft shattered, and Harruq struck down the demon.

"We have little time," Tarlak said, pointing upward. The demons were forming ranks. It would not be long before more waves descended. They looked to the king. "Go through," Tarlak said. "The people will need you."

"I will not abandon those still here," Antonil said. "I will defend to the death if I must."

"I thought you'd say that," Tarlak said. He snapped his fingers. A sudden gust of wind roared to life. An invisible force pushed up on his feet, stealing any chance he had to resist. Cursing the wizard's name, Antonil flew through the portal and vanished.

"Don't get me wrong," Tarlak said as Lathaar shook his head at him. "Honor and pride has its place, but I'm pretty sure intelligence and reason deserve a bit of respect as well."

"Jerico," Lathaar said, gesturing to his wounded brethren. "He's wounded. Please, get him through the portal."

"Forget me," Jerico said, his voice hoarse. "I'm not going anywhere."

"Like the abyss you aren't," Tarlak said.

High above thunder rumbled, and at its sound, Mira shivered.

"The goddess is strained," she said. "Please hurry."

"Just a hundred more," Lathaar said as people rushed into the portal. "We can hold."

Another crack of thunder, and as its force rumbled through the land the demons dove for Mira and her protectors. They were tightly packed, as if they would bury them in metal regardless if they died or not.

"For war!" they shouted, a communal roar that shook the hearts of all remaining.

"For Ashhur," Lathaar cried, rising his swords to the sky.

"And may Karak have them," Tarlak said, fire leaping from his fingers. Aurelia joined him, their barrages of ice and fire swirling together. Demons crumpled and shattered under the power. Harruq and Lathaar stood at either side of Mira, and as the bodies came racing in they cut and blocked, slamming away any who would dare strike her. Lathaar's swords blinded and repulsed the demons. Harruq's cut their flesh and broke their wings. Haern circled about, eyeing the battle for any opening. If Harruq faltered, Haern was there, killing the attacker. If Aurelia's lance of rock or ice missed its target, he was there, his sabers a blur of death.

Lightning filled the sky, some magical, some not. Fire joined it, and smoke blurred the clouds. On and on the Veldaren people entered the portal. The demons could find no opening, no weakness, but still they came. Antonil's soldiers joined the ranks of the fleeing, unable to fight any longer. The demons' attacks focused, more desperate and brutal. At last an elderly couple passed through the portal, and only the Eschaton remained guarding Mira. The ground shook, and the ethereal wind surrounding Mira vanished.

"It's time to go," Tarlak said. "Everyone, get your ass in the portal!"

"Someone take Jerico!" Lathaar shouted as he parried away the attacks of three demons. The light on his swords flared, and as the blinded demons pulled back, he cut them down.

The runes atop the hill cracked and exploded, showering them with chalk. The portal shrunk to half its size.

"Now or never!" Tarlak said. He tipped his hat to the others, hurled one last fireball, and jumped through.

"Harruq, help him!" Aurelia shouted. She lifted wall after wall of ice from the ground, trying to buy themselves time.

Harruq ran to Jerico, ducking blow after blow from demons that swooped above the walls of ice. He was almost there when he heard a horrible cry. He turned to see Aurelia on her knees, her hands pressed against her neck. Her delicate fingers were soaked in blood. A red-tipped spear lay beside her. Harruq looked back, and when his eyes met with Jerico's, he saw understanding without anger or pity.

"Go," Jerico said.

Harruq ran to his wife, took her in his arms, and disappeared through the portal.

More spears fell down, exploding whenever they neared contact with Mira's skin. Lathaar fought with a frantic new urgency. The demons flocked to the holy light of his blades like moths to a torch. Mira walked to the portal and stood there, shaking her head as the waves of death and suffering assaulted her mind.

"Does the tragedy destroy the valiant sacrifice?" she asked the battlefield.

"Get up!" Lathaar shouted to Jerico. He stood beside Mira, fending off demons one after another.

"We cannot save him," Haern said, joining his side. His sabers danced, demon after demon died, but at last he would wait no more. He yanked his blades free from a shredded throat, twirled his cloak, and leapt through the portal.

"Leave," Jerico shouted, his face locked in pain.

Lathaar stabbed his longsword through the eye of a demon, twisted it, and then kicked away the corpse.

"I will not abandon you!"

Jerico knew this true, and that was why he hurled Bonebreaker through the air. The mace struck Lathaar in the chest, and even through the platemail he could feel his bones trembling. He staggered back, his balance lost. Mira saw Jerico's intent and aided him. She pushed Lathaar through.

The ground shaking, the sky furious, and with demons all about, Jerico laid back to the dirt.

"Thank you," he said to Mira, who stared at him with an expression he did not understand.

"Die well," she told him. "And I'm sorry."

She stepped through the portal, and at her passing the blue vanished. Lightning struck where it had been, and at that final release of power the clouds lost their anger. The wind died. Light pierced through as Jerico lay on his back. He stared at the newly freed sun and prayed that Ashhur would grant his soul passage to the Golden Eternity.

Epilogue

Qurrah stirred as the sun crept above the dull horizon. He felt a weight on his chest and an ache in his temples. Tessanna huddled in his arms. In her hands she held a knife. She smiled at him as blood ran down her face from five vertical cuts.

"Pieces," she said as she slashed off her ear without a single grimace of pain. "Mommy left me in pieces."

A Note from the Author:

Are you having fun yet?

We're beyond the halfway mark now. If you're reading this, I want to extend my most heartfelt thanks. You don't read three novels out of impulse. You read them because you enjoyed them, and that's all I can hope for. I hope Death of Promises didn't disappoint.

Things probably look pretty dark at this point. I've sent my characters through hell, I've killed those close to them, and I've only been able to offer them the tiniest glimmers of hope. Aullienna especially haunts over everything. No one was glad for her death, not even me. I cried writing it, and I cried editing it. I see my real daughter in her, and no matter how hard I try, I will never portray Harruq's suffering great enough to match what I myself would feel in his place.

Perhaps it seems odd, then, for me to ask if you're having fun. One of my goals was to make sure the deaths of loved ones meant something. I would not bury a character without tears shed, graves dug, and hearts broken. More will die. It's not some sick promise. It's fact. The rough draft of the fourth book, The Shadows of Grace, is already finished.

I don't view myself as a novelist or fantasy writer or self-published author. I see myself as a storyteller. This story, these brother half-orcs, have a tale I'm dying to tell, and it won't be blunted. I wrote in the back of The Weight of Blood that this was a tale of redemption. By this point, you might think me a liar, although Harruq should appear a far better man than he was. There's not much I can do except ask that you trust me.

You've given me three novels worth of time, time precious to you and precious to me. Thank you.

Other than that, I hope to see you soon. I'm sure I'll be yammering in the back of The Shadows of Grace, a grin on my face, wondering if you'll be able to believe what just happened.

David Dalglish